THE SHADOW
CONSTANT

A.J. SCUDIERE

GRIFFYN INK

For further information, please contact:

Griffyn Ink

www.griffynink.com

Mail@GriffynInk.com

For ordering information or special discounts for bulk purchases or book clubs, please contact Griffyn Ink at Mail@GriffynInk.com.

The Shadow Constant

A.J. Scudiere

ISBN: 978-1-937996-21-5

ISBN: 978-1-937996-22-2

❀ Created with Vellum

Want a free story?
Go to www.ReadAJS.com/free-book to get free short stories.

Look for other novels by A.J. Scudiere.
Available in bookstores, online, and at AJScudiere.com.

The NightShade Forensic Files
Book 1 - Under Dark Skies
Book 2 - Fracture Five
Book 3 - The Atlas Defect
Book 4 - Echo and Ember
Coming soon: Book 5 - Garden of Bone

FORTUNE (red)
FORTUNE (gray)

The Vendetta Trifecta
Vengeance
Retribution
Justice

Resonance

God's Eye

Phoenix

The Shadow Constant

"There are really just 2 types of readers—those who are fans of AJ Scudiere, and those who will be."
-Bill Salina, Reviewer, Amazon

For *The Shadow Constant*:
"The Shadow Constant by A.J. Scudiere was one of those novels I got wrapped up in quickly and had a hard time putting down."
-Thomas Duff, Reviewer, Amazon

For *Phoenix*:
"It's not a book you read and forget; this is a book you read and think about, again and again . . . everything that has happened in this book could be true. That's why it sticks in your mind and keeps coming back for rethought."
-Jo Ann Hakola, The Book Faerie

For *God's Eye*:
"I highly recommend it to anyone who enjoys reading - it's well-written and brilliantly characterized. I've read all of A.J.'s books and they just keep getting better."
-Katy Sozaeva, Reviewer, Amazon

For *Vengeance*:
"Vengeance is an attention-grabbing story that lovers of action-driven novels will fall hard for. I hightly recommend it."
-Melissa Levine, Professional Reviewer

For *Resonance*:
"Resonance is an action-packed thriller, highly recommended. 5 stars."
-Midwest Book Review

This one is for Bear and Peas.
May you embrace the differences in all of us.
May you keep your eyes to the possibilities.
May you stand against giants.

ACKNOWLEDGMENTS

Special thanks go out to everyone who helped make this possible.
First, Wally Hebert, plantation restoration expert and all around great guy. The plantation tour was fantastic, and I cannot thank you enough for being willing to help me out. Your knowledge is woven throughout Hazelton House.

Secondly, thanks go to all the Aspies out there who post videos and talk openly about what it's like to have Aspergers. There are others who helped me, too, but they shall remain anonymous. Aspies are as diverse a group as any, and your invaluable information helped give Kayla a full life.

Lastly, big thank yous to all the usual suspects. My sister, Eli, who beta-reads everything, and organizes all. My husband, Guy, whose unfailing support makes all this possible. The kids, who respect the sign that sometimes appears on my office door: "You can come in, but you might have to wait until I finish killing someone." And all the fans--your posts, chats, and emails make me so happy to be doing this.

Want a free story?

Go to www.ReadAJS.com/free-book to get free short stories.

I hope you enjoyed reading this book.

If you did, please consider the following:

Share it! Lend your copy to a friend.

Recommend it! Tell people that you liked it. We all enjoy finding new authors that we love. I'll share with you authors that I've found. Feel free to share my name with others.

Review it! Reviews tell other readers what to get and what not to get. Even just the sheer number of reviews helps an author. Review on: Amazon, Barnes&Noble, GoodReads, iBooks, or your blog.

Thank you!

PROLOGUE

T hree Months into the Reconstruction of Hazelton House

THE MAN WAS BACK at the door again, his knocking soft but persistent. His clothes looked expensive, his left hand casually in his pocket when he'd come by. She waited while his right hand paused, then knocked again.

Kayla heard him from where she stood now just inside the carriage house; the sound carried well through these old plantation buildings, especially since this one stood nearly empty.

Switching her grasp and wiping her hands on her jeans, Kayla went out into the midday sunshine that flooded the small, grassy area between the buildings. There were noises from the creatures in the grass, but they were obscured by the rasp of the generator as it kicked up and the whir and chug got louder.

She climbed the short, wide staircase and headed across the back porch and through the standard double doors. So many things about Hazelton House seemed ordinary for its time frame.

Kayla was angered by his presumptions; he'd let himself in and turned on lights. Coming around the side and through the archway, she spotted him in the entryway, looking up at the brightly lit chandelier overhead, but he didn't give her time to ponder his presence.

"Excuse my intrusion. No one answered my knock and the door was unlocked." He smiled.

Looking him straight in the eyes, Kayla asked, "Where's Ivy?"

When he only shrugged in answer, she lifted the shotgun and shot him square in the chest.

1

Old Dining Room, Hazelton House

"W<small>AIT</small>!"

Kayla heard Reenie's voice, and she tried to shift her weight, change the arc, but a sledgehammer was hard to stop once it was going. That was the physics of destruction. There was also the issue that taking out walls was a good method of working through your frustrations.

She'd been told repeatedly to find a good physical release, to stop telling people everything she thought, and to keep potentially hurtful things to herself. But there were no guidelines for what was and wasn't potentially hurtful, no rules that made sense or were useful anyway. So the non-original walls had turned into a good way to release some tensions.

Like getting fired. Again.

Tension about Reenie becoming a permanent part of the family.

Frustrations about having been removed from society and told that the plantation would be good for everyone. Including her new babysitter. Which she did not need.

Kayla wasn't the only one letting a grudge loose on the wall; it had been getting a good bashing from more than just her. But while the others had managed to stop what they were doing, her sledgehammer was already in motion and Reenie was yelling for Kayla to defy gravity.

It didn't happen. The heavy, metal head dug deep, tearing through the horse-hair plaster and thin strips of wood that supported it. It went into the wall very near where Reenie's hand was reaching. Kayla watched as her probably-future-sister-in-law snatched the stray limb back with a sharp "Kayla!"

She was starting to sigh as the hammer finally rested at the bottom of its arc. But she didn't get to say anything. Evan, who had managed to simply stop mid-swing—who always managed to do what Reenie told him, when she told it—gave Reenie the 'let Kayla be' look that he had been employing with everyone since Kayla's second birthday.

But what he said was, "We told everyone to be sure that all hammers were stopped before anyone put any body part in the pathway. It's the only way we'll all survive this."

Evan was right. Reenie shouldn't have reached out until she was sure no one was going to bash off her limb. With four of them there, geared in thick lab goggles, face masks and heavy gloves, all swinging heavy hammers, Reenie should have waited.

Instead she had reached out, her pale fingers almost disappearing behind puffs of white dust wrought by the destruction of the wall. And she'd almost lost them because Kayla wasn't strong enough to stop her sledgehammer once it was going. And maybe, just a little, because Kayla wasn't Reenie's biggest fan.

Now, Reenie looked at each of them in turn. To Kayla she gave a raised-brow *are-you-done?* look. To Evan she nodded—a look that held a wealth of information Kayla would never decipher.

And to Ivy she gave her usual suspicious look. Then Reenie reached into the wall and began to tug at something only she could see. In a moment, she produced a packet of letters.

Kayla was unimpressed. This wall had been built later than the original house, and antebellum Southerners were known for hiding their valuables and private treasures. She already had a metal detector set aside to sweep the backyard in hopes of finding silver buried during the Civil War. They had found treasures galore in the attic and outbuilding. And with the paperwork Evan had talked Reenie into signing, it was one quarter Kayla's . . . that thought alone brought a smile to her face.

But Kayla didn't care much for correspondence. She knew little of the drama that was love in the 1870s—she knew little of love in her own era. She was just trying to become an unqualified adult, support herself, keep a job. It was more than a touch humiliating to be rapidly approaching thirty and not yet have completely mastered those simple tasks. So she didn't care that Reenie was oooh-ing and ahhh-ing over what looked like a packet of old love letters.

But Reenie did.

Apparently, she decided it was a good time for a break, because she sat her round bottom down in the middle of the white-gray dust and ignored the grit hanging in the air. Yanking her face mask off, Reenie tugged at the melted blue blob that must have been a wax seal at one point. The letters had clearly been in the wall for years upon years, and the hot summers had re-melted the wax any number of times, bleeding the color into the thick, porous paper that Reenie was working hard not to destroy in her haste to read yet another love story. Had Kayla cared, she would have recommended the woman read another poorly written romance novel over destroying something histori-cal, but this was no ancient cotton gin like the ones she'd found lined up and rusted in the carriage house. Or the rods of squared iron that stood sentry in the corner of the blacksmith's shop, still awaiting a smithy to transform them into hinge or latch. It wasn't a gear wheel, a cog, an axle that must have been a part of something, half buried in the dirt floor of the carriage house. This was just paper, likely coated with the ramblings of a Scarlet O'Hara type with a penchant for whining.

Kayla felt her face form into the familiar scrunch of brow that Evan still used frequently and her father had once shared with both his kids. It was the family "thinking face" and she could feel that she was making it. Attempting to find some zen, she tried to smooth her expression, thus missing that Reenie had opened the top letter and was already reading.

"*E.*" She paused. "That's it—it's just written to E. That sounds mysterious." Reenie smiled and began again to read.

"*I find it best that I be blunt in this missive. Normally, I would wish you well and remind you of my ever-present fondness. I would ask that you return posthaste to Hazelton House and to me. I have begged that you find more reasons to stay longer at Mulberry Grove, and to visit here more often. Previously, my besotted eyes believed that your unease was with my husband, with the man that I should revere above all others and mostly above you.*"

Reenie paused and looked up, her eyes hopeful that the others would find this as intriguing as she clearly did. Kayla looked to Ivy, still covered in her goggles and facemask. Even the long, wavy black hair that Kayla knew was there was hidden under a yellow bandanna. There was nothing to work with, no cue from Ivy about what to express, what to "feel". So Kayla stayed expressionless and confused by what made Reenie excited in a rambling letter that had started with being "blunt" then had been anything but.

The tone of her future-sister-in-law's voice went up a bandwidth, but Kayla focused on the words.

"*For long months I have seen your face when you are gone. But yesterday I saw your face in the newborn babe of the housemaid. Though I am great and increasing every day, I attended the birthbed of this servant who has been loyal to me for long months when it was just us two women in the house. Now I find fault in both her attentiveness and yours.*

"*I am unable to find regret in informing you of the passing of my servant and her child. The striking resemblance to your family nature has washed much emotion from my soul. I ordered them dug shallow in the far yard with the other slaves.*"

The voice stopped and Kayla took a moment to absorb what she'd heard. Given what she knew about mid-nineteenth-century writings—which was admittedly little—maybe the woman *was* being blunt.

After a deep breath and some fumbling with a third page that was stuck with wax, Reenie started up again.

"*I beg you not to journey again to Hazelton House. Find any excuses to give to M. for your perpetual absence. But do not come to see me or the babe I carry. It shall bear a resemblance to you moreso than to M. to whom I should have stayed a loyal wife. My great pain is no less than I deserve having been given by you exactly that which I have given my own true M.*

"*Find your reasons for not attending to M. and hold fast to them. He deserves nothing of that which we have sown. He will mourn the babe he believes is his and with the child I shall bury my own betrayal and we shall never speak of this again.*"

Kayla blinked. That part she understood. "That's a pisser."

Her words were echoed nearly identically by Ivy, from whom she'd picked up the phrase. If Ivy was upset at Kayla's blatant theft of personality, she didn't show it. All eyes were on Reenie.

But, as usual, it was Kayla who voiced what everyone else thought better than to say. "Do you think she killed it?"

HEFTING THE SLEDGEHAMMER, Kayla wandered to another room. The old sitting room was mostly free of the grit that hung in the air where they had been 'restoring' the house. Blessedly alone in the cleared and prepped cube, Kayla sucked in hard-won oxygen through the facemask and blinked at the tainted air even though the goggles allowed nothing in. The sun came in through the windows, causing the ever-present dust motes to glint in its path like fairies and for a moment Kayla stood there admiring the trapezoidal shape of light on the flat plastic sheeting.

Kayla had prepped the floor herself, anchoring corners with round river rocks and carefully unrolling the sheeting, folding and tucking away the spare edges. She would have cut it with a box cutter but dared not harm the floors. She was no Reenie with her love of woodwork and dentil moldings, but she appreciated the not-quite-square and -plumb rooms. She had done the wall-paper work in this room, pulling back the upper left corner from each wall to reveal the layers.

They had all agreed that the wall on her left had to go. It wasn't original. Reenie, the architect, had argued that it wasn't load bearing. Ivy, the art historian, had pointed out that the wall-paper was only two layers thick, not five, like on the window wall. Evan, the carpenter, had shown them how the floorboards continued from this room into the next, indicating they were laid at some time before the wall had been built over them. Kayla, the one with Aspergers, had pointed out that the offending piece was constructed of drywall—a product not invented until the turn of the twentieth century.

Never mind that she had one degree in mechanical engi-neering and another in electrical. Never mind that every job she'd held had paid her more than Reenie made, more than her brother or her father had ever earned. Never mind that she had no social life so—despite an expensive habit of collecting small machines—she had more money saved than any of them. Regardless of all this, she was the one who needed watching like a small child. She was the one who had been fired seven times, three of those since earning her master's. Two of those times had been after she and Evan had both read more than one manual on finding satisfying and sustainable work for a person with Aspergers. Satisfying, she'd found. Sustainable, no.

So she was out here on this country road, beyond the stone wall, up the long, rutted drive and behind the old, worn walls of Hazelton House . . . with a sledgehammer and the need to blow off some steam.

With a grunt, she pulled back on the handle and used brute strength and inertia to get the hammer up and over her head and into the wall. The resulting hole was small and did nothing to calm the irritation that bubbled up in her when she thought of her last dismissal.

With time and perspective, she'd come to understand the other times she'd been fired. Her focus often did not match that of the company—they wanted time-over-budget; Kayla focused on quality-over-service. She found it hard to cut corners and deliver a product that was less than her best, less than as good as it could be. But this last time was not yet far enough behind her for any real clarity.

She buried the hammer into the wall again, feeling the slight give that indicated she'd hit her mark. Drywall didn't offer the substance that good old lathe and plaster did. She moved over eighteen inches and struck again. Hitting a stud could change the way the wall came down. Well, if she were Evan, it might. But for her, hitting a stud would likely just send a wicked reverb down her arms.

With no crowbar handy, she was left punching holes the size of the hammer head into the wall. Since it didn't calm her, the physical activity wound her up, her brain wandering to the last conversation she'd had with her most recent boss at the mechanical design company. The problem was that her brain might wander to someplace, but it didn't wander away. When she hit a potent memory, it was like having a video playing on the wall of the room. She re-heard conversations word for word. To this day, she could conjure the look on her mother's face as they'd stood in the kitchen, Kayla holding an ice-filled towel against her bloody lip as her mother looked at her sadly.

Upon finding the high school quarterback harassing a boy at his locker, Kayla had pointed out that using the term "fag" often indicated homophobia. Many men acted out because of a deep-seated fear that they themselves were gay, which usually started with unwanted attraction to other men.

When Kayla cited the current psychology, he'd turned on her and punched her in the mouth. He'd split her lip, knocking her backward into a nearby locker and earning her a goose egg on the back of her head, too. The subsequent stumble and fall had garnered a handful of bruises. She was beaten up from every angle. The kid he'd been harassing had disappeared immediately. And Kayla had wound up first in the office of a principal who had never quite figured out what to do with a girl who was far too bright for special ed, and far too socially inept to ever fit in. Then she'd found herself in her kitchen with her mother looking at her, not as enraged at the boy who had hit her as she was frustrated with her own inability to help her daughter to learn when to speak up and when to shut up.

Though her lip was unsplit now and she had no outer bruises, she felt just as beat up. Her jeans were old and getting rapidly older. Her throat was dry from the dust, though her face sweated beneath her gear. Unlike Ivy, Kayla had not tied her hair back and she could practically feel it tangling as she hefted the hammer again and tried to find release in burying it into the wall. Again, she fell short of satisfaction.

She considered going off to find a crowbar so she could make some real headway taking down the wall. But the only one she knew where to find was in the other room with Reenie and Evan and Ivy. And the last thing Kayla wanted to do was remind them that she'd wandered off on her own and no one was watching her. So she stuck to the sledgehammer, punching holes in the wall and seeing again that last conversation with Mr. Williams.

"Kayla, you need to incorporate fewer measures into the machinery."

She'd put emergency stops at every workstation along the long conveyor belt system she'd designed. "Why?"

"Only the supervisor needs the override."

"No, safety dictates—"

"One stop meets all the OSHA requirements." He'd begun frowning at that time.

"But any employee should be able to override the line at any time if necessary. They do it at Ford." At many companies really. He should have known that. Maybe he did.

He'd tipped his head like she was a small child. "They're building cars. We're designing a cookie factory."

His analogy sucked and was simply wrong on many levels. But she'd learned not to tell people that. "Can you explain why we shouldn't put in the extra safety stops?"

Kayla had learned through the years that if she knew *why* something was important, it was suddenly easy to implement. And if she had no idea why something was necessary, she was just as unable to make it happen.

But Williams had said only, "I don't have the time to explain it to you."

More confused than she had been when the conversation started, she hadn't monitored her mouth. What had come out was, "Is that because you won't take the time? Are you insulting my IQ? Or maybe it's your intelligence that's at issue . . . are you not smart enough to explain it?"

Kayla buried the sledgehammer into the wall again. The problem was that she didn't know how to get past it. She lived a logical life, she worked logically, spoke logically, hell, she was even beating up this wall logically, placing holes every eighteen inches on center. Thus, she wanted a logical fix to her problems.

With Williams, she didn't know what to do differently to not wind up in the same trouble the next time. The obvious answer was: don't run at the mouth. But she also knew if she didn't get an explanation she would have gotten fired for not taking out the safety measures she believed were necessary and Williams didn't want. She simply wasn't capable of putting out a harmful product.

Williams' next words had been to the point. "You're fired, Reeves."

She knew her rights. She could have fought it through HR, but then she'd have to tell the world what she'd said to him. That she'd questioned his intelligence. She'd have to highlight that she had no understanding of what to do or say in many situations. And she knew Williams would have fought back . . . mean. As it was, he'd given her two months severance—as though he knew he was in the wrong, but he wanted her gone.

Swinging the hammer into the wall and making yet another unsatisfyingly small hole, she sighed. She'd planned to wait a week, goof off, and then tell Evan. She'd made it three days before she was stir crazy without a job. That day, she'd gotten up in time to go to work—just like every day—she'd showered, dried her hair, put on sunscreen and added lipstick because her mother had told her to wear it every day but had only convinced her when she shared the skin cancer prevention benefits of wearing it. Then Kayla had been halfway through her cereal, facing another hair-pullingly boring day, when she'd caved and called Evan.

Her brother had said the worst possible thing he could say: maybe this was an opportunity.

Kayla was not neurotypical, but you didn't have to be to know the old "opportunity" line was complete crap. Then Evan told her that he and Reenie were making plans, but he wouldn't say what. He just asked her to sit tight and not job hunt for a few days.

Why he said that, Kayla had not understood. Something big

was up, because Evan wasn't paying attention. He definitely knew better than to tell someone with Aspergers to just "sit tight" and not do anything for the next several days. Kayla figured he had asked Reenie to marry him or that Reenie was already pregnant. Both those thoughts wigged her out more than she cared to admit.

So she'd pulled up her "things to do when I'm bored" list that she and Evan had made when she'd first moved here for the job. She assigned herself an outing each morning and another each afternoon, stopping in at her apartment for meals from her own pantry. The first day, she ran part of the Emerald Necklace, a long green trail through the city. But it freaked her out and she marked it as "done." She hit the zoo that afternoon, marked it as "done-do again" and went back the next day, too. The Westside Market was too many people, too much noise, and too everything and she didn't stay long, but she'd thought that might be the case, so she had a backup plan in place. Next, she drove to the Submarine Memorial and spent the rest of the day quietly touring on her own.

Five days later Evan called back.

He wasn't marrying Reenie—though it was still inevitable that he would.

Reenie wasn't pregnant. What Reenie was, was a Hazelton. Or her grandmother had been. Her grandfather had brought the Carroll name and some money into the family, but recently the family had fallen onto hard times again. "Hard times" in the twenty-first century South meant that Reenie's cousin, Roy Weems had fathered three kids by three different mothers, two of the babies born only a month apart. And now he was in jail on some assault charge. His older brother, Billy, died in a motorcycle accident five years earlier with no children. According to the deed, Roy's current jail time meant he was no longer fit as proprietor of the rotting plantation, not that he'd ever been fit. But this left Reenie as the most direct descendant and thus the new owner of Hazelton House.

Kayla wasn't sure why Reenie hadn't been first in line. Kayla had no great love of her future in-law, but she was just as direct of a descendant of Charlene Hazelton Carroll as the guys had been. Reenie didn't have a penis or the Hazelton name. But Roy and Billy didn't have the name either, and now they both had jail records. No matter how Kayla felt about Reenie, the woman had managed to live a straight, solid life.

The sledgehammer swung again with a heft of her now-aching shoulders, and she produced the last of the second row of holes. The wall still stood and, in fact, could be completely repaired with some mesh and spackle. All that time and swinging and she'd done it no great damage. She hated taking down drywall without a crowbar. Honestly, looking at the wall, she was pretty sure she'd proven it couldn't be done, unless she was going to go with brute strength and aim for the studs. But that's not how they were doing this one, not in a historic home built in the 1700s.

Each space between studs now had a high hole and a low one. Each hole was just the width of the hammer head, except for one low spot about halfway down the wall, where she had the bright idea to bury the head, then use it to pull back on the drywall. It had worked, leaving a nearly two-foot gap in the wall, but it had been way too much work.

Kayla gave up and went looking for the crowbar.

2

B ack Parlor, Hazelton House

EVAN LOOKED up as Reenie came back into the room. "Did you get it catalogued?"

"Yup!" Reenie smiled, and he knew the letters were put away and written into her findings notebook, with date, location, and any identifying info. Reenie had probably saved a full page for these. They weren't like the armoire in the second upstairs bedroom—she'd dubbed that empty and slated it for cleaning and polishing. No, these needed to be read through, and he was pretty sure how Reenie would be spending the evening and probably late into the night. He'd fall asleep not getting any while she read about what other people did a hundred years ago, rather than doing anything herself.

"Do I get to read them?" Ivy glanced sideways at Reenie. Ivy was the art history major; she was the one who would know the most about the letters. But Reenie held the strings, and on Ivy she held them tight.

Reenie's smile dimmed a bit. "I should have them read by tomorrow."

Evan stayed out of the exchange. The two of them interacted merely as professionals, even though they lived on the same plantation. Ivy, obviously, was the expert. Reenie was the owner. He and Kayla were owners, too. It had been their money that had dug Reenie out of the back taxes on the place three months ago. It was their money they had all been living off, their money that paid Ivy's salary, meager though it was.

Kayla wandered back in—she didn't look at anyone, not in the face, but that wasn't unusual. Bending, she picked up the hand-sized crowbar at his feet, then walked back out with it. He'd been intending to pick it up again, and Reenie's eyebrows-up, *say-something!* expression conveyed that she understood that.

He frowned and walked across the room for the second hand-held prybar.

Reenie was overexpressive, and he wondered if that was part of the draw—that was often an exact counterpoint to Kayla's sometimes-blank countenance. But he didn't say anything.

Ivy, too, looked at him, a small shrug asking if she should follow Kayla. He gave a subtle shake of his head, though he could have simply said so out loud. Even if Kayla could hear him, she would ignore it. She was never sure if people were talking about her; it had bothered her when she was younger, but together they'd helped get her through high school by having her remind herself that it likely wasn't about her, and what did she care anyway? So now, he could talk about her pretty much any time he wanted and unless he specifically said her name within earshot, she wouldn't even pay attention. In fact, sometimes even within earshot she still didn't hear him, she'd be so buried in her own thoughts.

So he turned to Ivy, "I think I was unclear when we hired you."

He had pulled Ivy aside after the three of them had interviewed the only applicant to answer the ad they'd posted. He'd told her that there was another part to the job: keeping an eye on Kayla.

Ivy had easily taken this on herself, and with Reenie's mother-hen tendencies, Kayla didn't get a moment to herself.

Evan sighed. "She's an adult. She just gets so focused sometimes that she forgets to eat or she won't get any exercise. That's all I wanted from you, Ivy, just an occasional check in on some basics. Kayla doesn't need a babysitter; she doesn't have to be followed like a child."

Reenie snorted. She was beautiful, round-faced and big-eyed, too buxom and curvy to quite fill the genteel Southern role she'd been born to play. And one of the things that never failed to grab him where it counted was that her façade would slip sometimes, and she'd snort or give a full, real belly laugh, say something completely off-color, be anything but poised. But now the snort led to an opinion.

"I'd say she does need a babysitter. She can't hold a job, she's been fired from every one she's ever had."

He shook his head, this was an old argument, and probably the reason he hadn't married Reenie yet. He would, he knew it— hell, they owned property together—but he needed peace between the women in his life, and they didn't have it yet. "She's higher paid than either of us. She has plenty of savings. And you've been fired before, too. So have I."

Reenie stood up. "I was fired from waiting tables, not from a real job. And it was in college. She gets fired again and again and you support her."

She could have slapped him and done less damage. Evan staggered back a step as though from an actual blow. The pile of discarded lathe and plaster that he stepped into created an uneven ground that matched the emotional precipice she'd shoved him onto. He took a moment to get his bearings, then went ahead and blurted what had come immediately to mind.

"You have no right, Reenie. Her money made this place possible, not yours. Your net worth is negative. She's only at one-quarter share because she wanted each of us to have a bigger piece than she did, not because she was out of money. Yes, she's handicapped in that she can't read facial expressions and doesn't always fit in socially, but you're handicapped by your complete inability to manage your money or your time. You're always late to everything. And you're so focused on what looks right that you can't think about what's actually right. And I'm handicapped because I'm stuck between you two."

He dropped the crowbar, not caring that it would mar the antique flooring that was one of the only ones of its kind still in existence, and he stormed out of the room.

THREE DAYS LATER, Reenie still wasn't saying much to him. She used monosyllables here and there. She pointed. She frowned. And she always found she was needed in some room away from where he was working.

He took his aggression out on the walls.

There were ten walls in the house that weren't original to the design. Not that there were any floorplans anywhere. In 1714, architects didn't take blueprints to the courthouse and register the layout. In 1714, the town of Ebenezer had been the county seat of Effingham. Now Evan wanted to use the term 'Effingham' as an American-sounding swear word.

Using the back of his hand he rapped on a wall. Suddenly, Reenie appeared.

"This is added." He gripped the sledgehammer that seemed to be his near-constant companion.

"Don't you dare damage that! There's a bathroom on the other side."

He smiled. "Ivy would tell us to take it out."

Kayla's face quirked Mona-Lisa like. "When Ivy owns a plantation house, she can stay true to the original century and pee outside. I want the toilet."

Evan couldn't help but smile back at her. Reenie was a wonderful woman, but she couldn't see past her own nose where his sister was concerned. Just because Kay didn't fit her mold, Reenie couldn't deal. He wanted to spend the rest of his life with her, but not like this.

The thing was, Kayla didn't fit much of anybody's mold.

Crowbar in hand, she headed to the opposite side of the room, feet crunching on the spread plastic. Using a grease pen from the corner of her jeans she walked the wall and made a series of small marks. "Here. Take this one out."

The room had been divided into smaller pieces a century or so earlier. According to Reenie, records showed that the main building had served as a boarding house after the Civil War. These had likely been bedrooms for the boarders where a small ballroom had once been.

Bracing his feet wide at just the right distance from the new wall, Evan pulled back on the sledgehammer. He was going for the studs. He'd swung this thing enough times over the last weeks that he knew exactly where to plant his boots. He knew to take a quick glance over his shoulder each time before he swung. And he knew that he needed to aim with his left hand occasionally leading or he was going build some very lopsided musculature.

With a backward glance, he let fly.

There was a thunk and a crack as he hit the stud. Just by sight, Kayla had found and marked all the hidden beams in the wall. With a rhythmic step and swing he took them out one by one, easing his frustrations with Reenie.

Kayla came along behind him, prying away sections of plaster and the wooden strips that had formed the base for it. After the surface was cleared, they pried away the planks that had been nailed to the floor and ceiling to anchor the studs. Made a pile of dead pieces on a nearby tarp to be dragged out to the industrial-sized trash bin that was getting emptied weekly.

Just as they threw the last piece onto the plastic, Reenie sauntered back in with a huge smile on her face. Apparently, she wasn't too mad at him anymore. The notebook where she kept the documentation of everything they'd found was clutched in a firm hug. "That wall was a treasure trove."

He didn't ask, and neither did Kayla.

The wall where they'd found the packet of letters, the top one of which suggested that the writer would kill her child, had held other things, too. After he'd cooled off a bit, Evan had come back and finished the job by himself much later that night. But he'd found the need to make two piles—one for the dead wall pieces and a second for a few items hiding behind the plaster.

There had been a diary and a second stack of letters from another time frame. A baby outfit and a set of clothes for a grown man, stained with what must be blood.

Despite his find, Reenie had been angry that he hadn't woken her and let her catalog things as they came out. She'd been mad that he'd just made a pile, rather than marking each exact stud where the items had been found. It had only added to her ire from what he'd said earlier. And he found he couldn't take it back, so he'd let her stay mad.

Now she smiled. "According to Ivy, the wall was built around the late 1800s, but the letters were from 1803 to 1805. The clothes she looked up; they are from around the 1820s. I went out to the family plot, and guess what!?"

Reenie didn't wait for either of them to answer.

Evan had known his sister wouldn't guess, but Reenie didn't and so her next words covered right over Kayla's "I have no idea what to guess."

"There's a grave for an infant that died in birth, only a few weeks after that letter!"

"Wow." Unable to think of anything else to say, Evan glanced at Kayla. He could have predicted the look on her face. She looked like she was horrified and trying to cover it up.

Kayla, too, said "Wow." She said it just as Evan had, same inflection and everything. She'd learned a long time ago to mimic someone who fit in, someone that she trusted, so Evan wasn't surprised that she used his own word to cover the fact that she was appalled that Reenie was excited about the death of a baby . . . possibly a murder.

Though this wouldn't help Kayla take to Reenie, Reenie beamed at his sister, something that didn't happen often.

"I know! We have some twisted history, us Hazeltons. And that's going to bring people here to visit!" She turned and started away, calling back over her shoulder, "I'll tell you all about it at dinner!"

Kayla shrugged at him, and he knew she didn't think that selling the murder of an infant was the way to go, so he tried—as he always did—to smooth the way. "It happened, and it's history. That kind of thing occurred more than people think, and it will help educate the people who come here."

His sister nodded back at him as though accepting that excuse, but then she changed the subject, not swayed from the task they had been on for hours. "I calculate that we don't have time to get this whole wall out by dinner, but if we tackle the smaller one first, we should get done a little early."

Grinning at her, he started an old game. "When do you think we'll finish?"

Kayla pushed her glove down to check the shiny surface of her analog watch. It was a men's watch, gold, with roman numerals and a ticking second hand. It was only slightly different than the one he'd given her for her thirteenth birthday. When one died, she went in search of a nearly identical replacement. "5:42."

He frowned then looked at the wall, assessing the work needed. "Over."

She nodded and they got to it.

Kayla won. They had finished at 5:41. Evan had been on Reenie's case for years to triple her estimated time for any task, in hopes that she wouldn't continue to be perpetually late. Kayla, on the other hand, could figure a task to the minute. Which was why he only ever bet the over/under.

Dinner was at six, so they hauled the tarp out to the trash, dumping all the debris. They kept some pieces; they were after all part of Hazelton House history. But they didn't match the antebellum version of the plantation that they had decided to portray, so Reenie and Ivy had declared the dead wall parts interesting but not part of the final product.

He made a second run while Kayla poked at all the fireplace stones. The mechanical engineer in her and the OCD-like quality that came with Aspergers demanded that she check the rooms and structures for soundness. When he came back in a second time, he found her with a heavy stone pulled from the hearth, and she was unrolling a huge oiled cloth.

"Ev, check this out." She didn't look up.

He didn't look down. He'd had enough of women and their findings. "I'm taking a shower, then I'm going to come back in and get you for dinner."

He'd seen that intent expression on her face before. If he didn't come back, she would miss dinner, and maybe breakfast tomorrow, too. She might forget the value of the original hardwood floors and start making notes on them. Luckily, she only carried a grease pen.

If he hadn't been so exhausted and hungry, he might have stayed. Whatever she was unrolling had her enthralled.

3

K itchen, Overseer's House

"So."

Evan sat back as Reenie started up again. Actually, it was wrong to think of it as "starting up," she hadn't quit all through dinner. At least the information was interesting. Kayla was paying little to no attention, looking off into space.

"The infant grave that matches the letter we found, is for a boy. Alfred Elmore Hazelton. He's the fourth son and fifth child of Martin and Charlene Hazelton. And he's the only child not to survive to adulthood."

Ivy finished the bite she was chewing and asked, "Are these your ancestors?"

"They sure are. We are a pretty screwed up bunch. Martin and Charlene are my great-something grandparents. My grand-mother, Charlene Carlyle Hazelton married Edwin Carroll. She was the last of the Hazeltons; that's where the surname changed."

Evan didn't follow all the names and genealogies that Reenie was rattling off. But even mentally absent, Kayla did. "You're a Charlene, too."

Ivy looked at Kayla, then at Reenie, then back at Kayla. "What?"

Kayla pointed at Reenie. "She's Charlene Temple Carroll."

"So where does 'Reenie' come from?" Ivy was not Southern with a capital S. Not the way Reenie was.

Reenie sighed. "My mother was the second daughter born to her mother. No sons. The first daughter of the eldest Hazelton son is always named Charlene. So my aunt is the Charlene in my mom's generation. She actually goes by 'Charlene.' My grandmother went by Charlie, and she was a cold bitch, which you wouldn't expect from that nickname. Anyway, Charlie had no sons, so when my mom had me before Aunt Charlene had any children, she named me Charlene," Reenie shrugged, "Oldest daughter in the generation and all that. My mother was single at the time, so she waited a few years until she was married to come home and show me off to Charlie. Apparently, my grandmother went off her rocker and nearly disowned my mom for it, since the name belonged to my aunt's first daughter. The way my momma tells it, Charlie was more upset over the name than the whole baby-out-of-wedlock thing. And never mind that Aunt Charlene only had boys and the chain would have died out completely if my mom hadn't done it. So Mom immediately looked for something else to call me and apparently as a toddler I called myself 'Reenie' and it stuck."

Evan had never heard that before. He'd never thought to ask how she'd gotten such an unusual name. It was simply hers, it fit her, and she was Southern. If he knew one thing about Southern women, it was that they often had odd names. "So your great . . . great great grandmother might have killed your great . . . great great uncle at birth?"

She shrugged. "More 'greats' than that, but it's looking that way."

"Your genetics concern me."

She rolled her eyes, "You don't even know your genetics past your grandparents. Don't give me any guff."

Guff. There was a word that was pure Reenie. But he didn't have time to think about it, Reenie was already leaning forward to share more dirt. "It gets juicier!"

He wasn't sure he was up for more juice. But Ivy leaned in, too, and both the women glanced at Kayla, who showed only a passing interest even after joining the conversation for a beat.

Reenie dove back in with gusto. "So . . . those letters are addressed to 'E' and signed 'L.' It took me a while to figure out Martin's wife went by 'Lena.' But I'm still looking for 'E'—he's been harder to find. He's a friend of Martin's and visits the family periodically. She mentioned another plantation, Mulberry Grove, but it burned in Sherman's March, so there won't be anything there."

Ivy blinked. "You did all this today?"

Instead of tearing down walls or doing some much-needed planning, Evan thought. But he knew better than to say it. There was a modicum of peace in the house and he wasn't going to mess with it.

Reenie smiled. "I love the Internet."

Evan now regretted asking Kayla to install it.

He chewed the rotisserie chicken Ivy had bought at the local grocery store. None of them really cooked beyond the basics, and town was five miles away. Springfield had only a few thousand residents, which gave it two gas stations, one big and one small grocery, and a tiny handful of other businesses. Savannah was only about twenty-five minutes away, and that was a good part of why they thought this venture had a fighting chance. Still, at least one of them had to learn to cook. Anything other than the combo Taco Bell/Pizza Hut was a drive.

Reenie wasn't even eating; she was too busy talking. Wanting to point this out, Evan shoved more chicken in his mouth to quell the urge and keep the peace. Then Reenie turned her eyes on him. This could be bad.

"That diary was Carlee's diary. Carlee was fourteen in 1805 when the last letter was written."

Ivy interrupted, "Is she another Charlene?"

"The only daughter of Lena and Martin." A brief nod, then Reenie thought for a moment. "Well, given Lena's history, maybe she wasn't Martin's daughter after all."

Kayla smiled. "Maybe you aren't a Hazelton at all then."

Evan felt his teeth grind. Kay could be a trial. She honestly thought it was an interesting development that the family line could be skewed and impure. Just as Reenie had said. His sister had no idea that it could devastate someone to find out they weren't who they believed they were.

Reenie froze.

He felt his shoulders sag. They shouldn't have hired Ivy. They should have hired a man so that he wouldn't be left swimming in this shark-filled estrogen pool.

Reenie's head tipped as she thought about it. "Maybe. But I have legal inheritance of the house." Then she sighed. "And if you check out the house portraits, either I'm genetically related to Lena and Martin or else the painter was both unskilled and psychic."

Kayla laughed.

Evan almost choked on the broccoli he had swallowed in an attempt to look normal and stay out of things. This was epic. Maybe he should shut up more often.

Reenie missed the moment for what it was and kept rolling. "Carlee apparently had a crush on a young man who visited the plantation often. This was when she was fourteen. But the diary spans the later years of the letters. I haven't read it yet, but I'm hoping it will reveal more, like who E is."

Evan held back his groan. He was practicing shut-up-ism. It was going to be his new religion.

Kayla, now a bona fide part of the discussion, spoke up. "So what you need to figure out next is who put the stuff in the wall."

Ivy joined, too, nodding at Kayla. "That was an odd lot of items to put in together. They must all have been buried at one time. Something someone didn't want laying around to be found."

Evan kept eating even though he was full, the conversation roiling around him.

"So," Reenie paused for just a small moment. "It sounds like typical, Southern, hide-it-in-the-house-somewhere history. So the question is: who and why and when."

"That's three questions." That from Kayla. "But who was the right age to be involved in wall building in 1870? And what happened in 1805 that someone in 1870 thought was better removed from the family history?"

There was no answer to that, yet.

But if Evan knew Reenie she'd find it or die trying. She picked up her plate, her food only half-eaten. "When y'all are finished, just leave stuff on the counter. I'll be back to put it away." Then she disappeared down the hall, probably to get started on that diary.

Ivy's plate was empty, but she hadn't been storytelling the whole time the way Reenie had. "I'm going to clean up the rest of the chicken then head back to the big house."

She had her own room there with a window unit for air-conditioning and a space heater in the corner. She had an old four-poster bed that was original to the house. She'd cleaned and polished it the first day they were here, as well as fixing up the matching armoire. One trip into Savannah and Ivy had a sewing machine, fabric and some cutting boards. The next day she'd had curtains, bed drapes and a coordinating bedspread. If the wall paper hadn't been so old and peeling, it would have looked like Ivy slept in the 1700s.

In contrast, the house here—where he and Reenie shared the back room and Kayla slept in the old "office"—was 70s' crap. The kitchen counters had been updated with laminate, and the cabinets had been painted over several times, hinges and all. The stove was olive green and the counters robin's egg blue. Evan cringed every time he came in here.

He was convinced of two things: (1) If he put a marble on one side of the counter, it would roll to the other end and fall off. He refused to try. (2) The previous generation of Hazelton-Carrolls had suffered not just from tragically short life spans but tragically bad taste.

Forcing himself not to dwell on his current dwelling, he turned to Kayla. "What did you find in the fireplace? Were you trying to find loose stones?"

She laughed. "I've found several. None of them had anything hidden behind them until now."

"It looked big."

She went into her room and came back with the rolled and flattened piece in her hands. But then there was no clean spot on the table to lay it out. Kayla's desk would be cluttered with organized piles of papers, and if anyone touched anything, she knew and was bothered by it.

"Bring it back and we'll spread it out on the bed. Reenie will want to see it." Maybe he could continue some of the not-good-but-passable-will between the two women.

They followed the dark tan hallway to the end to his and Reenie's room. In the middle was a queen-sized bed from a big box store. Had the house not been so hideous in its own right, the bed would have looked crudely out of place. But the layers of paint obscured the fine work in the moldings, the carpet was an old, nearly-shag model, and the cheap corners of the low-slung bed fit right in.

Reenie sat cross-legged near the head, propped on pillows, the letters stacked to one side of her, her log notebook on the other, and the diary in her lap where she read.

"Kayla found something under a stone in one of the fireplaces."

His girlfriend perked. "Is it more letters? Lovers would tuck letters into secret places for the other to find. This was particularly true when they were courting and couldn't be together."

Holding up the thick paper, Kayla shook her head. "Blueprint." She sat and unscrolled it across the bed, carefully revealing labels, notes, and descriptions of materials.

Evan frowned. It looked like a machine. "Do you know what it is?"

Reenie said nothing; this was not her area of expertise. But Kayla spoke, "It looks like a generator of some kind, but nothing I've ever seen."

Still cross-legged with the diary in her lap, Reenie leaned forward to examine it. She grabbed at the corner and tugged it toward her, "Look, it says 'E.W.' and it's dated Oct, 1821."

Kayla spoke at the same time, pointing somewhere else on the diagram, "This gear is out in the carriage house."

Kayla sat in the carriage house on the packed dirt that still carried the imagined smell of old wood and horses. She told herself that the horses had never been kept here, only the carriages themselves, but there was something about lifting the hand-hewn T-latch and coming through the wooden door to where there were still ruts in the ground from years of wooden spoke wheels, and just a few treads from car tires.

The light was poor, the lack of windows standard in this type of outbuilding. There was space for three carriages—according to Ivy, a large amount for an average family, but typical on a wealthy plantation then—each with their own double doors for entry. Two spaces had seen far more use than the third, and a smaller, person-sized entrance was embedded at the far left side. That entrance was not the size of a typical household door today, but Kayla's healthy five-foot-eight frame could fit.

She'd brought in a standing light, running an extension cord from the Overseer's House. Though there was power in the big house, she didn't trust it. The Overseer's was the only part that had been in continual use until just a few years ago when Reenie's cousin had moved out to be closer to one of his baby mamas; it was the only part that had been pulled through time to anywhere near the modern century.

So Kayla flexed the neck of the lamp until a cone of light pointed the way she needed. There were ten contraptions lined up and stacked along the back wall of the third bay. She almost laughed at the thought of Civil-War families using their garages for crap storage just the way any modern person would. It seemed there were many more American traditions than just the Fourth of July and apple pie.

The rusted pieces stared back at her, hand cranks off to one side all at different angles. It would soothe her to align them all, but she didn't want to touch them. The wooden boxes built around them had started to decay, showing rusted wire-mesh barrels inside, bent and twisted comb fingers that had once sat perfectly straight, picking cotton fibers through the holes and leaving the seeds behind. Why there were so many on this particular farm, Kayla couldn't say. But they had all been put away at the same time, it seemed. All lined up neat, maybe a hundred or more years ago, and not touched again. Kayla respected that.

But she had come for something else.

There were long wooden moldings stacked into the corner, short squat pieces of wood, a large barrel that sported a painted label she could no longer read, and a handful of metal bands for other barrels long since dismantled. Other pieces sat in stacks, some neater than others; some pieces looked to be partially under dirt, probably having burrowed their way in with time and water.

She tugged the lamp further so she didn't get in her own light. There.

In the third stack, flat on its side, sandwiched between a stubby four-by-four and three useless pieces of molding, was the gear. Though she didn't want to disturb the history stacked there, she wanted the gear. She wondered if Reenie would be mad at her for moving something before it was catalogued, but not caring enough to stop. Reenie would be mad about something, it was really just a question of what. This would certainly fit the bill.

Kayla turned the gear over in her hand, paying no attention to the red dust it embedded into her skin. The heft of it pulled her in, the sharpness of the corners, the single seam that ran around one edge and had been worn almost, but not quite, non-existent. This had not been hewn at the smithy's here on the farm; it had been made from a mold somewhere else and brought here.

The problem was that there were two gears like this in the diagram—one larger, one smaller. Kayla didn't know which she held in her hand. The diagram had been clear on many things and decidedly vague on others. The overall size of the machine was definitely in the vague category. How exactly it worked and whether or not it actually did were two other fuzzy spots. Kayla loved a mystery.

Trying not to disturb Reenie's future catalogue, Kayla moved piece after piece, constructing new piles of odds and ends. She'd learned from experience, that though she would know at a moment's glance that everything had been touched, no one else would likely see it. They were as blind to that as she was to the nuances of propriety. Her only real concern was that Evan would ask her about it. She was a terrible liar, but as long as no one asked point blank, they'd never know she'd rearranged it all.

Once she found the second gear she could start to determine the size of the overall machine. Then she would know what to look for to find all the pieces.

THE EARLY DAWN was cool and wet, one of the things Evan loved about living out here. One of the many things that led him to think it might become permanent. He stood with his bare feet leaching some of his excess body heat into the dewy grass while the sun came up on the other side of the creek.

The big house, and thus the Overseer's as well, had been aligned east to west, so the front faced the sunrise, and the back the sunset. Long porches allowed the family to take advantage of the views. But Evan wondered how long it had been since another family had sat there.

This morning he raised his mug in a salute to Ivy as he passed by. Standing there in tight jeans and a snug white tank that didn't quite hide the purple of her bra, Ivy looked just a little on the slutty side of normal. It was enough to make him grateful that he'd called both her school and her previous employers for references, or he would have been hard pressed to say this was the same woman who'd interviewed in a standard, pale-blue suit. The same one who held the only doctorate degree among them. The one he couldn't now bring himself to address as Dr. Lopez. Her thick black hair and dark skin contrasted with her violet eyes, marking her as much Irish as she was Hispanic. Now the odd color of those eyes focused sharply on him.

"Is everything all right?"

He didn't answer, just asked another question, because honestly he thought things were fine, but he couldn't say for sure. "Have you seen Kayla?"

"At seven in the morning? She's usually gone by six." She came down off the porch to join him.

And his thoughts turned to his mistake at the interview. He'd really oversold the whole "keep an eye on Kayla" thing if Ivy already knew Kayla's standard schedule.

"Can I help? Is she okay?"

He smiled. "She's usually just fine. Often found something and just didn't realize the time had passed. Chances are when we find her, she'll be engrossed in some project and think it's still yesterday."

Ivy stopped dead. "Seriously? The sun went down and the temperature dropped about thirty degrees. How could a person not notice that?" She'd started sweeping the area visually like he did, probably also wondering where the hell a twenty-nine-year-old woman could have holed up all night on a plantation. She sure hadn't been in her bed or even her room.

"There." He spotted an orange power cable running along the left side of the house. Turning to follow it, he tried to explain. Not that anyone ever really could. "She's just so focused. You know how you read or get on the computer and don't realize an hour passed when you only planned to be on for a minute or two?"

A small nod from Ivy cued him.

"Now multiply that focus—that intent—by about a thousand."

Ivy made a face that said she understood the concept but wasn't sure she believed the reality.

So he tried to smooth it over. "I don't know what it's like either. But if we find her, you'll see it. Then you'll believe. The rest of us neurotypicals will probably never know what it's like to be that focused."

As he rounded the corner and saw the cord disappear into the far left door of the carriage house, she spoke up, "Neuro-typicals? . . . Never mind. I've got it."

He pushed open the door, the early dawn light falling perfectly into the empty space. The cord fed a lamp that was off, but aimed into a corner. Though nothing looked disturbed or missing, Kayla wouldn't have gone to the trouble to bring out a light to not touch anything. "Crap."

Ivy was sipping her coffee as she tucked one old Converse lace-up sneaker behind the other. Evan wondered if she had matched the purple in her shoes to her bra on purpose. She seemed to be taking cues from him about how worried to be and her voice reflected that. "I think I noticed the megawatt flashlight missing this morning from the set-up room, and I think the door to the smithy wasn't ajar yesterday."

He smiled. "Maybe you have a touch of it, too."

She laughed. "Just a touch. Or maybe a good solid smack of OCD. Nothing diagnosable, but I would have marched down and latched the smithy door if I'd noticed it last night."

They wandered across the property, silently sipping coffee and high stepping as the yard gave way to the open grounds where the grass was no longer bowed to the mower. He considered going back for shoes, but then decided against it. His time was best spent finding Kayla.

They went over the creek, walking the foot bridge that was in their most direct path. Three bridges had been built over the maximum width the water might take in high season. Evan had yet to see the need for a bridge so wide and high, but he couldn't help admiring the solid construction. He felt a strange satisfaction for some dead farmer or possibly slave who had done such great work that the bridge was strong enough to easily hold a horse or two a good 150 years after the building of it. The old wood had worn away where hooves and feet had passed probably tens of thousands of times and he wanted to stop and admire it, but he had to find his sister, so he simply crossed it. The only enjoyment he took was the feeling of well-loved wood under his bare feet.

Worry weighing in his chest, he traipsed on, his sweatpants ruined with dew and hitchhikers. He had always found Kayla before. Ninety-five percent of the time, everything was fine—

except his heart rate. The other five percent she usually wound up fine, too. Only once, in junior high, had she gone off with some boy and gotten herself far from home and far from safe. It was probably a normal teenage girl thing to do, but it had scared the shit out of Evan. And here, out in the middle of Southern nowhere, he remembered that feeling, remembered her scared voice over the cell phone and him rushing to get her, afraid he wouldn't be in time. That time there had been a bonfire, drugs, and a gun.

There were no gangs here, no mean girls in junior high, no guns. But maybe she'd decided to restart the blacksmith's fire, maybe she'd decided to rebuild the brick hut on her own, maybe she'd constructed a bandsaw and was harvesting soft wood trees and planking them. With Kayla you never knew.

And he reminded himself that she was smart and that it had been years since she'd needed anything more than a reminder to eat, anything more than a pathway back to the world the rest of them lived in. But old habits died hard.

"Do you hear that?" Ivy stopped, her head cocked to one side as she listened.

He did. Just a faint noise.

"Kayla!?" He yelled it, though that was often as useful as pissing in the wind. She could be ten feet away and not respond if she was in the zone.

"Ev?" The faint voice came from behind the blacksmith's, and she peeked around the side of the building, unsurprisingly wearing the same clothing as the day before. "Ivy!"

Of course, he worried his ass off and she lit up a smile for Ivy.

"Come see what I have."

She probably still had no clue it was seven in the morning. Kayla was clearly alive, healthy and happy. Maybe a little dehydrated, but he couldn't see it, so he followed Ivy who hadn't hesitated at all.

Behind the smithy's was a cleared patch of hearth stones and hard-packed ground. Littered around the small area were various gears and cranks, an old chain rusted into an unusable twist. She'd made piles of pieces, grouped them in some way that Evan didn't fathom.

Ivy seemed to understand even less. "You stayed out here all night?"

Looking up to the new sun, Kayla took stock. "I guess so. The moon was brightest back here, and the pieces were all over the place."

Evan sipped his coffee and quietly looked Kayla over. There was dirt on her jeans and shirt, her hair had slipped her ponytail, and much of it had come down around her face in wisps that he knew Reenie was jealous of and Kay couldn't care less about.

Ivy didn't seem to put much stake in the other woman's appearance one way or another, "I guess you'll be sleeping most of the day, huh?" Her surprise at both Evan and Kayla's quick answers was evident.

"Nope."

"No, she won't." He followed it up with the same thing he did anytime someone didn't understand his sister. "It's the Aspergers."

Ivy frowned at him. "I wouldn't have thought so. I haven't read anything about lack of need for sleep."

She'd been reading about it?

A small smile split her face as Ivy seemed to read his mind, too. "I read about everything that interests me." Then she turned to Kayla. "I'm guessing it's because you're so smart. They say daVinci only slept a few hours every night, and lowered need for sleep is most common in the highly intelligent."

"I am highly intelligent." Kayla smiled.

Evan had almost said it. He knew it sounded better coming from him. From her, it was often taken as arrogant.

Ivy nodded as though Kayla had simply stated that the sun rose in the east, and he felt an iron weight lift from his shoulders a bit. He'd carried it even when his little sister had lived in a different city. He'd fretted for her daily, been angry with the people around her for not understanding her. He even hated her old boss, Williams, though he'd never met the ass. But maybe here in this insular world he could stop worrying. He could focus on Reenie. On him.

So he decided to give a little more explanation. Bring Ivy into the circle a little more. "They say it takes ten thousand hours of practice to become an expert at something. That's five years at full time. Most Aspies hit that mark in their chosen interest before age ten." He looked from one to the other. "Do me a favor and head up for breakfast in about twenty minutes? I'll get Reenie to fix us something, or maybe I will."

They both nodded at him, then he did something he rarely did. He turned and walked away.

The last thing he heard as he moved out of earshot was Kayla's voice. "I'm building it."

4

B ack Field

EVAN TURNED off the old tractor engine for a moment and went through a small handful of soothing rituals. He adjusted his bandanna from where it had worked itself askew and took a long drink from his water bottle where the ice was already nearly gone. Then he stopped and just enjoyed not having his bones rattled.

There would be no new tractor.

Though it was planned for, the plantation account was steadily dropping. Kayla had even added fifty percent beyond the calculated total for new ideas, increased-from-expectation costs, and—as she called it—"random plantation finds." She'd already had a handful of those herself.

Just yesterday, Kayla bought a second metal detector, thankfully from her personal savings, and today she and Ivy were scanning the yard behind the big house. They'd been digging up all kinds of things. Kayla had already run the half-mile across the field once today with Ivy in tow to show off the silver tea pot they'd found.

Kayla and Ivy's unflagging enthusiasm had turned the yard into a Civil-War-era treasure hunt. Reenie was still asleep, having begged off the day, not feeling well again. Since he was pretty sure she wasn't pregnant, and since he suspected her late night work would pay off in the end, he'd let it go. Now he was grateful that she wasn't up to see the series of holes the two other women had dug into the backyard. Grass seed already waited in sturdy bags to help put the place back to rights.

Kayla smiled and told him that Ivy had the great idea to flag the backyard with references for the big items—like the teapot and a gold and pearl necklace. They could then post a sign at the side of the yard explaining how antebellum women had buried their valuables to keep them from being confiscated by Union troops, marauding bandits or even the Confederate government to help pay for the war.

Highlighting the finds was a great idea. But it meant they needed engraved brass plates for each piece. They needed an all-weather-proof plaque at the side of the yard explaining the markers. And so Kayla's extra fifty percent dwindled as fast as the calculated amounts did.

That meant there was no new tractor in the budget.

And the old one shook him in a way he hadn't thought possible. It was like being on a five-hour-long wooden roller coaster. He hated those things.

But he loved the idea of cotton.

Evan cranked the engine back up and looked over his shoulder at the rows he was digging behind him. They were a little blurred in his vision because of the vibration of the machine under him. They probably also didn't look quite straight, because they weren't. But he was a carpenter, not a farmer, and the growing cotton plants would obscure any small deviations in a short while.

If they wanted the plantation running cotton by next year, he had to get the crop in.

Obviously, they couldn't run a whole plantation with four people. And they couldn't run a museum with just four people either. But they were nowhere near ready to open the doors, and so for now, they were on their own.

He'd already decided that—as cool as having the plantation running as it had in the 1700s was—there was no way he was planting all the fields. One would be plenty to show people what it would have looked like. To show them a cotton plant up close and, when the season was right, let them pick some of the stiff, fluffy heads. Kayla would set up a room with carding equipment and working cotton gins for people to use and there were plans to put the originals in the garage on display.

The museum had been Reenie's crazy idea to save Hazelton House. She wasn't rich enough to own it outright. She didn't want to sell it, it had been in her family for generations. And one night, distraught about the options, she'd said, "Do you think I could get a loan to turn it into a museum?"

There had never been a snowball's chance in hell of Reenie getting that kind of loan with her negative credit. But then Kayla had gotten fired again, and here they were. There wasn't enough money to start a full-scale museum. But they could rent out the back fields—Reenie was already talking to several farmers about that. And they could open the doors with parts of the house and main buildings ready to show.

It was Kayla who'd said, "Do enough, just enough. Then charge a low admission and get a lot of foot traffic through. Have something fun. As we make money, we'll add more things, and the same people will want to come back again. Then we can slowly raise the price of admission."

Leave it to Miss Math to calculate it all out. While Reenie

pondered the idea, Kayla had hung up. Fifteen minutes later, Evan and Reenie's phones had beeped with an email. There was a spreadsheet with start-up numbers, cost analysis, underestimated attendance and profit, and the subject line "This works."

Reenie had nearly cried.

But never once had she thanked Kayla for saving her family home. She was blind to the fact that Kayla had done it. It was just his weird sister, crunching numbers again.

So Evan was out here riding the tractor, getting his back chiropracted in the worst way while his heart clenched at the thought of the two of them. He wondered what he would do if never the twain met.

Dammit.

He had to quit letting his thoughts wander. When his thoughts went astray, so did his lines. Nothing too bad, but the local farmers might make fun of him. Still, his back would kill him tomorrow if his head didn't kill him today. He needed some drugs and a good foot rub, and he knew just the woman to blackmail into it.

With those simple needs firmly in his sights, Evan polished off his water and started through the last turn. He faced away from the house now, the sight of Ivy and Kayla working with some kind of excited frenzy lost to him. He didn't much think he was one to jump up and down and wave his hands like a girl, but he was jealous that their work—though no less hard than his—brought them such fits of joy.

The sun was lower than he'd expected it to be when he rounded the last turn. Coming from somewhere east, a slight breeze had kicked up, bringing with it the scent of ripe and slightly gone greenery. He smelled the nearby creek, even if he couldn't hear it with the sound of the engine obliterating everything short of nuclear war. And he found himself hoping for a good rainy season ahead.

It was nearly summer, late for cotton. But it was either plant late or plant not at all. They hoped to open doors in late August and—though the bolls would not yet be busting open—have a field full of plants to display. For the first visitors there would be bought rather than home-grown cotton to hand pick and to gin.

From day one Reenie had been working at the museum calendar. They would follow the dictates set forth by the owners in the past. Once a month they would spend a day making candles—and invite people to participate and take some nearly authentic pieces of the past home with them. They would make lye and scented household soaps. Bring in experts to teach embroidery. Weave scarves with cotton fibers. They could charge for the classes and materials. Reenie hoped to be the proud owner of a sticky trap for the local and touristy historians and crafters alike.

Evan had asked if they would be killing pigs and salting bacon in December. While slaughter certainly didn't appeal, putting up meat and making his own bacon definitely did.

Reenie had refused, but why just do women's work? A man could dream. He figured men would like it . . . get your hands dirty, learn something and go home with bacon.

Ivy lobbied for a greenhouse. She wanted it to stand where the old one had—she'd already located the stone outline of the original foundation, the only thing left of a hundred-year-old glass and wood structure.

Reenie had immediately bumped that idea down the list and tasked Ivy with researching the oil paintings, writing up the history of color schemes, and so on. Ivy had taken it upon herself to preserve and re-do the stenciling on the walls and floors and also to look further, into the slave cabins and cemetery for original art that might be buried or dismissed there.

Evan shook his head as he finally chugged toward the barn. The four of them were an amazing mix. Ivy had been a lucky find . . . the only one to answer their oddly worded ad in several local papers and online. But Reenie had quoted from "*Little Women*" the night they'd interviewed then hired her. "You only need one, if it's the right one."

Locking the tractor into the barn meant for horses and plows, he still felt an odd sense of satisfaction, of completion, of home. Then again, maybe he'd just shaken his brain too much. Because, as amazing a team as the four of them were, they were all nucking futs to be doing this.

Checking his water bottle, he found it as empty as he'd expected to. He needed a drink, but didn't think he was fit to stand in the kitchen before he showered. Hopefully Reenie would have woken up and driven into town to get some dinner for them all.

Though Kayla and Ivy were in sight the whole time, the plantation was big, and the breeze and still-lingering rattle in his head stole their voices until he was nearly upon them.

Spotting him, Kayla came running up, her hands cupped together. Kayla wasn't one for catching frogs, and when he got close his curiosity was rewarded: coins. She pushed them closer to him, suggesting he pick one up, but he held his grubby hands away from her shiny treasure. Unaccepting of his refusal, she took his free hand and poured a couple into his palm. Kayla didn't notice the dirt on him, and it took a moment to see that she too was covered in it. Hers was, of course, a rich topsoil rather than the dry dust that had kicked up in the field. But she was just as filthy as he was.

Tucking his water bottle under his arm he used a dirty fingertip to flip one coin over.

The letters *CSA*. Two men on horseback.

On another, a draped woman and the words "Confederate States of America."

He almost dropped them.

His eyes first caught Kayla's and he stared at the smile on her face. Then he swept the area where he stood. Small white boundary flags from the local home store littered the area, popping up like flowers growing randomly through the yard. His brain shut down.

Ivy then came into his narrowed view, hauling Reenie by the wrist.

As though time was in slow motion, he surveyed the three women. Kayla and Ivy were each in old jeans and t-shirts—Ivy in her usual slightly tight version and Kayla wearing something printed with a math slogan. Reenie was dressed and made up to go into town, and she now bore a bucket and bag labeled with a big red KFC. Evan felt his stomach turn at the idea of another piece of chicken. But the wonder and confusion on her face stopped all thoughts of food.

Ivy looked back and forth between them all. Then she announced, "We found enough stuff to have a display and enough more to sell to help fund the museum."

Evan stared at Reenie. "What do you mean they lost it?"

Her eyes were wide and they were about to overflow with the tears she had held back. She shook her head. She held the phone away from her, the speaker a touch grainy as the voice on the other side of the line came through again.

"I'm sure we'll find it. There are only so many places it can be. But I don't have it ready for pick-up right now."

He watched Reenie take a deep breath before she let fly. "That was your *only* job. Protect it and have it finished by today."

"We did protect it."

Reenie's lip curled. "Well, I'm soothed knowing that someone else has my historical document well protected."

Evan heard the clear message lurking under her sarcasm and the man from the preservation company responded in kind. "I assure you ma'am, this has never happened to us before."

Reenie's volley back was fast and angry. "I assure you, sir, that this is the last time I'll use your company. That document had not been assessed, and thus I can sue you for its *possible* value."

"Ma'am, you didn't purchase the additional insurance on it. Our policy is that—if we fail to produce it within three more weeks—we will pay you our minimum $100 insurance fee." He paused, but not long enough to let Reenie form a rebuttal. "We will continue to look for it. I'll keep you posted of our progress."

"Certainly." Evan spoke through gritted teeth. He knew the little man had heard him when he first came into the room, but now he wanted to remind the shop-keeper that he wasn't just dealing with a woman close to tears who hadn't insured the document in question. "We'll call and visit regularly. Good-bye."

Her face a mask of self-irritation and outright anger, Reenie huffed. "He's over an hour away! I called five different places and he had the best recommendations of anyone. Why is ours the first thing that he ever loses?!"

Evan was pretty sure it wasn't a question, and even if it was, there was no answer, so he practiced his shut-up-ism and offered her a hug. He needed the hug, too. His brain was on fast forward. That diagram was nothing, but it was the first thing to leave the borders of the plantation. Reenie wanted it protected right away, since Kayla seemed hell bent on working with it.

They hadn't even tried to sell any of the coins yet. A new seller on the market could start a frenzy; they needed to do it right, get the money and not alert anyone what was here. They didn't need people sneaking onto their land looking for a confederate gold mine. Not that it was; probably much of it had been recovered from the preceding generations.

He had once wondered out loud why no one had gone out with a metal detector before. Reenie thought someone probably had, pointing out that Kayla had insisted on the best equipment, no hobbyist metal detector for her. So she'd likely found stuff others hadn't. And then Reenie had asked him, "You never met Roy or Billy did you?"

It had been rhetorical and she didn't wait for an answer, "Well, let's just say rocks are smarter. And when it comes to Aunt Charlene those apples fell right under that tree. It's why so much of the place is in such bad shape."

So they had kept their finds close to home, and he hated that the first thing out appeared to be gone. He was trying to comfort Reenie by saying, "I'm sure they'll find it. They've never lost anything before, so why would they start now?" when both Kayla and Ivy wandered into the office with identical bowls of cereal in hand.

As tight as his chest was about the lost diagram, it did him good to see the friendship that was developing between the two women.

Kayla didn't have a lot of tight friends. Now, as best he could tell, Ivy was becoming a real friend. The two hung out together for no reason. They'd gone to see a movie on the other side of Savannah four nights ago—dropping off the diagram on the way —and it seemed that Ivy was invested for herself, not because he'd asked her to watch out for his sister.

Reenie stiffened in his arms as she noticed the other women. Neither had said anything, taking in the scene the two of them made; Reenie in his arms fighting tears, his jaw clenched to the point of breaking.

Kayla paid no homage to the stiff silence and broke it. "What's wrong?"

Reenie looked up at his sister. "Oh, Kayla." She sniffed. "They lost your diagram."

"What?" Both Ivy and Kayla asked simultaneously.

Finally losing it, now that she had to put it into words, Reenie began to cry great sobs and punctuated her sentences with gulps for air. "The company that was protecting it! They can't find it. It's gone!"

Taking the half-full cereal bowls, Ivy set them on the desk. But once Kayla's hands were empty she turned to Reenie and—

Evan could only guess she was mimicking him—took Reenie into an awkward but genuine hug. "It's okay. I know what was on it."

"But—"

Kayla didn't let her finish, "There are lots of historical documents in this house. It was just one. And one that didn't make a lot of sense. I've been building the machine in my spare time, and I honestly don't think it works. Ivy's been helping."

Ivy shrugged. "'*Helping*' is a generous term. I hand her things she needs. Ask me about the oils used in the paintings or the stencil patterns chosen for the walls, I'm all over it. But gears are not my thing."

Plus Kayla was working from memory, Evan knew. He'd been there. When Kayla worked out of her head, there was no list of steps for the other person to follow, no diagram to know what would be needed next, how to proceed.

But Reenie shook her head. "We need to sit down." She looked around; there weren't enough seats in here for all four of them and she headed to the dining room. That she'd left the cereal bowls unattended on the desk indicated that things were worse than he thought. He didn't grab them either, just shut the office door behind him and followed.

She pointed to seats and took one herself, wringing her hands as she did. His chest tightened again.

"I didn't know when we turned it in, or I would have insured it." Her voice was small.

"Didn't know what?" He loved his sister, but she could never wait for a reveal. He did. Reenie would get there.

"I know y'all did the partial tear down on the last wall by yourselves. And I didn't feel well that day, but it was because I'd been up all night reading and doing research." After a breathy pause that barely masked tightly held tears, Reenie continued. "I read Carlee's diary. All of it. The boy she had a crush on was an apprentice or assistant to the man who visited. There's eventually some information about him. I think that's why the diary was in the wall with the letters and the clothing."

Kayla and Ivy frowned, but as usual, Kayla didn't wait. "What does this have to do with my diagram?"

Reenie shook her head, breaking free. "I'm so sorry."

Kayla shrugged. "The attic is full of papers and things to put on display, most of it just as useless as the diagram. The bloody clothes will be much more intriguing to the visitors, as will the diary."

Evan knew she was just repeating what he'd said. Kayla actually found the idea of displaying what was probably associated with a crime as abhorrent. But she was trying to soothe Reenie, and trying to do it in a way that would actually *soothe* Reenie. When she'd been younger, Kayla would have simply stood up and walked out, figuring that since she wanted to be alone when she was upset, so would someone else. Now she knew better, and though her motions were awkward, she tried.

Reenie sniffed and started talking again. "The young man was named Edward, and I thought at first maybe he was the 'E' in the letters. But seventeen seemed young for an affair with the house mistress. Edward was the apprentice to an unmarried man who visited frequently. Apparently that man had an affair with Lena, Carlee's mother. Carlee was suspicious of this, but didn't put into so many words. So it was hard to figure out for a bit.

"Both women mentioned that the men, one listed as 'E' and the other referred to as 'Edward,' visited from a nearby plantation but didn't live there. That plantation was Mulberry Grove." Reenie looked heavenward as though asking for forgiveness. As of yet, she was the only one who seemed to think she needed it. But since it seemed cathartic for her to talk it out—as it always did with Reenie—Evan motioned for Kayla to wait and see what happened.

"Edward was Edward Temple. According to the house Bible, he married Carlee Hazelton in 1810. His is the name that my mother pulled for my middle name." For a moment Reenie smiled. "Anyway, as best I can tell, Edward traveled extensively with E, landing often at Mulberry Grove. . ."

She waited.

No one moved.

"You don't know who owned Mulberry Grove?" She asked them all, clearly surprised that no one did.

Evan wanted to point out that none of them came from a family with a plantation and that her shock was misplaced. But he just shrugged.

"Phineas Miller did."

That clue still left him nothing and the thick silence reinforced that Kayla and Ivy were with him.

"He was business partners with Eli Whitney. That's why there are ten cotton gins in the carriage house. No one plantation needed that many. . . . I'm pretty certain that Eli Whitney is the 'E' in the diary."

Kayla raised her eyebrows, but it was Ivy who spoke for them all. "Then the diagram was possibly of an unpatented later invention of Whitney's?"

Reenie nodded.

"Oh shit." Ivy slapped back into the chair as though blasted with buck shot.

And that was when Reenie lost her composure. "I didn't know! I didn't think—ever!—that the initials E.W. would mean *Eli Whitney*. Or I *never* would have sent it out." Her face plunged into her hands and she began to cry again in earnest.

It took them three full minutes to gather themselves enough for someone to figure out to get Reenie a tissue. Then they had to go get her another one. And another. By the third trip Kayla brought the whole box from the other room, absently slapping it on the table. Reenie must have interpreted the sound as anger and she began crying harder.

"I'm so sorry, Kayla."

His sister shook her head. "It's okay." She frowned and even Evan had no idea what she was thinking. He didn't try, just sat there with his arm around Reenie, trying to comfort her over the loss of something priceless and a piece of her own history.

Finally, she looked up at him. "It gets worse."

Three pairs of eyes turned to look at her. Her own were red-rimmed and getting puffy. They were wet with tears still over-flowing and making dirty tracks down her cheeks. No one moved while they all waited for Reenie to get it together.

At last, she did. "There was a cufflink in the pocket of the pants . . . the bloody pants from the wall. If all the things were put there for one reason, then the shirt possibly belongs to Martin Hazelton. The cufflink said 'MH'. I was confused by it, but it fits."

Ivy shook her head, not following.

"If Martin found out about the affair then . . . Anyway, Whitney died in 1825 and there are no real records about how or where that happened. And the bloodstain on the shirt looked *spattered*. If the shirt is Martin's, then the blood could be Whitney's."

5

Dining Room, Overseer's House

"Don't you think you're jumping to conclusions?" Kayla immediately regretted not adding a "maybe." She had long ago learned that a "maybe" or "often" softened the blows she didn't mean to deal.

Luckily, Reenie was so distraught that she didn't seem to take offense, something Kayla measured only partly by Reenie's actions. The rest she measured by the fact that Evan hadn't frowned at her. She was reassured again by the speed with which Ivy jumped in to say much the same thing.

"Yeah, Reenie. That blood could be anybody's. You may be right, but just because we have a bloody shirt, a page signed 'E.W.' and a diary in the wall doesn't mean it all goes together that way." She tipped her head. "I can think of lots of options, and about eighty-five percent aren't hinky at all. Also, Kayla and I found so much today."

Reenie found a smile for Ivy, but only a small one. Evan had said that Reenie just tended to keep to herself, but Kayla was pretty certain that she was so fond of propriety and her Southern ways that she didn't have many truly friendly bones in her body. Still Kayla figured there had to be more than what she could see. Her brother wouldn't love someone as closed up as Reenie always seemed to be—that attitude must be reserved just for Kayla. Of course, what could be worse to a belle than a woman with an engineering degree and Aspergers? Except maybe Ivy. Regardless, it was nothing that could be fixed. She was who she was.

Still, Reenie was willing to be led off the path of self-recrimination, "Do you know what you found? Like what era it's from and how much it's worth? Does your degree cover that?"

Ivy's eyebrow went up, but Kayla had missed something.

"No. My Ph.D. is in antebellum art and artistic endeavors. So I know some things about the teapots and some of the hand painting on the china and not much about the rest." Then her voice took on a certain tilt that Kayla couldn't quite identify, "But I do have this really great cell phone that gets the Internet. It's pretty fast. Oh, and there's eBay."

Evan looked back and forth between Ivy and Kayla after that and Kayla wanted to jump up and shout *"What did I do?"* But since she felt that way on a nearly daily basis, she reined the impulse.

Reenie remained blank-faced. "I bet your degree left you with a lot of student loans."

A small smile played across the dark-haired woman's features. "No, it didn't. I left school with all my bills paid and a bit in savings. My mother was a stripper and a high school dropout. She told me to get an education and have a better life. So I stripped my way through college and grad school."

Oh. That explained a lot. Maybe Ivy thought she was dressing conservatively. And Kayla had to ask, "Did that cause a lot of trouble with your boyfriends?"

Evan started to stand and walk away, but just before he did he gave her that look, the one that she knew meant she had 'stepped over the line' and could expect an awkward silence in return. And she wanted to shout at him again, but though she held her ire, she did ask it. "What? It's a legitimate question!"

Ivy laughed. "It wasn't a problem. There were no boyfriends—"

"But you're so pretty!" With her almost-violet eyes and long wavy hair, Ivy had a classic face with a touch of the exotic. Even her skin was pretty. And if she was taking it all off . . .

Ivy laughed again. "I'm gay."

"Oh." Kayla struggled with what to say next. But that was a problem she was deeply familiar with. So she *almost* knew what to do. Almost. Kayla figured if she'd already dug herself into a hole, she should say something nice to get out of it, right? "That explains a lot."

Over Ivy's shoulder she could see Evan put his face in his hands. But Ivy just laughed again, a deep, rich sound that went straight to the heart.

Kayla smiled. And then she looked at Reenie, surprised to find that her surely-future-sister-in-law was almost smiling herself.

"REALLY?" Kayla stared incredulously at Ivy, who stood there with a shovel propped under one arm. Kayla held her own shovel, but with much less authority.

"Of course." Ivy made her "serious" face, but Kayla didn't trust it.

"I really don't think digging it up is wise. In fact, it seems like the exact opposite of wise."

Ivy smiled. "It won't smell. There's been plumbing in the house for over a hundred years."

Reenie came out then, old jeans and a T-shirt, a shovel in hand, though she didn't seem to know why. "What are we doing, ladies?"

That's when it hit Kayla. Reenie had been jealous of Ivy—afraid that the slightly slutty doctor would steal Evan away. That was just bad math, as far as Kayla could tell. Evan loved Reenie. He loved her when she was "on," when she was the star of the party and talking to everyone and running everything. And he loved her when she was "off"—sour and brooding like she was to Kayla a lot of the time and to Ivy all the time.

Then at breakfast, Reenie asked Ivy how she wanted her eggs. She'd asked Kayla, too, but it was clearly Ivy she was suddenly much more relaxed around. Because she'd learned Ivy was gay. Ivy was not going to steal Reenie's man. Case closed. Happy face on. Then Kayla and Ivy had come out here to do Ivy's digging and now here was Reenie, dressed to match, shovel in hand, not a clue in sight.

Ivy smiled. "We're digging up the outhouse!"

Reenie recoiled. "That seems like a bad, bad idea."

"That's what I said!" Kayla found herself facing Ivy, siding with Reenie for once. "Why are we digging up old people's poop?"

Ivy sighed. "How many times do I have to say it? There's no crap down there! It's all gone, decomposed. To everything, there is a season, turn turn and all that. What *is* down there are all the old *dishes* . . ." She looked pointedly at Reenie on that one. "Silver maybe. Anything a house slave may have chipped or bent. Rather than getting punished for it, they made it disappear. Down the outhouse."

That snagged Reenie's attention.

And then Kayla was the only one standing there. Ivy and Reenie—now best buds—had moved to where the bathroom first stood, and they were breaking ground. Chattering like magpies, they didn't notice that she'd walked away. And Kayla began to wonder if Ivy hadn't seen Reenie's jealousy problem and announced that she was gay to help smooth things between them.

Maybe she wasn't even gay. Maybe she'd just said it so Reenie would get that stick out of her butt.

Regardless, the two of them were now in business and Kayla was off on her own again, shovel forgotten. The blacksmith's was down the hill and Kayla had adopted it as a workshop. In the last week she'd hauled a generator down there to run her lights and a small machining tool. She'd been ordering random gears online, causing delivery guys to have to drive their clumsy trucks up the long, rutted drive on five different occasions over the week.

Ivy had talked her into redrawing the diagram. First on paper, then on an oilcloth that Ivy had taken two days to fabricate the way the original would have been. She'd found the proper ink and made Kayla duplicate all of it with a quill.

Ivy and Reenie both let out soft swear words when she finished. Reenie almost touched the still-wet ink, but pulled her hand back at the last moment, saying, "It's uncanny."

Evan shrugged. He'd always known they'd never starve: Kayla had the skills to be a first-rate forger, able to mimic anyone's handwriting. Sadly, her non-existent lying skills got in the way. So she was limited to lost oilcloth diagrams.

The paper one was now in the smithy, spread out on a workbench. For Ivy, not her. Kayla could still see it all in her head. Hell, she'd drawn two exact duplicates of the thing; she didn't need a reference in front of her. Which was a good thing, because the place Reenie had sent the original for 'protection' still hadn't found it. Though they had promised they would not give up searching, they made it clear that they were claiming the loss and marking it as "unfindable" on their records.

Reenie had also searched what she could on Eli Whitney . . . which wasn't much. There just wasn't a lot to be found. A handful of books existed, all at the fifth-grade level. Reenie had first scoffed, but then gave up and read one. She did find a sample of handwriting someone claimed was Whitney's. And Kayla had to admit that it looked nearly identical.

Reenie was beside herself, convinced that she'd lost a priceless document.

Kayla was much less certain.

For one thing, handwriting was an art in those days. Students were taught to write by mimicking their teachers. Whitney's early work was as a tutor, so there were likely a handful of his pupils around the South who had attempted to copy his penmanship. And between the four of them here at Hazelton House they had exactly zero knowledge about handwriting analysis. So Kayla didn't put much stock in the handwriting.

Secondly, the machine didn't work. Whitney had invented the cotton gin. He also designed interchangeable gun parts—and possibly invented the concept. Why would he make such a crappy machine? No, while this was fun to build, it wasn't likely the work of one of the greatest inventors of his time.

She threw open the shutters on the north side of the building and flipped on the light, shoving the dark back into the corners. Still, the awning over the firepit and work area was blocking much of the sun. She sat down and started chipping out teeth in the latest wheel she'd turned on her small lathe. Most people would have checked the circumference to be sure they had it scaled to the correct dimensions. Most people would have measured twice and cut once. But Kayla didn't. She didn't even pre-mark the wood. She didn't count the number of notches in the gear, check the width of the wheel or the angle she cut the teeth at.

She just saw what the wheel needed to be and she chipped out what didn't belong.

She smirked to herself. She was the Michelangelo of gears.

Gears for a machine that likely didn't even work. Still, it beat digging up shit.

EVAN HAD FINISHED PLANTING the cotton seeds in the back field. He was hot, sweaty and in that strange state where he was both miserable and elated. No one saw him slip into the back door at the Overseer's House and that was probably a good thing. If anyone tried to speak to him he'd likely just grunt and walk away.

Hauling back the door of the avocado-colored fridge, he pulled out a very modern glass pitcher of lemonade. That was all Reenie—the pitcher and the fact that it was always full of home-made lemonade—and for a moment he had the vicious dual thought of both enjoying that something here wasn't of completely shitty quality and wondering if Reenie had bought it on a credit card and was still paying off the pitcher.

He slapped an equally pretty glass onto the equally ugly counter and poured it full. Chugging it down, he then poured a second glass and a third before heading out to the porch to decompress.

Every muscle felt like screaming. One day in the cotton field was too much. Three days was ludicrous. And for a moment he stood at the railing of the long back porch realizing it wasn't coin-cidence that he could see all the fields from this spot. He was only the most recent man to stand here and sip from a glass of lemon-ade, exhausted after a full day's work.

The setting sun illuminated the land and he could imagine it all plowed and almost see slaves out there putting away the day's equipment. What Evan couldn't conjure were the thoughts of those slaves or the overseer. His own body sweated from every pore, and his satisfaction was from a job well done, work that was his and his alone.

The history here denied that satisfaction to anyone who would have come before.

Ivy would not have been welcomed. With her Hispanic heritage she would have been relegated to slave quarters and set to mending for pittance wages. Kayla would have been locked in a closet for her oddness. The fact that she was incredibly smart would have only exemplified the disparity in her. Only he and Reenie could have been happy here, and he didn't believe he could ever have a happiness built on the backs of others.

So he drank his lemonade and sweated in response to a job already finished and chose to think of more pleasant things. He surveyed the women, all clustered in the space between the back of the main house and the nearby outbuildings.

Kayla stood in the doorway to the carriage house, the sun setting behind her. The red sky was a beautiful sight, but she couldn't see it from where she lurked. Reenie and Ivy were still digging the pit they had started that morning and had sorted a decent collection of broken pieces of things that he couldn't understand the value of.

He thought for a moment that he saw Kayla squint, but then she went into the carriage house and closed up, latching the main carriage door she'd left open. She resumed her post almost out of sight at the small door on the far left.

Evan watched each of them one at a time, simultaneously feeling oddly protective and thinking that he needed a shower before anyone came within smelling distance of him. As he turned to take care of it, he saw Kayla cock her head at something in the distance.

It wasn't unusual for her to look at something intently. She could be watching the way the grass bent in the slight evening breeze for all he knew. But he always checked. Kayla was still his little sister, so whatever she was staring at intently was always his concern. Following her gaze required that he turn and look out the front windows. The continuing lack of curtains in the main room made it easy to see through from the kitchen.

With a small jolt, he realized what Kayla had been staring at, and why she'd been so reticent to come out of the shadows.

A man in a dark suit was making his way up the long drive. His wingtips pressed into the gravel with each step he took.

Though he wasn't trying to conceal himself, neither did the visitor announce his presence. The drive was long and once anyone was past the small concealing trees that lined the first fifty-plus feet off the road, they were clearly visible to the household. Again, Evan applauded the careful design of Hazelton House.

He stood still, not even lifting his glass for another drink, and watched the figure coming up the driveway.

As he approached, the man took off his suit jacket and pushed up his sleeves; he loosened his tie and tipped his head as though cracking or stretching his neck a bit. He looked left and right, surveying the grounds, then—bold as day—walked up the front steps and knocked on the door.

Evan considered going over and answering it for a second or two, but decided his rank smell left him in no position to greet anyone, let alone a newcomer in a suit and tie. Briefly, the thought passed through his head that the man was an antebellum historian, coming to interview—too late—for Ivy's job. But they hadn't posted any location information in the ad . . . so it couldn't be that.

No one seemed to hear the knocking and Evan thought about yelling for Kayla, but something stopped him. There was something in the way his sister had stared at the man as he'd come up the drive. She hadn't come around to greet him, and Evan knew that she knew it would be the polite thing to do. She'd been carefully trained how to greet people, what to say, and that she *should* welcome people to her home. Had she tucked herself into the shadows at the carriage house on purpose?

As though he were familiar with the place, the man in the suit stepped off the porch and headed around the back of the big house. Evan positioned himself in Kayla's room, where he could see the back area clearly.

Ivy and Reenie were still digging, their heads together like girls at a slumber party. Evan had no idea why Reenie was suddenly okay with everything that was Ivy. But he didn't want to question it; Reenie had always been what his mother would have called "mercurial" in her moods. So he didn't pay attention to their new friendship, only that they still did not see the stranger who was rapidly closing the distance.

He could see Kayla, still lingering in the shadows of the carriage house. The setting sun and the doorway obscured her to anyone who wasn't looking, but Evan could tell her gaze was aimed around the side of the house. She knew the man was coming and she knew from where, too.

Evan felt better that at least one of them was paying attention and disliked his own instantaneous concern. When had he become so paranoid?

As he came into view, the stranger put on a smile and threw out a warm "Hello!" to Ivy and Reenie.

It never failed to amaze Evan how Reenie could paste on a sincere-looking smile at any time. "Hello." She spoke it as though the stranger were an old acquaintance and she walked forward to him in a way that would have had Evan questioning whether or not she knew this man if he didn't know her as well as he did.

Adjusting his jacket to his other shoulder, the man held out his open hand to the land around him. "I just wanted to say hello. I noticed someone was fixing up the plantation. The place looks great, by the way."

He turned in an admiring circle, and Evan faltered back a step, hoping to not be seen by any of them. He still wanted to keep his eye on Kayla, who for some reason hadn't moved.

The man offered another smile, his voice holding just a hint of awe, "May I take a look around?"

"Oh, of course." Reenie smiled. And no wonder, her pride and joy was being admired—even before it was in its glory again. Even as she dug up the pieces of the past from the outhouse.

Stepping forward, the man checked out the pieces of broken dishes, "That's the family china pattern, huh?"

This time it was Ivy who beamed at their holdings. "Yes! According to my cell phone, it's a pattern that started around the early 1800s—Crown Bavaria. There's also some Spode and Wedgwood."

"Wow." He sounded sincere. Evan almost laughed. He would never be able to get that level of interest into his voice over broken china. But then the topic turned. "Do you mind if I walk around a little? I'd love to see the outbuildings."

Only then did Kayla step out of the shadows, surprising Evan and the women. If she shocked the stranger, he didn't show it.

"No. I'm sorry, but we aren't ready to show the place."

Reenie's eyes narrowed to daggers, but she smiled to cover her ire. "Oh, sure, it's not ready but—"

She was cut off by a smooth but firm Kayla. "None of us is clean enough to lead a tour. But we'll be open to the public in about four months. We'd love for you to come back then."

This time she smiled at the man and Evan barked out a laugh that had him slapping his hand over his mouth. Kayla's mimicry skills had made a show; she had become Reenie—Reenie with an agenda. She did not want this man looking around.

Reenie had her own agenda. "It'll be fine, I'm sure. Are you a neighbor?"

Ivy watched the back and forth like it was a tennis match, growing more confused with each volley. The man watched, too, and tucked his hands into his pockets, rocked back onto his heels. "Right over on Docket." With his head, he nodded in the direction of the subdivision down the main way.

But as Evan watched, he saw Kayla step behind the man and shake her head at Ivy. She'd bypassed Reenie, knowing there was no ground to be gained there. But Ivy was still a possible ally. Evan was getting ready to step out on the porch, dirty and sweaty clothes be damned, just as Ivy stepped up.

Softly, she put her hand on Reenie's arm, looking regal in the gesture despite the too short cut-offs with white pocket liners hanging slightly past the hem. Despite the once white wife-beater that did nothing to conceal the black bra beneath it, clearly delineated against her dark skin in the fading light. "Kayla's right." Then she looked to the man. "We can't. There'd be legal issues if anything happened."

Something in Reenie shifted, and she conceded.

Laughing warmly, the man stepped closer to Ivy. "I promise, I won't sue you. I've just always been fascinated with this place, and this is the first time I've had a chance to see it."

Ivy nodded at him sympathetically, but she glanced to Kayla, whose whole posture visibly tightened, and she continued. "We just can't." She made her voice seem so sad about it, "Some of the structures haven't even been tested for soundness."

That was a bald-faced lie. Ivy knew they'd done that first thing. Braced some roof lines and shored up the icehouse where the earth was bulging behind the old walls. But finally the man stepped back.

"I understand. Thank you though." He took a last sweeping look around, not that he could see much from where they all stood in between the main house and the outbuildings.

Reenie pulled her arm away from Ivy's touch and put her smile on again. "In four months we'll open the doors."

"Looking forward to it." With that, he turned and began the long walk down the drive.

Silent, they all stood in their places, the women clearly listening for his footsteps. Moving as a unit, they peeked around the edge of the building, probably watching the man's slow progress off the property. Evan took that as a cue that he could come out.

No one said anything for another few minutes. Then—as the man passed between the low rock walls that marked the entrance to the property—Reenie turned on Kayla.

"What was that?!" But she didn't give anyone the chance to respond. "He was a potential customer! You were downright rude."

Ivy stepped up, and again Evan had a moment of shock that his sister's protection no longer fell solely to him.

"He obviously said something that upset Kayla."

"Exactly!" Kayla jumped to her own defense, and for a moment Evan envisioned them all as lions jumping on Reenie's dead carcass. He stepped back, but Kayla stepped forward. "Where's his car? He's in a suit, but where's his car?"

"Jesus! He didn't want to drive up the driveway, Kayla. Parking on the street and *walking* up someone's driveway is not a suspicious activity." Reenie's jaw clenched tighter as she spoke.

But Kayla didn't cave. Instead she pointed behind her. She hadn't looked, but she pointed. "Do you see him? Down by the stop light? He's still walking. *Where's his car?*"

Evan was about to step in, when Reenie exploded. "He's a *neighbor!* You were mean to someone we should be kind to!"

Kayla shook her head. "He's not a neighbor. He's a liar."

"He lives on Docket! Right over there! How would you know that he doesn't live there?!" Reenie turned to Evan now, furious. Speaking as though Kayla wasn't there, she spat out, "Aspergers is not an excuse for bad behavior. You've let her get away with this for too long, and I won't have her treating people like that on my property."

He staggered back as though she had slapped him and Reenie used the opportunity to stomp by. He felt the now empty lemonade glass nearly slip from his fingers. For a moment, the world spun. He did let Kay off the hook a lot, always telling himself it was the Aspergers. For the first time, he wondered if maybe he hadn't gone a little too far, been a little too protective, spoiled her more than he should have.

When he finally opened his eyes, he saw his sister staring at him, raw pain and simmering anger in her eyes. "She thinks I'm an idiot."

"She does not." It just came out—a rote response intended to level a certain amount of peace between the two women. Peace that was never going to be there. Just the thought was a hot knife slicing through the deepest part of him.

Kayla saw the remark for what it was. Saw that there wasn't a single grain of truth to it. Saw that it was just a saying that had tumbled out of his mouth too many times in too many different directions. It was a band-aid on a canyon and so she turned to Ivy but didn't try to hide the conversation.

"Thank you for supporting me. That man shouldn't have been here. He was trying to find something. But I don't know what."

Ivy nodded and took Kayla's hand. "I don't know what you saw, but you saw it." She shrugged, then turned to include Evan. "The legal issue is real."

He nodded, unable to form words.

His sister kept talking to Ivy. He didn't listen, just watched. From behind, Kayla's long reddish-blond hair seemed animated as she spoke. It always did when she was passionate. Her free hand waved in the air and he heard her tones if not her words. She went on about something, assuming that everyone else wanted to hear all the details. When she was distracted, frustrated, angry, or overly happy, she forgot to monitor herself. Otherwise she counted sentences and stopped to let someone else speak. He knew this. He had taught her the technique at a young age.

She'd gone over four. She wasn't paying attention. Not to the fact that she was babbling. Not to the fact that his heart was breaking. Not to the fact that the gulf between her and Reenie had widened exponentially today. She was paying attention to Ivy, who still clutched her hand, who nodded and motioned for Kayla to go on for as many sentences as she wanted.

Watching the two of them brought him a little back into the present and he began to hear Kayla's still-heated words.

"—and the lawns all get mowed at the same time. It was the first thing I noticed. All the houses have these small orange stickers on the front door. So I went up and read one. No one lives on Docket. All the houses were bought up by the government for a through road about two months ago."

6

O ld Office, Overseer's House

KAYLA ROLLED over and tried not to ignore it, but the heated conversation from the other room was unavoidable. Laying her head on the pillow made every word become that much clearer. Though she knew that sound travels better, faster, through solids than air, that knowledge didn't stop the argument from continuing like it was happening in her head.

The worst part was that it was about her.

Kayla didn't particularly like or dislike Reenie. Well, that was wrong; she both liked and hated the woman, and not much in between. Sometimes Reenie was like an awesome big sister, and other times she expressed some pretty low opinions. Like now.

"She's *handicapped*, Evan. Handicapped! When are you going to get that through your head?"

"She's not handicapped. She just doesn't think the way you and I do."

Bless her brother for defending her, but Kayla knew it was tearing apart his relationship, and he hadn't had that many through the years. Maybe because of her.

The sound traveled so well through the old house that she could even hear Reenie's sigh, "Don't give me this 'non-neurotypical' shit. It's just as bad as 'handicapable.' She's just not able to be anything else."

Kayla had to disagree with Reenie on the first. Having Aspergers was just a spot on the scale. And actually, she kinda liked it. But she had to agree that she was incapable of being otherwise.

Reenie yelled again. "She can't do what I do! She can't understand the people around her. My mental capabilities span hers. That's the definition of handicapped, Evan."

Lying there in her bed, wishing she wasn't hearing this, Kayla gasped along with her brother. But he shouted back.

"No, Reenie. You *can't* do what she does. You don't have her focus. You don't have her dedication or her math abilities. That diagram would be lost without her skills. Skills that she gains because of the Aspergers. You can't even balance your checkbook!"

Kayla gave up. Standing, she looked around the room for a moment. She loved the symmetry of the double, glass-paned doors both to the hallway and the back porch, but she had to get out. In the moments it took to pull on jeans and a sweater, she was subjected to more of the fight.

"I can learn to balance my checkbook—"

"Clearly you can't!" Kayla could just about picture Evan's red face. "You said you wanted Kayla off 'your property' earlier today. Well it was your lack of skills that led to you needing her investments in the first place. Her money that she earned. You sure didn't. And she—"

"Don't start that, Evan."

"No. You're no better than anyone else. Certainly not her."

"You always choose her!"

"No, I don't. I chose you. I asked her to help out so you could save your family plantation—"

"I should have gotten a loan. I'll get one and buy her out."

"From where, Reenie? Who would loan you a penny with all your debt and bad credit? *Kayla* did. That's who. And she gave it so you don't have to repay it. So you can shut up." He was breathing heavy.

Kayla was grateful that it covered the sound of her turning the knob to the porch.

Then she realized if she went out that way, she would leave their house unlocked. She couldn't do that, not with that strange man around today. If he found a way into the house, it would be because Reenie welcomed the liar with open arms, but not because of Kayla. She would have to head down the hallway.

Sadly, that made the sound of her brother's marriage ending before it started even more clear.

"We worked it so that Kayla only owned one quarter of the property and we could always outvote her. Well, surprise, Kayla and I together own five eighths and *we* can outvote *you*, Reenie." Kayla cringed as she crept softly away, "I don't want to. But I won't have you acting like a bitch to my sister. She's a good person. She may not think the way you do, but she has a good heart. Right now, yours looks pretty black to me."

Kayla heard the tears in his voice, the frustration, and she heard the knob to his room turn. There wasn't time to move; she was obviously sneaking out, a pillow and blanket roughly tucked under one arm and hindering any speed she might have had. The wet tracks down Evan's face weren't a surprise.

Though Kayla had always had a hard time understanding why, he loved Reenie.

She mouthed the words to him, "I'm sorry."

At that moment, Reenie appeared behind him. Red-faced, her expression turned hard as she caught a glimpse of Kayla. There was nothing to do except explain. "I'm leaving. You guys won't have to worry about me tonight."

"Where are you going to go?" Evan looked at her, checking out the bedding she carried. Clearly, she wasn't headed to a hotel.

"The big house."

He shook his head, "It's cold."

"Ivy has a heater." It had been Reenie yelling that Kayla was handicapped, but it was Evan acting like it. "I'm not stupid."

He sighed. "No, you're abnormal. Abnormally smart. And I need to quit worrying about my little sister so much."

She shrugged. "Sometimes I forget to eat or I miss appointments. I know how it goes." With a brief hug by way of the one arm she had free, she turned and headed out the front door.

She could feel the lone key pressed into her pocket. The grass reached up and brushed at her bare ankles above where she'd shoved her feet straight into white Keds. Initially, she tried not to make noise as she came up the back porch, then realized that scaring the shit out of Ivy in the middle of the night wasn't a good plan, either. So she didn't avoid the creaks of the old porch, and she didn't worry when the door moaned on its 200-year-old hinges.

Then a smack of a door behind her preceded Evan gunning the engine on his small car. Turning, she spotted Reenie standing at the railing at the back of the Overseer's House. For a moment, their eyes met and no love was lost. Giving up, Kayla headed into the house.

It was colder than outside, the air sneaking around her feet and under the hem of her jeans. She could feel it at the small gap where her sweater didn't quite meet the waistband on her pants. She was through the kitchen and halfway up the servants' staircase, the steps worn to a smooth curve beneath her feet and countless others, when she heard Ivy's voice at a harsh whisper, "Kay? Is that you?"

"It's me." Then she wondered if Ivy was putting away her

nine-millimeter gun right now. She could very well have pulled it out and thumbed off the safety if she was hearing footsteps inside the house at night. Kayla slowed just a bit and hoped Ivy got it put away before she arrived. She didn't want to know.

The door was open to Ivy's room. The warm reception was as welcome as the knowledge that she was now on the far side of the house, away from the Overseer's cottage. Ivy's open curtains let in silver moonlight and a view of wide fields. There was a shimmer off the roof of the blacksmith's shop, and she knew in the far back of the property, obscured by the shadows were the small slave cabins. Abandoned and having lost much of their insulation over the years, they lingered just out of sight, a testament to a time that was both much gentler and far crueler. For the first time, Kayla surveyed the property and thought, *mine*.

"Reenie drive you out of your own house?"

Kayla jumped. She'd known Ivy was standing behind her, but hadn't expected the conversation. That was stupid; she'd showed up after midnight with a pillow and a comforter tucked under her arm and she owed Ivy an explanation.

"What are those for?" Ivy pointed to Kayla's furtively stripped bedding.

"I was hoping I could sleep on your floor. This is the only temperature-controlled room in the whole house right now." Kayla needed her own room. "Tomorrow, I'm going to buy my own AC and heater. I was thinking I'd set up next door if you'd be willing to share your bathroom with me." Then she shrugged. "But I keep odd schedules, so maybe I should go to the opposite end of the house."

She didn't leave an option for Ivy to claim the whole house. Kayla was part owner. And there was no telling how things would turn out after Evan and Reenie cooled down, but she wasn't going to quit on the plantation. She was invested--literally. But she needn't have worried about Ivy.

"You're welcome to stay as long as you like. And you can sleep on the floor, but it's cold—the room doesn't hold heat all that well. The bed is plenty big and if you want you can share with me until you figure out what you want to do."

Kayla tilted her head. "You don't mind?"

Ivy laughed. "I don't. I've been a stripper and a grad student. I keep odd schedules too."

That wasn't what Kayla had meant when she asked if Ivy minded, but she nodded and pushed her comforter over the back of the chair in the corner. The room was beautiful, with thick, soft curtains pulled back by tassels lining the windows and framing the view. Gauzy drapes topped the four posters where the bed sat plush in the middle of the room and for just a moment she felt like a princess and wondered if she would feel a pea under the mattress.

"You can't wear those into bed." Ivy stopped her, pointing at Kayla's jeans. Down at the hem they'd gotten soaked, and Kayla could even see cut grass clinging tentatively to the material. She wouldn't put that into Ivy's fluffy bed, so she made a face and peeled them.

A hand appeared in her view, holding out worn pajama pants and in a moment she was warm under the covers, Ivy sliding in on the other side of what must be a California king. Princess or not, she was upset, and the words tumbled out. "Reenie thinks I'm stupid."

She waited for Ivy to tell her it was wrong, that it was all a misinterpretation on Kayla's part—lord knew she was capable of that.

Rolling up on one side, her head propped in her hand, Ivy sighed. "Reenie can't see past her own nose."

"No. She can't." Something settled in her chest. She wasn't wrong and she hadn't misinterpreted Reenie. Someone neurotypical—Ivy—agreed with her. "Reenie's still so pissed that I was rude to the man before he lied. And Evan is defending me like he always does." She rolled onto her back and stared at the ceiling. It was a raw plaster, troweled on, sanded and painted by someone over a century ago. Others had lain here and stared at it, wondering what to do with their lives. It was oddly comforting. "I wish he wouldn't do that. It's destroying his relationship."

"You don't want him to defend you?"

Still not looking at Ivy, she followed the patterns in the trowel marks, noticing that the craftsman was right-handed, and she shrugged. "He loves Reenie. I think he would have married her before now if she and I could get along."

"That's his choice."

This time Kayla looked at Ivy. "It is. I know that. But I also know that it's a choice he wouldn't have to make if I didn't have Aspergers." She held up her hand as the other woman started an ardent protest. "Or if I weren't here."

There was a gasp, and Ivy was no longer leaning casually on her hand. She was sitting upright, looking down at Kayla. "You aren't thinking about leaving are you?"

"No. She pissed me off when she said that thing about 'her property.' It's not really hers. Evan and I paid for all of it. She's broke." Shaking her head a little, Kayla sighed. "I'm not big enough to walk away from that. And I'm afraid that she thinks she'll marry Evan and he'll make all her money troubles go away."

Settling back into the covers, Ivy asked, "Are there real 'troubles?'"

"No. It'll be fine. Reenie's not bad, but she has no real savings and she's got credit card bills to pay every month."

They were silent for a moment. She didn't know what Ivy was thinking, but Kayla was deciding which room to take. Probably the one on the other side of the bathroom; Ivy already knew her well enough to know that she wasn't going to read the hint that she should be somewhere else, that if Ivy said something, Kayla was going to take it at face value and follow through. She also should know that Kayla had a thick enough skin that if Ivy said she didn't want to share the bathroom, Kayla wasn't going to be offended or take it personally.

She was finally taking deeper breaths, finally coming down off the high edge of her anger, when Ivy spoke again. "So what did you see that made you not trust that man right away?"

Kayla only shrugged at first. When he walked up, she'd just known something didn't fit right. And she told Ivy that. "It was his suit and his shoes." She didn't know how to say it. "Who would wear shoes like that to walk up a plantation drive or to try to get a walk-around tour?"

"That was it? He seemed shifty?"

"I realized later that he said some things that didn't match. Like, he didn't know anything about plantations, but he called the carriage house an 'outbuilding'. I never used that word until I got here."

Ivy nodded and Kayla kept going. "He made a comment about the things from the privy. How did he know that? Why on earth would anyone assume you were digging up an outhouse? Or that the broken dishes would be used to piece together some of the history of the house? Even Reenie and I didn't know that until this morning when you asked."

Ivy was reclining against her pillow and Kayla hazarded a glance over at her. Her dark hair seemed to spill out around her head and shoulders, but it was her eyebrows—neat, inky slashes framing very expressive eyes—that showed her shock. "You're right. He knew way too much to be an amateur."

"Then he said he lived on Docket, and I knew that was a flat lie." Kayla looked at the ceiling again. "I just wish Reenie would have trusted me."

Ivy sighed and Kayla thought it must have been out of exasperation for her. She appreciated the backup. She wasn't used to it from anywhere other than Evan and she hadn't expected it. She'd thought Ivy was asleep, but then—just as Ivy rolled over and really relaxed—she heard, "Reenie will learn. One day."

Evan sat at the desk, running his hand along the smooth leather inset. It had been neglected, cracked and baked, but he'd pulled it from the desk top and worked it. He'd somehow decided that he had the time to rub in an Old World looking stain and conditioner. Then he'd settled it back into the shallow space carved just for the blotter.

There had been other things to do—there would always be other things to do—but Evan had decided that he was entitled to one nice thing in this godforsaken house. The bones were beautiful, but everything over them had been done to a horror of misperfection. The peel-and-stick tiles in the bathroom weren't even straight. But there were other, more important things first.

He couldn't change the fact that every surface, which had once been well-crafted and beautiful, had been replaced by something cheap and discordant. The bathroom and kitchen were only two rooms, but sported three colors of laminate. So when he'd lifted the protective sheet and found this desk, he knew he had to pull one body from the wreckage and revive it.

He'd dusted and polished, in all that spare time he'd found since they got here. And now he found irony in the fact that he sat here to pay the bills. That he worried, unsure until he hit the end and again totaled everything, if they were still okay. Sadly, the hundred dollars from the lost diagram had helped a bit. They needed everything they could get and it was the only income they'd seen in two months.

The other sad fact was that paying bills was the highlight of his last eighteen hours. He'd come in after his fitful drive and lay down beside an already sleeping Reenie and stared at the ceiling. Only then had he realized that Reenie not trusting Kayla wasn't the only issue. There had been a stranger on their property, asking for a full tour and lying about being a neighbor. While

Evan could think of several reasons a person might lie, he couldn't come up with one reason that fit everything.

No one had mentioned anything about it this morning. He'd seen Kayla and Ivy only in passing. They'd had their heads together and he'd decided not to speak or push the fragile peace of the day. So he was surprised to hear his door open and find Ivy standing just inside his domain.

"Is Kayla with you?" It was the first thing to tumble through his brain, the first thing to come out of his mouth.

"No." She stepped in and pushed the door closed behind her. Pulling up a chair, she sat herself down and looked him in the face. "And that's what I wanted to talk to you about."

"Oh?" That couldn't be anything good. But he tried not to show that his precarious day had just taken the much-feared nose-dive he'd expected. "What now?"

"That! Exactly that!"

He'd learned a long time ago, and not just with Kayla, to voice everything and assume nothing. "I have no idea what 'that' is."

"You assume there's something wrong with Kayla. She's fine."

That made him feel better and he was just letting out a bit of tightly reined air when Ivy ruined it.

"Reenie needs some adjustment, though."

He held up his hand. "I'm glad to talk about Kayla with you, or Reenie, but not Reenie and Kayla."

"Fair enough." She crossed her arms and leaned back, her long-sleeved shirt for once covering but not concealing the color of her bra. No wonder the woman gave Reenie the jitters. "When you hired me, you asked me to keep an eye on Kayla."

He jumped on that immediately, his worries starting to come to light. It was the perfect day for more shit to go wrong, that was for sure. "Do you need a raise?"

"No!" Now she looked offended, and Evan was once again on shifting ground. "I'm not doing it anymore. I'm glad to help out like a friend—meaning if I see she hasn't eaten, I'll say something. But I'm not 'keeping an eye on her'. She doesn't need it."

"Oh." That was news. "She doesn't? She stayed out all night making that machine once. She's missed a handful of meals since we've been here. Why do you think she doesn't need it?"

"Because she's in no danger of starving to death. She'll eat extra later. If she gets sick or goes missing I'll be all over it, but she's not a child and you keep treating her like she is."

He leaned back and contemplated that. He was of two distinct minds on that one. Who was this woman to come in here and in just a few weeks think she was a better expert than he about the sister he had cared for since she was born? On the other hand, she probably saw things he was blind to. He didn't get a chance to say anything though; Ivy jumped in again.

"Look. I want that stricken from my job description." She stood up. "I'm going to grab some lunch for us. But I will say that I don't ever want to find out how much it hurts her that you thought that and that I went along with it." She stood and was practically out the door before he untangled that mess enough to ask a different question.

"Did she spend the night on your floor last night?" With Kayla, she might have found a way to curl up in one of the unheated rooms, not wanting to disturb Ivy. You just never knew.

"No."

His heart stopped for a moment. But once again Ivy set him straight.

"She stayed in my bed."

"With you?"

Her eyes narrowed at him. "Don't worry, I didn't lay a hand on your precious baby sister."

As she went out the door, leaving the room as though she'd never been there, he could have sworn he heard her say "yet."

Burying himself in work, Evan tried to erase the thought from his head. He wrote payments and checked due dates. Sadly, the account was almost exactly where Kayla had predicted it would be two months into this venture. She'd made up some formula that included a variable for what month of the year it was and how much the unexpected expenditures of the previous month had been . . . and she had it figured out.

For a moment, he shook his head at the thought of it. Buying a car with Kayla was fun. The dealer would name a price and Kayla would glance up then rattle off a car payment. The first time she did that, the salesman would always give her some "don't jump the gun, little lady, let me calculate this" comment. Then he'd narrow his eyes when his number was incredibly close to hers. Kayla would barter him down, rattling off payments and rattling the salesman. At one point he'd said, "The car is for me, but you'll have to pass her to make a deal." That salesman had sputtered and asked, "Well, if the car is for you, why are you letting *her* do the bartering?" Evan had just smiled back and asked, "Wouldn't you?"

Reenie had accused him of making work for Kayla, of creating situations in which she could feel good about herself. Evan had accused Reenie of being an idiot for paying too much for her car because she had no grasp of what was going into her payment and not letting Kayla help. That had been the first sign —that long-ago argument about the car—that Reenie would never come around. His sister operated outside the bounds of Reenie's understanding.

Just like last night.

He'd been able to ignore the sandpaper roughness of the two women's personalities gritting against each other when their interaction had been occasional. But putting them together like this, in the same house, on the same job, was too much. He asked himself if maybe he hadn't done it on purpose. If maybe it hadn't been a test. He knew he was testing Reenie, not Kayla. Kayla couldn't change. She was diagnosed. Reenie could; she just refused to.

Could they hold out? Could he wait until the job was finished and the plantation was opened and Kayla found another place to work? Or would he and Kayla move away, sell their shares eventually? It was the first time it had crossed his mind to leave Reenie behind. But they'd been together for three years now, and he hadn't passed through that final eye of the needle. He'd never hit that point where he knew he wanted to spend the rest of his life with her.

And maybe last night he'd gotten his answer. Well, he'd been getting that answer for a while, but last night had felt like a two-by-four whacking him solidly between the eyes and leaving him with a splitting headache and twisted heart.

He was stuck in a crappy spot. He didn't want to leave. That was *his* cotton in *his* back field. He'd earned it with cash and muscle cramps. But this was Hazelton House and Reenie was a Hazelton.

A noise roused him from his decision-making/sulking fit and as he looked up he saw sneakers at the edge of the door. Sneakers equaled Kayla, so he tried to push a smile onto his face.

Reenie stood there in jeans and a fitted T-shirt—unusual attire for her, but he guessed he'd been seeing it more lately. Her face held the beginnings of a grin, one she was fighting. She came into the room, pushed by Kayla and Ivy who were crowding the space behind her.

Moving aside like the graceful belle she was, Reenie took a step back so she could face them all at once. "First, I want to say that I'm sorry."

She turned to him. "Evan, I love you more than anything. And I know I'm hard-headed sometimes. I'm working on it. Kayla, I shouldn't have yelled. I shouldn't have started that fight with Evan last night, and I'm sorry you had to hear it."

Evan heard only what the words didn't say. Reenie didn't accept Kayla; she was only sorry that she'd fought and that Kayla had heard. He pushed the half-smile all the way, faking it for now.

"That's nice, Reenie." Ivy butted in, "But what did you get?"

"Well!" She was all wide grin, apologies forgotten or forgiven. "They found it!"

She held up a cardboard roll he hadn't noticed she carried. He'd noticed so many other things, but missed the obvious. Evan frowned, "What?"

"The diagram!" She gently pushed him aside and began opening the tube, unrolling the oilcloth on his desk over his bills and carefully laid-out thoughts. "They called me two days ago to tell me that they had found it and it would be delivered. They also graciously offered the protection free of charge!"

Evan snorted at that. *Free of charge, my ass.* They owed this family some money for distress or something. But as he looked he saw that the diagram was encased in a flexible, snug-fitting plastic that appeared liquid and tear-proof. He was impressed.

But he didn't get to be impressed for long. Kayla and Ivy eagerly wormed in, effectively shoving him back. There was a low murmur between them as they looked.

Standing straight and catching his eye, Reenie smiled broadly, "Aren't you excited, Evan?"

But Kayla announced, "This isn't it. It's a forgery."

7

O ld Office, Overseer's House

"I'm telling you, it's *wrong*." Kayla touched the diagram where a small rod had been removed from the picture.

As though Kayla were smearing an original document, Reenie sighed and swatted Kayla's hand away. Hadn't that been the whole point of sending it out for a protective cover in the first place—so they didn't have to worry about who touched it?

"How could it possibly be wrong?" Reenie pointed now, her manicured nail hovering over the clear plastic, "It's initialed. It's dated the same. It's the same kind of paper and ink." She sighed. "I'm sorry, I just don't buy this idea that the preservation company switched two diagrams by Eli Whitney. *I* recognize this one. It's ours."

She crossed her arms as though all was said and done, but no one was paying attention.

"It looks good." Ivy ran a hand across the surface as though she were caressing the document itself and not just the plastic coating.

Exasperated, Kayla spoke before thinking. "Of course it looks good; you don't forge a Van Gogh with a box of crayons. But even I can forge the handwriting."

"I think Kayla's memory is just off. It's preposterous that there are two nearly identical documents that got switched." Reenie gave an unladylike huff.

"I'm going to go get my copy." Kayla took off without waiting for anyone to reply. She bolted through the back door at the Overseer's and bounded like a kid, making a gazelle leap from the top step to the worn ground. Crabgrass had sprung up where people had once walked frequently, but hadn't for too long. Now, she and her family had worn it to nubs.

Rounding the carriage house, she passed through tall grass and over packed dirt. The blacksmith's shop was her personal place, and she'd left her copy of the diagram here. Not even breathing heavily, she went to the rough-hewn workbench and picked up the smooth river rocks she'd stolen from the stream and freed the paper she'd tacked down with their weight.

Pushing back up the hill, she didn't even break a sweat. That was new to her. In two months, she'd done enough physical labor to change her physique. Her lungs pumped, taking in the clean country air, sweetened with the scents of grasses, running water and freshly turned earth.

She'd folded the paper as she ran and had it in hand as she popped up the four back steps onto the porch of the Overseer's House.

Evan held out his hand, and Kayla handed over the paper. Only then did she feel the need to suck in a little extra air. She opened her mouth to tell Ivy how excited she was—what a coup it was for a girl who worked at a desk most of her life to feel actually physically fit. But she didn't get to say it.

Reenie laid out the oilcloth drawing they had made for the

museum, the two copies spaced out on the leather blotter on Evan's desk. "They look pretty much the same to me."

"Yeah, they do." The need for breath caught up to her, as though she'd outrun it on the way here. Kayla tried to disguise the deeper inhale, and she pointed at the drawing. "But look here . . . and here."

"Your memory must have been wrong." Reenie turned to the returned "original."

"It's a fake." Kayla declared it quietly. She hated confrontation, but she and Reenie had been at each other for a good twenty-four hours straight. Her stomach might just churn her inside out if this continued.

Reenie nodded. "It's actually very impressive that you remembered as much as you did. That you were able to forge the handwriting so well. It's understandable you made a few errors."

"But I don't make errors." Why didn't Reenie understand that? She felt her jaw clench and she was suddenly seven years old again when no one believed she'd drawn the print in art class. Suddenly fourteen, in high school, where all the academics were too easy and the people too hard. Here in this plantation house, defending herself yet again. She looked at all three of them. "I don't make errors."

"Everyone makes errors." Reenie shrugged. "It's not a big deal except that you won't let it go."

"Because it's not an error." She was starting to panic and she knew Ivy could see it.

There was a nod and a hand on her arm. "I believe you." Ivy smiled, but it didn't stop the rapid beat of her heart that she wanted to attribute to the run; it didn't stop the sting at the back of her eyes.

"I'm sorry," Reenie said it to Evan, but Kayla could tell she didn't mean it as an apology. "I just don't buy that your sister has a disorder that renders her completely error-free."

Evan's weariness showed in his sigh. "Reenie, you know—"

"And I read up on it. I didn't find anything saying that Aspergers patients are error free. It does say they have a hard time lying, so I think your sister actually believes she's all that. But she's not. Why am I the bad guy here? Because I won't put your sister up on a pedestal?"

"I tried to stay out of this." He held his hands palm out in a classic surrender. Kayla felt bad for him. "But you put me in the middle, Reenie."

With his hands still out, he plopped down in the chair behind the desk, as though he needed to be seated for whatever was about to come. "Reenie, you know the Aspergers gives her intense focus. You freely admit her limitations, but you refuse to see the advantages. I've put them in front of you in print form from respected sources, and you still refuse."

"Nothing in there said she's a demi-god who's always right."

"I'm standing right here." Kayla pushed it out through clenched teeth.

But Evan ignored her. "Kayla is bright, incredibly bright, but even beyond that, there's tons of evidence about autism spectrum disorders producing photographic memories. Hell, just look online." He slashed one hand through the air in an angry gesture. "She's often wrong about things. But she's learned to keep her mouth shut when she doesn't understand. So if she spoke up now, she's *right*. In all my life, I've never seen her make a mathematical error. It *is* preposterous to think there are two nearly identical prints that got switched. If it were anyone other than Kayla insisting this is a forgery, I'd laugh at them. But it *is* Kayla."

He leaned forward, his elbows resting one on the fake, protected document and the other on the copy Kayla and Ivy had made for the museum. He looked at Kayla and Ivy this time, too. "If it's incredibly unlikely that anyone had another nearly identical print *and* that someone mistakenly switched them, then we have a bigger problem on our hands. The only other option I can think of is that this is a fake they purposefully gave to us."

Reenie blinked. "What?! You've gone nuts." She threw her hands up in the air, and made a face Kayla didn't understand. But it didn't look good.

Evan didn't react. He'd perfected that over the years. "A fake added to the fact that we had someone here wanting to see the plantation—but clearly lying to us—is very concerning."

Kayla nodded.

Reenie's breath escaped her as though it were fleeing hell. Kayla thought it might be . . . She'd liked this woman once.

Gesturing dramatically, Reenie shouted. "All of this is based on what *Kayla* says! Kayla says the document is a fake. Kayla says this man is lying, Kayla says Docket Street is foreclosed, Kayla says people shouldn't wear nice shoes or park away from their destination. Since when did Kayla—of all people—become the arbiter of social mores?"

Evan nodded, "You're absolutely right. Kayla has no concept of what's socially acceptable, which is why she catalogs what people normally do."

Thanks, Evan. She didn't let the sarcasm roll off her tongue like she wanted to. There were rules: No more than two sentences at a time. Three or four only if the person was leaning toward you and had their focus on you. When there's an argument, stay quiet.

It wasn't enough that she had to fake her way through the system. It wasn't enough to have her brother out her. It was that he was explaining to Reenie *how* she tried to fit in. That she made this into math, too, because that was the only way any of it made any sense. But Evan kept talking. "If someone is out of the norm, Kayla notices. He did several things out of the norm. Statistically, he's off."

"People don't act by statistics, Evan. Maybe your precious sister does, but regular people don't."

He didn't even flinch.

"Reenie, go. Check it out. I believe Kayla, but you don't. So go over to Docket Street. If anyone lives there, if this guy might, I'm sure Kayla will apologize."

She wasn't going to have to apologize. She wasn't wrong.

"You can get empirical evidence on that one, Reenie. Get it. Take your phone; if you see anything damning, get a picture for us. And we'll all try to work this out."

Reenie nodded. "What I'm going to show you is that there's nothing to work out. And I'm going to get pictures of how normal it is, so you all don't hunker down and form some sort of shotgun militia because *she* thinks things are wonky."

She stomped down the hall and Kayla heard Reenie's purse slide off the kitchen counter. She heard the screen door slap shut and a moment later gravel kicking as Reenie sped down the driveway. Off to gather evidence against Kayla's mental stability.

Kayla sometimes doubted her own mental stability. But she didn't doubt her facts.

EVAN LOOKED CAUTIOUSLY UP at Kayla and Ivy. Still standing there in front of him, they had very different looks on their faces.

Kayla's was blank. She probably had no doubt that Reenie would find exactly what Kayla had described on Docket Street. In fact, his sister was likely right now calculating the odds that someone had started work on Docket, or that they'd overturned the highway ruling and had sold off the houses in the last . . . however long it had been since Kayla had gone exploring. Evan put that guess at less than a week.

She'd always liked to go for walks. As a toddler she screamed for her stroller. Parked it by the door and rocked it, yelling until someone took her out around the block. Later, as a disenfranchised teen, she'd confessed that walks were soothing and that she catalogued the changes since the last time she'd passed. She could walk every day, point out which toys in which yards had been played with and which hadn't. She noticed right away when someone repainted, replaced a window, or just trimmed the hedges.

Ivy, on the other hand, did not look blank. She looked like she could chew iron and spit nails.He did what he could, shut his eyes and started. "If either of you ever repeat this, I'll say you're lying."

Kayla would never tell. But Ivy was an unknown quantity— an angry unknown quantity.

"Reenie is just as handicapped as she calls Kayla. But she'll never see it."

Ivy's eyebrows rose at that, and for the first time she didn't look like she needed to be kept away from all sharp objects.

He said things that made his throat catch, but since he believed them to be true, he said them anyway. "She simply doesn't fathom how anyone could think otherwise. And because she was raised this way, told she was good and perfect by a whole community, there's not been a reason for her to shift her views. This is hard on her, too."

Ivy's brows rose again and her mouth started to open, but she closed it quickly, looking a little fishlike.

Kayla's face was still blank. She'd heard the "Reenie" speech before. And probably didn't care to hear it again. "Can we talk about the diagram?"

"Sure."

Even Ivy seemed willing to let the conversation shift, although Evan wouldn't put it past her to come back in here and let him have it later. For a woman who was so often quiet in groups she had no qualms about ripping him a new one when they were alone. He wondered if she was always like that or if he was special.

Kayla paid no attention to the undercurrents between the other two; she just leaned over the nearly identical documents, her hair spilling over her shoulder in a straight waterfall of red-gold. She was pretty, he knew, and plenty smart. Maybe too smart. If she weren't like she was, she might be married with a young family by now. If she weren't like she was, *he* might be married with a young family by now. The friction between him and Reenie might not exist at all. But Kayla was Kayla, and he was her only family. And he loved her more than he loved anything else on earth. So he waited while she examined the oilcloths and he tensed when Ivy reached out and pulled back Kayla's hair, pushing it familiarly out of the way so she could see.

"Here." Kayla pointed to one then the other. "A small rod is missing, and . . . this bar—which I honestly can't figure out *what* it does anyway—it's different here."

The change was so miniscule, he didn't know if he'd see it even if he'd been told to look. The bar, originally octagonal with perfect corners, was now slightly rounded.

Evan blinked.

"Here, too." She pointed to the largest gear. "I think it acts as a kind of flywheel, though I'm not sure why. But look. These lines are doubled."

In the version Kayla had drawn, the lines appeared to represent insets into the outer circumference of the wheel. In the returned, protected copy, there were two lines—as though the insets were in insets themselves. He frowned. "That's confusing."

Kayla smirked. "The original is confusing. And it doesn't work." She looked at her watch.

"Why do you keep checking the time?" Ivy asked.

A shrug was belied by the confidence in her voice. Not only could Kayla not lie, she didn't even fudge the truth very well. "I'm trying to figure out when Reenie will get back."

When she would get vindicated. But Evan knew there was no watch in the world that could predict that. He bit his tongue.

Luckily, Ivy stepped up. "Okay. I'm going to start with this: If we trust what Kayla says—"

She was cut off by Kayla's jerking to attention, the sheer hurt on her face, and it took Ivy and Evan talking over each other to soothe the wound that had been opened.

"I believe you!" Ivy jumped in.

Evan spoke on top of her. "Ivy is posing hypotheticals!"

"Oh. Okay." The words were soft, and her eyes were more wary than they had been a moment before. And though he walked on eggshells, missteps were unavoidable. Evan couldn't correct everything, so he motioned for Ivy to continue.

"There are two options. One: that we trust Kayla's drawings and two: that we don't." She turned to Kayla, casually laying her hand over his sister's. "*I* trust them. But we have to look at both possibilities."

And just like that the clouds in her face disappeared and she was ready to listen with an open mind. He'd have to remember that trick.

"If she's wrong, then there's no reason to believe anything other than a mix-up. We do need to figure out why that man was here, but that will be resolved—hopefully to everyone's satisfaction—when Reenie gets back."

Evan nodded.

"Here's option two—" Ivy looked at them both pointedly, and he figured he wasn't going to like option two very much. "Kayla's right. Let's say this isn't the original. Let's assume this document is forged and it's altered. That's a *lot* of work for someone to go to for an old document."

Evan nodded. It *was* a lot of work. He'd been trying to figure that out himself. "I believe Kayla, but I can't come up with any good scenarios that explain why on earth someone would go to that kind of trouble."

One deep breath told him that Ivy had an ugly one.

"I'm sure we can come up with more options if we think on it, but here's what I suspect: if they took the real copy, it must be worth something. Worth more than the cost and trouble of replacing it with a fake so we don't even come looking for it. My guess is that Reenie is right: it was done by Eli Whitney."

"Thank you." Reenie's voice came from the doorway, clean and clear, with her usual edge of sophistication despite the fact that she was obviously out of breath. She came further into the room, faking having herself together and faking it well. "Kayla, I'm sorry."

It was bestowed upon his sister, as though by some royal decree. But Evan knew what it cost Reenie to apologize in general. It wasn't that she was a know-it-all or a control freak, she just stuck to what she knew, what she believed with all her heart. Apologies came with an uneasy look and a hard push from somewhere deep within.

And that was the end of it. Error admitted, she turned to the group. "Docket Street is shut down. The houses were foreclosed about four months ago. There's no way anyone lives there or would even claim to."

"Shit." It was low and disappointed. Ivy's shoulders sagged almost imperceptibly. He wondered if maybe she'd wanted Kayla to be wrong. What she said next confirmed it. "Kayla, it's not just that they went to the effort to replace the diagram, they *altered* it."

Kayla shrugged. "It doesn't even work. Sure, replacing the whole document means they expect to have time to sell the original before we notice. But I have no idea why they would do such tiny changes. There are a few radii that are altered, too." She pointed to a couple of different places. Evan would need a ruler to confirm that, but he didn't doubt her.

Kayla couldn't figure out why they would change it, because she didn't have a devious bone in her body. She couldn't think like a liar. But apparently Ivy could.

"In that case, maybe it isn't the document itself that's important. Maybe it's the machine that is. They altered it so Kayla couldn't make it work."

His sister spoke again, emphatically. "It *doesn't* work."

Ivy's smile concerned him.

"It will." She pointed to the places where the new copy was altered. "Focus here, here and here. They altered these, because changing them ensures failure. Figure out what they covered up, and you'll make it work."

8

A
Store in Savannah

KAYLA COULD TELL that Ivy didn't like something. What exactly that might be was a mystery.

Maybe she didn't like that she'd been pushed into chaperoning this odd supply run. Maybe she thought they should have searched the Internet first. Kayla conceded that point even though Ivy hadn't actually made it. They could have just done an online search for parts for the machine, but Kayla had become paranoid—and probably rightly so.

The document was a fake, which meant someone was paying attention. How they were doing it and how much, she didn't know. For an Aspergers patient, being paranoid was about the worst thing that could happen. She had no clue what was truly going on. No idea if the couple in the far corner were looking at her funny because they were keeping an eye on her or if they just thought her T-shirt was stupid. Or maybe they didn't get the joke. Or maybe they desperately wanted to understand the Schrödinger's cat reference and simply couldn't read it through rheumy eyes.

There were a thousand scenarios that were plausible. She might be simply misinterpreting things, and lord knew, she was good at drawing wrong conclusions. Statistically, the highest probability was that they were eyeing her, but for completely non-nefarious reasons. They were an elderly couple, and it was extremely unlikely that they were spies sent to follow her and unearth bad nineteenth-century generators designed by one Eli Whitney.

Which was why Kayla decided that if she ever had to tail someone, she'd send the elderly. No one suspected them.

Turning away, she pushed her focus back to the racks in front of her. The magnets were round, and many were in blister packs. That was about the stupidest thing ever. It wasn't like they didn't attract anything because they were in plastic. After she and Ivy struck out at Home Depot, Kayla hadn't known what to expect. She'd thought they would find those cardboard bins lining a row of shelves and she would reach in, wipe off the chalky dust that always permeated that place, and count out how many she needed. She loved Home Depot. She certainly hadn't expected to wind up in an electronics store, doing short order math to figure out how many blister packs she had to buy. Didn't expect to feel her friend's bare skin against her arm as she counted, or the warm fingers that curled through her own, lacing their hands tightly together. And she hadn't expected the soft tendrils that steadily crept their way through her system at the touch.

She almost yanked her hand back.

She'd had her hand held before. She rather liked it. But it had its own time and place—like a walk maybe. Not in the electronics store. Not when she was counting magnets. And she'd never had it slip in and scramble her thoughts. She started counting again.

Ivy's mouth came close to Kayla's ear, warm breath reaching out like heat from a fire. She felt her own breath hitch, tried to pull away. But Ivy's hand had hers in a firmer grip than it appeared and she couldn't pull back.

The whisper stole into her soul before it permeated her brain. Then Kayla's thoughts flipped suddenly on.

"Grab them all. Pay cash. Now."

Kayla tried to turn her head and look at Ivy in response to the missive, instead she was greeted with a firm kiss against her cheek and the embarrassing knowledge that she was being led, not seduced.

Ivy's hand released hers and began quietly loading the magnet packs into the basket she carried. In an effort to ignore the flush that had stolen onto her face uninvited, Kayla aimed her focus on the display and she, too, began slipping pack after pack in with the others.

It still took all the cash they had, and Kayla handing back two of the least-likely-useful packs in order to not use a card at all. The clerk told her that she wasn't putting back enough, but Kayla had accounted for the tax and assured him that she had. They had seventeen cents left between the two of them when they hauled the heavy, triple-bagged sacks of magnets to the car, their loot congealing click-by-click into blocks.

Kayla waited until they were pulling out of the parking lot before she asked, "What was that about?"

Teeth clenched, Ivy looked one way then another. She glared in the rearview mirror and didn't answer until they were turning onto the main road. "Do you see that green sedan in the parking lot? The slightly older one?"

"Yes."

Kayla was cranking her head over her shoulder for a better view when Ivy's hand nearly slapped her back. The accompanying hiss commanded, "Don't look."

"Then why... ?"

She didn't finish the question.

"I saw it behind us back in Ebenezer. They didn't follow us all the way here, but they're here now."

Kayla frowned. She'd only gotten the one look at the car, but it was an older model Chevy, heavyset with silver handles. "That car isn't that uncommon."

"But the long scratch down the left-hand side is. And so is the man who climbed out."

Kayla called the image in her head. "He was wearing jeans and a white T-shirt, work boots and a long flannel shirt over it."

"Oh shit." Even Ivy could see that was wrong. "Do you think he had a gun?"

There was a shrug that Ivy somehow managed to choreograph with turning the wheel and leading them onto the main road. She took the direction away from Ebenezer. "Why else would anyone wear a flannel overshirt in seventy-plus weather?"

She sighed and went with the flow of traffic, away from the plantation, away from the machine, away from Evan and Reenie. "Should we call?"

Ivy shook her head. "I need to think for a bit." Her eyes darted to the rearview mirror then around the car in a distinctive pattern that said she hadn't found what she was looking for. "I'm afraid to use the phones. I'm getting really paranoid right now."

Kayla didn't say anything. What could she say? That she thought Ivy was right to be paranoid?

"Did the green car follow us in Ebenezer?"

Ivy shook her head. "It seemed that way. But I thought I was just being overly suspicious, so I didn't say anything. Ebenezer isn't even a town, it's a fistful of stop signs. So it makes sense that everyone there was headed the same way—out of town. Then the car disappeared and I thought I was being silly. I was glad I hadn't said anything and made an idiot out of myself. But now . . ."

Kayla nodded. "We should head back. We can catch I-16 then hop over toward home."

Merging carefully into another lane, Ivy nodded. Kayla, too, checked the mirrors, but she was looking for the green sedan, which was luckily nowhere in sight.

Ivy spoke only once on the way back toward Ebenezer. "I think we caught him with timing. He couldn't climb back into his car when he'd just gotten out. He'd look suspicious if he didn't go inside and at least examine something."

Nothing more was said until they parked in the space between the buildings at Hazelton House. They had started keeping the cars out of sight so no one could tell when they were home and when they weren't. They managed to get one car in the carriage house, but there was enough room behind the main house to keep the other two from being viewed from the street. So it was a short walk up to the back steps. She was thinking about carrying the magnets up to her room, because she didn't want all the parts down in the blacksmith's shop. Night was settling in, and it would become easier for someone to sneak down there.

She had two heavy bags in her arms and was crossing the back space, passing by the open small door to the carriage house, when it hit her. The thought—the idea—washed over her with certainty just as Reenie stepped out onto the back porch of the Overseer's House. "Did you get all the magnets you need?"

Kayla nearly growled, but she couldn't. "Nope, we didn't find anything. In fact, I don't think it needs magnets at all. I think it was brass inlay."

The expression on Reenie's face was clear as day. There were many of Reenie's looks that Kayla didn't understand, but she knew *did-you-suddenly-go-batshit-crazy?* when she saw it. Shaking her head 'no,' Kayla climbed the steps as fast as she could. She had to get to Reenie and shut her up.

Moving into the other woman's space, she clearly mouthed, "Don't say anything." But she didn't make a sound. Aloud, she wondered, "Did you make pie? My birthday is coming up."

It was, and she did want pie.

"Sure." The drawn out tone of the syllable left no doubt that Reenie was still parking Kayla in the crazy camp. But Ivy followed up the stairs with faith and silence.

As they entered the bedroom they'd been sharing—but that Kayla still thought of as Ivy's—her friend whispered, "What's going on?"

It was only possible to be so quiet when pushing bags laden with heavy magnets under a four-poster bed situated on an old wooden floor. But she did her best. Then she didn't answer Ivy's question. She wasn't ready to commit to what she feared. "Do you have a gun?"

A frown that Kayla couldn't interpret seemed to ask a question, but the answer was a statement. "I have a twenty-two and a shotgun."

"Load them both."

She pushed out the doorway, leaving a startled Ivy in her wake. Kayla was afraid. She was certain what she'd find. And she didn't want to find it.

Dark was dropping like curtains as she made her way back out. Evan was coming in from the far field. Sweaty, he had clearly spent the whole day tending his cotton. But that meant he would have had an eye on her smithy while she'd been gone.

He smiled and wiped his face with the hem of his shirt. "Hey, Kay. How was your trip?"

"Useless. There were no brass fittings anywhere." Evan recognized the evasion, the misdirection. He knew what she'd gone in search of. But instead of becoming confused, he grew wary. She'd imitated something Reenie said, borrowing the cadence and accent of the words. Hopefully the tones didn't tip her hand to all around.

His eyes focused, and he mouthed some words to her. It took just a moment to interpret, "Do you need a hand?"

Yes, she did. The nod gave her answer but failed to tell him how to get started.

In her mind, she replayed the images that struck her on the walk in. When the man in the shiny shoes had come while they were digging up the privy, he had walked around the corner. His hand had touched the house, the wall, the railing.

Kayla went there first. Pointing, she turned her head, and carefully checked the wood. She motioned for Evan to do the same. Nothing.

Evan silently conveyed a question about a flashlight, but Kayla shook her head. With two fingers she motioned eyes all around. So they kept looking. When the porch didn't play out, they moved to the next spot—the second place the man had stopped.

Fifteen minutes later, they found the first bug.

EVAN ROLLED OVER IN BED, his hand snaking up under the pillow to the gun that was waiting there. Reenie didn't know about it; it was enough that he knew. He had a snapshot memory in his head of Ivy cross-legged on her bed, checking the clip on a nine-millimeter. Kayla had smiled at him as she stood at the edge of the window, having just peeked around the curtain, a shotgun propped beside her, no doubt loaded and ready.

The bug had scared them all. Reenie had been doubtful at first, but then—when Evan had pulled her over and quietly pointed it out to her—she'd gotten very still. Between the houses on Docket Street really being foreclosed and now this, she was starting to worry, too.

Tides of ideas came and receded. Why would someone follow Ivy and Kayla? It had to be tied to the forged diagram. But why would anyone forge the damn thing in the first place? Reenie wanted to tie the whole incident to the bloody clothes and a probably-murdered baby from nine generations ago.

Evan knew they needed to protect themselves, but the gun didn't make him feel any better. It made things worse. It was tangible proof that things were wrong.

The first issue was the bug; the second issue was the man who put it there. He'd come to their place of business, their home, looked them in the eye, and lied to them. Then he'd placed surveillance listening devices and left. Someone was monitoring them and they were sleeping with guns.

All day he'd felt the hair on his neck rise as he worked the cotton field earlier. The field probably would have been fine without him. He'd planted several varieties of seed, as it was more important that he produce *something*. As long as it was cotton, as long as visitors could play with it, pick the seeds, run it through the gin, and take a piece of history home with them, it didn't matter. But he desperately needed sprouts. So he'd hedged his bets and planted the most likely seed strains.

He'd spent time today, crouched down in the dirt, checking for saturation in the soil, checking that the earth was undisturbed. And his spine had prickled—that tiny change in sensation when you know something is about to go wrong, when you feel you are being followed. But he hadn't seen anything. Well, not until later.

After he'd looked around, searched for faces in the nearby woods and found nothing, he'd seen footprints in the soft earth at the edge of the field. He couldn't identify them nor could he rule much out. They could even belong to Kayla; she had relatively big feet, as she was somewhat tall. The prints might even be old, where he hadn't plowed, and only partially imprinted. Only Ivy had small enough feet to be off his radar. Hell, the tracks might even be his own.

But they'd disturbed him, made him wonder.

Still, he'd quelled the unease. Told himself that he was being swayed by Kayla's concerns. Kayla dealt in black-and-whites a lot. Kayla found things to be suspicious, so something must be suspicious. She knew it was unlikely, but the thing that was suspicious didn't go away. She hadn't overreacted and so neither had he.

Still, it had made him look twice into the woods to see if he was being watched. It made him pay attention to the feeling at the back of his neck, at the base of his spine. And it had made him shut up and look when Kayla had motioned what she needed.

If the diagram had been questionable, the bug was not.

Had Kay and Ivy really been followed? He didn't know. But he knew enough to slide the gun—loaded—under his pillow. He knew enough that sleep was going to be hard won and that he'd never be able to forget the image of his sister, in another woman's bedroom, smiling and saying goodnight to him. Shotgun at her side.

He closed his eyes and listened to the sounds of the plantation at night. He heard crickets and owls. There were some scuttling noises and in the far distance coyotes voiced disapproval. But he didn't hear footsteps, human sounds, or anything that would make him suspicious. Still, he was suspicious.

Evan took a deep breath and wondered if he could force himself to sleep.

KAYLA CHIPPED CAREFULLY at the wood in the gears she had made. At the time, the wood had been a cheap option, a lightweight way to build what was needed without investment of time or money. She hadn't thought it would work anyway. And it hadn't.

But she'd put the magnets into a backpack, in hopes that no one watching would know what she had, and she'd taken the food Ivy had packed for her and headed down to the smithy to tinker with it. The magnets couldn't be altered, so she altered the gears to fit what she'd bought. And while Evan tinkered in the cotton field again—presumably to be able to keep an eye on her —she popped the magnets into place, one by one.

The gear grew heavier as she added the iron pieces to it. Carving each spot carefully, Kayla took into account any variations from piece to piece. They should all be the same, but she was snapping them into place, no glue, no fastenings of any kind. So she worked slowly, meticulously, not certain the magnets would make any difference, but seeing how they might.

She'd slept soundly next to Ivy, glad that she hadn't gotten her own room yet, and beginning to wonder if she would. Sleep had been easier to find with the loaded guns standing guard. The creaks and groans from the old house were a comfort; they would hear anyone long before he reached the upstairs room. So she'd dreamed of magnets and cotton fields and schematics in lead ink.

She awoke and headed out, only to be stopped and mothered and handed a sack lunch by Ivy.

A glance outside revealed that the day had waned while she carved. So she pulled a sandwich from the bag and forced herself to eat it, if only to show Ivy that she'd paid attention and that the watchfulness was appreciated. It was peanut butter and jelly but tasted like nothing since her brain was elsewhere.

Finally, the gear was finished. A quick shake revealed all the new pieces to be tight in their homes, the gear itself ready to be reinstalled into the machine. It took a while to get the re-engineered piece situated, to shore up the struts meant to handle the weight of wood, not iron. Giving a test spin, she found a little oil cleared up the friction. But still the machine did nothing.

She spun the wheel several times, waiting for something to catch. Each gear turned another, eventually heading to a crankshaft that looked to be useful for output of some kind. It would be attached to a turnbar, or a generator, or . . .

Kayla was beginning to wonder if maybe she'd been wrong—if the machine wasn't a generator at all. The magnetted gear didn't turn anything else, because it wasn't really a gear at all. And now she'd altered it to fit her cheap, blister-packed magnets, but it should be doing the right thing.

She then turned her attention to the bar that had also been altered in the second diagram. This time something about the lines and the way they'd been drawn grabbed her. In the original, she'd seen a change in the thickness of the lines and she'd duplicated it on her own forgery. It made her think there was a connection between the pieces she'd just spent the day fitting into place and the changes in the bar.

No one had asked for her help today; she'd come out to work on the machine, no questions asked. Ivy and Reenie had stayed at the house, though Evan had insisted that there be a loaded gun nearby and that they not answer the door to anyone. He'd told all the girls to call him; he wanted to be notified of anyone who made them nervous and anyone who didn't.

Kayla had been left completely alone. But she'd been so engrossed in her work that nearly the whole day had passed. Ivy and Reenie had probably re-painted the front room in the oxblood shade that Ivy had chosen to match the chips of original paint they had found. The parlor would be a bright, rich yellow and beyond that, the sitting room would be coated in a soothing green. If they could get the edges right—Reenie insisted that they paint the borders by hand—they might have gotten through painting all three rooms while she'd been here today.

She reminded herself to comment on the work they'd finished and to find something nice to say about it when she got in tonight. She was spending the day wrapped up in her own projects, and they'd lost a hand to help with their deadline; the least she could do was say something kind. Maybe it would help her shift focus after a day here by herself.

Kayla had tinkered with magnets, taping them together and

working on an idea. She resisted changing her original piece until she was more certain how it should work.

Three iterations later, she spun the wheel and this time it caught.

9

T he Blacksmith's Shop

EVAN KNEW Kayla was fine the moment Ivy came in the back door. Ivy's eyes had grown wide-eyed and dewy looking since she'd trotted off to find his sister.

A quick glance at Reenie revealed that she was irritated by the arrival of only one person, by the lack of attendance at her meal.

Ignoring Reenie's dark mood if not the woman herself, he asked, "What?"

"She did it." Ivy opened up a radiant smile and turned away. The now-empty doorway revealed the dark sky beyond, and the knowledge that Ivy was headed to the smithy.

When Reenie announced that she was tired of holding dinner and had insinuated that she was even more tired of holding meals for someone with no sense of time, Ivy had gone in search of Kayla. Ivy's sudden solo return, the light on her face, and the hasty exit all indicated something big. "She did it" could mean anything, but Evan knew the machine was now working; that was the only reasonable "it" here. So, he too passed through the doorway with no further explanation and left it standing wide in hope that Reenie would follow.

He watched his footing, moving slowly through the deep gray. Unlike his sister, he didn't know every blade of grass and dip in the ground. If he went faster, Evan would turn an ankle. But he risked looking behind him and saw Reenie had put on her shoes and was reluctantly following.

Stopping at the crest of the bridge, Evan leaned against the railing as she picked her way toward him, her slim form a shadow to his now-adjusted eyes. He held out his hand, a gesture of love, welcome and thanks. She'd come when she didn't have to. She'd stopped what she was doing, interrupted a meal she'd fixed for everyone and been abandoned at. But still she put on her sneakers and come out to see "it." She probably wasn't even interested in the machine itself; but she was here, and he was proud.

"Oh!" Reenie startled as she finally spotted him waiting in the dark. Her hand came out and she laced her fingers in his, an old gesture from before the plantation started erecting walls between them even as they tore the physical walls down.

"Come on." He tugged her along, offering stability and impetus. But he didn't say more. The journey took a while and as they came around the trees, he saw Ivy in the distance. The light emanating from the smithy made her into a silhouette as she stepped lightly over the packed earth around the shop, much more familiar with the terrain than him. She disappeared through the doorway, and closed it, cutting off the illumination.

Warm air snaked currents around them and the sounds of the night closed in. Evan could feel Reenie inching closer, clinging as the darkness seemed to overwhelm them. She'd grown up in a town with nothing like the open spaces here. Her land had been populated with people and stores, not trees and insects and vacant historical buildings.

Just before he pulled open the door, he thought the wind brought him a scent of iron, as though the smithy still functioned in its former incarnation. Kayla was mostly working wood in there, no iron had been heated at all that he knew of. The heavy door swung open on its ancient hinges, revealing a scene he wasn't all that comfortable seeing.

Kayla knelt near where she propped the machine on blocks to keep important pieces off the dirt floor. Ivy crouched behind his sister, her arms around Kayla, a hug of excitement. But then his attention snapped back. The wheel turned. And at the far end he could see motion—a gear in constant rotation.

Kayla looked up at him, eyes bright. "She was right. It was exactly those two altered spots on the diagram that made the difference. I fixed the wheel, inserting magnets. The trick was to alternate the polarities in the gear. I'd already noticed it had an even number of cogs, so that was an option." She pointed to the moving wheel, too involved in the work to count the number of sentences she was saying or to notice that no one else spoke. "This gear doesn't attach to anything, so that didn't make sense, except that it tipped me to the magnets, but even that didn't make it work."

"But the rest of it was right. Except the rod." Ivy was looking at him and Reenie now. Reenie had remained silent, and Evan was grateful that she wasn't criticizing.

"The rod was the final piece, it has magnets, too. I tried the round ones, but eventually found that the bar magnets worked better and they provided better balance, or the physical turning of the wheels and gears gets out of sync. I oiled it a lot, too. It has to be incredibly low friction or it doesn't run very long. I had it running before but it petered out. I could almost directly calculate the kinetic friction coefficient from the angular velocity." She didn't even seem to breathe, the norm when she was so focused.

"But then I oiled it, and oiled it again. And then I cleaned it and changed the oil to the synthetic engine oil I stole from your trunk, Evan."

She didn't apologize and he didn't see the need to suggest she remember to ask before she took or borrowed things in the future. He was looking at the machine, listening while she spoke.

Kayla must have noticed. "It takes setting motion to the bar, then a crazy hard wrench to the flywheel here. But you have to do both, and you have to do the bar first, with a small spin, then the wheel with a serious push. Like starting a gas engine with a pull cord." She pointed to the largest gear that she had spent the day setting magnets into. "But once you achieve that, it goes. It's been running for three hours and forty two minutes." She didn't look at her watch.

Reenie clutched his hand tighter, eyeing the machine like it was a strange animal that had wandered into her house.

Evan asked what he was wanting to. "Kay? Is there a power source?"

"That's just it, Ev. I have no idea what force I input. I can't even guess a Newton conversion number, but I can't believe I put in energy anywhere near necessary for what the output is. I want to see how long it goes." She kept her gaze on the machine; only her hand came up and clasped Ivy's arm where it hugged around her neck, otherwise everything was ignored. She spoke to him, but didn't look; only touched Ivy, leaving Reenie a non-entity in Kayla's attention window.

He leaned down to her. "I don't think you can. I don't think it's safe to leave it here, especially not running, and I need you to come in tonight and get some sleep."

"No, Evan. It needs to run. If it truly is over-efficient then it will keep going. I need to time it."

Reenie spoke for the first time. "Over efficient?"

Though she didn't look up, Kayla smiled. "Perpetual motion, over one hundred percent efficiency. It outputs without input."

Eyebrows up, Reenie was the only one who reacted. She shook her head as though she could shake out the thoughts. "I never even thought of that. Do you think that's why we're being watched?"

Urgency hit Evan with a slap. "Then it's even more important that we shut this down. We can't leave it here tonight—"

"I'll stay with it." It wasn't an argument, but he had to argue back.

"I don't think it's safe, Kay." He took a deep breath. "We have to shut it down and keep it safe."

When she looked up, concern finally settled in her gaze. "Do you really think people are going to come after it?"

"I think they already have."

She nodded. The logic of his argument was irrefutable. She was the one who said the man in the suit had lied to them. She'd been in the car when Ivy insisted they'd been followed. And she knew what the ramifications might be if someone was looking for this. "We can't move the whole thing. It was assembled here and I don't know why anyone would look here. Well, that's stupid." She recanted her own thought almost before she'd finished saying it. "If anyone is watching us and saw all of us come here together . . . Satellite images could even show the lights on here and pinpoint the smithy's if anyone is that advanced. Shit."

Evan agreed. It was all bad. "What can we do if we can't move it? Covering it with a sheet won't be enough and there's not one here." He looked around; there wasn't even a tarp, only a half-eaten lunch that lay lonely and dried out on the bench in the corner. Evan would lay better than even odds that Ivy had brought it to her.

Ivy stood and looked the machine over. After a moment, Evan joined her exasperation. It couldn't stay here. He wouldn't be surprised at all if they came back in the morning and it looked as though the device had never existed.

At least Ivy gave up and turned to other tasks. She went

through Kayla's backpack, then she focused on the food, gathering up the sandwich remnants and throwing a few chewed-on pieces out the doorway to the tall grass behind the building.

It was Reenie who asked, "Can you dismantle it?"

"No!" Immediately Kayla reacted. "It took so long to set it up, it's covered in oil."

That much was true. But Reenie didn't let Kayla's outburst stop her. "Okay, but maybe part of it? If it really works, it will work when you put it back together tomorrow."

This time there was no immediate negative response, only the murmur, "Like a bicycle. Like taking the front wheel. But what to take . . ."

"Exactly." Reenie smiled. "Which pieces are small enough that we can carry them?"

It was the strangest conversation Evan had ever witnessed. Reenie had just solved Kayla's problem. And Kayla had let her. Kayla was making eye contact with his sister, there were no raised voices and both women were smiling.

"It's not a matter of size but of access and value."

Reenie nodded back. "The question is: what's the front wheel here? What's easy to carry, easy to put back and makes the whole thing impossible to use if anyone finds the remaining parts? Could the wheel be the wheel?"

Kayla grinned suddenly. "Yes, I think you're right. We just have to stop it." She sighed, her heart clearly breaking at the prospect of shutting down her beloved machine.

Reenie put a hand on his sister's shoulder, and for a moment Evan thought that maybe the miracle here tonight wasn't the possibility of a real free energy machine, but that Reenie and Kayla were patching things up.

Kayla sat in the dirt as she looked the machine over and Reenie now crouched down into her line of sight. "I know you don't want to stop it. Neither do I; it's crazy cool. But getting it stolen is worse. And when you start it tomorrow, you'll know that today wasn't a fluke."

"Today wasn't a fluke."

His muscles clenched in automatic reaction, and Evan noticed that Ivy's did, too. In her short time here, she'd absorbed the dynamic. Then the tension suddenly dispersed when Kayla recanted.

"Well, running it again tomorrow will *prove* that it's not a fluke. Now I think we can stop it if we can get the bar . . ." The word trailed off as she tipped her head and watched the octagonal piece as it rotated with less than smooth motion. She reached out as though she could grab it but stopping it was going to be no easy feat. Even just getting a grip on it would be problematic as most of the machine was operating under a fine sweat of a mixture of oils, and getting a solid grasp might just peel a layer of skin.

Evan reached out to stop Kayla from her usual focused daze even as Reenie said, "Honey, no. There has to be a safer way. Could we use that old towel?"

Kayla nodded without looking up, her hand still snaking out as though she just reach for a wheel or a cog.

Snapping up the rag and stepping in front of his sister, Evan reached over and took hold of the turning bar. He lasted through three tries before he gave up.

Kayla just watched passively. Or so it seemed until she spoke. "Try grabbing the bar and the wheel at the same time. They seem to work in conjunction so it stands to reason that it might take both of them to get it to stop."

He tried again with Kay talking him through in her long, run-on sentences.

"Grab it at the end and apply pressure, just to slow it. Now see if you can put just enough kinetic friction on the big gear to slow it, too. Good . . . now release. See? It's running slower, so do it again, just that same way."

And so it went until the machine stood still. Kayla marked the hour with a sad sigh as though it were a time of death. "Run time: three hours and fifty-eight minutes."

Then she sat down and undid a bolt, then another, and a third, until she had the top wheel where she could lift it free and wrap it into the filthy, oily towel Evan held out. He hoped no one would think there was ever anything of value in such a horrible-looking rag.

Kayla still looked at the machine as though it might bite her, but then she said, "I think we should take the bar, too. The two work in tandem. Someone might see that."

Before he could stop her this time, she reached out and grabbed it. Unlike the great gear, it pulled easily from its slot, not attached to anything.

Without a word, the foursome wrapped the second piece in with the first and gathered Kayla's things. Ivy looked around as though there was more that should be done, but there was no way to hide anything. The remaining part stood sentry with a few long, pointed iron bars, left leaning in the corner and rusted with a century of air.

Shrugging, as if to say, "anyone who comes in here will already know what they are looking for" Evan turned away. Ivy seemed to understand. The two of them had a good non-verbal shorthand going. Maybe it came from being in the middle so often. Maybe they were in the middle because of who they were, and that was why they understood each other. But now he turned away, one arm cradling the bundle, the other around Reenie's shoulders.

It was a silent procession back to the house, the group splitting as Kayla led Ivy along the shorter path through the trees, and he and Reenie took the more foot-solid route around and over the bridge. The women waited for them at the back door where Kayla took the bundle from him, wanting to keep it to herself overnight, and he wondered what she'd gained from taking the "short" path.

But he didn't mention it.

They all met for a re-heated and relatively quiet dinner before everyone dispersed. Even Reenie seemed willing to let the dishes slide, her eyes tight with concern she hadn't shared. She held it to herself through the rhythmic slush of toothbrushing and the choreographed change into her pajamas. But she slid into bed beside him, turned off the light and started talking in a rushed whisper.

Fear poured fourth just as the words did. "Evan, I'd heard a rumor . . . maybe an urban legend about Eli Whitney inventing a free energy machine. I didn't even connect it until tonight. The story was that he invented it and then was killed for it."

Waiting for his chance, Evan tried to jump in, but was railroaded.

"I always thought it was like that story about the hook, or the guy in the back of the car at the gas station. But I'm beginning to wonder. If I heard a story like that, couldn't others?"

"Well, sure, but—" He was run over again.

"Then someone could be watching the area—could have been watching and waiting for a while. There aren't many books on Whitney, and most of it is for kids, but he lived in this area, he worked at several plantations here, tutoring the children before he teamed up with Phineas Miller and invented the cotton gin—"

"I don't get where this is going, Reenie." Having not found an opportunity, he'd made one. "Whitney was rich and famous, how could he have been killed? And with no one knowing about the machine?"

"That's just it. He wasn't rich and famous. The cotton gin was so easy to make he couldn't protect the patent. He went bankrupt defending the rights in court. He also invented some interchange-able parts for guns and managed to support himself, but it's widely believed that he stole or at least borrowed that idea and wasn't the true inventor. But he traveled these plantations a lot, and it stands to reason that if he did invent something else of real use, he would guard it with his life the second time around. I'm just saying—"

"Wait." He held up a hand, palm out, motioning her to stop. Even in the dark she could see it, and she did. "Can I tell you something? You sound just like Kayla. You aren't even punctuating your thoughts."

She took it better than he thought she would. "Does that mean that I'm limited to three sentences at a time?"

"Maybe." He smiled into the dark. Hope welled in him at the thought of Reenie and Kayla maybe finally beginning to understand each other.

"Okay." She breathed in. "One: there are only a few plantations left around here; they'd be easy to monitor. Two: there's only the one good specialty shop around here for protecting historical finds. It would be easy to monitor, too."

He didn't correct her, didn't tell her that she was undercounting her sentences. She was right about the rest.

"Evan, we'd be easy to find. I'm not really sure why it's valuable, but the fact that someone seems to be following us around says that it is. I'm worried."

He knew why it was valuable. But he didn't say it. The fact was, he was worried, too.

KAYLA SAT on the floor and unwrapped her parcel as though it were candy.

To her it was. This grimy, oily wheel was as wonderful as any Halloween treat she'd ever been given, more fascinating than any present. She touched it reverently. The oil had gotten gritty as hands had touched and brought small flecks of dirt into the mix, but still . . . it *worked*.

She ran her hand around the edge of the magnets, testing each one for fastness. They held. They should; she'd worked very meticulously to be sure that each was carved perfectly into place.

In the room, Ivy went about her bedtime routine. The day hung on her, the weight borne in her slim shoulders, shown in the haphazard way she kicked off her shoes and let them flip under the bed, unguarded. With a sigh, she disappeared through the door and into the bathroom.

When she returned, Kayla glanced up, only to see a scrubbed face, brushed hair and changed clothes. It seemed that Ivy had just stepped from the room half a moment ago. Kayla blinked, but held up the wheel. "I need to fix it. Do you have a chisel?"

Ivy blinked at her blandly. "No. I don't keep chisels under my pillow."

"Oh. Of course not. Maybe a flathead screwdriver?"

"It's my bedroom, Kay." Ivy's body language was ignoring her, crawling into bed, and turning up the covers. But her mouth was in the game. "Why do you need it?"

"I need to pry out the magnets."

"What!?"

Kayla took a deep breath and admitted what she didn't want to. "It worked for today, but these magnets aren't good enough. The machine will run better with stronger pieces. I can find some roughly the same size, but I'll need to pry these out and fit the others into the spots. Also, I'll need to re-machine the gear itself soon." She ran her hand around the edge, leaving yet another oil streak on her palm, the mark of a day well spent. "The wood is already showing signs of stress. Heavier magnets will add to that. The electronics store didn't have anything but dinky ones."

Ivy's head was already on the pillow, but her voice was clear. "Is 'dinky' the scientific term for that?"

Kayla smiled.

"Really, Kay, it took us all day to find those dinky ones. Where are we going to find better magnets?"

"In my storage unit in Cleveland. I had a good set. I was also thinking my friend might have some and he could machine a great gear for me. Maybe even weld some hollow pieces that will create a gear only slightly heavier than the iron itself. I think that machine would sing."

This time, she saw that Ivy had propped her head up on her hand and was trying to make eye contact. "When are we going to go to Cleveland? I thought we were re-starting it tomorrow with the gear as is."

"Well, tomorrow we could go to Cleveland instead." Kayla turned the gear and held the bar up until she could feel the attraction between the two. She didn't dare let them get close enough to clack together.

There was a sigh from the vicinity of the fluffy white bed. "We can't get to Cleveland and back in one day."

"Yes, we can." Why were people always saying that? "I'll drive. It's only an issue of whether or not Charles can machine the piece we need that fast. I don't want it in the mail."

"No, we don't want that." A small puff of noise hit her as Ivy flopped back onto the pillow. "We can't go tomorrow. But we should pose the idea to Evan and Reenie in the morning when we start up again. You should come to bed."

"Yes." She should. Kayla didn't move. "If this really works. If I can measure the input and show the efficiency, then I can radically alter fuel consumption. I want to work on it. I don't really care if someone else puts their name on it. No one needs to try to steal it. We can name it after them. I just want to make it work."

"That's not the issue, Kay."

"Then what is?" She wasn't willing to hand the mechanics over to someone else to adjust and refine. She wanted to tinker. She wanted to *know*, to *see* it work. To be part of the process.

"Kayla. If that's a free energy machine, if it really is even just *slightly* over-efficient, then no one wants to steal your invention, your discovery. Do you have any idea how much of the economy is tied up in fuel?"

Oh. Kayla didn't say it, but at the single syllable in her head, every cell in her body stopped.

"They want to shut it down. They'll want to silence you. And it."

10

C leveland, Ohio

Ivy HELD the new gear loosely on her lap as she slept soundly if not completely peacefully in the passenger seat of Kayla's little car. The Cleveland trip had been successful if long. Her friend Charles had been happy to help, too. But it had taken more time to weld the gear than Ivy had allotted for. Kayla didn't mind. When he explained that the metal he had in shop wasn't the best quality for that kind of heavy-use application she had in mind, he suggested they go out and get the right kind. Kayla had agreed instantly. Ivy had not.

Thus it was now long past midnight when Kayla had texted Evan in code that they were on their way back.

So her brother knew they would be getting in late, and her companion was out cold, leaving Kayla to concentrate only on the driving. The freeway lights passed by her in a rhythm that she drove to, almost like a visual music. The fifth one in front of her was out, a missing beat.

She didn't really think that their phones had been tapped—in fact, there was logic to the contrary. Wouldn't it be easier to hack email than a cell? All four of them had online accounts that they used regularly. Reenie was constantly placing orders and shipping materials. And all the accounts were on free systems. A good keyword search could have brought the seekers right to them.

If someone was watching for important historical items to pilfer, then the system was near perfect. Idiots like them would bring in important historical items and anyone with any reasonable knowledge could fake a second one and keep the original. Which was what Kayla thought had happened to them . . . almost.

In the back of her mind, she wondered if there was a way to check up on the restoration shop. They claimed they had never lost anything before the Eli Whitney diagram. But if the shop employees or owners were stealing things then they could legitimately state they'd never lost anything. Also, the Hazelton House piece would never ultimately be claimed as a lost item, because eventually it had been "found." It might even be a single employee feeding information to someone who could fence the items.

She wondered what kind of a journey her original document had gone on, where it might be now, who might have it. But the fact remained, if she and Ivy could make a reasonable facsimile to show in the museum, then anyone could.

The road changed as she exited Ohio, the new asphalt creating a sound that mimicked the clop of horse hooves beneath the tires. The light out here was limited to that provided by trucks, as the moon had lost even the sliver it had shown them a few nights ago.

Glancing at her roadmate, Kayla saw that Ivy slept on. Even the hard beat of the pavement didn't disturb her. To Kayla the sound was a pulsing reminder of where she came from, the visit to Charles a hint of what she'd given up. They hadn't spoken to each other since she'd left. But Charles had Aspergers, too and he was thrilled to see Kayla, though she hadn't called ahead. He'd readily dropped the project he was immersed in to help her with her gears.

That was how Kayla measured their friendship. Not by calls and emails, but by how high they ranked to each other in attention. It had taken him five full minutes to even see that she'd brought someone else with her. And Ivy, soundly ignored in the frenzy of ideas that had spilled forth between them, had seen to food and drinks. She'd texted Evan that "buying the groceries" would take a little longer than expected. She'd read a book on her phone when she wasn't able to participate at all. And now she slept, cradling the big gear as if it were her child.

It had been lightly oiled and wrapped in canvas, and it had to be cutting off some of the circulation to her legs, as she hadn't moved since she passed out about three hours back. But Kayla didn't have the heart to wake her, didn't need her to drive, only needed her to be Ivy. To be willing to step back and let Kayla be Kayla. Something neither of her parents had ever quite gotten the hang of. Only Evan had been able to hold on to her without strangling what she was.

Though she wasn't tired, Kayla sped up, altering her rate until the thump of the tires on bad road matched the beat of the song on the radio. The second song was too slow, and though she changed the stations several times, she couldn't find anything that matched the road so well. Kayla turned her thoughts inward.

Evan and Reenie had reported the day as fine and simple. No one had come to call, they had not left the plantation and they didn't see anything suspicious. They were all monitoring their conversations out in the space between the buildings now. Because Kayla was able to recount the conversations she'd been involved with in that space and a few she had overheard, they'd reached several reasonable conclusions.

One—no one had unknowingly given away any details about the machine or what it did. Two—leave the bug and let whoever it was go on idyllically monitoring it. Kayla had also swept the house with a radio-frequency detector she'd rigged and found nothing. Reenie had worried, but Kayla pointed out that the man had come into the courtyard area and placed a device where he put his hand. He'd never made it into the house. Someone would have had to break in to do something like that. And while Kayla didn't think anyone had, it didn't stop her from spending three hours tinkering with the detector then sweeping the place.

Kayla didn't stop the whole way back. Pulling into the long, rutted drive brought the unexpected sensation that Hazelton House was "home." Cleveland had never been that. It had been a place to explore. A location with a job she liked. The next in a line of square-built apartments with white walls.

As Ivy bumped awake, Kayla stayed silent, watching the big house grow in size as they approached. She like the squareness of it. She'd measured the outsides and squealed with delight the day she found out the base had golden rectangle proportions. Even Reenie had liked that one. The house boasted both internal and external lateral symmetry, something Kayla found soothing.

In that moment, as Ivy awakened and whispered, "Are we back?" Kayla decided that if she was home, she needed an office.

"Yes, we're home." She spoke it in the same hushed tone that Ivy had used, an old trick of trying to blend in. Speak as the other person speaks, say what you wish, but mimic the volume and cadence.

Ivy was gathering herself, rubbing her eyes, looking around the car for trash and handing wrapped gears to Kayla. But Kayla's thoughts were upstairs on the second floor. The far right window fit a smaller room. It had another window on the side of the house, lending a nice symmetry within the room, too. She could watch out the front drive as she worked.

Following Ivy up the steps, she mimicked the wave Evan gave them as he stepped back into his own home, able to sleep now that they had returned safely. It was 3:17 a.m. and he had waited up. Kayla smiled to herself, but she was debating whether to start the machine or start on her office.

After tucking the gears safely out of sight under Ivy's bed, she listened to the cadence of Ivy's toothbrush, and the pattern she was familiar with that signaled Ivy was about to climb into bed and fall dead asleep. But Kayla went into the front room, shadows wrapping around her. Hands on hips, she surveyed the layers of paints that had colored the room, first deep green, then later lighter blue, and at one point a disturbing burnt orange. Newspaper covered all the upstairs windows after Reenie had freaked out about someone watching them.

Mentally, she placed her furniture around the room . . . a desk, a drafting table, a deep swivel chair. Though she loved the idea of the office—an office of her own without a bed in it—she pushed the plans aside; She had to start the machine. It was logical really, if she did the office first, the machine would sit stagnant. Putting the machine before the office would mean she could collect data while she decorated.

She was still standing there in the dark, smiling, when Ivy's voice came from behind her, "Kay, you have to come to bed. It's nearly four a.m. and I won't sleep until you're in here."

She was turning to say she was plenty wide awake, but Ivy caught her off guard. Ivy was neurotypical, the dark circles under her eyes indicative of less than seven hours of sleep in the last day. Her face bore that slack look of exhaustion, and Kayla's heart tugged a bit. "I'll be there in a minute."

"Mmm hmmm" seemed to be all Ivy could muster. Soft, dragging steps shuffled back into the bedroom and Kayla kept looking at her new office, seeing a design station and a building station, a communication spot with a phone, computer, etc. But in her head, her mental count of time ran out, and she turned to get ready for bed.

EVAN STARED. His hands dripped oil, his knees ached, his eyeballs felt like he'd rubbed dirt into them, but his heart sang. Kayla smiled up at him, much the way she had as a kid building architecturally sound sand castles on their beach vacations. The other kids and parents had admired her skill. His mother worried that her only daughter didn't run and play, didn't try to surf or collect shells like the other kids. No, Kay had been building even before she could speak.

He felt the turn of a circle inside him somewhere. His sister looked much the same as he. She was dirty—filthy, really—with oil smears on her jeans and on her legs where her skin peeked through the rips in the denim. These were not trendy tears, but wear in spots where Kayla put them through the most paces. She often worked on her own lap, creating stains and thin spots. The lower part of the butt had worn through, and Evan had seen a peek of the plaid boxers she'd slipped under rather than just getting a different pair of jeans.

Her shirt looked better than his, but only because his was white and betrayed his tasks to the world. She'd worn an old favorite tee bearing the logo "I failed the Turing Test." She'd probably put it on special this morning to commemorate the new gears going into the machine.

They'd run it for four hours and thirty minutes before stopping it. They'd eaten a sandwich lunch that Ivy had brought them. Luckily, Reenie had been right behind her with antiseptic hand wipes. She'd monitored both Kayla and Evan like children, checking their faces before letting them eat. But even Reenie hadn't complained that they were starting to get behind on the plantation schedule.

It wasn't anything they couldn't fix. The business licenses had been filed, the custom paints ordered. The company that specialized in washing historic buildings had Hazelton House on their calendar for three weeks from now, and the cotton had gone into the ground. Reenie had a strict plan, but they hadn't lost anything they couldn't catch up. At least he didn't think so.

The machine was running again while they ate. Kayla didn't like to leave it stagnant; just because she wasn't doing anything with it during lunch didn't mean it couldn't be doing something. And she'd become quite adept at starting it. She would grab the bar and rest her hand on the wheel, then twist both at the same time, watching it spring to action, running without further input from her.

After lunch, they all went their separate ways, and he left her to check on the cotton field. He wanted to see the soil, be sure it was wet enough, dry enough, right enough. He really didn't have a feel for what cotton needed. Hell, previous to this, he had trouble keeping his houseplants alive. But he'd done okay with a patch of corn and beans one year, so he had reason to hope.

The black earth sifted nicely through his fingers, still moist from the watering he'd done the other day, praying that rain didn't come. It hadn't. The water had been the right choice.

Footsteps behind him caused him to turn around. Ivy approached with her hand up, shielding her eyes from the bright glare of midday. "Is everything going okay out here?"

He smiled and was getting ready to tell her that it was, when he glanced to the edge of the field. "Come here."

Uncertain of what was to come, Ivy followed him. He'd told Reenie about the prints, but they hadn't made a decision to do anything about it and thus had done nothing. There was no need to worry everyone further, when the prints were likely just leftovers from one of them. "Could this be Kayla?"

"No way." Ivy tilted her head. "Those are men's shoes."

Shit. "That's what I thought."

"Are they recent?"

And with that worried tone in her voice, he'd done exactly what he'd intended *not* to do. "No. I'm hoping they're just old tracks that didn't get stomped or plowed . . ." He sighed, knowing that wishing didn't make it so.

Then Ivy pointed. "What about those over there? Are they yours?"

And there, in between some of the rows, was a second set of tracks. His stomach clenched.

Silently, they looked at each other and followed the path set by the strange prints. He didn't say it—he suspected Ivy already knew—but there was no way these were his tracks. They were in dirt he had turned two days before, leaving only a narrow window for when they might have arrived. In a moment, it was pretty clear that the footsteps had come out of the wood area, walked over and looked at the plants, then headed for the barn.

"They go under the door." Ivy pointed to where the steps backtracked and then disappeared, showing that the man had stopped to let himself inside.

Furious, Evan reached for the door—he didn't lock it, and looking back that had been an incredibly stupid decision. But it had been one he'd made before the lying man had planted the bug and aside from the blacksmith's Evan hadn't revisited the idea of leaving the outbuildings unsecured. His stomach turned with the combination of anger and fear, but Ivy's hand on his arm stopped him. "Wait."

His breathing passed through the forced rhythm that his emotion created, but he clenched his fists and tried to be logical.

It seemed forever before she said, "Okay, I see steps leading away. I didn't want you to barge if someone's still in there."

But he already had the door wrenched open before she finished her sentence. In the darkness, he scanned his equipment. It didn't appear that anything had even been moved. Yanking the flashlight from his back pocket, he tracked the footsteps around one large farming machine then another. It looked like their intruder had stopped and looked under a tarp here, checked a box there. The dust had been disturbed, or there were obvious fingermarks and sometimes he just had the deep sense that the space had been violated.

"Is anything missing?" Ivy managed to remain calm through so much. From the looks of her—the visible, dark bra straps and tight jeans—he would have expected her to squeal over a new top or nail polish color. Instead, she was almost sedate. She held her tongue until she had something important to say and she rarely spoke without meaning. That she'd spent a good part of her life on the pole just made her a bundle of contradictions that Evan didn't think he would ever sort out. But he shook his head.

Without a word, they continued following the footsteps back out of the barn. As soon as the man stepped out of the dirt and into the grass, all was lost. Evan could only make out a general direction—if he kept going straight, he'd walk right into the slave cabins.

Ivy's voice was soft but firm. "We need to tell the others."

He shouldn't have discounted the first set of prints when he'd seen them the other day. These were clearly the same—someone had a pair of "trespassing at Hazelton House" boots. His face must have displayed his frustration, because Ivy threw out a gambit at obvious distraction. "So, I didn't understand Kayla's shirt and I looked up the Turing Test online."

He just nodded again. As distractors went, it wasn't much.

But Ivy continued. "I didn't know how to ask her if she gets the irony."

"What do you mean?"

"Well . . ." Clearly Ivy didn't really know how to ask him either. "Because of the Aspergers. She has social miscues, an almost Google-level of knowledge on some things, and some days she sounds like a computer. She really *could* fail the Turing Test."

Without warning, Evan threw his head back and laughed. Full from his belly, the sound nearly doubled him over, and he missed a few steps before he caught back up with Ivy. He was wiping hysterical tears from his eyes as he choked out, "You know. I didn't get it, but I bet she does. I'll bet she's been wearing that shirt all this time just because of that."

He sobered up as they reached the blacksmith's, but neither of them headed for the doorway. Without talking, he and Ivy started moving around the outside of the building, searching for prints. He didn't find any, and Ivy rounded the last corner shaking her head no. He hoped that was good news.

Inside, they found only Kayla; Evan and Ivy looked at her, speaking simultaneously.

"What's with the buckets?"

"Is that a thermometer? Is the engine overheating?"

Kayla grinned up at them, an evil sprite as she held up a screwdriver with a large bore drill bit that she'd converted to run a gear. "I'm testing the engine."

"Come again?" Ivy leaned forward.

That brought a wider smile, Kayla loved explaining things. "So, I found out how long I have to run the screwdriver to start the engine. It's approximately forty-five seconds. That's because I'm not moving the bar at all. I didn't want to touch anything and input extra power into the scenario."

Ivy nodded as though this made sense, and Evan followed. "So you've found a new way to start it?"

"Yeah, a measurable way. I still don't know the exact force I'm inputting, but forty-five seconds of the same speed of the drill should give me roughly the same input repeatedly. So I created a relatively closed system—" She pointed to the covered buckets, both with thermometers sticking out as well as a gear. "And I'm trying to see if I can measure temperature change."

"Why are you trying to heat the water in the buckets?" Ivy frowned.

Kayla shrugged. "It's not that I'm *trying* to heat it, it's that I'm trying to show that putting the same amount of energy into the machine produces more energy than putting the energy directly into the liquid."

"Oh." Ivy didn't sound like she understood, but Evan asked, "You're looking for some proof of over-efficiency."

"Basically." She turned to a post-it pad and noted the time. Then she wrote a few things down after looking at the pieces sticking out of the sealed lid on the bucket on the right. Next, she hooked the drill into some part of it and ran it while clocking time on her cell phone. After what Evan figured was a minute she stopped and recorded a few more things.

He'd waited, because he knew better than to talk to her in the middle of an experiment, "You set all this up in—" he checked his watch, "under two hours?"

"Ev. It's two old paint buckets. I poked in holes and used a drill bit and an old gear. It's pretty simple. I already ran a few trials." She waved her hand at the bench.

Ivy nearly choked. Maybe she wouldn't after she knew Kayla longer, but she put her hand to her throat and walked over. "Is each of these a trial?"

Kayla nodded.

The surface of the bench was nearly covered in green squares, each with the same organization if not the same numbers.

Kayla's voice came to them. "Every single trial has showed the machine to be far more productive off the same initial input. And —you'll see on each note—the machine was halted. It could have gone longer and given more output."

He didn't want to stop her, but the day was waning. Every night, they would have to pull it apart and keep the pieces separate. Kayla's data today made that even more important than ever.

Three trials later, he stopped her.

She smiled at him, "I filled the bench. I think I have enough evidence."

He'd been counting on that. He noted the careful arrangement of post-its, waiting until she'd filled the final gaps. Then asked what they could do to help.

Kayla set Ivy to arranging the sticky notes into a spiral notebook while she and Evan pulled the gears and thermometers out of the buckets, packing certain pieces into her backpack. They unbolted and wrapped the main wheel and pulled the magnet bar from the body of the machine. Then, like silent soldiers, they trekked the material back to the main house.

They stashed pieces under the bed in Kayla and Ivy's room, then headed over to see what Reenie had for dinner. Heading up the back porch steps, each veered near the edge on the middle board. He made what was probably his fifth mental note to fix it and acknowledged that it was a low priority on what had become a very long list. He didn't smell anything as he approached the back door. The kitchen had been added into the back of the house, and he perked his ears to listen for Reenie bustling about, but there was nothing.

So he was shocked to find her sitting at the table watching him come in. She had an odd look on her face.

He had only the warning of a stray footstep behind him before she flinched and he turned.

In a moment too short to process anything, a small man came through the doorway holding a big gun. He waved it wildly between Reenie and Evan, then snapped his head at the sound of Ivy and Kayla coming through the door and nearly piling into Evan's back.

Moving his hands, palm back, to his side, Evan used the subtle gesture to corral the two women behind him. Reenie was too far away to shield without lunging for her.

The man held the shotgun in their general direction and faced Reenie, his eyes angry, "You said they weren't here."

"They just walked in." Reenie delivered her line in her crisp southern accent, as though this man was foolish for doubting her. She looked calm sitting there at the table, her hands clasped in front of her where the intruder could see them. Sometimes Evan forgot that this small woman possessed one fine pair of brass balls.

Then Reenie clenched her jaw. "Ask them. I told you I wouldn't just hand anything over. We all have to vote."

Frustrated as hell with Reenie, and sweating from every pore, the man shook his gun at Ivy and Kayla where they stayed behind Evan. "Get me the diagram."

11

The Overseer's House

KAYLA WAS SURPRISED when Reenie reached out and took her hand. Her first response was to yank it back; Reenie was the last person she expected to make a move like that. The touch made her uncomfortable, but because it did, Kayla analyzed it and decided that maybe the best thing she could do was accept it. She even offered a small squeeze in return—she'd seen people do that and it always seemed to comfort the squeezee.

They were all still breathing heavily as Evan returned to the kitchen after having watched the man drive off. "He was smart enough to put some mud on his license plate, but I still got the first letter and last number and can narrow down the second letter. And I got the make and model of the car." He jerked open a drawer, pulling pens and paper, then scratched out some notes. Whether his movements were tight because he was angry or scared or just coming off an adrenaline rush, Kayla couldn't tell.

Turning to where they all still sat shell-shocked at the kitchen table, he passed out pink grocery list pages. Then he handed out orders along with pens. "Write down a description of him. Note the time now at the top of the page. And note the time you think he left here. Reenie, write down when you think he arrived."

Kayla blinked twice, then checked her cell and began writing: Caramel blonde hair. About five inches long, all over. No sun highlighting. Straight. Pale skin, peach tones. Freckles across nose and some on forehead. Black suit. Cheap brand. Single-breasted. Slightly too short in the leg and too big at the waist. Only two buttons attached. White shirt. Top button undone, no tie. Wide nose. Green eyes – moss. Round shape. Eyebrows same color as hair.

She chewed on the pen a moment before adding information about his shoes, socks, lack of a watch, height, weight, general build. Then she looked up to see that Reenie and Evan had both stopped writing and Ivy was struggling to make her pen work. Her hand was shaking so much that she couldn't create legible words. Her voice shook, too. "How are you writing?"

Kayla shrugged. She just had a lot to write. Describing a whole person was extensive. But she tried what had already worked once that night and reached out to squeeze Ivy's hand.

It seemed to work. Gathering some calm around her like a blanket, Ivy turned to Evan. "Shouldn't we be calling the police?"

He sighed, "That was my next question . . . right after—" he turned to Reenie and yelled, "What the hell were you doing?!? Just sitting there? Why didn't you just give him what he wanted?!! He had a gun for God's sake!"

Kayla jerked back at the venom in Evan's voice. She'd never heard him yell like that. Ever. Reenie flinched, too.

"I—"

"I'm sorry." Evan's demeanor changed on a dime. His head and shoulders dropped as though his strings had been cut. Suddenly, he reached out and grabbed for Reenie. Pulling her onto his lap, he ratcheted his grip until she squirmed and said she couldn't breathe. "I was so scared for you. And you were so calm. I knew I couldn't get to you in time if he tried to do something."

On that last word, his voice hitched, letting them all know exactly what had caused the outburst. This time his words were stronger for the quiet with which they were delivered. "Kayla and Ivy were behind me, but you . . . what were you thinking?"

"Well," Reenie smiled. "I decided if Kayla was right about the last one, maybe she was right about this one, too."

Kayla leaned back at that. *When had this happened?* "Last what?"

"Maybe it was the adrenaline in my system, but I had time to think. It was like he was moving very slowly, so I looked him over and I tried to think like Kayla. He looked like an amateur. His hair was uncombed but his eyes were focused, so I didn't think he was actually crazy or doing drugs. So I thought I could try to stall him. I wanted y'all to get a look at him." She smiled at Kayla, then turned within the scope of his arms and shrugged at Evan. "He didn't look like he was going to shoot me. He just wanted the diagram and he was very clear about that."

Evan pushed her off his lap. "Did he tear up the house?" He was down the hall before he even finished the sentence.

Reenie answered in a louder voice, but didn't seem to be able to make her legs work well enough to stand. Collapsing like a rag doll into her chair, she yelled back, "He just said he was looking for you."

Emerging back into the kitchen, Evan gave a slight nod. "It looks like he didn't touch anything. But all the doors are open, even some of the closets."

Ivy looked at them all like they were crazy, and Kayla thought they probably were. "Someone just came in with a gun, held Reenie hostage, and took our property. Are you all going to call the police or not?"

"That's a good question." Evan, now calm himself, stayed in the doorway, his arms spanning the space, making it impossible for anyone to come or go.

"What?!" Ivy stood up now. "It shouldn't be a question at all. And in about five more minutes, we're going to have some serious explaining to do about why we waited to call."

Evan walked over and sat down and Kayla straightened in her chair. They had always been a democracy, even after Evan pulled Reenie into the group. So his next statement didn't surprise her.

"Ivy's right. We have about five minutes if we're going to call. Let's put it to a vote."

Ivy's hand immediately shot up, and she looked at the rest of them as if they were nuts. "What?"

Kayla pulled Ivy's hand back down and continued to hold it. "Let's look at the facts first."

Yanking her hand back, Ivy glared at them all, but didn't say anything.

Kayla threw out the first issue. "Reenie said this guy looked like an amateur. And he seemed perfectly happy taking the fake diagram. He didn't question that it was protected and didn't really check it. He just took what I handed him."

Reenie nodded. "That would indicate that he isn't involved with the people who changed out the diagram for the repro-duction."

"And probably not with the guy who planted the bug." Evan added, "I'd guess he's with the reprint guys. Or else there's a third faction at play. You're right, this guy didn't seem like a pro."

"Holy shit." Ivy jumped up. "*Do you hear yourselves*? You think there are three possible 'factions' after something you have and you aren't considering calling the police? Unless you're mafia, you're stupid." Then she sat back down, eyeing all of them warily. "*Are* you mafia?"

Kayla laughed. "No, silly."

"Sadly, that doesn't make me feel any better." She leaned back and crossed her arms. "Two minutes, by the way."

Reenie jumped in again. "It does sound worse now that we said all the pieces out loud. We do have to call the cops. A forgery is one thing, a gun is another."

Kayla nodded. "But we don't tell them about the bug or the forgery. The machine works. But we aren't in any place to go public with that, I can't hook it to machinery or a generator yet."

Ivy squinted at her. "Wait a minute. What's the harm with letting people know about your machine now? It works. You've proven that. Isn't it time to go public? That seems like the safest way. Telling everyone about it means there's no need to shut you up. You sound like you're guarding the Hope diamond."

Kayla sat back in her chair, pushed there by the weight of the world. "It's not the Hope diamond."

"Of course not." Ivy sighed. "Now will someone *please* call the police?"

"Ivy, the Hope diamond doesn't *do* anything. Sure, it's a national treasure and all, but this machine could change the way the world runs. It can conceivably reduce oil and coal consumption. You were right—the government will want it and big oil will fight us all the way. Do you really think the police can protect us better than our own silence?"

KAYLA WATCHED the sheriff's deputy drive off. He'd seemed young and green. He'd seemed confused. But that was possibly due to how they'd played it.

Ivy had turned traitor and called the cops before a vote was taken. She wasn't a Reeves. Reeves' voted. Apparently, Ivy Lopez got upset with people and took action.

The police had declined to show up and the case was diverted to the sheriff's office. Hazelton House was "county," and thus the police didn't serve and protect them. Reenie ran her hand through her hair and muttered, "I knew that. Why don't we have a direct line to the sheriff?"

She'd already corrected that with a post-it on the fridge before the officer even arrived. And once the operator had determined that no one had been hurt, no one was still hurting, and the event in question was over, their estimated time of arrival was delayed even more. Everyone sat around getting hungrier and crankier while they waited, not touching anything of the crime scene as instructed.

But Ivy acted again. She'd lined them up—and while their stomachs rumbled—devised a plan. Point number one: they had no idea why the man wanted this diagram. They should tell the officer that it had been misplaced by the restoration store. Might as well sic the police on that company.

Point number two: No mention of the machine, no mention of the altered diagram, no mention of the fact that they still had a copy of the schematic. They were to say that Ivy and Evan had been working in the cotton field and Kayla had been exploring the slave cabins—no mention of the blacksmith's shop.

This lie led to point number three: Tell everyone that Kayla had Aspergers and didn't speak. Thus her bad lying skills wouldn't get them all caught in the carefully tailored web they were spinning.

Officer Junior had bought it hook, line and sinker. He had no problem believing that Aspergers patients were sometimes completely unable to speak. Kayla's work had been not in lying but in keeping her mouth shut and refraining from yelling at him that he was an idiot. And—had he just pulled out his smart phone—he could have found out that nothing of the sort was true. So she kept her mouth shut and nodded some times, and he wrote her off completely as a valid witness.

Then Evan handed him the lists they had written.

"Who wrote this one?" He waved the list that covered both the front and back of the sheet in neat print.

"Kayla." Evan pointed at her. "She's not talking right now, but she isn't dumb. Plus, her memory is phenomenal. That's all going to be accurate—all the details."

Kayla nodded to reassure him. That list was their best chance of finding the idiot who'd tried to rob them—Kayla couldn't count his efforts as a success since he'd gotten away only with a fake.

Later, after the officer had bid them good night and told them how lucky they were, Reenie had fixed them a dinner of soup and sandwiches. Kayla ate just enough to tamp down the protests of her stomach and finally crawled into bed beside Ivy. "That sucked."

"Yeah, but you did good." Already snug under the fluffy covers, Ivy looked like a princess, but spoke like a sailor. "That had to be fucking painful to keep your mouth shut."

"It was." Kayla stared upward at the gauzy drapes over the bed. It was comforting, this fairy bed. A bed she had never wanted and wasn't sure she fit in, but it was all Ivy, and thus comforting at times like this.

Ivy's smiled, but her sigh spoke volumes. "I don't hold any real hope that they'll find this guy. I'm not feeling really safe with the sherriff's department. I hope this guy isn't indicative of the whole department, because I was not impressed with his investigative skills."

"What about the guns?"

"I don't think he could have used it if he needed to. I think he would have pissed his pants first."

Kayla laughed. "No, I meant, do you feel safer having guns here? Does it help?"

"Oh. Sure. But I don't think they're good enough. When she needed it, Reenie either didn't have one or didn't have it in reach, which is just as bad."

"So, are you thinking what I'm thinking?"

"Yup." Ivy tucked the covers up and turned away from Kayla, but she kept talking. Kayla decided to read it as Ivy just being tired, just getting comfortable. She was about to do the same thing herself, so it was hard to deem it an insult. "Family meeting in the morning?"

"We'll start it at breakfast." Kayla felt a warmth flush into her system. Ivy had said "family meeting." Ivy was "family."

~

EVAN LOOKED BACK and forth at Kayla and Ivy.

He wanted to believe the two were nuts, but after last night he was hard pressed to say otherwise. He hated it, but—"They're right, Reenie. You got held at gun point last night—"

"And I was *fine*." Though her voice stayed calm—something Reenie was a master at—her emphasis could not be missed.

Both Kayla and Ivy dove into the murky argument at once, so Evan sat back and let the sheer mass of the opposition do its work.

"He wasn't a professional. He was an idiot." That from Ivy.

Kayla hit with a different attack and Evan had to applaud her. "Reenie, you did great. You talked him through and bought us time to all get a good look at him. But if he had been on drugs or . . . who knows, even you wouldn't have been able to do that."

Evan liked the "even you." It was a nice touch, and coming from anyone else he would have believed it, but coming from Kayla . . . well, he knew it was calculated. Reenie didn't seem to catch that though, and he took advantage, adding his own straw to the camel's back.

"Reenie, I was so scared when I saw you there. I couldn't get to you. If he had shot you, there would have been nothing I could do. And that was even after I came in the door. Before that, all I could have done was hear you scream, and that scares the shit out of me." His argument had the added advantage of being entirely true. He was grateful that Reenie had held her own the night before, but he'd almost died several times in the process. "If you won't do it for you, do it for me. Or else always be in the company of one of us so that we can keep you safe."

At least Kayla and Ivy seemed ready to holster up and go full out Annie Oakley. He'd countered their eagerness by suggesting that they not just carry weapons but be reasonably proficient with them. At the mention of target practice, both girls had gone positively gleeful. While he was afraid they'd just go around shooting people, after last night there was no denying the need to act and to be at the ready at all times.

Reenie nodded slowly. "Won't they know if we take a class? Or get a license?"

Evan looked around the table. "Which is why we won't do that. We have two handguns?" He looked to the other two.

Ivy smiled. "I have my own nine-millimeter. I can handle it. I have a carry concealed license already."

Reenie's eyebrows popped up, followed quickly by Ivy's shoulders. "My mother was a stripper. When she said 'Always carry protection' she didn't mean condoms."

Evan skirted that one, not waiting to see what would happen when Reenie's southern sensibilities let that sink in. "Then we have three hand guns and four people. We need at least one more. And I, for one, wouldn't mind a spare."

"A spare!?" Reenie leaned back in her seat. Evan knew he was crossing her line with the idea of an extra.

"Yes. We got invaded last night. They want what we have, and it isn't theirs. The sheriff's office isn't close enough to protect us. And that means it's up to us to keep us safe."

His gut twisted even as he said it. He didn't like the idea of leaving, of splitting the group and having at least some of the women defending themselves. But there was still work to do to get the plantation ready. They still had to find a way to earn a living.

He didn't foresee Kayla surviving a bidding war with Big Oil over her machine, and that meant his gut was probably going to stay tied in knots for a while. It was the safest option he saw right now.

"Someone needs to go to a distant gun fair or shop today and pick up two extras. I'm thinking a nine-mill and a twenty-two. Kayla and Reenie can take the twenty-twos—" He gave Kayla a look as she was clearly gearing up to balk. "And Ivy and I will take the nines."

Just then they all jumped as a doorbell chimed loudly throughout the house.

"Jesus." Reenie put her hand to her chest and started to stand up. Her breathing turned heavy as Evan searched the air and asked, "What was that?"

"It's an electronic doorbell—wireless—that I put in yesterday." Kayla stood to answer it.

Evan stayed with Reenie, even as he hollered to Kayla to be safe. Quickly, he motioned Ivy to the door with her. He stayed where he was, torn by not knowing what was the right place for him, but he didn't like the waxy pale shade of Reenie's skin or the fact that the air she was breathing didn't seem to be soaking in. "Reenie?"

She looked up at him, eyes brimming with unshed tears. She was fighting something, he just didn't know what. Her voice was a whisper. "That chime was the last sound I heard before I opened the door and that man came in here. There were times when I was certain he was an idiot and I could talk him right out the door. But there were a few moments when I was pretty convinced he was going to kill me."

She sniffed and Evan pulled her into his arms, onto his lap. There was nothing he could do to take that away from her, no matter how much he wished otherwise.

That was how the deputy found them.

Officer Junior had returned, Ivy and Kayla trailing him into the kitchen. Behind the officer, Kayla motioned a zipper across her mouth, reminding them all that she wasn't speaking. Evan was glad she'd remembered that—he might not have.

"I'm glad you're all here." The officer refused the seat Ivy offered him at the table. "We did some follow-up work this morning. Given that you used the historical preservation services in town and that they knew you had this diagram, that was where we started looking."

Evan smiled and said, "thank you" but privately he thought the officer was acting pretty proud about a deduction any third grader who'd read some Hardy Boys mystery could make. He was not expecting any grand deductions.

He was wrong.

The officer opened the notebook that Evan had assumed he always carried. Apparently, today it was transporting useful things. "We found some pictures of the employees there," He laid out three security camera photos of male employees, all wearing the same shirts and khaki pants.

Immediately, Kayla slapped a finger on the one who'd been here last night. Evan recognized him, too. In this grainy shot, he didn't look upset, his hair was combed and he was smiling at a customer. But it was him, no doubt. Evan said so.

In a few more minutes, Officer Green left, supposedly to apprehend the wayward employee. Or maybe to talk to his boss about finding out what the thief was going to do with the diagram now that he had it.

With breakfasts either finished or abandoned, Reenie stood and cleared the table. Kayla, who had silently shown the deputy to the door, now returned to end the conversation. "So who's going to buy guns?"

"I say we split our best shooters until everyone gets some practice in. That means Ivy and I each take one of you." He turned to Ivy, pleased to see that she had no qualms about being named as a gunman. Evan was starting to develop a bunker mentality.

It was Reenie who said what he wanted her to. "I think Evan should go ... and take Kayla, not me."

Kayla looked a little surprised at that—as though she was shocked when Reenie expressed logical thoughts. Kayla needed to start adding up the number of times that happened and work her statistics so she could stop being so surprised by it.

Reenie faced her. "You know mechanics better than anyone here. I'd suggest that you go together, and stick close but actually not shop together. You'll be less obvious if you stay a little separated from each other."

"That's a good point." Kayla conceded.

Reenie didn't respond with *Damn straight*," but offered the sensible, "Ivy and I will stay here and work."

Ivy nodded. "I'll wear my gun."

Evan felt bad for her. Their one employee had a PhD in Art History. She'd lived what sounded to be a traumatic life and had picked herself up by her own bra straps to make it better. In her initial interview, she'd been fascinated and awed by the opportunity to restore an actual historic plantation.

There was some of that involved, and she'd get to paint today with an antique brush and probably spend several hours in one of Reenie's favorite pastimes: cataloguing shit from the attic. But mostly, Ivy had been oiling a machine that wasn't supposed to exist. She'd been driving to Cleveland to machine gears. She'd been babysitting his twenty-nine-year-old sister.

And now he'd just asked her to strap on a gun.

They'd cleared the table after breakfast and Kayla hopped off to research any not-quite-local gun shows or shops. No one left the Overseer's House before Ivy headed out the door; Evan quickly grabbed her arm and stopped her. "No one goes anywhere alone until we're all armed."

Ivy nodded, taking yet another thing in stride and pacing him over to the big house and up to her room where she opened several drawers in her nightstand for her clip and gun.

Standing there in the shiny white room with all its pomp and fluff, he had to say it. "Ivy, I'm sorry."

She slid the clip slickly into the gun and smiled at him. "For what?"

12

T he Old Kitchen Building

EVAN FOUND Reenie in the old kitchen building. A bandanna in her hair, she was scrubbing the brick oven with a stiff-bristled broom. Her face looked much like the oven, a layer of soot having turned to a fine patina. She turned as soon as he walked in, hyperaware of everyone around her today. "Hey! How did it go?"

It didn't matter how it went. "You're *alone*. Reenie, we agreed—"

She cut him off with a word and a quick, sharp wave of her hand. "Later."

His frown came without his bidding; his worry strong and genuine. They had all agreed not to split up, but here she was, alone. And he'd only come here because he'd discovered Ivy alone in the attic with a notebook in her hand and dust in her hair. It was the first place he'd looked after realizing the women weren't digging up any latrines and that the downstairs rooms had been painted and were just waiting to dry.

What wasn't logical was that Ivy was by herself. He'd initially figured that Reenie must be in the bathroom and he took in the scene. Piles of random things lay quiet around their employee perhaps already logged and discarded. There was clothing draped over an old, upholstered chair. There were toys carved of wood, their paint chipped, faded or rubbed away. Glass and crystal pieces nestled in clumps of newspapers from when they had last been paraded out for guests.

Ivy smiled up from the middle, the fading sunlight coming in through the dormer window giving her a sepia look, as though she were part of the history she researched. But what he noticed next was that Ivy was pinned in to her spot on the floor. And there was only room for one person in the middle of her little kingdom. He'd asked immediately, "Where's Reenie?"

Ivy had sent him here, and from the reclaimed looks of the old hewn-wood table and bench seats, the ancient butcher-block counter and white enameled sink, Reenie had been here, cleaning—by herself—for a while. Which meant both women had decided to split up. "Do you at least have a weapon?"

She shifted the broom in her hand, suddenly grabbing it with two fists and wielding it as protection. He had a fleeting image of Wonder Woman, deflecting bullets with her magic wristcuffs. Reenie looked just as tough and almost as implausible. Evan was getting ready to point that out when she leaned over and picked up a whiskey bottle.

"You're drinking?" Whatever the story was here, it just kept getting better and better.

"No, I have a glass bottle to smash and wield. And . . ." She reached to the edge of the strings that held the apron around her waist and pulled out a long knife.

Evan nodded. Though she was poorly armed, her expression

was all badass. He had to respect that. She was here, and she was safe, and tomorrow she'd have a gun and he'd breathe a little easier in a world that was spinning away from him.

So he took a breath and tried to grasp what he could. "Can you tell me why you and Ivy split up? I thought we all agreed to stick at least to units of two armed."

Reenie looked around as though she thought there might be a bug in this place, too. "Did you see Ivy?"

He nodded, weary. There was no easy space in the middle of the triangle of Kayla, Reenie and his own need to step up and be the man.

Reenie took her broom to the door and offered up a quick glance out. Then she turned, her eyes suddenly serious and worried. "I found Ivy's phone. I was snooping and I know it's wrong, but it buzzed. She had a text and she never talks to anyone. She has no friends."

Evan shrugged. He'd noticed that. "I figure she's an ex-stripper with an art history doctorate, there is no one else in her crowd."

"Right, but I was so excited that she had a friend."

"So?"

"It was from her service provider." Reenie leaned in. "But then I tried to make it look like I hadn't opened her text and I screwed it up. I wound up in a huge string of photos on her phone. Of a lot of historical items here at the house."

Evan frowned. It wasn't damning evidence; there were many logical explanations and only a few sinister ones. But Reenie's next words dropped the bottom out of his heart.

"Then I went back to erase the message." She furtively glanced out the door again. "There's a string of texts with a lot of those pictures on them. She has bidders on things she found in the attic. Things I didn't know were there. Things from my grandfather."

"What?" He thunked down onto the bench seat, momentarily grateful it wasn't still covered with spiderwebs and mouse turds.

Reenie plopped next to him, looking dejected in her cute and dirty outfit. "I know."

This was why she'd separated herself from the woman with the gun, why she'd come out here and taken her chances with just a broomstick, whiskey bottle and poorly wielded kitchen knife.

Evan looked at her then at the bottle. "Can I drink some of that?"

She laughed. "I wish. I'm pretty sure it's rotten. It wasn't well stored. You can drink it, but I'm not responsible for you having to visit the ER because your insides are burned out." Her smile was weak, but he was glad she could joke with him in the face of a betrayal.

They'd wandered off topic, probably to avoid the point, but he had to get back to it. "I can see why you wanted to come off on your own, but why do you think Ivy let you?"

"I think she's up there, cataloging things and setting who knows what aside. I just wasn't in the mood to start a fight. Not after that clerk came in here with the gun."

Evan didn't like the pattern his thoughts were forming. "Do you think she had anything to do with that? With the missing diagram?"

Reenie looked straight ahead, though it was clear she wasn't seeing anything in particular. "The thought had occurred to me. I haven't come to any conclusions. In fact, I've been doing a stellar job of pushing them aside." Back in her own skin, she waved her hand around, showing off the damage she had dealt to the dirt and time that had tried to take over the kitchen house.

Evan smiled, again glad to be off a dreaded topic. "It does look great." Then he popped up from his seat. "Shit. Kayla just went up to be with Ivy. She sleeps in the same room as her."

He was three steps away, but Reenie's hand locked on his and tugged him back to the bench and reality. "Ivy isn't an immediate threat. I don't think Kayla's in any danger from her. At least . . . what's up with the two of them?"

Evan pushed a hand through his hair. "I really have no clue. If we were anywhere else, I'd think the amount if times she says 'Ivy said . . .' would be an indicator. But she's not going to tell me what *I* said, and it's only a little more often than the number of times she says 'Reenie said,' so I have no clue."

"Really? No clue. Evan, they are grown women sharing the same bed."

"I don't think they're . . ." No, it wasn't that he didn't think it, it was that he didn't *want* to think it. He admitted at least that much to himself. "I don't know."

Reenie nodded. "Is it going to break Kayla's heart if she finds out Ivy's turned on us?"

He sat there, still holding Reenie's hand in the dim glow of the old yellow bulbs dangling from the ceiling by thick wires. The walls of this plantation were strong and stable; he never doubted their ability to stand up to time. But the secrets they harbored within were going to kill them all. One way or another.

KAYLA SAT cross-legged on the bed facing Ivy. They had a big bag spread out between them with guns scattered across the plastic as Ivy showed her how to push the bullets into the clip with little clicks, how to pull back on the slide and chamber the first round. She knew all the steps, but enjoyed watching Ivy with her smooth motions and clever hands.

They stashed the guns under books or pillows on the sweet bedside tables Ivy had placed there, before clearing the remaining parts and pieces. Ivy went off to get ready for bed, but Kayla stopped her. "Nowhere, Ivy. Nowhere without the gun."

Ivy rolled her eyes. "It's the damn bathroom." But she picked up the gun, tucked it in her waistband, then sighed when it sank and nearly removed her pajama pants. "It's just the damn bathroom, and you're here."

She set the gun back down and went off with confidence but also without the gun. Kayla left the door open and her ears, too. All she heard was Ivy brushing her teeth, flushing the toilet, the usual sounds, nothing sinister, and she figured Ivy had a point. So she kept the twenty-two in her hands and sat waiting, keeping what watch she could, but the old house stayed silent. Eventually the two women curled up and found sleep.

But Kayla's dreams were vivid.

In them, the machine was blown apart by the historical clerk with the shotgun. Then she built another and another and hooked them up in a chain, each one turning the next, and when she woke up the next morning she had an idea.

Armed now and allowed to wander off on her own, she left Ivy and Reenie to the job of cataloguing the attic. She left Evan to the barn and outbuildings. He'd been talking about restoring one of the slave cabins.

But Kayla was headed back to the blacksmith's shop to fiddle with the settings on the machine. She had a problem with one of the mathematical constants she'd worked out. Her brain on other things, she fell into her own world until Evan came in to check up on her.

"Kayla?" He looked around the room, the question more a "what are you doing?" than a "hey, are you here?"

Smiling, she brought her gaze up until it connected with his. "I did it."

"I see. But what exactly did you do?" He had to raise his voice a touch to be clear over the sound of the constant chug of metal and magnets.

"Did you re-engineer some of the gears?" He put his hand out, but then pulled it back as it got close to the running machine.

"Mmm-hmmm." She turned back to the machine, watching it run, watching the link between it and the generator, and finally doing what she had thought of that morning. First, Kayla had spent her morning replacing the last wooden gears out of the original setup. Next she'd unhooked the small generator that she'd brought down to the blacksmith's earlier. Using only the sunlight coming in through the open doorway and window, she'd linked them. And spent all her time trying to figure out how to make it work.

Now Kayla smiled as she plugged in the light and watched it come on. "I made light."

"You're like God or something."

She laughed. "I just might be." Then she pointed. "I altered it so the gears would run longer, faster, handle more force. Then I hooked it to the generator."

"Huh." Evan looked at all the pieces and then to the light.

"I made electricity." She stopped work for the first time that day. "I actually did. I started the machine by pushing the wheel and that runs the generator so I really made this electricity."

"Can you explain this, Kay?"

She laughed. "No. No way in hell can I fully explain it. There's no way I could ever turn this thing—" she pointed to the gear linking the machine into where it powered the generator—"this fast or for this long, but it really is running on my power. So no, I got nothing. Though I keep trying to solve it."

"You show this to Ivy yet?"

She shook her head. No one had even stopped by . . . she checked her watch. Four thirty. "Not Reenie either." Consciously, she calculated her breakfast against the time. She should eat. "I should have lunch . . . or food at least, but I don't want to leave."

Her eyes were trained on the machine, the turning wheel was mesmerizing, fascinating, and exhilarating. But she wasn't hungry. The machine was better than food. "Should we show it to them?"

"No."

It wasn't the answer she'd expected and it made her look up, but she didn't get to ask a question. Evan dove in. "We should head back and get you some food. You should stop it. Unhook things, don't leave anything obvious."

Reluctantly, Kayla did as he suggested, spending nearly half an hour taking the pieces apart and separating them into different piles. She didn't worry about remembering what went where—she knew and she would still know fifty years from now. So she stacked things haphazardly, in a way she hoped would keep others from making the connections she'd made. She directed Evan to move things, switch things, and he did as he was told. Then he led her up the hill to find some food.

"Evan, are you okay? You're acting weird."

He gave a quarter laugh, "Kay, you may not perpetuate the myth of the weak woman—for which I am eternally grateful—but I grew up in a culture that tells me I'm the man and I need to protect my womens."

"We aren't your harem, Ev. We're good. And all carrying guns now." She smiled, knowing the gun had her walking taller, more forcefully, even though she knew it to be a false confidence. "I get to tell them what I did."

"All right." He plucked at the front of his T-shirt trying to dispel the heat or sweat he'd built up there. "I get to take a shower."

"Well, if you aren't going to be there, then I'll tell you now. I solved the first shadow constant, so tomorrow, I'm going to see if I can power one of the buildings."

"Holy shit, Kay. Do you think it will?"

"I have no idea if it's going to work or die or blow a fuse. So I'm thinking one of the smaller buildings."

"You could try the kitchen. Reenie was cleaning in there the other day. It got wired at some time."

Kayla laughed. It would be good. "Yeah. That's a smart bet.

I'm guessing it got wired around the time of Jesus, so if I burn anything up, I won't feel bad." She shoved her hands into her jeans pockets. It was warmer out here, hiking across the grass. Evan paced her on her straight route. She hadn't yet worn a path across the field and through the trees, but she'd cleared a little, just by going through every day.

Evan pointed as they approached the back of the Overseer's House, "Do you think the generator's big enough to power that? It's a small one. Not intended for the kind of power a place like this draws."

"Nah, I don't. I don't think it's the machine but the generator that will be the failing point if we go for a big building first. But if round one works, I want to upgrade and try it."

Evan nodded and went inside, sending her up to the attic where she found Ivy and Reenie with notebooks, hangers and boxes. They didn't notice her and she watched silently for a few minutes. The two women worked in a fluid tandem, skirting around each other in the small space, reading each other clearly.

It took Kayla a few minutes to recognize the tightness in her chest as jealousy. Ivy and Reenie fit together well. And Reenie had Evan, but Kayla wanted to have that with someone—that counterweight, that other half that she read about and sometimes saw on TV. On shows, she'd always written it off as choreography and practice. Her parents had never had it; they had been very verbal people, always working things out by talking and writing down lists and rules. Evan and Reenie were somewhere in the middle, but not like this. Not like a dance that was clearly improvised but no less graceful for it.

Reenie asked Ivy several times, "Do you know what that's worth?" and each time Ivy had responded in the negative until the last.

"Holy shit. I think that's a sugar chest."

Reenie stilled, her hands on her hips, "And that's a 'holy shit' because?'

"There aren't many of them left. Most were destroyed during the Civil War. I hear they're worth tens of thousands a lot of the time. But I'm not positive that's one." She didn't touch it, didn't pick it up from where Reenie had placed it in the middle of their findings.

Kayla stayed silent and out of the way, but as she moved her hand to the doorframe she saw the black smears of used motor oil everywhere. They ran across the back of her hand and up her arm; she likely had them on her face, too. And, since she wasn't sure she liked what she was seeing, she turned away to go get a shower without ever having been seen.

Ten minutes later, she was clean and sitting in the kitchen at the Overseer's House when Evan came in. He too had wet hair plastered to his head, but his eyes were quick and they darted only once to the sandwich and chips she'd made herself before he quickly set to making an identical set for himself. He knew exactly what was in the sandwich. Though Kayla would eat many different dishes, when left to her own devices she made one kind of sandwich, the same way every time, same chips, same drink. She also had one soup, served with Cheezits. One dish—chicken pasta with pesto, cheese, and sundried tomatoes—and her repertoire was done.

Three minutes later, he sat himself across from her at the small table with an identical meal in front of him. Evan frowned. "What's wrong? You made light. Like God."

She laughed but didn't want to say she'd felt odd and out of place watching Reenie and Ivy sort through the attic. That once in a while she saw people interacting with each other without any words or instructions and she got jealous. They read a language she didn't understand and had no hope of learning. It was akin to being deaf: she was never going to hear it. But she shook off her self-pity and smiled at Evan. "I did make light. And I took a shower, so I smell better. I'll probably need to go into town later tomorrow for that bigger generator."

"Why would you need a bigger generator?" Reenie stuck her head through the doorway, clearly having just caught the last part. "Are you planning on knocking the power out or something?"

"Almost." Kayla laughed, then frowned again. "Where's Ivy?"

Reenie gestured to her dust-covered self. She didn't seem to know that she had a wisp of spiderweb clinging to her hair, and Kayla wasn't going to tell her. "Ivy looks as bad as me, if not worse. She's showering in the big house."

Evan pointed at Kayla. "Tell her what you did."

Kayla finished her bite and smiled. "I made light."

"Like God?"

Inside something clicked. She wasn't sure when or how it happened. But—while she knew that she and Reenie were going to bump heads again, that it was inevitable—she knew now that Reenie sometimes got her. Not always. But enough. "Yeah, like God. I hooked the machine to the small generator and powered the light with it for a while."

"Wow." Reenie's eyes and mouth opened and she appeared genuinely amazed.

Kayla held her hand up, though. "That's a really small power draw. It's not as impressive as it may sound. I need to power something bigger. I was thinking the old kitchen is about right." At that point she consciously shut herself up. She'd passed her three sentence limit, and while she was ready to launch into a full explanation of why it was the right building to test on, she knew Reenie only gave a crap that Kayla didn't blow the power. Instead, she switched tacks. "If it passes all the tests, you get to do the big one, Reenie."

"Me?"

"You're the biggest power draw here. You use your hairdryer and curling iron, you do all the cooking, you turn on all the lights wherever you go."

"What?" It had clearly been taken as an insult and Kayla had to pull back a bit.

"What did I miss?" Ivy slid beside Reenie in the doorway. She took care not to brush her clean and still-damp self against Reenie's still-dirty one.

Reenie gaped at her. "You're already done?"

"I'm fast." Ivy smiled and seated herself next to Kayla, stealing a chip and taking a drink from her glass. "What did I miss?"

A wry smile and a shrug passed through Reenie's body. "Apparently, I'm the biggest power suck in the household." Then she shook her head and started to turn away. "I'm going to go practice for your big test, Kayla. Don't anyone bother me. I'm seeing how much power I can draw at one time."

"Thank you!" Kayla hollered as Reenie headed down the hall. But she couldn't see Reenie's face and had no way of knowing if Reenie understood that it had been kind of snarky. But she turned back to Ivy. "I made light."

KAYLA PICKED a bolt from the lot in Ivy's palm. How she stayed clean and pristine remained a mystery. Ivy handed parts, wiped down messes and buried oil drips so no one kneeled into them by accident.

"There." Kayla stood back, her set up identical to yesterday's. She'd only managed to get in one trial before Evan showed up the night before. But an early night led to an early morning, and when Kayla rolled out of bed with the sunrise she'd woken Ivy. But her roommate hadn't minded; in fact she'd seemed as excited as Kayla to trek down here and reset everything.

Kayla started to grab the wheel and bar but then had another thought. "You do it." It was scientific to have Ivy start it, she'd decided. "And I can talk you through. Someone besides me needs to start it."

"Why?"

"What if I'm magic?" Kayla shrugged. It didn't make any sense, but she felt she had to test it. "If it's as good as we think it is, if it really works, then anyone can start it."

Ivy laughed at that. "You might just be magic, Kay. But tell me what to do . . ."

Kayla talked her through several frustrating attempts to get the wheel and the bar headed in just the right directions and at just the right speed. On the fourth try, Ivy managed to get it to catch. "Ha ha!" She jumped up and down and clapped like a schoolgirl—a schoolgirl in tight jeans and dark eyeliner—and smiled at her accomplishment.

Kayla nodded. "Excellent. Now we have proved that it isn't magic. Plug in the light."

Just as she suspected, with her new, altered constants, the machine smoothly and quickly picked up speed from the pace it had assumed when Ivy started it. Kayla noticed that yesterday, too. It ran one speed on its own, but the light seemed to draw on it.

Ivy's voice cut through her thoughts. "Is it going to break? Did I do it wrong?"

"No." Kayla didn't look at her. The higher tone indicated Ivy was nervous. "The light is drawing power; the machine is speeding up to produce it."

"I thought power was a constant."

From the reaction on Ivy's face, Kayla had made a "*what-the-hell-are-you-thinking*" face. "No. Every time you plug something in you draw more power through the system. It's why they come read your meter every month, to see how much you drew. That's why you can blow a fuse. It's not a constant at all."

"Oh." At least she didn't seem insulted, because Kayla was realizing—after the fact, of course—that she could have come across as though she thought Ivy was stupid. She didn't know how to say she thought nothing of the sort.

"So, if I unplug the light, the machine will slow down?"

"It should. Try it." Yeah, Ivy was nowhere near stupid.

They plugged in the light and unplugged it several times and had Kayla wishing for a good hairdryer. Those things sucked power like nobody's business. At one point she'd calculated the number of years of ozone life span that could be added to the earth if everyone quit using their hairdryers.

"Kayla." The harsh whisper was accompanied by Ivy's hand on her arm, and Kayla went suddenly still.

Ivy silently turned off the light, then put her finger to her lips. Breathing softly but heavily, she turned to the doorway and peeked outside, only to snap her head back in. "Shit." She mouthed it, but Kayla understood just the same.

With wide eyes and a panicked expression, she mouthed, "Stop it!" The finger pointing at the machine made it all clear. Quietly and efficiently, she began unplugging and dismantling peripherals. She made panicked movements, changes in decisions as she tried to place things far apart, like they did each time they dismantled.

Kayla knew from Ivy's face that there wasn't time to do it right. She could fix it later. So she reached out and grabbed the bar.

She was smart enough to choose a grip that went with the rotation of the magnetized bar rather than against it, but there was no choice that kept it from burning through her skin as she brought it to a rapid halt with no towel for protection or stepwise reduction in speed. Her palm screamed in pain as she yanked the bar from its spot even as it made its last rotation.

Even as she wrapped the still-hot bar into the hem of her shirt, she looked for something else to take. The big wheel was too time consuming to take out, but she managed to yank a cog and pull a support from under it. Ivy kicked dirt at the overturned apparatus and grabbed the biggest and heaviest piece from Kayla. Then she pointed at the window.

Too quickly to pay attention to technique, the two of them

pushed through the opening, stopping for one moment to plaster themselves to the side of the building. Then Ivy turned to her, chest still heaving and pointed around to the other side of the building. She mouthed the words, "They're over there."

And Kayla had one thought, *they?*

13

T he Icehouse

"THEY?" Kayla mouthed the word to Ivy only to be answered by a very worried nod.

They stood, clasping their gears and cogs, Kayla ignoring the rough burn on her palm, their backs pressed against the hard casing of the blacksmith's building. *They* were coming.

Ivy pointed in one direction. They were coming from the woods, from the edge of the property. No one up to any good came from the edge of the property by Kayla's reasoning.

Ivy clutched her gear closer and pointed toward the old icehouse. Kayla understood. Ducking low and running, she tried to keep the blacksmith's between her and 'them,' tried to stay low, disappear into the tall grass. She wasn't stealthy, and she feared she'd give them away.

Tucking in right behind Ivy, she tracked her friend's graceful lead until they came up against the doors to the icehouse. With her free hand shaking and nearly thwarting her, Ivy pushed the latch out of the way and ducked sideways through the door. Kayla followed quickly as behind her she heard voices.

The voices came from back at the blacksmith's, carrying around the side of the old building and across the tops of the grass between them, so she couldn't distinguish the words from this distance. Hardly able to hear over the harsh chop of her own breath, Kayla stepped to the side and reached out to pull the door shut, and found she couldn't latch it.

Plastered once again to a building, she and Ivy stood for just one moment, backs against the wall—this time inside the icehouse, inside the darkness they'd created by closing the door behind them. The thin sliver of light disappeared into the gaping space in front of them.

Kayla turned her face to the side and whispered, "I can't latch it. We have to go down."

Ivy blinked, and tipped her head down to look into the sharp and sudden drop-off. "No."

"Yes." If they didn't go down and *they* opened the door, Kayla and Ivy could step back and fall.

They were standing on the stone rim that hovered near the door. The icehouse appeared squat from the outside, as it was mostly cut into the ground rather than built above it. Thick rocks lined the walls over a story's depth into the earth and the cool air inside—air that had maintained ice from the frozen winter pond through the summer months in the old days— wafted up to them, chilling Kayla to the bone. Or maybe that was just the fear.

"Down." She said again. Into the dark, toward a bottom that was simply a pool of shadow and cold.

But the steep staircase descending the side went down three steps and disappeared into a pile of the rocks it was built from, long ago having succumbed to the pressures of earth on the walls. The icehouse had lasted over a hundred years but not a hundred and fifty. The well was no longer round, the twenty-foot diameter no longer consistent.

When they first arrived at the plantation, Kayla and Evan climbed down here and shored up the bulging walls with a few well placed beams per Reenie's directions. It had been the first piece of reconstruction on the farm. Evan planned to take out most of the north wall and replace it with Plexiglas so that visitors could look down in and see what it had once been. It would likely never be safe for tours or even use. The pond no longer froze six- to ten-foot-thick sheets of ice to cut and store here; global warming was a fact, but one Kayla couldn't feel now as she stood on the ledge and motioned Ivy to go down.

Ivy shook her head, forcing Kayla to lead the way.

One of the thick beams that braced the walls came to rest about a foot below where they stood. Kayla tested it warily, putting weight on it with one foot, before turning and carefully backing down. The sharp, near forty-five degree angle required that one hand grip the wood and the other wrap around her middle, trapping the gears she carried. If they clunked to the hay-covered floor, the noise would carry. Maybe a *clink* off each other, maybe just a dull thud, but they'd draw attention she and Ivy couldn't afford.

Facing the wall, Kayla saw Ivy shake her head and pull out the gun from the back of her jeans.

This time it was Kayla who made as fierce a "no" gesture as she could with all her limbs preoccupied with not falling the remaining twenty feet to the hard ground herself. Never be the first to pull a gun. It made people nervous.

"Did you see a gun on them?" She hissed.

Ivy shook her head no.

"Then put it away and climb down!" It didn't matter that her friend was scared. She was scared, too. But they had to get away. They had to stay out of sight and keep the machine out of the wrong hands. Until they could put it in everyone's hands—until they knew if they even should—Kayla would fight to keep her secrets close.

Ivy turned reluctantly to the wall and stepped down onto the beam, her foot searching around in open space until finally landing on solid wood. At the wall, her pressure was well placed, but as she slowly scooted further down, the beam started to shift, bowing just a little under their combined weights.

About seven feet above the ground, Kayla tilted precariously and almost fell. Though it didn't sound like much, it was a huge drop she wasn't ready to take. Looking up, she saw Ivy clinging to the four inches of wood like a frightened monkey. There was nothing she could do except whisper, "Come on. You can make it. We have to be fast."

She thought she heard *them* give up on the blacksmith's shop. She thought she heard *them* coming across the grass. She couldn't be certain from down here. But if she was right, they could be dead.

At four feet above the ground, she jumped off. Not the quietest of landings, but it needed to be done. She was now at the bottom of the icehouse, almost directly across from the door, and anyone looking in would see her. But first they'd see Ivy, shimmying down the beam right in their frame of sight.

Kayla ran and set the gears she held onto the hay-covered ground just below the doorway. Unless someone stood at the edge and leaned over to look directly down, they wouldn't see this spot. It was cloaked by shadows and angles, a good spot for Ivy and herself, too.

Having stashed the parts, she ran back and reached up, but Ivy was still too high to touch. Climbing onto the beam would only bow it more and further disturb the already frightened Ivy. Instead, Kayla reached her hands up. Standing underneath Ivy, she spoke softly. "Drop the gear to me."

It was the heaviest one, and her palm screamed in pain as it smacked, but Kayla was running the twenty feet to the other wall even before she fully had the grasp of it. When she turned, she nearly smacked into Ivy, who must have suddenly shimmied faster.

Ivy grabbed her hand—her good hand—and yanked her.

They plastered their backs against the wall as the door opened twenty feet above their heads letting in a swath of early morning sunlight. Immediately, the space filled with two distinct human-formed shadows.

Voices came from directly above. Kayla held her breath and listened, but didn't look up, just clutched tighter at Ivy's hand.

"I thought I saw some movement here."

"It's cold. What is this place?"

"The icehouse." That was it. No explanation, no comment on the beams. This person knew something about plantations. But it wasn't the man who had visited before. Not the man who had come in his nice suit and shiny shoes and planted the bug. Wrong voice. Still there was something reminiscent that made Kayla think the two were together. The second man, the one who'd asked about the cold, didn't know about plantations. His response was the norm.

For a moment there were no sounds and Kayla guessed they were looking around. Through her eyelids she could see that the light was changing, which told her something was happening in the doorway. They were probably checking out the cross beams, probably considered the slim staircase and recognized it for the hazard it was.

For a split second a thought rocketed through her brain.

Evan.

Reenie.

What if they came out now? What if they ran into these two? What if these two were armed?

Kayla opened her eyes. Letting go of Ivy's hand, as silently as she could, she moved to pull the gun from her waist band.

She couldn't chamber a round; the sound would ricochet

around in here worse than a bullet and draw the wrong eyes directly to them. It would do the exact opposite of keeping them safe. So Kayla stood still and watched while Ivy slowly followed suit.

After what seemed forever, the light finally changed and as she heard the words, "Maybe they just went around this building." The doors were pushed shut. Her vision sunk into the deep dark again.

Ivy held her hand tight, keeping her pinned with her back to the rocks that were ice cold even through these hottest days of July.

Kayla leaned in until her lips brushed Ivy's ear, and she whispered. "Reenie. Evan."

Then, as they stood still, they heard the door get one final push into place. And Kayla's heart sank when she heard the latch click home.

"Shit." It was whispered, Ivy's voice reaching only to Kayla. "We're stuck, aren't we?"

"I think so." She wasn't sure it was worth risking the climb in near total darkness. If they fell, they would have no hope. They could be here for days. Bones broken, knocked out. And even if they reached the top, they likely couldn't open the door. The chance of stepping backward off the slim outcropping was too high. No, they were better off here.

Kayla switched her grasp on the gear. "My hand is burned."

"What?"

"From stopping the machine." She pressed it, palm flat to the cold rocks. They were soothing against the damaged flesh, but not to the rest of her. She figured the two of them had maybe an hour before they started to get too cold, medically concerning cold. In Kayla's mind it would suck to die of irony—getting hypothermia in the middle of July. On a Georgia plantation at that.

No, she wasn't going to die here, and she wasn't going to let Reenie or Evan get hurt either. She turned to Ivy. "Phone?"

Next to her, she heard and felt her friend shuffle around, presumably checking pockets. "Shit. No. I must have dropped it."

If it fell back at the blacksmith's then it was certain *they* knew someone had been there. It was hard to make a place look abandoned or at least unused when there was a cell phone lying around. Kayla pulled her hand from the wall. Reluctant to set down the gear, she sucked it up and pulled out her phone.

Looking up and listening for a moment, she didn't hear anything. Then she ruined the adjustment their eyes had achieved by turning the phone on. Had someone been standing up there looking down, they couldn't have missed the light, but if they were outside, they'd never see it.

She called Evan.

"Kayla?"

Her heart beat easier just for hearing his voice.

EVAN HEADED out across the expanse of field, his gun tucked into the back of his pants and his heart tucked into his throat. He managed to convince Reenie to stay back at the house, armed with her phone, but wishing for a sniper rifle. He considered her aim for a moment, deciding that he was grateful they didn't have one. Instead, she had opted for the attic of the big house, hoping to find a way onto the front of the roof—for safety, lookout purposes, and cell phone contact.

He saw the two men down by the big barn and had the fleeting thought that maybe one of them was wearing boots with the right-sized tread. He kept one hand fisted at his waist near the butt of the gun, but the other he raised high and yelled out to them as though he just spotted some friendly neighbors on his property.

Friendly, my ass, he thought.

Then he wondered if maybe they weren't all on overkill.

He hadn't had a chance to ask Ivy and Kayla if they had been threatened in any way. At least, this morning, by these two men. Maybe these were just neighbors coming over to check out the activity on a prominent house in the area that had previously sat neglected. There had also been talk around the small town, he knew. Reenie had been asked at the grocery store what the plans for the plantation were, and she hadn't been shy about telling everyone that they were opening a museum and all would be invited.

So it was possible that Kayla and Ivy had hit the deck for no real reason. But then again, these two were trespassing even if they were trying to be friendly. And Evan didn't think Kay and Ivy were much for hysterical reactions. So he yelled out "H-e-l-l-oooo!" and thought, "Get the fuck off my land."

"Hey." The straighter one waved back.

The second guy—the one who didn't wave—struck Evan as uncertain, even from this distance. He appeared to be the same height as his friend, but he stepped to the back, clearly letting the first do the talking. His shoulders stooped just a little, and his posture said he was unhappy with the whole situation. He even looked a little frightened, lagging just a beat or two behind the first.

As they all headed toward the center of the field to meet up, their faces became clearer, and Evan's initial judgments appeared to bear out. The second's eyes shifted one way then another; he only nodded and didn't reach out a hand or make any overtly friendly gestures.

The first was the polar opposite. He smiled grandly, looked at Evan like he was glad to see an old friend. He gestured wide and asked about the plantation with enthusiastic questions.

He seemed to have nothing but lies.

Still, Evan questioned his own perception. He'd come out

here because of a frantic call from Kayla. He was primed to believe the worst. Then again, the bug in the back area also primed him to assume the worst. It had been planted by another friendly neighbor who had been all smiles and innocuous questions.

Evan, still keeping his hand at his waist, close to the gun, fed them the usual lines about being busy. About the plantation opening in two months and to come back then. He told them he worried about liability, what with so many untended buildings and who-knew-what out there.

They took the news the way they had done everything in the interaction—the second one hanging back, looking into the distance, often at the icehouse. The first one smiled and said of course he understood.

But he lied. Because instead of getting off the property, he asked more questions. What had they found on the plantation? Clothing? Chests?

Evan made the mistake of saying, "Of course." Instead of telling him to go the hell away.

The first one still hadn't provided a name. Did he think Evan wouldn't notice? Or was this just one big farce? The three of them standing there having a pretend conversation while they all knew Ivy and Kayla were at the bottom of the icehouse. Probably freezing their asses off. Did these two catch a glimpse of Reenie? Evan didn't look up toward the front of the property, didn't want to give her away. But she had to be up on the roof of the big house by now, watching.

The first kept talking. "Did you find anything else? I hear there are lots of hidey holes in these places. You can dig up coins and stuff from the yard, from where they buried it during the Civil War. Lots of famous people came through this part of Georgia, you know. Maybe you'll find some interesting letters or papers. Sherman marched right by here. Longstreet came this way. Phineas Miller's ranch is right over the hill. I hear he and

Whitney invented the cotton gin there. Cobb was here, too, in Ebenezer."

But Evan had stopped listening. He'd heard enough. So when the man paused and waited for his fish to bite, Evan didn't.

He shook his head as though he was saddened by it, rather than near murderous. "We haven't found much but an old teapot and some broken dishes. I'm really sorry, but I have to get to work. We have just so much to do to open on time. But we'd love for you to come back then." He lied through his teeth.

"Oh, I understand." The man smiled and clapped him on the back, not seeming to notice, or maybe not to care, that Evan stiffened as he did.

He hadn't been able to fight it, to pretend to be okay with any of this.

The man kept talking. "I'm a collector myself. It's why I live here in the Old South. Here's my card—" he handed over another slick smile along with the small rectangle—"give me a call if you find anything interesting or unusual. I'll make it worth your while."

Evan took the card—it was that or pull the gun. So he nodded and tried to casually use his right hand to untuck his shirt and cover the gun before he turned and walked away.

He was more than several steps away before he turned and looked at them. They hadn't moved. The first offered a nod and, as one, they turned and began walking toward the edge of the property.

For a moment, Evan frowned. They were headed to the far corner. They would have to climb the low rock wall that skirted the whole front of the land, or they'd have to head out through the woods. Neither option seemed normal. But these two didn't change direction. They didn't head to the front or down the drive.

Then Evan gathered his thoughts and headed back to the house. Still he didn't look up to see if Reenie was perched on the roof. If she was good, she'd be out of sight anyway. He didn't glance at the icehouse but walked right by. There was no way he was going over and letting Kayla and Ivy out while still within eyeshot and earshot of these two guys.

He had to admit, he didn't know that the two weren't going to go park themselves in the woods, likely just out of sight, and watch everything. Who was to say they hadn't been doing it all along?

Turning again, he surveyed the land. The two men were now nowhere to be seen. They'd left or taken cover—he didn't know which. What he did know was that even though they were gone, the fear wasn't.

KAYLA MOVED her hand three times. Each time her palm warmed the rock she'd pressed it against, she pulled it back and checked to see if the burn returned. It did.

She and Ivy didn't speak much as they strained to listen to the sounds outside. She wanted to hear Evan throw the bastards off their land. She didn't want to hear gunshots.

But there was nothing. No one came close enough to over-power the resonant echo of their own breathing as it bounced off the cold, dry walls. There were no outside noises save for a low hum with a long cadence. It had taken Kayla a while to figure out that it was the sound of the water from the creek, transferred through the ground and finally the rock, getting caught in what was essentially a sound chamber now that the icehouse had no ice to absorb it.

Her phone buzzed in her hand and scrambled to stop the sound. The harsh whisper of her answer reverberated back to her tenfold. "Evan?"

"Hey, Kay. They're gone. There were two of them, and they offered to buy unusual things that we found while renovating." He sounded resigned.

"Those bastards!" Kayla heard Reenie in the background and nearly smiled at the woman's cussing.

Evan started speaking again. "I didn't know how to escort them off the property without being really suspicious. And I went with the 'if we don't act like there's anything to protect, there mustn't be anything to protect' theory. So I can tell you that I can't see them anymore, but I can't be sure they're actually gone."

Kayla nodded, then squeezed her eyes shut. "Yeah, Ev. I got you. You want us to stay down here a while to be sure they're really gone?"

"Do you mind?"

"I don't, but it's cold in here. We're good for another forty minutes maybe."

Ivy was leaning into her, trying to share the call. Even though Kayla knew what was coming, she wasn't able to prevent it.

"Evan," Ivy spoke in the direction of the phone, "Kayla burned her hand stopping the machine. I know we need to wait. But the sooner the better."

Kayla pushed at her, trying to keep her out of the conversation. "I'm good. I did burn it, but the rocks are cold in here, and I don't think there's anything anyone can or needs to do for me at this point. I don't think it's going to do anything more than sting a bit. I grabbed the bar when it was spinning."

The hiss of Evan's breath told her what he thought about that. "Oh, shit."

"Ev. I'm okay. I'm not in need of a hospital or even a doctor. We can handle it in a while." But it was cold and this time when Ivy plastered herself to Kayla to get to the phone, Kayla didn't protest.

"She's not going to die Evan, but we need to look at it when we get out."

"Okay." He sighed, "I'll be there relatively soon. And hope to hell these guys are gone."

They said good-bye and hung up. Her phone battery looked

good. There were twenty-three things she did as part of getting ready for bed; charging her phone was always one of them.

Then the screen went black and their unadjusted eyes plunged them into total darkness again.

Ivy snuggled up against her, probably trying to stay warm now that they knew help would be a while. But Kayla didn't worry. She told Ivy not to, too.

"But I do worry about you, Kayla. Haven't you figured that out yet?"

Ivy shifted and shifted again, and in the inky black that seemed to press in on her, Kayla couldn't figure out what Ivy was doing. Not until she felt Ivy's breath on her cheek, soft and warm. Slim hands found her arms and slid up slowly until they framed her face.

As Kayla caught on, Ivy's mouth closed over hers, soft and gentle and bone melting.

14

B ack Field

"WHAT?" Evan yelled to Reenie.

"I need to look at it to see." Under the protective headphones, gunfire came through as clear, distinct pops, but voices sounded like they'd traveled between two tin cans and a string.

Ivy had surprised him, hitting her target dead center, then done it again, putting her bullets so close that they ripped into previous holes. Then she had smiled, tucked her gun away, and gone off to do whatever she was doing with her day.

Evan wasn't sure what that might be or if it was even anything good. But he was certain he didn't like the brightness that came into Kayla's eyes when she said, "Go have fun," to Ivy.

He hadn't said anything to Kayla about what he and Reenie suspected—that they were curious if Ivy was maybe doing some fencing on the side. Then again it could be worse, she could be bringing these people to their door. And now it looked like it was already too late to do anything about any of it.

How was he supposed to tell his sister that one of the few true friends she'd had in her life was neither true nor a friend? In not knowing, he had procrastinated. And in procrastinating, he had clearly raised the cost for his sister.

The three remaining shooters signaled, took off their protective gear, and quietly put the safeties on their guns before tucking them away. Then they headed to the hay bales he'd constructed into a stack and pulled their targets. Evan had spent the morning with his heart pounding in abject terror that a stray bullet would hit something of importance. It was their land, but shooting a trespasser wasn't in his cards. He hoped. He didn't want to accidentally hit a neighbor's dog or even take out a random Bambi. He wasn't that kind of guy.

But he was forced to acknowledge that could change.

Kayla pulled her target from where he'd stabbed shims into the bales to hold the corners. She had a cluster of holes around the heart area. She might have killed her target with that. The several head shots she'd landed looked better. He did a quick count and saw that over half her bullets had made no holes. Which meant she'd either put them directly through these holes —which was incredibly unlikely, even for Kayla—or she'd just missed.

Reenie's target looked the same. But the cluster of holes was smaller. Her accuracy was better. And she had fewer misses. She had a hole where an arm would be. One in the lower torso—a gut shot. But mostly, Reenie had nailed the kill.

Kayla looked over at Reenie's target as she was pulling it down. "You did better than me."

It was just a statement. Reenie shrugged, but Kayla smiled. "This means, when the shit goes down, I'm getting behind you."

At Reenie's laugh, Evan felt some of the tension in his shoulders seep out and disperse with the sound. At least the peace between them appeared to hold, even as it went to hell everywhere else.

The three of them decided to call it a day, and Evan stayed behind to dismantle the hay-bale stack into something that looked more like it belonged on a plantation. The last thing he wanted to do was advertise that they were improving their gun skills. Or that they had caught on that they needed to improve them. He completed the sweaty work and contemplated his own paranoia while he was at it.

When he made it back up to the buildings, he was in need of a shower he wouldn't yet take.

He found Kayla out in the sun behind the old kitchen, hooking up the generator and the machine. She'd rescued the gears from the bottom of the icehouse and used a wheelbarrow to cart the whole machine up the hill herself. She'd done it in pieces into the evening the night before, commenting on the old wheel barrow and how it was a quality tool and had lasted well over a hundred years. But then again, there was something to be said for rubber wheels and ball bearings. Things that could be had cheap in today's market.

He wanted to stop and help, but Reenie was peeking around the back corner; a rumbling somewhere in the distance signaled that their shipment of wood had arrived.

The rumbling of what had to be the delivery truck came closer and he could almost hear the ruts in the drive. He looked at Reenie and knew she had her twenty-two tucked on her person, somewhere. Just the thought scared the crap out of him. But he nodded as though it were perfectly normal to be getting a delivery of wood while everyone was armed and strange people had been sneaking onto the property.

He directed the truck, then was invited to climb into the cab to share the bumpy ride down to the barn where he'd set up his shop. What Evan actually shared were faked smiles and a cover of friendliness while all along he assessed the driver, wondered what he was up to, if the man was really just delivering wood.

For a moment, he imagined the truck as a Trojan horse, considering the possibility that there were armed soldiers in the back who would burst forth and pour across his land as soon as the truck was deep enough onto the property. They would take the machine.

And in that moment, Evan decided they could have it. It wasn't worth being a farmer with a gun and a set of suspicious people hanging around. If his hand was forced, Evan knew he'd hand the damn machine over before he put his family in trouble, before he had Kayla shimmying down support beams into dark, cold wells again, and with a burned hand.

Besides, Kayla could just build another one.

And right at that moment, he realized that he would have to defend that machine to the death.

Because if anyone figured out that she could just build another one, then Kayla would become expendable too.

His thoughts were interrupted by the truck jerking to a halt. While Evan had been woolgathering, the driver had expertly turned the small rig around and backed up toward the barn door. And that, Evan realized, was dangerous. He couldn't afford to drop his guard anymore. Not for a moment.

The driver climbed down and with a few short sentences established where Evan wanted the wood. With motions as efficient as his words, he unloaded it down a short ramp. Luckily, the only thing stashed in the back was the order itself and a super-dolly that made Evan's presence nearly useless. There were no soldiers waiting with Kevlar vests and spare ammo.

Evan watched carefully as the truck drove off and set to arranging the wood. He had enough now for the backs and casings of many of the display pieces Reenie had designed. With an architect's eye, she had created boxes for each purpose, something unique to house each item on display. Had Evan not loved her and had he not also loved a challenge, he would have pitched her complicated designs back at her and demanded they buy prefab cases. Instead, he would use found and re-claimed wood from the plantation as designed. People would be able to touch part of the history. He would take out the steps on the back porch of the Overseer's—one of these days—and use some of that as well.

The boxes would suffer wear from the oils on the hands of people who would come to see the place. Reenie understood that. She also knew the plantation itself would wear with use, but she found that much preferable to being torn down, unused or unloved. She'd played here as a child and remembered her childish appreciation for the bridge, the chipped paint in some of the rooms. Only as an adult viewing it in disrepair, seeing it as a designer, did she develop an understanding of the dip worn into the bridge from untold numbers of feet, the smooth patina in the center of the steps, the chair rail, dented and nicked by chairs over more than a century. Better used than neglected, she said. So Evan would build her display cases.

He was halfway through the first construction when Kayla came by.

Looking up at her, her image slightly distorted through his goggles, he immediately pulled his earplugs and asked, "Have you eaten yet today?"

She tilted her head and gave him a sour look. She probably didn't appreciate his immediately directing the conversation to her care. "No, I was coming down to see if you wanted to join me for lunch? I'm headed up now."

He looked around at his work. Checked his watch. Then nodded.

Kayla just stood there, a blank expression on her face as he unplugged the table saw and hung his goggles on a pull switch, stacking his gloves on top. He ran his fingers through his hair, shaking out the sawdust that had surely gathered. He was rewarded by a pale tan cloud that sank through the air to blend into the barn floor in front of him.

But Evan waited. He couldn't tell if Kayla was angry or just off in Neverland. When they were about fifteen feet away from the barn, she looked back over her shoulder, then told him.

"I came down to see if you wanted lunch, but I wanted to look around, too." She sighed. "I didn't do it last night, I didn't want to look like I was looking, you know?"

He nodded, not sure that he did know, but having a bad feeling that he just might.

"There's now a bug inside the blacksmith's shop and one just outside your barn door, over on the right, toward the stables. When I came in to get you, I'm pretty sure I saw one inside, too."

"Shit." He sighed it out. "Shit. Shit. Shit."

"That's pretty much my thought, too." I called Ivy on her cell and told her and Reenie to sweep the inside of the big house, just in case. We can help when we get there. They are going to act like they are checking each room for something checklisty, in case someone is listening in."

Evan sighed again. "If they've got devices inside the houses, I think we'll need to remove them. I don't see how we can go on playing like we don't know. It's one thing when they're outside, but..."

He didn't finish and he didn't need to. Kayla understood him. Nearly thirty years of shared history meant they could probably have a whole conversation in front of a listening device and no one would be any the wiser. Where other people would do that with facial expressions and nuance, he and Kayla would be strictly in code.

She led him back through the tree line, places they didn't feel a bug would be likely and they came up behind the old kitchen building. Evan looked up. Built of brick and painted white, it had the old kitchen downstairs, with storage and a full root cellar the likes of which he'd never seen before in the crawl space underneath. But at one point, the building had been wired for electricity and the second floor converted to an apartment. As old as it was, it wasn't really useful as living space. It had an old wood stove in the corner for heat and cooking. The windows were double hung and leaky as hell. But now the building itself looked loved.

Every light in the place was on. Nothing flickered. And, as they approached Evan heard the sound of the generator overlaid with the slight hum of Kayla's machine.

He stopped cold. "How long has it been running?"

She checked her watch. "An hour and seventeen minutes. And not a flicker yet, not that I've seen." She smiled.

"Holy crap, Kay." He watched in awe. "How much of it is the machine and how much is the power line?"

"It's all machine. And it hasn't hurt the wires inside at all."

He wanted to ask, *And you know this how?* But he didn't. The question wasn't had she tested it, but what with. It turned out he didn't even have to ask.

"I got out my voltmeter and checked it with the power line still intact. Read the meter, cranked the numbers. Then I completely disconnected the power here—" She pointed up where the wire attached at the roofline and ran down through a protected shell on the outside of the building, right up to the power box. It was obviously an add-on. Nothing on this plantation had been built with electricity in mind, anyone's mind.

He interrupted. "Isn't that a big deal, and dangerous?"

"Nah. It's an old building. Wiring was additional. And compared to today's systems, it's poor quality without any safety backups. It was basically plugged in at the breaker box." She shrugged as though altering the power source to a building was normal. Then again, she was a mechanical engineer. He didn't know all the details of all the jobs she'd held. Only that she'd done a stellar job on each until she'd perfected something they hadn't wanted perfected or refused to cut corners that the owner had insisted be cut. "Then I hooked the machine to the generator and hooked the whole thing to the building. So far, so good. I rechecked all the numbers before I came to get you, and I'll check all the outlets again after we eat."

He looked up. "*All* of them?"

"Evan, it's *old*! It was wired back when there were only about five different things that could even use electricity." She laughed. "It doesn't even have an electric source for the oven or heat. So there are about six outlets in the whole building—which was apparently very forward thinking at the time."

Evan nodded and they headed inside the Overseer's for lunch, and for the more somber tasks of telling Reenie and Ivy about the new bugs.

KAYLA HAD SLEPT FITFULLY.

It had been hard to fall asleep and harder to stay asleep. Her dreams had been plagued by men chasing her and Ivy into the icehouse. In her dreams the two of them fell and didn't hit bottom. They were shot at, yelled at. Sometimes, the machine was destroyed, stolen or modified to become a nuclear weapon. Even asleep Kayla hadn't grasped how they had done that. Even in her dreams she clung tight to the laws of physics.

She'd woken Ivy twice with her jerks and yelps as she yanked herself from nightmares. She'd eventually given up and rolled out of bed quietly, thinking she might as well start the day early as fall back into another nightmare. She kept the gun on the counter in the bathroom while she showered. It was always kept closer now, since the icehouse incident. Since there were more bugs. There was no longer talk of not needing it somewhere like the bathroom. There were no longer heavy sighs or arguments of overkill.

In the predawn she'd scanned the area and had gone out to

check on the machine. She'd wanted to purchase a larger generator last evening, but Evan had argued her down and eventually she'd given in and given him her specs and watched him leave to buy her toy.

While he was gone, she dismantled the machine, storing parts in separate places. Most were in the carriage house, but several were now in her backpack, having been tucked there last evening and spent the night under her bed. At least she would have known had someone come for them.

Now as the sun rose, Kayla worked behind the big house, reassembling pieces of the machine. With no functioning kitchen and only she and Ivy giving the main building other than occasional use, she reasoned that it was the best test for the big generator. Not only was it the next level up in power, but they could test its capacity easily just by turning lights off and on. And if the whole thing went to hell, then she and Ivy could move into her old room at the Overseer's or over the kitchen. Testing the big house would be much easier than explaining to Evan and Reenie that she'd blown their power and they would have to get their house rewired.

After this, it would be time to start on a second machine. So she'd call Charles and get him the specs for the whole thing. Since he'd already machined three critical parts, she wouldn't have to send those, a fact that soothed her worry about where her information was getting tapped that she didn't know about.

A rumble came from the distance, a deep hum that got slowly louder. The sound concerned Kayla until she realized it came from a combination of airplane and paranoia. The Savannah International Airport was closer to here than it was to Savannah, even though planes rarely came over the Ebenezer area. But the paranoia gave her a thought, and thirty minutes later she was working in the shade of the tarp lean-to she had rigged. It was nice that it kept the sun off of her skin, but more important, it would keep planes and helicopters and satellites from seeing what she'd built and where it was.

Ivy came out then, wearing cut-off jeans in homage to the heat. Her legs were about a mile long, ending in work boots that had only been laced halfway. It shouldn't have looked good, but it did. Today's bra was bright pink under a skintight white tee. "What can I do to help?" She stretched and yawned, making Kayla yawn, too.

"Bring coffee?" She hadn't wanted it until she saw that Ivy was in need, but suddenly she craved it, and knew she wouldn't last long without.

She'd changed out here under the Georgia sun. She'd become more daring, less in need of her routine. She still had it, but it had changed, too. She now lived with options. Everyone on the plantation had been generous, allowing her to build the machine rather than helping Evan with the construction of the display cases or painting edges as Reenie had hoped she would—Kayla's were machine precise. Reenie had opted to let Kayla continue her work and suffer through with only Reenie and Ivy's own "human" painting skills.

But Kayla was going to pay them back with this machine. After the past few days she was convinced that they could operate completely off the grid. She could save them the entire power bill for the plantation . . . and that was a big bill. They just needed several of these little babies, and she would have contributed her part. She wasn't sure what she'd do when Hazelton House opened its doors for business. The construction and wiring part of the job would be completed. And while she could easily see Reenie and Ivy dressed in period pieces and giving tours, she couldn't see herself doing the same.

Pushing that thought out of the way to be dealt with later, she reached up to take the coffee Ivy held out as she ducked under the edge of the tarp. With a deep inhale, Kayla went through her coffee ritual. Breathe in, blow on it, repeat. Sip. "Mmmmm."

"I know. Reenie's been getting into some local stuff at the grocer's. It's really good." Ivy picked up a metal piece and fitted it into place in the machine before setting down her mug and reaching for a bolt.

More and more, Kayla was becoming convinced that the machine was important. She'd have to fight for it. Have to prove what it could do. But Ivy was on her side. She smiled at her roommate and sipped her coffee while she watched as Ivy handed her the next several pieces.

Over the next hour they worked mostly in silence. When Reenie checked in later, they said they were great, that things were going well. Kayla told her the new coffee was wonderful.

When Evan came by, they gave him a projected hookup time. In another hour and a half they expected to have checked the power in the big house, unhooked the existing line, and hooked up the machine and generator in its place. In ninety minutes they expected to be running on Whitney power. Free power.

Evan wanted to be there when the switch was flipped. Ivy promised to call, then Evan went down to the barn to check out the bugs, look for any new tracks, and maybe even build something so they could open the museum on time. And Ivy handed her the next gear.

Heavy and laden with deep cogs, it was tipped just so. Ivy angled the piece into Kayla's hands ready to slide into its spot. The cogs fitted neatly against their counterparts on the smaller wheel, and Ivy handed over a bolt and nut to hold it into place. Before she'd tightened the nut, Ivy had oiled the spot, just enough to make the gear run smoothly.

Kayla looked up then, and as Ivy smiled, Kayla realized she'd found her dance.

Improv and necessity blended together with a friend. She smiled back.

Before she had paid much attention, they were finished. The sun was at an angle, peeking in under the wide seam of the tarp, sneaking up on her feet, and pushing her to be ready to test what she had built. Ivy was on the phone with Evan so Kayla decided to hop into the Overseer's.

"You're ready?" Reenie was holding up a dress that was about a foot shorter than anything she could have worn. Without any qualms, she set the dress aside and carefully closed the book she'd been making notes in, then followed Kayla outside nearly as excited as Kayla was herself.

Evan appeared over the hillside as Kayla gathered the two cords in her hands. Anxious to plug them together, she gestured to him to hurry. Though he was clearly tired, he did, and as he approached Kayla pushed her two pieces together and nearly squealed with glee when the lights on the second floor came on.

"That's it?" Evan asked.

With a huff, Kayla turned to him. "Yes. I only turned on a few lights inside. I didn't want to overdo the power. But let's give it a shot. Go. Turn on lights."

She stayed put while the other three traipsed through the back door and fanned out. Through the window above her she heard Evan heading up the stairs about the same time as lights flicked on in both sides of the first floor. As quickly as Evan made it up the stairs to the third floor, he must have come right back down.

The second floor landing window, located just over her head, popped up with a squeak and a crack and Evan stuck his head out. "Someone's coming. Turn it off."

She shook her head no. "Best thing is to leave it and act normal. I'll stay back here."

Then Evan turned as someone must have called him. "One minute" he told her, then disappeared, leaving the window open.

Kayla heard the knock at the front door as loud as any of them. The house was only about a third as deep as it was wide. A single hidden door connected the front lobby to the back room the stairs climbed over. But she didn't head through the house toward the front door. She heard Ivy's voice piping up the closest, "I'll get it."

Stepping back out of the way, Kayla strained to hear as she stood guard over her machine. She tried to put enough distance between her and it to hear what was happening over the constant, additive chug of the Whitney Machine and the generator. She only made out a few words here and there.

It was a man at the door. He offered something to Ivy.

Frowning, Kayla scanned her area, then ducked into the back room, sliding sideways until she could get a glimpse through the space where the door no longer quite met the wall. Another man in an expensive suit. More shiny shoes. This man was heavier and older than the last. He was less happy, less inquisitive, more demanding.

He told Ivy to get the lady of the house—a term Kayla had not heard in quite a while. She wondered briefly if he was trying to sell them a vacuum cleaner. Then figured that would make life much too easy and that was therefore most likely the last thing he was interested in.

On cat's feet, she went back and forth. Outside to scan the area around the machine, to make sure no one had come with him. Inside, to try to glean bits of conversation.

Reenie appeared quickly, "I'm the lady of the house. What can I help you with?"

"Are you the owner?"

"Yes."

Where Kayla would have demanded to know why this was important, Reenie had pushed a smile into her voice and probably onto her face and answered him point blank.

"Then you are the owner of the properties and all the items herein."

This was not going well. She should be darting back outside to look at the machine, but Kayla couldn't move.

Reenie hadn't spoken. Maybe a nod had sufficed, Kayla couldn't tell.

But she heard his voice loud and clear from where she had plastered herself to the space where the wall met the old hidden door at the back of the foyer.

"I buy antiques. Diaries, clothing, machinery, diagrams, dishes and even sometimes broken pieces of things."

"We aren't selling anything." The smile remained in Reenie's voice, so bright that even Kayla could hear it there. "I'm sure you've heard we are opening the plantation in several months as a museum."

"You'll never survive as a museum. Your best bet is to sell to me."

"I don't think so. Thank you." Kayla imagined Reenie shutting the door in his face. But that wasn't what happened.

"I heard you were robbed a while ago and that the police located the thief but not the document."

Silence waited a beat and Kayla was torn between staying to listen and running outside and pulling her gun and waving it around to make sure her precious machine was okay. The lights were still on, so it was still running. But that didn't mean someone wasn't there, hadn't snuck up to look it over, steal her improvements . . .

She couldn't move. Her indecision held her where she was.

Reenie's voice was quiet and Kayla strained to hear.

"Are you threatening me?"

"No ma'am. I'm pointing out that your finances aren't sound and your security is lax and you'd be best off selling me your plow and your cotton gins and all the other treasures that are here. I'm sure you have other documents, diaries. I'll pay for them. Others won't." His voice rumbled deep with the resonance of menace.

Reenie's didn't. Louder now and full of steel, she offered a sugar-sweet threat of her own. "You, sir, are on my property uninvited. That's trespassing. You've offered thinly veiled threats. Also illegal. The sheriff is aware of our recent break-in and is nearby. Sir, I think you would look just dashing in handcuffs. You have five minutes to not find out."

"I'll get the things from this plantation. Either now or when you go bankrupt."

15

T he Overseer's House

EVAN ATE his breakfast while talking shop with the girls. Sometimes he felt odd being the only man. Somewhere deep inside he knew what he needed was a beer and a football game. But football wasn't on yet, and the beer wasn't the same with Reenie.

He wasn't ready to leave the others alone yet, and he couldn't invite anyone over. It wasn't that kind of a home, at least not yet. He hoped one day to have the Overseer's remodeled to resemble something from the previous century, but function like the next. He wanted a room with a leather couch and a big TV and a minifridge for beer and cheese dip. Sadly, that day was a long way off, Evan knew. And he wasn't relaxed enough to talk himself into believing it would come anytime soon.

A week and a half had gone by in relative silence. The women were relaxing their guard. Evan could see it in the slow draining of tension from shoulders, the longer gaits, the way they focused on each other when they talked. They had definitely dropped their vigilance. So he upped his.

He'd asked Kayla at one time about how she and Ivy were getting along. Did they watch out for each other, make sure there was protection nearby? Kayla said they did, that they didn't even shower unless the other person was nearby and on watch. But Evan figured that may very well have followed the other practices to the wayside now too.

Their last visitor had been the heavyset man in the suit. He had threatened. He spoke like he knew too much about the robbery, but he'd left when Reenie had threatened him back.

Immediately following his departure, Kayla had conducted another sweep for bugs and found none on her initial visual inspection and none when she came back through with her radio frequency tester. She'd shrugged and called the man a well-dressed thug. She'd pointed out his similarity in dress to their first visitor, but also the lack of matching MO and the fact that half the adult males in America wore suits. Kayla wasn't convinced the two visits were related.

So Evan enjoyed his eggs even as the girls all got up. His mouth was full but he asked around the food, "Where you off to?"

Kayla smiled. "Building number three!"

Kayla had machined some of it herself, joining him in his shop several days last week. And she and Ivy had made another trip to Cleveland, picking up pieces from Charles.

After having the pieces back for one day, Kayla had assembled the second Whitney Machine and was powering both the Overseer's and the main house. Evan had no clue what she was going to do with the third one, but with eggs in his mouth he didn't get a chance to ask.

Reenie leaned over and kissed him. "Thank you for pulling down the attic ladder."

Then she and Ivy went down the hall to see what had been

stashed in the space over their heads here. He didn't expect any great treasures. And neither did they.

The attic and findings in the big house were catalogued and finished. The wine cellar had given up two bottles of wine, one red, one white, both rancid. Evan was building their display case today. The myriad things in the attic had been sorted for the museum by quality, historical pertinence, and any proof of authenticity Reenie could find.

Reenie had tasked Ivy with writing out the first drafts of the display tags while she spent the morning ordering a machine that would make a museum-quality sign. She wasn't ready to order one, nor tell the world that they had one of only a few remaining antebellum sugar chests—a truly historic find. It was enough that they'd had to pay someone to build the outside displays for Ivy's idea of showing where they'd dug stuff up.

The attic in the Overseer's was just a last-ditch effort to delay Reenie's new tasks another day. She had to figure out how to make candles, lye soap, and hand lotions. Evan knew she was not looking forward to boiling a big vat of tallow in the late-August heat. But she had to do several batches—and do them well—before she could teach the skill, plus she needed enough candles to put around the house. She'd hoped the weather would cool off, but instead, it had kicked up again.

He, on the other hand, was enjoying the small green shoots the heat had peeking through his tilled earth. People would be able to pick and gin cotton here at Hazelton House. There would even be a spot with a few spinning stations. But first he had to insulate and air-condition the upper floor of the barn. Maybe that's where Kayla's third machine would go.

He was scrubbing his plate to put into the avocado colored dishwasher that did not actually seem to wash the dishes, but merely spit at them, when Reenie came back in. Grinning through the dust, she smiled. "Look what I found!"

"We. We found it." Ivy gave her a half-hearted frown.

"We." Reenie smiled back at Ivy, but Evan could tell it was forced. He didn't think Ivy could.

He and Reenie had been watching their historian like a hawk. But nothing had come of it. Reenie had even tried to play I Spy and check out Ivy's phone. But she hadn't found any incriminating evidence, only additional pictures of the items found in the house.

Where he had just vacated the table, Reenie sat herself down with a nearly audible plop. The leather-bound pages she held made a noise well beyond the audible. Ivy thunked down opposite her with a nearly identical stack. Dust rose in small puffs but neither woman seemed to notice.

Frowning, Evan looked at the stacks more closely. Each had dates inscribed across the front in scrolling, lyrical handwriting. "Ledgers?"

Reenie nodded, her eyes alight. He'd never seen anyone get bright-eyed over ledgers, but she and Ivy both looked as though they'd found Midas's own account books.

He doubted there was anything in there besides dust, so he pushed a grin and gave them a half-hearted "Y'all have fun." And with that he was out the door.

KAYLA TIGHTENED bolts and added grease to otherwise pristine gears. She didn't sand or buff any of the edges. She didn't have to. Charles had made these for her, and Charles did quality work.

She'd sent some of the measurements by text and some by email. She'd left a few numbers out here and there and told him those over the phone. No one method contained everything Charles had needed and it had made her feel like a child playing at spy games. Again her paranoia superseded her reason. But the alternative wasn't worth thinking about.

Evan had mentioned that they'd gotten lax, but she disagreed.

She was working in the barn, building the third machine on site while Evan created cases. She didn't comment on the machine or its parts while she worked. The damn bugs would get nothing from her. It didn't matter anyway. She found it particularly funny that someone had been stupid enough to put a listening device in a wood shop. She hoped the whine of the saw busted their eardrums.

Her brother was putting together the frames of the cases, adding moldings that he'd found here in the barn whenever possible. He worked with dovetails and occasionally wooden pegs. Not all of his construction was original; he'd used hinges from the hardware store, and occasionally added a false latch at the front of the display, something he'd found, or that she had brought from the blacksmith's or the carriage house. Then he pointed to her.

She was on sanding duty.

Yes, she had a master's degree in mechanical engineering. She could construct a building. In fact, she was pretty damn sure she'd modified Eli Whitney's design to create a true free energy machine. She'd figured out all the math except that shadow constant . . . but she was apparently also her brother's apprentice and she was on sand-paper duty.

The sand paper turned out to be an expensive version of the cheap foam sander blocks she sometimes got at the hardware store. For a moment, Kayla just stopped and ran her fingers over the surface; the grit was so fine that she almost couldn't feel it.

"Kay?" Evan's voice broke her thoughts. "It doesn't work from over there." He pointed to the case he had just finished. Both tall and wide, it had a cleanly framed Plexiglas front. Inside there were two dowels near the top, pointing out at her. A shallow divot was smoothed into the top of each dowel. Two dresses would hang here, on the hangers Reenie had found and Ivy had confirmed as originals.

The dresses were long; luckily, the people had been short. So

Kayla was able to reach the top and smooth the whole thing from where it stood.

About fifteen legal type post-it flags graced the surface on various sides. Evan had tagged any spots he'd found in his last run. Kayla knew it was for him, not her. She wouldn't miss. She had a pattern, and she'd get all of it.

It was two hours later that she declared it done. The box—already basically finished when he'd given it to her—now was smooth as a baby's butt and glowed with a low sheen from a thorough cloth polishing. They made a good team. Even Reenie did not believe in cutting corners. Kayla had calculated how long it would take to get the plantation up and running. Then she'd calculated how long it would take to do it right. They were doing it right, she thought, as she ran her hand along the edge where the back joined the front. Thanks to Evan's very excellent workmanship, the box appeared to have no seams. Hopefully, no one would feel tempted to break in.

Finishing the job shattered her reverie and she looked up at Evan. "Lunch?"

He agreed, nearly finished with the stain he was rubbing in. He lovingly pushed the liquid into the wood, down to the last corner and smiled. "We shouldn't be in here for a while. That stain is serious. After lunch, we can add the wattle to the slave cabin."

"It's not wattle." She deadpanned.

"It's our wattle." He grinned. He'd read up on the original grout then discarded what he'd learned and created his own and deemed it "wattle." Kayla was not amused by his historical inaccuracy. At least it looked right when it dried, even if it was definitely remastered for the twenty-first century slave cabin, a fact that Kayla found quite ironic.

"It's not wattle. It's 'Evan's goop'."

"Um. Kay? Don't call it that."

She frowned at him as they hiked up the hill. Plucked at her shirt, as though that would make the heat lessen. "What? Oh." She sighed. "You have a dirty mind, Evan."

"Yeah, well yours is maybe just a little too clean."

They talked about how to do the next layer of wattle, and though it was beneath her skills, Kayla was looking forward to it. When they were kids, their parents often tasked them with jobs together. As an adult, Kayla could see it for what it was—a ploy to keep Evan's watchful eyes on her—but something about this task, about the things here at the plantation, though they weren't the things she would prefer to do with her life if she could just choose, were comforting in the way peanut butter and jelly were.

They chatted about nonessential things as they approached the back of the main house, letting the bug pick up their menial conversation. Evan even motioned Kayla into her usual nonstop Aspy mode when she started ragging him again about the wattle. Let them enjoy listening to that, if anyone even was.

Because she'd started, it was hard to stop. She was critiquing his choice of neither sticking with the original recipe nor for going straight for a good everyday grout, but having to mix and test his own blend. She wandered right into the kitchen and practically into Evan's back.

Reenie and Ivy were at the table. To say they were sitting at it would be a mistake.

Books where draped across each other, open to various pages. The old ledgers were leather bound and likely hand stitched, they didn't stack or hold form, and they appeared to almost melt across the Formica.

Kayla had time to take all this in, as did Evan. The two women were heatedly debating a timetable, but not against each other, more like on top of each other.

"No, this was in 1825. That's too late if you're following the other time frame."

"That was a fast turnaround. What could have done that?" Ivy grabbed one of the books on the table and started flipping through pages. "I don't see any notes on it . . ."

"Let me look."

Reluctantly, she handed the book to Reenie, but immediately picked up another one and began reading and muttering.

Still neither of them noticed Evan and Kayla standing there.

But as she watched, Kayla realized the two were incredibly focused. They were so deep in whatever they were doing that they didn't notice anything around them. They were acting as though they had Aspergers.

For a brief moment she smiled, maybe now they would know what it was like to be her. She was like this far more frequently than they ever would be, but at least they would be able to relate. She would point out what they had done.

Then she frowned. She didn't do *this*. Reenie and Ivy were in it together. Kayla had never shared her drive with someone, and an acute pang of jealousy hit hard enough to force the word out of her mouth before she realized it would startle the crap out of them. "Hey!"

They both jumped, Ivy reaching for her gun and getting her fingers around the grip before she grabbed her heart and let her breath gush out. Reenie sank to her chair looking like someone had set a firecracker off in her ear.

Wanting to feel bad, Kayla lied. "I'm sorry."

Evan stepped in before anyone could call her on it. "Did you two eat lunch? It's nearly three."

Reenie reached somewhere under the pile and pulled out her cell phone even as Ivy grabbed for her back pocket and frowned. Reenie showed her the screen. "Look at that. We were so involved we didn't even think about food."

Ivy's stomach chose that moment to growl audibly.

The laugh that burbled out of Kayla was covered by Evan's commentary. "Are you two developing Aspergers now?"

Reenie shrugged. "Maybe."

Bless Evan. Kayla looked at what they had as the two women got up to see about food. It wound up being a bit of a throw-together, with Ivy ending up making three-cheese macaroni as they all talked. Stomachs protested the wait but went largely ignored as the two rushed to tell Kayla and Evan what they'd discovered.

"These are all the ledgers from the plantation for . . . close to seventy years. From 1740 to 1837. There are gaps." Ivy stirred the water as though that would make it boil. The macaroni sat at her side, unmeasured, but in Ivy's mind ready to go. Kayla fought the urge to weigh out four servings.

Reenie spoke over Ivy. "There are some big gaps. But the interesting parts are around the early 1800s."

Evan was washing his hands now at the sink, even as he listened attentively. When he finished and stepped out of the way, Kayla stepped into the vacated spot and took up the job. As she went through the motions of hand washing—a constant series of movements and beats—she filtered the words she heard without any visual input.

Reenie's voice filled in more of the story. "The plantation was doing well enough until one Martin Hazelton got his hands on it. It's hard to tell where he takes over. His father died in 1801, but it looks like Martin was running things before that, and all accounts we read said that Reynold—his father—was ill in his later years. So that much makes sense."

Ivy dumped in the macaroni directly from the box. Kayla held back from commenting only because she'd eaten macaroni and cheese before that Ivy had made, and it had tasted fine—whether or not she'd measured it properly. So, statistically, what she did was likely fine. But Kayla still itched.

Her brain was struggling to stay on the topic of discussion. Reenie didn't seem to hear the near-simultaneous grumbling of stomachs, so she kept talking. Interrupted occasionally by Ivy.

"Martin was not a good manager."

"He was actually pretty bad. Married Charlene—Lena—the first Charlene Hazelton—just after he turned eighteen himself. Reenie's right, it's hard to tell where it started, but the plantation went from thriving to barely surviving."

Reenie pointed to one of the books. "He ran the place into the ground by 1807, just a few years after his father's passing. But catch this: by then, Martin wasn't keeping the books. Nor was the overseer. The housegirl did it."

"What?" Even Kayla knew that was highly unusual. "Was she a slave? And how would a housegirl even read the books?"

Reenie and Ivy both stepped up to bat on that one, talking over each other.

"They were so poor—"

"It was *very* unusual—"

But Ivy waved for Reenie to go on and turned at least half her attention back to the macaroni.

"It seems Lena considered herself a great forward thinker once upon a time. And when she taught her oldest to read, she taught several of the house slaves, too. I read that in one of her diaries. Apparently having met with some success, she took it upon herself to see just how much she could educate the slaves. This matches with costs for primers, number books and chalks and slates over the years. She even taught one of them to play piano!

"There are withdrawals from the family coffers, first in the older Overseer's hand, then in the housegirl's hand. There are deposits where they sold off some of their slaves bit by bit over the years. So apparently, when the overseer was dismissed, several of the slaves were substituted into his place. The house girl took over the accounting. She notes several instances where money disappears from the coffers when she counts it each week."

Reenie turned one of the books, flipped pages and then

pointed while Kayla and Evan squinted at the embellished cursive. "Wow, it's beautiful. Even the ledgers were an art form."

"Well, only with the housegirl." Reenie cradled the ledger almost as though it was a baby. Then she looked sad, and Kayla started putting some of the pieces together while Reenie talked. "It was an art form until the abrupt departure of the housegirl from the record keeping in 1805. There's a note about a payment in cotton from the housegirl's husband for baby supplies in late April."

Kayla cringed. She recognized the year. "Oh no."

"Yeah. Then there's an abrupt ending to her entries in May of that year. No entries at all until about a week later. Then, there are several entries backdated for the missing days, but there's one for supplies purchased from the plantation for two pine boxes by the housegirl's husband. And that's the last record of them. The records go on from there in some scrawl that's clearly by a different person."

"It matches the letters from the wall, doesn't it?" Kayla asked.

"Really?" Evan had given up the wait and grabbed chips from the pantry. Kayla could tell he was trying not to stuff his face. It wasn't working.

"Yes, it does." Ivy stirred the pot and Kayla finally smelled melting cheese. Her head floated a bit, and her stomach felt like it would invert. She wasn't certain that it wouldn't.

None of the other words that were said made it into her brain as Ivy served her first, the plate containing a heap of mac and cheese with a fork set on the side. Kayla wasn't sure how Ivy did it; Kayla always measured. By sight sometimes—she could just tell how long a foot was, or a meter. Maybe Ivy could just tell what was the right amount of cheese. Kayla sniffed the air again and her body relaxed as the food went in.

It wasn't until Reenie answered a question Kayla didn't hear, that the words around her came into sharp focus again.

"Yes, I think Lena killed the housegirl. And not much later, there's an entry for a fine coffin from town for a baby. It matches the dates, and I'm more convinced than ever that's what she was talking about in the letters. I think she killed her own baby, too."

EVAN AND KAYLA were back at work in the barn when the late afternoon sun finally slanted enough to come through the back door. It hit Kayla squarely where she was working. While she contemplated the sad story told by the accounts in the ledgers, she'd assembled her third machine. It would power this place for the tourists so they could get their hands on plantation life—or at least tiny pieces of it. It would heat and cool and provide light for classes that Reenie wanted to run. That could be a drain on the bills, but not with this, not now.

As she oiled and set gears, her brain adjusted for the change in size from the other machines. But the strong sun in her eyes was an indicator that once again time had passed and she had not paid attention.

Straightening, she felt the protest from her knees and ankles, a sign that she had not moved from that position during the time she'd not been paying attention. With a cock of her head one way, then another, she stretched her neck, then her arms, loosening her shoulders as she stood aligned in the open frame of the doorway.

Not speaking—she knew Evan wouldn't hear her over the singing of the saw—she motioned that she was stepping out. A nod was all she needed in return and she was on her way. Out the door and down the short hill to the wall formed by the woods. Her short sleeves left her arms exposed to the sun, but she had on sunscreen. It was part of the many steps she took in the morning; she had to trust that it was still working. The hem of her shirt moved around the gun as she walked, the hem of her jeans disappearing into the grass as it got higher. Approaching the tree line, she found her eyes squinting.

There was something back there in the trees.

Thinking it was a deer and hoping to catch a glimpse, Kayla slowly crouched down and tried to become more silent, more stealthy. She could watch it if it didn't see her.

On the slow downward slope she approached, hoping to be silent, trying to sink into the grass.

And that was why the two men didn't see her.

Kayla drew her gun.

16

T he Barn

WHEN EVAN FOUND KAYLA, she was shaking. The gun was loose in her hands, but from what he'd heard, she'd been holding it plenty tight just a moment ago.

Putting his arms around her, he tried to still her movements, but nothing he did worked. She rattled like a machine about to come apart. He wondered if that might be exactly what she was.

And then he realized he was shaking, too, and with his own disturbed hands he took the gun. It had that feeling—an almost-ringing—that let you know it had been fired recently and it liked it. Evan was less happy than the gun.

He'd done exactly what he made everyone promise not to do: he'd let down his guard.

Kayla had motioned to him that she was heading outside. She was going out where he'd seen strange tracks and suspected someone was casing their property when they weren't around. And he'd just let her walk out, hadn't thought twice.

Back in its heyday, this place had been bustling. Animals in the barns and the slaves in their cabins guarded every corner. But now the guards only numbered four. And four clearly was not enough to do a good job of keeping the outside from creeping across their borders.

Evan had been working, thinking that it had been a while, that Kayla must be doing more than stretching, when the gunshot pierced his musings. At least, he'd thought that's what it was. With the saw buzzing and his ear protection muffling all sounds, his brain hadn't been certain what the noise was. Even so, he'd jerked to cut the machine off, stopping the board mid-rip. He'd yanked his ear plugs and goggles, tossing them before the saw blade even began to slow.

First he saw the men in the woods. They stared at him for one brief minute, hands in the air. While he'd gotten a good look at their faces, his memory of their features had been distorted by his fear for Kayla.

She stood in a ready stance, hands firm on the gun he could practically see smoke rising from. Glancing back to the men, he'd seen that they weren't shot. No one wore growing blooms of bloodstain; no one stood awkwardly, protecting a limb.

But as he looked them over, they looked at him.

The change in them, the direction of their glances, had Kayla looking for him, for just a fraction of a moment. And as his eyes met hers, saw that she was threatening the men out of raw anger more than fear, he caused her to lose her grip on the standoff.

Taking advantage of her distraction, the two men slipped away, counting on cover of trees to at least thwart any shots Kayla might try to get off. They crashed like fumbling beasts through the woods, but because of that Evan could hear that they were heading off the property.

Kayla rapidly scanned the area, seeming to see nothing. And

it took Evan a second to grasp that—as loud as they were—Kayla couldn't hear them. Her ears must be ringing from the shot she'd fired.

He'd turned to her then, as the men left his own hearing range, and he pulled the gun from her now-lax grip. Jerking, he remembered at the last minute to put the safety back on before he tucked it into the waistband of his jeans where it butted against his own gun. If the weight of one gun wasn't enough to make him rethink his choices, two—one smelling of fresh-fired cordite—definitely did the job.

A rustle beyond their sight had him jerking around to check that direction, too.

There wasn't much to see, a slight rise blocked the view of the big house from where the barn sat on the flat ground below. But someone was definitely coming.

By feel, Evan pulled his gun—the cooler one, the higher caliber one—from the back of his jeans. Leaving one arm around Kayla, he thumbed off the safety and lifted the piece, aiming toward the person who was coming. At high speed.

He could hear it now, the sound of running feet, and though he knew that anyone coming from that direction was likely Reenie or Ivy, he still raised the gun. Kayla had subsided to small tremors, but the way she was reacting indicated that she had no idea why he was aiming where he was. Probably a sign that her hearing hadn't yet returned. Or that she'd shut down. Nothing like firing a gun to set off some bad side effects of Aspergers.

Shit.

"Ev?" the voice was small, tinny, Kayla wanting to know what was going on. But he didn't have time. The plantation was big. The grass tall and loud in its dry August stage. It was taking the running person a while to get to them. Or so it seemed in his adrenaline-fueled brain.

"Shh, Kay." He didn't take his eyes off the hill. "Shit."

Reenie topped the crest, running strong, her gun out, held

stiffly at her side the way she must have seen on some cop show. And his eyes threatened to go blurry, squeezing to mimic the sensation in his chest. What had he done?

He lowered his gun, thumbed the safety, and shoved it haphazardly back into his waistband before he could do something stupid. Or rather, so that when he did something stupid, it didn't involve twitchy fingers and random bullets.

"What happened?" As she reached them, Reenie's words revealed she was slightly out of breath, but not as much as he would have expected for the run she'd just completed. She'd been hauling ass, too. "I thought I heard a gunshot."

"You did."

"What?!" She looked them over as she took in a deep breath, but it didn't bend her over or change her stance. It seemed his Reenie was made of sterner stuff than he'd given her credit for. She must have decided that his two words were insufficient, because she repeated herself. "What happened?"

He wanted to reach out and hold her, but she didn't come nearer and he was fully aware that he was keeping his sister upright. He couldn't move to Reenie, so he settled for an update. "There were two men out in the woods, Kayla shot at them."

Reenie's gaze went to Kayla, still tipped against him for support. "Why?"

The muscle twitch in his shoulder was the only response to his surprise that Kayla answered Reenie. Not only did she answer, she did it in a clear voice, shocking the shit out of him with both her steadiness and what she revealed. She did the opposite of what he expected, standing straighter, pushing out from under his arm and taking a breath.

"They had cameras, each of them." Her voice modulated up and down and it took him a few beats to realize that she was trying to find the right volume. "They took pictures of the barn, used telephoto lenses to try to see what was inside. One was the same man who came here the first time."

"Holy shit." Reenie gave a hard blink and darted her eyes away for a moment. Her comment was about the men. Evan almost said the same thing about Kayla standing tall. She hadn't snapped loudly, or crumbled quietly.

And that worried him even more, because it meant Kayla made a rational decision to shoot at those men.

Her words confirmed his concern. "I didn't shoot *at* them, just aimed into the trees. I wanted them to know I wasn't afraid to pull the trigger. I yelled that I was giving one warning shot, then I put it right near their heads."

Reenie looked for a moment like someone had punched her in the stomach and Evan knew she was thinking about what could have happened if Kayla had missed and hit one of them. But this wasn't the time to discuss that. She turned to him instead. "You didn't hear any of this?"

"No." He was ashamed and appalled that he hadn't. "I had my earplugs in and the saw turned on." And apparently his common sense turned off. "I barely heard the shot and came out to check."

Kayla didn't let their conversation sidetrack her from her own. "They both wore holsters. And when I warned them they were trespassing and asked for their cameras, they reached for their guns. I already had mine out." She smiled a bit. "So I was faster."

"Oh, Jesus, Kayla." Reenie stepped up and gave her a hug.

Evan cringed. Kayla was sensitive about who touched her and a hug could be a near violation on some days. But she did nothing. Just squeezed her eyes and allowed Reenie to embrace her.

With that one motion—or lack of it, no shoving Reenie away, not even a step back—his world completed its inversion. They were wearing guns; he was tilling fields and planting cotton; they were fending off invaders after Kayla's machine; he and Reenie were convinced Ivy was a mole; and Kayla had just let Reenie hug her. Had the moon risen and subsequently fallen from the sky just then, he couldn't have summoned the energy to find it strange.

Reenie let his sister go and Kayla looked back and forth at both of them. "They didn't seem surprised that I had a gun or that I shot at them. Only that I was so close before they saw me."

There was silence between the three of them for a moment. Evan could see that Kayla was slowly reorganizing the fragments of her thoughts that had been scattered by the surprise visit. He and Reenie scanned the area, at least until Reenie let out a tiny, "Oh, crap!" and dove into her pocket for her cell phone.

With a few touches of buttons she was on it and talking, clearly to Ivy. "Yes, it was a shot. . . . no, don't come down, stay there, keep a lookout." She turned her eyes to his, conveying some message that he failed to intercept, but then her focus went back to the call. "Everyone's okay. We're going to stay here and see if we can find anything they left behind, that kind of thing. . . did you see anything up there?" Reenie gave a short shake of her head at him, telling him that Ivy hadn't. "Well, you stay. Keep your eyes peeled and your hands ready and we should be up in a bit."

She hung up then and they went about the business Reenie had suggested, searching the near woods and finding only one small broken digital camera. Kayla pocketed it and mentioned trying to pull something off the drive. Given the shape it was in—it looked stepped on—Evan could only wish her luck.

Reenie turned and pointed. "They ran off that way."

Evan and Kayla already knew it because they'd seen it, but Reenie was pointing to obvious damage caused by someone, or two someones, leaving in a hurry.

Kayla spoke up. "Those are the same tracks from earlier. The smaller ones."

Evan and Reenie looked at each other, but Kayla didn't. She just kept talking. "That means that our guy came and talked to us in his suit, planted at least one listening device, and then come back several times to case the place."

KAYLA LOOKED AROUND. "Here. This is probably our best bet."

It made perfect sense why they shouldn't talk in the barn, but she had no clue why Reenie and Evan didn't want to head back to the big house, or the Overseer's. Or why they clearly didn't want to include Ivy.

Evan looked back, scanning the woods, tipping his head as though he could see farther that way, as though the trees might part and give him a better view if he held his head just right. "We're in the open. I don't like it."

"Then we can go over the hill and sit down." Kayla suggested.

Reenie gave a tight shake of her head. "Here is good."

"Why can't we—"

Evan put his hand on her arm, effectively cutting her off. It had taken her a long time to learn that one. But her parents had used it often—hand-on-arm meant *Kayla, be quiet. Now.* "Just wait. We have some things to tell you."

"Things you can't say with Ivy around?" It just didn't sound right or good. And as she looked up the hill again she realized why Reenie didn't want to go over to the other side. To the side *away* from the men who had carried guns . . . because then they would be in sight of the big house. Especially if Ivy had gone up to the third floor or even the roof to keep a lookout. She was probably there now, gun in hand, while they sat here and talked about her.

"I don't like this." Kayla protested.

"I know." Evan seemed sad about it at least, but she couldn't figure if he was sad about what he was going to say or just unhappy that he had to be the one to break the news.

"Sit." Reenie ordered, then proceeded to gracefully smooth her knee-length jeans and drop to the ground like an Indian princess. She twisted in a series of yoga-like movements that took Kayla a moment to identify as prying her gun free. Reenie cradled it in her lap like a puppy. "There's more that you don't know yet, Evan. Things we found this afternoon. Things I found."

As her brother sat, too, he left Kayla to be the last to look around and find a space in the tall grass. Her ears, which had finally stopped ringing, were now assaulted by the swish and rasp of the grass surrounding her. Evan's voice broke the strange sound shield as he pushed down the grass between them, creating a small cocoon. "That's not good."

"No." Reenie sighed. "I checked the old family bible against the dates in the ledgers and I found a letter in between some of the pages. I think I've pretty much put it all together."

Kayla put her hand on Reenie's arm to soften what she said. Lord knew her tone would convey that she thought Reenie was an idiot. Reenie just looked at it, but Kayla spoke anyway. "I think it's cool that you're finding out about your past, but we have men with guns here—"

"Hear me out." Reenie interrupted, "Eli Whitney was here, more than once. He worked with his business partner at Mulberry Grove, not very far away, and he visited Hazelton House quite a bit. He apparently had affairs with both Lena and the housegirl and maybe a few others in the years before that."

Kayla had a fleeting thought that Whitney had gotten around.

Reenie kept talking with a low constant tone that Kayla appreciated. "He was also friends with Martin Hazelton, man of the house and husband of the woman—or one of the women— that Eli was sleeping with. When the cotton gin bankrupted Whitney, he got into guns. But he also tried at least one other way out of debt."

Evan was paying rapt attention, so Kayla kept her focus on Reenie's words although she didn't yet follow the importance.

"Martin Hazelton was also in severe financial trouble, but one of the things he wasn't able to sell off was a handful of coal mines in Kentucky. So, instead of selling them, he and Whitney cooked up an idea to get them both out of debt and make the coal more valuable. They convinced all of Hazelton's plantation owner friends to invest in the mines and in Whitney. Eli was supposed to deliver a machine that ran on coal, and thus increase demand, but Whitney didn't give them the coal engine they wanted. He gave them your machine, Kayla." This time Reenie was looking right at her.

But it wasn't really Kayla's machine, was it?

She didn't get to pose the question. Reenie let her gun rest in her lap, and she began plucking at a blade of grass. Kayla had noticed that Reenie fidgeted with nearby objects when she was unhappy. But she kept talking. "This is where the family bible came in. I was checking the dates of the baby who died against the accounts of births and deaths in the front of the bible and there was a letter tucked in the pages. Carlee—Martin and Lena's oldest—wrote it and put it there. It's a letter to God, asking that he forgive her sins."

"What?" Evan frowned.

"Yeah. It seems Carlee was up late eavesdropping and heard her father accuse Whitney of stealing his last penny—I assume the investment in the machine—and the two men argued. When Lena came in to break it up, it came out that the baby who had died was Whitney's and so Martin grabbed a gun and shot Whitney right there in the house." Reenie paused and for a moment Kayla was hit by a vision of the two men, one bleeding badly and near death.

"Wow." Kayla hadn't been able to stop that, and she was geared up to ask what she wanted to say, when Reenie spoke again.

"What this means, Kayla, is that someone was already killed over that machine. It didn't use coal like it was supposed to. It would put Martin Hazelton and all his cronies *out* of business rather than helping them. And they funded its invention. Carlee says she stayed quiet, but over the next few days, Hazelton called the other investors in and explained Whitney's betrayal—the investment one, not with Lena—and they created a story, disposed of the body, and covered the whole thing up, even putting the diagram into the hearth, so Hazelton would always be able to keep a lid on it."

"That's nuts."

"Years later, Carlee hid her father's bloody clothes and the evidence in the wall when she and her husband remodeled. She'd didn't want that past to come back on her family. Her younger brothers had died by then and she knew she was the only one to survive to the next generation. But she lived with it all her life."

Honestly, it was a great story to put into the museum. *But?* Kayla wondered, "What does that have to do with now? And why can't Ivy hear this?"

"Ivy has been taking photos of things in the house and getting bids on them."

"What?" For a moment Kayla's brain folded the words and Reenie made no sense. Kayla turned to Evan, only to find that he was not shocked by this. He'd known.

Evan blinked before he spoke. "Kay, it looks like she's been trying to sell off some of the antiques online. She could do it, she has connections in the antebellum antique world."

"The Antebellum Antique World?" Evan was being stupid. "You make it sound like an underground mafia organization."

"It may be." Reenie frowned. "We're concerned she's involved with the people who keep coming here."

"What!?" Kayla couldn't look back and forth between the two of them fast enough. When had they completely lost it? "You cannot be serious. Ivy risked falling and breaking a limb in order to hide in the icehouse. All while making the whole thing more dangerous because she was carrying a heavy gear to save the machine."

"That doesn't mean she wasn't involved."

"It sure as hell lessens the possibility." Kayla shot back. "And she's the one who heard the noises and told me they were coming. If it wasn't for Ivy, they would have walked right into the blacksmith's and right in on me working with the machine. So I don't know where you get this idea that she's doing anything other than just taking some pictures."

Reenie looked to Evan and Kayla could not interpret what passed between the two of them, only that she had missed something of importance.

"She was texting with someone and getting prices."

Kayla sniffed once. "Then why isn't she gone? Why hasn't she just taken the most valuable pieces and left?" Then she had a fast thought. "Nothing's missing, is it?"

"Only what's been missing all along." Another look passed from Reenie to Evan, and she seemed to say the next part directly to Kayla. "We never recovered the original plans. Someone out there has the Eli Whitney diagram for this machine."

"So?" Kayla refused to believe that Ivy had done something wrong. "Then if she's involved with these people, she would have what she needs. Why is she still here?" But Kayla knew she had a tendency toward absolute loyalty. That was the Aspergers; she formed strong but variable bonds and she only chose to be friends with people she could believe in faithfully. She'd chosen Ivy.

Evan finally entered the conversation. "Maybe she's trying to learn the modifications you used to make it work. Think about it logically."

The snort escaped her, disbelief in audible form. "I *only* think logically. I'm not capable of much else, so please don't go insulting the one good thought process I have. I'm telling you it's not logical for Ivy to be stealing from us."

Reenie put her hand on Kayla's arm, a tactic she was coming to easily recognize and just as easily dislike.

Kayla shook off the hand and stood up, dusting off her butt and her bruised emotions. Evan and Reenie didn't understand

and didn't really seem to be listening. "We're sitting in the grass accusing someone who isn't here to defend herself. And if she was cheating us out of our money and museum pieces by way of her cell phone she wouldn't go losing the damn thing so much."

Angry and irritated, Kayla started to walk away, but Evan was on his feet, hands going to his gun and it took her a second to realize he was handing hers to her. Somehow it felt heavier in her hand this time. Technically it would be lighter, the clinging smell of cordite letting her know she was one round shy of a full clip, reminding her that she'd fired it.

But it wasn't just the gun Evan wanted to give her, it was advice. "We're sitting in the grass because there were people spying on us. People who had to be shot at to get them off our property. We're in the grass because there are listening devices around our home and because one of us has photos and bid prices on our museum pieces. . . . Kayla, if she takes or sells those pieces, the quality of our museum goes down. As does our chance to earn a living here."

Kayla was liking the idea of earning a living here at Hazelton House less and less. But her options weren't rosy. She'd been fired again. It was now definitely a pattern and would haunt her hiring options. The machine was her one true love right now and it seemed everyone was trying to take it away from her.

She traipsed back toward the barn, trailed by a sigh and Reenie's words.

"Kayla, they killed Whitney over that machine. And that was back when the country ran on coal. Now, if you can reduce the need for power, you're going up against Big Oil, and that's scary. Very scary."

It was exactly what Ivy had told her.

Kayla didn't say that though. She just walked away, back to the barn where Evan trailed her and helped her dismantle anything obvious. Helped her pack a few of the parts onto a dolly. Since she'd made the machines bigger, she was no longer able to transport what she needed in her backpack. She'd become a larger operation.

Quiet all throughout dinner that night, she spoke only to assure Ivy that she was fine. Just getting the words out was a challenge. She was anything but fine and she hadn't fooled anyone. Clearly she was worried, tangled in something. She wouldn't have been able to utter the lie at all except that Reenie had convinced her that the words were often code for "don't ask" and she used them that way now.

Until she could find a way to ask Ivy what was really going on, she would stay silent.

Sleep was hard fought and hard won and didn't seem to accomplish much. When she woke up the next morning she was convinced she'd shut her eyes only a moment before. The light filtering in around the drapes called her an idiot. But she got dressed and went out to start her day.

She'd been in the barn for several hours, when she decided to take a break. The morning had been uneventful, but in her tied-up state of mind, she'd forgotten to eat breakfast. Abandoning the third machine she went back up to the big house.

It was ten a.m. when she realized two things.

One—the man standing at her front door was wearing the gray shirt with red stripes that indicated he was with Georgia Power. His presence meant she had screwed up big time.

Two—Ivy was missing.

17

H *azelton House*

KAYLA FOCUSED on the symmetry of the steps as she descended the right-hand staircase. Telling herself that next time she would take the left, she hoped for a little balance in her life.

But the thought didn't right the tilt of her world.

The knock came again at the door and she yelled out to it, trying to keep her voice steady while her thoughts scrambled and her breathing went erratic. "I'm coming."

There was no one else in the main house. Evan had gone to the barn to work, and he would have his saw on, his earplugs in, and his goggles narrowing out any part of the world that was not directly in front of him. But he should have his phone set to vibrate...

Reenie was supposed to be in the attic at the Overseer's house; she, too, should have her phone on. Kayla texted them both. She quickly added Ivy to the group, wondering where her friend was and hoping the text would bring her back. Kayla didn't believe that to be the case, for a number of reasons.

"Ma'am?"

As the voice came again through the door, Kayla reached to the back of her jeans and gripped the handle of the gun. Just touching it, grabbing it, brought a small measure of calm, though it should have done the opposite. For a second, she thought about switching the safety, but she knew she should *not* answer the door with a loaded gun in hand. So she had protection at hand, but not at the ready, her heart pattering in her chest as she faced the unknown alone.

"Coming."

She had to get the door. She had to play dumb. Because she had *been* dumb. Very dumb.

The man was from Georgia Power, a fact she had sent out in her text. And though she would pretend she didn't know what he was here for, she did know. And it made her heart twist slowly. Her brain tried to fold in on itself, take the easy way and tap her out of the situation, which did sometimes happen to her when things got to be too much. Kayla fought to hold it together. Even if both Reenie and Evan ran over, they wouldn't know what to say to the man in the gray shirt. Kayla stood the only chance of bluffing him out.

Gas.

She would try gas.

"Hello?" Using Reenie's company voice, she swung the door wide and gave her best smile, knowing full well that it was often considered fake looking. It was the best she had.

"Ma'am, I'm Tom Collins with Georgia Power." He touched the brim of his baseball-style logo hat, a gesture she had never understood the use of in modern times.

Kayla, still nervous as hell, smiled again and nodded, opting not to say anything. She'd known who he was with.

"Are you the owner here?" He said it as though he expected her to say no. And she wanted to say no.

If she went to fetch Reenie or Evan it would buy her some time; instead, she felt she had to stand on her own and save that time-out for when it would be best played. It was a wild card and she was going to need it. "I'm one of the owners. What can I help you with?"

Kayla had appropriated Reenie's voice before, but right now it grated. So she used it as little as possible, instead waiting for what he was going to say.

"Ma'am, it's not our usual time to—"

Interrupting she tried to gain an upper hand. "Are you here to read the meter? I thought you usually didn't need to check in for that."

She knew what the meter would say. And that was exactly the problem.

"No, ma'am."

He smiled at her again and she wondered if he was getting frustrated with her. She couldn't tell.

"What I was saying is that it's not our usual time to read the meter. But I am here about your meter reading just the same."

Deliberately misunderstanding, Kayla gave her best fake smile again and said, "Oh, well feel free to go ahead and check it."

"Ma'am, we think the issue is with the meter itself. We're pretty sure it's not reading correctly."

Shit. "How so?"

He proceeded to tell her what she already knew. "The 'wattage used' reading has been declining steadily for about a month or so, and now it's down to almost nothing."

"Oh. Good for us." A split-second thought passed that she should clap her hands together with some kind of odd glee, but she passed on that idea and waited.

"I'm afraid not, ma'am." He looked up and around, finally tucking his clipboard/computer pad under his arm as he did.

It allowed her the first, momentary glance she'd gotten of the info he carried with him, but a second's sight was all she needed, the numbers were now embedded in her head. The printout he was using had gray highlighting on it, delineating dates and meter readings. It went back almost a year, starting with a small string of zeros while the place had rotted before it came into Reenie's possession. Then there was a note of the exact date they'd had the power turned back on. Kayla had been part of that, it had been after they'd all traveled here and toured the grounds and decided to rebuild.

For a moment, she could see the old walls behind where the man now stood, the way the old paper had been greasy and peeling from around the wide double front door. Now everything was smooth and painted a beautiful burgundy color, Pompeii-inspired in the antebellum style. Just the thought of the color brought back Ivy's arguments. She was a stickler for perfect restoration—no modern advancements, just exactly the way things had been before. She'd suggested they grind the original plaster from the walls, mix it with fresh horse hair, just like in the Civil War days, and reapply it. That had been too much, Reenie wanted low VOC paints with no fumes. She wanted sealed wood that wouldn't rot. She wanted modern restrooms.

Kayla's breath caught at the thought of what they had done here. At her pang of worry for Ivy she re-fortified herself. She had to get rid of this man.

Collins spoke again, a slight accent matching his slight smile. "Your lights are on, and this is a big house. You're clearly using air-conditioning. The way this summer has been going, I'd guess you've been using it a lot."

"Oh yes." Another attempt at being Reenie with a layer of brick-wall will.

"If that's the case, we've been undercharging you. The meter's been steadily reading lower. Unless you installed some solar panels or such?"

He looked at her sideways from under his cap, waiting to catch her.

While solar would have been a great answer, it didn't fly. Any decent installation should have netted them an occasional power gain—which would have fed back onto the grid causing a negative reading. Kayla had read the whole Georgia Power contract when they'd signed up. She always did. And she remembered what it said. They were not allowed to hook a negative system into the Georgia Power grid without express written permission. It was punishable by fines and even jail time. Kayla wasn't stupid enough to tell him that they had solar panels on the roof.

"No sir. No solar panels." She almost told him she knew it was illegal, but that didn't fit with playing dumb.

"Do you have another power source?"

Time for the card.

"Yes. We do have some gas generators going. We invested in some, hoping to reduce the power bill." Gas didn't feed back onto the power grid. People used gas barbecues, gas water heaters, gas fireplaces all the time. But these were separate systems. Kayla just wasn't sure she was ready to say she was running the entire main house and the Overseer's on gas. That would be expensive and potentially stupid.

"May I see the generator?"

"Oh, I'll have to call my brother. He's another owner here." She plucked her phone from her back pocket and smiled again at the man while she dialed. No one had texted her back. *Shit.*

Evan's answer just barely saved her from voicemail. His "Hello?" overlapped with Reenie's voice as she finally came in through the back door. "Kayla? Did you need something?"

"One minute, Ev." She was turning to say something to Reenie, as she pushed through the hidden door to the foyer, and Kayla realized her façade had fallen away, and she'd lost her Reenie face. Quickly reinstalling it, she smiled up at Reenie and watched as the other woman frowned. "I'm on the line with Evan now."

"Evan. There's a man here from Georgia Power, he wants to see your gas generators."

Reenie looked at her oddly again, but Kayla had no idea if Reenie was trying to send her a signal. Then again, Reenie knew Kayla couldn't catch that with a net, and she wouldn't try. Then Kayla calmed herself a bit. "He wanted to see the generators and I told him that you would have to take care of that."

"You're really fine?"

"Yes. Reenie is here now, too. Just come up."

With Evan on his way, Kayla turned to find the man from Georgia Power looking back and forth. He introduced himself again and reached out to shake Reenie's hand.

Her actual smile was nowhere to be found so she had also plastered on a fake. "Tom Collins? Like the drink?"

"Yes, ma'am." His grin was genuine as he glanced back and forth between the two of them. "Are you two sisters?"

Reenie looked shocked. "Oh no!"

"Just old friends." Kayla stepped up and gave Reenie a hug around the waist.

He probably thought that because she was using Reenie's expressions. Never mind that their skin tones, builds, and heights gave no hint of kinship, her mimicry skills were supreme. She smiled Reenie's smile again and wondered how the hell they were going to keep Collins occupied while they waited for Evan to arrive from the barn.

EVAN WAS BREATHING HEAVILY when he topped the hill, but not from the run. It was from what he'd been doing when he got Kayla's text. He'd thought she would handle the issue with the power guy the best she could. He guessed she had—faked her way through, handed the torch to him and bought them all some time.

It was all going to shit. He didn't need the Georgia Power guy on top of everything else he'd found. Now GP had to be convinced their meters were wrong. They had probably sent someone out to fix things and possibly charge them back bills. At this point, Evan would happily pay whatever they wanted.

The Hazelton House budget had been set with exorbitant bills in mind. This place was a power suck, the insulation literally paper. Even Ivy hadn't balked at upgrading that. Stuffing the walls with old newspaper was realistic to the original era but incredibly foolhardy in this one. And would possibly cost her her job when the building burned to nothing but a clean brick shell. And in the meantime, they were lighting and cooling and running all kinds of power-hungry equipment on the plantation—all split from a single main power input that had been added long before they knew that that, too, was incredibly unsafe.

Even so, Hazelton House had probably been a beacon on the GP grid—a huge power suck and a primary source of income. While Big Oil was slowly cranking prices on all petroleum-based products, electric companies were squeezing out every last penny they could just to stay in business. As he picked his way up the back porch steps he thought about Kayla's hint at gas and how he was going to play it.

He could pick out Reenie's voice and that of the man from Georgia Power—the only male voice. No Ivy. And he was pretty sure he heard Kayla doing her best Reenie impression. The two women were laughing like old friends. And Kayla was playing "dumb me."

"My brother has been fiddling with the generator, trying to see if he can get us off the power grid."

"We're sorry," That was Reenie, and he pushed open the door in the middle of her sentence to find her hand out to the man in uniform. "Should we have notified you that were going to be using less power?"

"No ma'am." The visitors' eyes made clear contact with Evan's. "Sir?"

"Hello." He held out his hand, "I'm Evan Reeves. I understand you have some concerns about our generators?"

Pleased that he didn't pick up any bad vibes, but not willing to use that as any kind of yardstick given his recent track records, Evan engaged the man.

The man pushed his hat up. "Can I take a look at the generators? I have to be sure they're offline from our system and not violating any safety laws."

About to protest, Evan almost swallowed his tongue when Kayla talked on top of him. "Oh, is that all you wanted? I could have showed you that." Then she smiled at Reenie. "*We* could have. Couldn't we? Come on back. I'll show you the one right here."

She led them out the back door, walking strangely. It took Evan a moment to realize the walk wasn't odd at all, just odd for Kayla. She tiptoed as though she were in heels. He could imagine that in her mind her hair was done and she was in a day dress, her feet in dainty shoes. Instead she was in jeans liberally speckled with dirt and holes, all of it at odds with her Southern Belle demeanor, and all of it spot on. He almost smiled.

Out back, she pointed out the faulty middle step and used it as an excuse to keep them all up on the porch. *Go Girl*, Evan thought.

"Here," she smiled over-brightly. "Evan can you show him the hook-ups from here? I just don't want anyone to get in trouble on that old step."

Evan leaned out on the railing, on the sturdy boards he'd already replaced. "You can see the incoming power—yours—is completely unhooked from the insource to the building."

The angle was bad, the incoming power went to the top

corner of the big house, and the GP employee couldn't not notice that. "Can I go take a closer look?"

He started gingerly down the steps.

It was Kayla who grabbed his arm and yanked him back. "Wait! It's dangerous." She pulled him along the way she wanted him to go. Who knew she'd get such an education from hanging around with Reenie? "You should go out the front, and we'll walk around the side. I'd just feel so bad if you hurt yourself."

He nodded, seeming to buy it. It was the best they had to keep him from walking straight back and seeing what they had. Kayla had tented all the machines. She'd covered two sides on each, giving her access from one open side. But if he so much as glanced inside, the power man would know this was no gas generator.

They took a field trip to the side corner as a group, where Evan once again pointed out the disconnect: that he—actually Kayla—had properly capped the old power line. He showed the split line running to the barn, the only place left drawing any power from the grid. He offered to walk Tom Collins down to the other building to see the connection there. Anything to draw his attention from the Whitney Machine chugging away just beyond a blue two-ply tarp. Even a good wind could ruin everything, but luckily the day was still.

It didn't work.

"No, sir. I don't need to see that building. The connection looks secure and the numbers match up for that." He looked down at his clipboard again, then back up. "Can I see the generator?"

He didn't know what sounds were going to come out of his mouth, but Evan opened it, hopeful that he would find some words. His heart hammered. He had to say—

"No, sir. Evan!" Kayla looked him in the eyes with reproach. "Evan, you *cannot* let people see it."

Startled, he tried his best to play along. She simply couldn't throw it all under the bus at this point. Not still in Reenie's voice.

She put an awkward hand on the man's bare forearm, but he didn't shrug her off. "I'm sorry sir. But my brother has made a few modifications to his generator. He's getting an efficiency of almost forty—oh! I'm sorry again. He's hoping to sell his designs."

Reenie picked up the thread. Pointing at Evan she said, "That's my future husband, and he's banking on getting me a nice ring from the sale of that generator design."

That earned her a laugh and a questioning look from the power man. He still wasn't sending off any odd vibes that Evan could pick up, but the feel of the gun in the back of his pants was eating a hole in him. There was just no way to know if he could get to it in time. Evan smiled back, trying for a "that's my girl" look and having no idea if he succeeded.

But then the joke was over.

Collins straightened. "I'm afraid I need to see the generator. I didn't see a gas tank for the size you would need. And I have to be sure it's not hooked into our system." He turned to make his way toward the blue tarp—to uncover everything they'd worked for. And with what Evan had seen today, that simply couldn't happen.

He considered threatening the man with his gun. He was contemplating knocking him out with the butt when Kayla's cold words brought them all up short.

"You cannot look at it. I'm a lawyer, Mr. Collins. I read every inch of that Georgia Power contract. We don't have solar, haven't applied for any energy-saving discounts, and aren't hooked into your grid—as you have clearly seen." She pointed back at the corner of the house. "That's my brother's design, and I cannot let anyone get to it before we get his paperwork filed with the patent office."

Reenie stepped in. "I'm sorry. I know you wouldn't steal anything, but anyone who saw it could claim the idea as their own. We just aren't taking chances with anybody."

This, at last, brought a nod from Collins. The lawyer threat seemed to work. "Yes, ma'am. I understand. Once you get that paperwork filed, I'd love to see it. People have been trying to get better power out of gas generators for years. Hasn't been much success."

Reenie led him around the front of the building and before Collins could say anything else, Evan asked, "Can we alter our power intake as needed? I mean, at some point I'm going to have to take my generators offline. That's why we didn't change our status. It isn't permanent."

Ignoring the sharp look he received from Kayla, and glad that Mr. Power had his back to her, Evan waited.

"If you'll be hooking back into our line—" He pointed up to the incoming source line--"You'll need to be sure to have a pro do it."

With a small nod, Evan accepted the answer at face value. "We have an electrical engineer come help with that." *Yes,* he thought, *she'll come down from the second floor.*

"Yeah, it's good work." Collins looked up at the cable. They could still see it where all four of them gathered at the front side of the house. "You know, you get that engineer to sign a paper for you, you could have him take a look at that generator of yours. Might help." Collins went back to hunt-and-pecking notes into the computer pad attached to the back of his clipboard and completely missed Evan's ironic grin.

It was likely his only smile of the day.

Collins left, thanking them for their help with his mystery and saying they were welcome to draw more power any time they wanted. But they stood and waited while Collins ambled down the long drive. Eventually Evan felt like an idiot and figured they all looked suspicious just standing there, so he ushered them into the house where they continued watching through the windows. But the Georgia Power man got into a car bearing the same logo and simply drove away.

Reenie's relief was audible as she gushed out a question before anyone could say anything else. "Do you think he was legit?"

"No." Evan answered as fast as she'd asked. And right on top of Kayla.

"His name was a mixed drink. But his paperwork looked pretty real."

Both the women had gears turning in their heads and their thought processes were nearly visible. But all Evan could think was that Collins hadn't really pushed. He'd tried to see the generator, but he'd also given up relatively easily. "That was a good ploy about being a lawyer, Kayla."

She smiled. "I didn't have to threaten them about the overbill they did in July either."

"They overbilled us in July?!" Reenie looked as though this was the biggest sin of the day.

With a shrug, Kayla made a simple statement of fact. "I read the wattages on his printout. It didn't match the billing rate. You're the one who pays the bill. Didn't you notice?"

"No." Reenie's shoulders sloped. You just didn't go up against Kayla and numbers.

But his sister was onto another subject. "I can't find Ivy anywhere."

"What?" Attention snagged again, Reenie lost her concern about overbilling. "Nowhere?"

Evan broke in. "I'm sure she'll turn up." When he had both women's attention, he told them what was really important. "I didn't come up when you texted, Kay, because I was scuttling your machine."

He waited a beat, his heart breaking at telling her that, and knowing that he needed to tell her more. "Someone was inside the barn this morning. After you were there, and before me. Or you would have seen the prints. They were all around the machine."

18

K ayla and Ivy's Room, Hazelton House

IVY WAS GONE and Kayla had no idea what to do next. She'd tried Ivy's phone repeatedly, until they found it on the floor by the bed, a long list of incoming calls from Kayla posted on the screen.

Reenie looked back and forth from Kayla to Evan. Evan was checking out the room.

Neither Reenie nor Evan thought it was a big deal that Ivy was nowhere to be found. They both wanted to go immediately to the barn. And her brother was right: if there had already been tracks around the machine, she would have noticed. Which meant that someone had been there in the very small window of time between when she'd left and Evan arrived. Her brother had been out on the property most of the morning. So the only way a person could have gotten in and back out of the barn without being noticed was to know when people left and how far away the others were. Kayla did have to allow for two other options, though, one—psychic skill and two—incredible luck. Both seemed equally unlikely.

Evan broke into her thoughts, which was probably a good thing. Her famous focus was for crap right now, with her eyes here in the bedroom and her brain in the barn.

"There's no sign of a struggle." He waved his hand around. "Nothing obvious anyway."

Grasping at straws, Kayla blurted out, "She left her phone."

Reenie even shrugged at that one. "It *is* odd we can't find her, but she's always leaving it lying around. That doesn't mean anything."

Evan sighed and Kayla tried again. "Well, then, we know she's not doing anything illegal. Or she'd guard it and never let us see. And she wouldn't have told me her password." In a few clicks the phone was open again. The calls were all to Kayla, Reenie, Evan, the line at the Overseer's and about three other numbers. One was labeled "Mom" and came with a picture of an older woman wearing too much makeup and hairspray. Kayla cringed. Another several calls came from a Dr. Biernacki. And one to Charles dated from when they'd gone to pick up the batch of gears he'd made. Thrusting the phone to Reenie, Kayla pointed to it. "You might as well search now. You'll never have a better excuse."

There was no perceptible nod to Reenie's agreement, only the fact that she took the phone and began punching buttons.

Kayla broke in. "If you could find any hints to where Ivy is while you're checking her phone log for criminal activity that would be nice, too."

Reenie frowned at her, and Evan spoke softly. "She's not being sarcastic." He turned back to Kayla, his large presence making the space seem both smaller and emptier. "How worried about her are you?"

"Very."

"You don't seem it." He looked at her closely, as though words or runic clues might appear on her skin.

"How do I not seem that worried, Evan?" She had studied behavior, tried to imitate it and sometimes did well. She knew that when people were worried their voices rose in pitch and that hers often didn't. And Evan should know that. As though the room stretched somehow, she suddenly seemed farther away from the other two than she had before. Reenie was frantically punching in things on Ivy's phone, Evan was staring at her funny and she was wondering if maybe there *were* things on her face.

"You haven't suggested that we call the police or file a missing persons report." He waited for her answer.

She stared at him because she was in shock, not because she wanted him to understand just how far off base he was. "Evan, are you on crack? The police may be part of the problem, and we only have a sheriff out here anyway. And you can't file a missing person report on an adult for forty-eight hours."

Reenie looked up from where she was neck deep in Ivy's phone logs. "Is that right?"

"Yes." Kayla eyes dodged back and forth between them. Why did no one think Ivy was missing? "And there's no obvious sign of a struggle. We aren't even related. We'd have to get a hold of her mother to file a report."

Somehow, she'd managed to remain calm until now. But standing here in the bedroom with everything around her, things became more serious and her heart rate rocketed. The fact that the phone had been on the floor was disconcerting. Ivy was constantly leaving it behind—in the desk drawer, by the bed, even the Overseer's dining table—but there hadn't been a single time that Kayla knew about when it hadn't been somewhere safe.

"Okay." Evan had his voice-of-reason tone on. "Why do you think she's missing?"

She wanted to be more eloquent, but she didn't have it in her. Thoughts pinged around in her head, scrambling her thoughts. Screw the machine. The idea of the footprints kept trying to weasel into her brain and pull her off track. It made her wonder what was happening with her machine now and what exactly Evan had meant when he said he "scuttled" it. But instead Kayla nearly wailed. "Because she's missing! She's not here. And her things *are*! Strange people keep coming here and lying to us and stealing our things and now they've stolen *Ivy*!" Tears were forming in her eyes and by the time she finished, several had escaped and were making their way down her face.

"Okay." It was as much as Evan would give. It was his answer when she started to lose it. But 'okay' meant he would do something. "Reenie, maybe you can save the phone for later."

Reenie looked once at Kayla and with an odd look on her face, pocketed the device.

"Let's look for Ivy here first." Holding up a hand, Evan stopped Kayla before she could start. "If she's here, we'll find her. If she left of her own accord, maybe we can find out that she did, or how or where or even when she'll be back. If she didn't, then maybe we can find something to take to law enforcement."

Fighting back the sting in her eyes and failing, Kayla found a way to agree with her brother. He made sense.

Before either of the women could formulate a response, Evan was issuing orders and making a plan. "We'll get the walkies from downstairs, then we'll go over everything. We'll start by combing the houses. Reenie and Kayla take this house, start at the attic, and work your way down, room by room. I'll be at the Overseer's. When anyone finishes, let the others know, and we'll decide what to search next until we've done the whole plantation."

He started out of the room, Reenie right behind him and Kayla bringing up the rear. Since she was simply following the person in front of her, her mind wandered. Given the size of the property and depending on how thorough a search they did, they might not get finished before nightfall. She checked her watch. Not even near lunch yet. There was time for a good look, but not the best. She chose speed over thoroughness.

"Umph." The noise came simultaneously from both Reenie

and Kayla as Kayla plowed into the other woman's back. They were standing in front of the storage door, Evan looking at them weird even as he checked the walkies.

"Sorry." she muttered, then she snapped straight. "Okay, I saw Ivy at five fifty-seven this morning. That's when I left the room. I snuck out, she was sleeping." They had to put together what they each knew, so they could make sense of what they found, or didn't. "I went to the barn to work on the machine. When I came back at nine forty-two she wasn't here. By the time I realized she was gone it was fourteen minutes later and that man was knocking at the door. He was driving a small car, and I didn't see anyone else in it. If Ivy was taken in that car then Collins would have needed a second person and then hidden both of them below the window line in that tiny space. So we can pretty safely say it didn't happen that way. Maybe someone drove up?"

She'd been speaking at a rather high speed and so Kayla paused, holding the walkie talkie Evan had pressed into her hand and waiting for the other two to catch up. When they did, Reenie spoke first.

"Do you think Collins was a distraction so someone could take her?"

"No." Kayla shook her head nearly violently. "I knew Ivy was gone before he knocked. So that wasn't it. It had to be before he knocked."

"Could he have taken her then come back and knocked on the door?" Reenie's thoughts were clearly jumbled and Kayla's panic fought for control.

"*NO!*" The words shot out of her mouth with the intent to destroy everything in front of her. The uncertainty was fear and the fear was a physical pain that she could feel in her chest and taste in the back of her mouth. It made her skin feel too tight and made her long to kiss Ivy again. The longing only twisted her tighter. "I already *told* you. There was no place to keep her in that *car*! It wasn't him! It was *someone else*!"

Her fingers contracted and the walkie slid from her grip. A fraction of a second later it smacked the floor at her feet. In her brain she saw it camera lens like, the corner hitting the oak flooring at just the right angle, cracking into three main pieces that each went a different direction. The beauty of the mist-like shards spraying out from the impact told her it would never go back together even with duct tape. And duct tape could fix just about anything. Except this. And Ivy.

Tears pushed at the backs of her eyes and the hand that touched her arm was flung off with a violent shrug. In her brain, she heard the equivalent of a public service announcement, "This Aspy has gone 392 days without incident." Over a year. Shot. And she hadn't even gotten a coin to mark the occasion.

She wasn't an alcoholic; she hadn't done this to herself. She deserved to let go, deserved the shaking and the sound like a roaring alarm in her head. In spite of wanting to claw her way out of herself, there was something familiar in the feeling. She knew this place. She'd spent time here. And it was better than thinking Ivy was gone.

Evan's voice droned on the other side of the buzz. He was speaking to Reenie; he had to be warning her not to touch Kayla. That if she put her hand out again, she might not get it back. Ivy's name came through the thundering noise. The pounding in her skull pushed out the letters in Morse code. Short-short-short-short-short-long . . .

"K-a-y-l-a-a-a."

Her muscles tightened and her ears physically hurt as the consonants of her brother's voice dragged. She turned to the sound, her eyes finally pulling an image out of the noisy blur before her, her lungs cracking and suddenly, painfully expanding at the sound of his voice. She could see his face, hear him, smell him. And this, too, was familiar. Comfortable. An anchor in the storm that was in her and of her.

Using all the skills she had learned over the years, Kayla did something she had not been able to do even ten years ago. She pooled her thoughts and pushed her focus toward her brother. She concentrated hard on his voice. Even in the storm the irony was not lost on her that she was having to fight so hard for the focus that was usually legendary in her.

Evan kept speaking, his words coming in warped and breaking up. She didn't understand what he was saying, but was grateful that he knew to keep saying it. He spoke with a steady cadence, not breaking rhythm as he worked from one sentence to another, one thought to the next. And finally, after swimming through depths and following the sound, she was able to grasp some of the words.

"Need . . . . get . . . Ivy . . . sooner . . . if . . . will . . . can get . . . fix it . . . we can find . . . will come home . . . okay. It will be okay. . . find Ivy, but we need you with us Kayla."

The last sound came on a sigh and Kayla blinked as he hugged her. She stood very still, breathing steadily, wondering as she always did why he hugged her so tightly after bringing her out when a hug could send her right back in. But he'd told her once that he couldn't not do it. That it was payment for bringing her back because when she went it always scared the crap out of him. Well, news flash, it scared her too.

She pressed her lips together and took three small breaths, feeling the last tight squeeze of the hug. When she blinked and opened her eyes she could see both Evan and Reenie looking at her, Evan with satisfaction. Reenie with open curiosity and concern.

"That was pretty short, Kay." Evan reached to pick up the broken walkie.

"Not even duct tape, Ev."

He seemed to know what she was saying, but he probably didn't know that she would be able to replay that film of the walkie breaking—the battery door hitting and shattering—in her mind whenever she thought of it. Even Evan didn't know that every time she walked in here she would unerringly see the tiny nick in the flooring that was exactly the shape the plastic corner had been with an added trail from the largest shard as it flew off towards the desk.

"I'll grab you the other one." And he turned back to the closet while Reenie apparently decided to be useful and pick up pieces.

Deciding to be helpful, too, and knowing that Reenie would never find it on her own, Kayla walked to the far side of the room and picked up the largest piece. "Here."

Somehow the other woman took it from her without allowing their fingers to even so much as brush. "Thank you." But the words sounded stilted. Kayla catalogued the sound though she couldn't imagine when she would ever need that tone.

"Okay." Evan held out the fourth walkie to her. "Are you ready to start?"

Kayla nodded while Reenie tried to shoot Evan subtle "are you mad?" looks. Even Kayla could interpret that one. "I'm fine now, Reenie. I am. I need to go look for Ivy. I'm starting in our room."

And she turned, walkie on and crackling, and took off up the stairs.

∽

EVAN WAS EXHAUSTED. They had searched the house top to bottom. Apparently poorly, because they found no evidence that Ivy had left the property willingly. Nor had they found anything suggesting she had left unwillingly.

Her purse was missing, but her car was in the carriage house. Her phone was here, her clothing here, all of her other things were here. But what wasn't here was anything suggesting where she had gone or when she expected to return. No paper, sticky note, or text message. Hell, at this point he would have gladly taken a hieroglyph. Anything to make things easier for Kayla.

When he realized his teeth were clenched, he tried to loosen them. Success came not through his own efforts, but as Reenie curled into him, quietly watching the news on the small TV at the far end of the bed. The room felt crowded, the walls closer than anyone with money would have built them today. It was a room made for a generation when any man of six feet was absurdly tall. And it left Evan feeling absurd in the room. He felt useless to his sister and he knew that he had hijacked Reenie's day.

In the curve of his arm, she took a deep breath while the news reporter tried to convince them that their refrigerator was trying to kill them. Sensationalistic crap was what it was. He didn't know why Reenie watched it, so her voice was a welcome interruption.

"I wish I could have apologized to Kayla before she went to sleep."

He shrugged, only after he did it realizing it had moved her "pillow." "I wish she would have slept here. I'd be willing to go over to the big house and sleep on the floor, but I'm afraid she'd shoot us if we tried to creep over there now."

"I feel like shit."

He felt a wet spot forming on his chest where silent tears had leaked from Reenie's eyes. He had no clue what to do with them, but consoled himself that if he could learn what to do when Kayla freaked out then he could surely learn something for Reenie's tears, too. "You'll apologize to her tomorrow, tell her what you found. Kayla's a very loyal and forgiving person."

There was a nod against his arm as she turned back to watching the show and his thoughts, once again untethered, wandered. Reenie had played with Ivy's phone off and on during the day. She'd sat in the barn going through all the numbers and texts. She'd used her own phone to connect to the Internet and look things up while he showed Kayla what he'd done to her machine, where he had buried or hidden some of the pieces. It had been nearly dark by the time they made it there and they spent some of the time blinking in the waning light.

Kayla had packed up a few of the remaining parts. She said she could tell that someone had touched them, and it clearly gave her the willies to be touching them, too. But she put all she could carry in her backpack and hiked them up the hill in the deepening night. Reenie had trailed one step behind them, her attention on her phones, Evan's attention on the shadows gathering around them.

They hadn't made it to the slave houses. The crumbling row of huts wouldn't have been a good place to keep a hostage or to hide out. Many of the walls were missing or had gaps wide enough to see a white tank top or brightly colored bra through. But they would go at first light and look for evidence anyway. Kayla had set her alarm, but he knew she would wake on her own within the five minutes before it went off.

She'd gone reluctantly on her own to the big house after leaving her pack with Evan and Reenie. They'd all eaten just a little, Evan in his office, Kayla standing at the counter nearly falling asleep in her soup. When Reenie might have eaten something, he didn't even know. And sometime later, Reenie had come into his office, holding out Ivy's phone and saying, "I fucked up."

Not used to hearing the f-word from Reenie, Evan was shocked. "What?"

"Ivy wasn't selling things online. She was protecting us."

He'd set down his pen, admitting that doing the books wasn't soothing. He'd been just filling time, trying to do something positive today, and he'd failed at this, too. "What did you find?"

She showed him a text in a string about the sugar chest, then she told him, "That sugar chest? Ivy told me to put it away. Not put it on display, not to even tell anyone we had it." She was looking at the phone and scrolling through messages again. "She told this guy to delete the pictures. She was trying to keep us from putting out things we didn't have the means to protect. She told me there were things here that were too valuable to display." Reenie shook her head. "She wasn't trying to fence anything. The things she said to me fit perfectly with this other text string. I guess she decided not to work with the guy I found. She never contacted him but once again after he sent her a text pushing her to sell some pieces. She went to this other guy."

And now Reenie would have a hard time sleeping because she felt guilty. So he wasn't surprised that Reenie was restless, or that she rolled away and threw back the covers declaring she needed to eat.

Eyes glazed and unable to sleep, he stared thoughtlessly at the TV. When Reenie reentered the room, he blinked to focus and saw that she was holding something. The odd tone in her voice went perfectly with the strange stance. "There was a small plate and a cup in the sink all day. I thought it was yours. But I just saw lipstick on the edge of the glass and it isn't mine. So it has to be Ivy's. She ate breakfast in the kitchen here."

"So?" They all ate here. It was the only stocked kitchen on the plantation. There was nothing off in finding evidence that Ivy had eaten breakfast.

Holding up the object in her hand, Reenie showed him a wallet. "It's Ivy's. I checked the ID in it just to be sure."

Too quickly for any grace, he sat bolt upright, reaching out for the piece even though she was at the other end of the bed. As though if he felt it with his own hands that would make her words more true.

"Where did you find it?" He spoke the words as the leather slid into his extended palm.

"It was on the seat of a chair. Pushed under the table as though someone had set it there and then hid it."

"Holy shit." Ivy really had been taken.

Immediately, his thoughts shot to Kayla. She'd been right, again. She'd *known*. And he had to admit Ivy wasn't going to come in and say she'd gone to Alabama to visit her aunt or something. She'd taken her purse and car keys but not her car and she'd been gone all day with no money or ID.

Just then the TV snagged his thoughts, the name "Collins" sinking in like a baited hook.

Both their heads turned to the small screen and watched horrified as the picture flashed.

"Georgia Power employee Tom Collins was found this evening outside the Springfield area. He had been beaten then shot point blank and left within ten feet of the company car he was driving today. He was declared dead at the scene.

"The search for Collins began when his wife called the Georgia Power switchboard to see if he was working late when he didn't show up for dinner . . ."

Evan didn't hear any more of the broadcast and he only partly felt the smooth surface of the wallet slip through his fingers.

19

B ack Porch, Hazelton House

EVAN WAS out the door of the Overseer's and into the night illuminated by the pale glow of a soft yellow lamp someone had
attached to the top corner of the kitchen building long ago. He
was across the small space before he knew he had decided to
check on his sister. The hard pack of earth beneath his bare feet
was still heated from the long days. Small pebbles bit into his
feet, trying to steal his attention. Where they failed, the sharp
sensation of falling succeeded.

The board on the back steps gave way, sending his arms
flailing and his mind careening in another direction. Luckily, at
the last moment it held, springing beneath his left foot more like
elastic than wood and he knew it was probably the last time
anyone would successfully step on it and not go through.

But the interruption halted all his forward momentum and he

sat down hard on the back porch realizing as his head hit his waiting palm that he hadn't thought this out.

Tom Collins had been beaten, shot, and dumped in a ditch after leaving the plantation. A brief and sad chuckle nearly escaped Evan at the thought that had really been his name. It seemed like such a ploy at the time—and a good one, too. If Evan wanted to get into someone's house, he would have dressed as a utility employee and claimed there was something wrong with their system. But, as Kayla had expertly pointed out, there really was something wrong, at least from the power company's point of view. A plantation of the size they were running should draw massive amounts of current all the time, so Georgia Power had actually been lax in waiting as long as they had to send someone out. Still, the man was now dead. And Evan desperately wanted to check on Kayla.

But there were a handful of major problems with his plan. One was that she was likely to meet him at the door—with a gun trained on his chest. Option two violated the premise that you didn't wake an Aspy from a deep sleep and you sure didn't fuck with their schedule. He would be doing both. And the combination of the bad wakeup and the gun was likely to wind up with him getting shot.

Besides, there was nothing to indicate that Kayla was in any danger. Except for the fact that everything was falling down all around them. Collins was dead. Georgia Power knew something was up, as would anyone who could hack utility records—something all four of them had failed to anticipate. The machine in the barn had been checked out, and they didn't know what had been done. And Ivy was missing—really missing.

After finding Ivy's wallet, he had no doubt that the woman was truly missing. And it had taken them all day to even figure out they should be looking for her. For a heartbeat, he wondered if she was even still alive.

He had no evidence that they would keep her that way,

whoever had her. They had killed Tom Collins, after all. But Evan could only believe that Ivy was more valuable than a Georgia Power employee and he hoped to God that she was singing like a canary and keeping herself as safe as possible. There was nothing on this plantation that was worth any of their lives.

Sitting there, Evan let the wild winds of the late summer night whip by. They came around the corners of the buildings, snuck past barriers, and ruffled the tops of the trees and even the few blades of grass that were hearty enough to grow back here. He could only hope the whistling of the wind irritated the ears of whoever was listening on the other end of that stupid bug.

He could see it from where he sat, a small bump on the otherwise perfectly imperfect lines of the wood siding. No wonder Kayla had found it. Though it was mostly out of sight, she was a master at finding patterns. Sometimes he wondered if that was the only way that she could deal with the world around her.

One of the prevailing theories on autism spectrum disorders —of which Aspergers was right up there—was the lack of mental filters that neurotypicals had. Everything came through, everything that normal people were able to ignore. The feel of the elastic in your underwear. The pinging noise in the distance. The fact that the twenty-third fencepost from the west end of the property had been knocked over even though the barbed wire stayed intact. Kayla saw all of it, counted all of it. So she would have noticed the bug disrupting the sharp-in-and-sloped-out pattern of the siding against the backdrop of the sky. And she would have seen the footprints in the barn had they been there before she arrived. Others might miss that. Others might be focused on the machine and miss the subtle changes in the hard dirt floor. He'd only seen them because something had niggled at the back of his brain and he'd scanned the place. If he hadn't done that, he'd never have noticed.

But because of Kayla, he knew—*knew*—the short window of time in which someone had come in. Because of her, he had faith that the house itself had not been bugged. And because of her, he had some bizarre machine that generated power with no electric or fuel input. He also had a missing employee and a dead man that he was convinced were related to that machine somehow.

Knowing he wouldn't get any sleep and unable to leave the area unattended, Evan traipsed back over to the Overseer's and went in through the kitchen door.

"Evan?" Reenie's voice greeted him, low and harsh.

"Yes, just me." He was unsurprised to hear the click and slide of her gun and the shuffles as she put it away before coming into the kitchen to hug him.

Good girl.

"Did she say anything?"

He shook his head. "I didn't wake her. It just didn't seem right. I didn't make it past the back porch."

Her frown sunk into him a little deeper than maybe it should have. "Have you been wandering around this whole time?"

"No." It rode a sigh as weary and confused as he was. "I just sat there, trying to figure things out."

"And?" She wore a soft smile, as though she had already forgiven him for not figuring any of it out.

"Nothing. You?"

Her head moved slowly back and forth, followed by a bone-tired shrug. Guilt ate at her pretty features, and he reached a hand out to brush away a tear that had escaped her lashes and was making a dash down her cheek. "You didn't know."

"Kayla did." Another layer of guilt settled like a heavy drape around her. "You told me, but I hadn't ever lived with someone like her. I didn't believe anyone could memorize like that."

He almost laughed. "You've been on the Internet! You've seen that pencil drawing of New York by the autistic kid who flew over it once. Yes, they can do those things."

"No." Her head shook slowly back and forth as if her thoughts might lose their harsh grip on her. "He was unusual. A rare case,

Rainman. Kayla is just Kayla. She doesn't say the right things in company and she leaves the room when I have friends over. She doesn't shut up at dinner sometimes while she starves because she won't eat things cooked in batter." Reenie brushed at her own tears this time. "But she's really brilliant. I guess that's why she always had a good job. And while she's eating the same peanut butter and jelly every day, she sees things the rest of us just miss. Sometimes I think if I asked her, she could tell me how many blades of grass are on this plantation."

Taking her into his arms, Evan hugged her. "She'd never give you an exact number. She'd have to take into account loss and new growth."

She smacked at his shoulder even as she finally smiled.

"I love you, Reenie, and you see things she doesn't." Then his mood turned somber again. "I want you to go back to bed and get some sleep. I can't. I'm going to sit watch tonight." He saw her protest before she said it and headed her off before she could start. "You know how I am when I've had too little sleep. We need one of us to be clear-headed tomorrow. We have to tell Kayla what we found and she's going to be up early."

Reenie nodded. "Take a gun."

Kayla came awake at her usual early hour, but even as she rose she knew in her gut something was wrong. Though the room held the summer warmth, the other side of the bed felt cool to the touch. Ivy had not occupied it last night. With a sharp breath, Kayla came fully alert to reality.

For just a few moments, Kayla had forgotten her friend was missing. Forgotten that Evan and Reenie were only just starting to worry about her. Forgotten that the nosy Georgia Power had accused them of bypassing the meter. She wanted to smile at that, but she couldn't, because Ivy was gone.

She sprang from the bed, getting dressed faster than usual, her uniform of jeans and a T-shirt more than adequate for the day. She brushed her teeth, her will to go and wake up Reenie and Evan and start the search warring with her need for routine and the full two minutes she usually brushed for. She fought the hairbrush as well, her hair up into a ponytail without the usual fifty strokes, and then she was jumping down the servants' staircase, her favorite place in the house. It was closed off with doors at either end and followed the curve of other rooms. Barely wide enough for a tray, the staircase hugged her on both sides, the weak overhead lights filtering around the corners as she ran her hands down both walls at the same time. Kayla popped out the back door and leapt down the porch stairs before she realized she'd jumped right over a dozing Evan.

He lifted his head and blinked at her. Almost gummy in his just waking speech he said, "Ivy's gone."

"I know." She sat down beside him upset that she was being proven right—she didn't want to be—and glad that at least now they would start really looking. Then Evan said something that surprised her.

"Reenie's in the kitchen making us breakfast."

"Why is she up so early?" Usually, Kayla had this small amount of time to herself.

"Because she knew you would be up, and because we need to start looking for Ivy."

Stunned, she sat back on her hands for a moment. Beside them, behind the blue tarp, the generator chugged and under that the soft whir of her Whitney Machine made a backbeat to their problems. She leaned a little and bumped Evan's shoulder with hers.

He sighed and grinned at the same time. Then he explained about the wallet as he walked her over to the Overseer's back porch, her steps spry and nearly bouncing with anticipation, his soft and blurry like his thoughts seemed to be. That was okay. She was on.

Kayla was talking at fifty miles per hour as she came into the kitchen to find toast and eggs scrambled hard with cheddar cheese mixed in. So she stopped to say, "Thank you, Reenie."

Though she didn't say it, the thanks was for everything. For finally believing. For believing enough in the first place to look and find the wallet. For the eggs that were just as she liked them, which meant they could go directly into her mouth without thought of picking out stray pieces of tomato or chives or any of the extra things that ruined food.

But the stream of thought that held those ideas in no way interrupted the one coming out of her mouth. "The wallet means Ivy was forced to leave. It means she was taken from here, probably from this room. They may have told her to take her purse. Chances are, she was sitting and having her breakfast when they came in. They came in too fast for her to get her gun. But made her clean up." Kayla was eating eggs even as she talked. "Maybe it was someone she knew, or recognized?"

She paused for a microsecond, then kept going. "It may have been someone coming in with a gun on her. She wouldn't have fought. But she left the wallet." She looked around. "There's no evidence of a fight. Nothing is broken or missing."

Reenie stopped her with a held-up hand. "I checked while the eggs were cooking. I even counted all the plates and silverware. I accounted for the rest, but I could only find seven of the forks."

Perking at the news, Kayla jumped on it. "We had all eight of those. Is it around here?" Immediately she started looking across the floor, even got onto her hands and knees and checked under the edge of the cabinets and tried to peer around the old refrigerator. Nothing. She stood up, dusted off her hands and sat back down to her breakfast.

Evan, who had been silent, asked, "Well?" just as he polished off the last of his eggs and toast.

Kayla shrugged. "It looks like she may have pocketed a cheap fork. So she's out there with her purse, no wallet, and a fork. And .... her gun!"

Jumping up again, she ran back to the big house. Maybe it was still in the bedside drawer, but if Ivy had come to the Overseer's in the morning with her purse, she should have had her gun in it or on her. They had all been carrying them everywhere. Or at least they were supposed to.

Breathing heavily from the quick run, she scrambled through the bedside drawers as she heard Evan's feet pounding gracelessly up the stairs. She reached under the edge of the mattress and even flopped down on Ivy's side of the bed, swinging her hands around for any place a gun could be in easy reach.

She popped up again as her brother came to stop in the doorway, one hand braced on a bent leg and the other gripping the frame to keep himself upright. She blurted out one word, "Nothing!"

His lungs soughing, Evan ground out, "You're about to have something when I puke all over this floor."

"Ew!"

Finally prying himself upright, he gave her a stern look. "Don't go anywhere alone. We—"

"There's three of us. That's not divisible by two, someone has to go somewhere alone."

His sigh was deep and self-pitying, but he'd told her to do something that was mathematically impossible. "Kayla, don't make me go chasing after you in the middle of a meal. Or I will yak on your floor."

She ignored that threat; she'd never seen Evan heave up anything in his life. "So we all go together?"

"Yes."

"Then where's Reenie?"

"At the table." His "don't speak" hand shot up, palm out, his breathing still interfering with his words a little. "From now on we all try to stay together. Which means no one hops up and runs off, and preferably no running is done in the middle of meals."

He couldn't swim after eating either. Kayla stared at him. Waiting.

"I'm done." And his breathing was about back to normal. "That's good that you didn't find her gun. It means she has it."

Kayla started back to the Overseer's House. "It means she *had* it. Which is better than nothing. Probably they searched her and took it. Anyone with half a brain would."

"Aren't you a fucking ray of sunshine?"

"I'm just saying."

They were in the middle of the space between the buildings when Reenie came out to meet them. Tears were streaming down her face. Even an Aspy could figure that one out and Kayla blurted. "Ivy may have her gun, so what's wrong?"

"It's my grandfather."

"What?" Evan had brusquely pushed his way around Kayla in less than a heartbeat, bumping her in his haste. But seeing the way he pulled Reenie into his arms, she didn't think anything of it.

His words were a soft murmur, "Honey, your grandfather's been gone for years. You said he died when you were a kid."

"Yes!" She was sniffling, hard. "Remember I said he was kinda crazy? He gambled on all kinds of things."

Kayla was nodding. "He's the one who ran the family fortune into the ground?"

"Well," Reenie heaved a wet sigh, "They all did. I'm coming to grips with the fact that all the Hazeltons and Carrolls were bad with money."

Evan shot Kayla a 'don't you dare' look, as though he knew she was going to make a statement about Reenie's poor money habits. Sure, she'd thought it, but at nearly thirty years old she'd learned to keep her mouth shut. Sometimes. She frowned at them. "Reenie, why is this bothering you now?"

"Because I was looking through Ivy's phone again when you ran off. Thinking I'd be helpful with the search, maybe find some clue, and I saw her texts about the sugar chest." She gulped and almost became incomprehensible. But Kayla managed to piece it together.

"My grandfather was always doing crazy things, ignoring my grandmother, spending money they didn't have, but he was good to me. Built me doll houses and a tree house. He fixed up the attic in the big house so I could play there. And I used that stupid sugar chest as a clothes hamper! It's worth tens of thousands of dollars. And he changed it. He built me a trap bottom in the drawer."

She hiccupped. Then sniffed.

Evan still looked confused. Kayla waited.

"He told me he had something that was going to change the world. Even at eight, I didn't believe him. Then he died. Anyway, I remembered and just went upstairs to check the false bottom, and everything's been tossed around in the Overseer's attic! Someone's been up there."

"What!?" Evan immediately pushed past her to head into the house. "Is he still there?"

Kayla leapt between them, but Evan was having none of it. Even her verbal break in, a loud "Ev!" didn't stop the conversation.

"No, it must have been yesterday. I haven't been up since a few days ago." Reenie was shaking her head and sniffling, but managed to pull a letter out of her pocket. "He wrote this to me. Thought I'd find it long before now. It says he broke the machine and hid the instructions and that he was packing, but if I found this, I'd know he was safe. He intended to disappear, but he died!"

"What?" Evan stared at her.

Kayla tried again, "Evan! Reenie!" she kept her voice at a reasonable level but tried to make it as sharp as she could.

Evan held up his "don't talk" hand. She ignored it.

But he ignored her better. "You think your grandfather built a Whitney Machine? And was killed for it?"

"His death was very suspicious, but my grandmother was fed up with him and she didn't demand an autopsy." Finally getting Kayla's attention, Reenie spoke directly to her. "You know those gears you found, I think they were my grandfather's. They weren't old enough to be Whitney's, were they?"

Kayla shook her head, they weren't. Holy crap. "Did he make it work?"

"I don't think so, but he said he was close." Turning tear-streaked eyes back to Evan, she whispered. "They killed my grandfather over this thing, and they took Ivy and they're still here, looking."

"It was right in front of them." Kayla whispered, holding her hand out to the generator-Whitney combo she had running under the blue tarp. "I'm guessing maybe they don't want the actual machines. They want the schematics before they'll dismantle it."

Reenie whispered again. "They killed my grandfather."

Kayla spoke as softly as she could. "And they just heard this whole conversation."

She pointed to the bug at the side of the building.

T he Barn

KAYLA KICKED AT THE DIRT, ruining the footprints. She didn't need
to see them; they were seared into her head.

"Hey!" Evan protested. "The rest of us don't have your photographic memory."

She nodded. It was as close as she could come to admitting
that she'd screwed up by kicking the dirt. She was getting frustrated and knew she didn't handle it with any grace at all. The
gun shifted in the waistband of her jeans, making her sweat
against the warm metal. She hated the feel of it. And she could
detect all of it, the loop of hard metal that protected the trigger.
The small indentations along the side of the barrel where the
pieces slid against each other as the gun fired. Sometimes it
turned and in the middle of her back she could feel the safety.

There were better safeties on the market now, but she didn't
have one. Evan and Reenie seemed not to notice theirs. But then

again, they didn't notice a lot of things. Like the fact that Evan's omelets were usually a bit runny. Or that Reenie always had the same tone of voice when company was around, whether she liked them or not. And they didn't notice how sticky it was being glued to each other all day.

They'd first checked the slave cabins, hoping to find something, but expecting nothing—which was exactly what they'd gotten. Some of the cabins were just a few old timbers jutting out of the earth where corners had been, or a stone here or there from a truly primitive hearth. Glancing through open walls ten or fifteen feet from Evan or Reenie was as much alone time as Kayla had been allowed today. Even when she had to pee, they decided they should all go pee together. And it was just too much.

Evan set down the shotgun he'd been carrying and went to crouch at the area where the footprints had been. She was pretty sure she heard a muttered "Dammit, Kayla" but she didn't really care.

They were the same prints that they had seen before. Someone with a roughly size-ten-foot and good work boots liked to come see how things were doing. He'd been shot at, and he'd come back. Kayla didn't need his tracks there. She sighed. "They never took anything because even the lighter version of the gears that Charles made for me are too heavy to carry the whole thing off. Without a cart, they'd have to steal it bit by bit."

Evan glared at her. Eyebrows slanted down toward the thought-knot just above his nose. His mouth was in a straight line, his lips pressed together. In case she'd missed that, he jabbed one finger at the bug on the far side of the open space.

She shrugged back at him. She wanted them to hear, wanted them to know that she knew. Kayla had had enough.

Grabbing the shotgun, she headed out the door.

She was cresting the hill when she heard the noise, a muffled rhythm from up by the house that had her jogging faster. Logically, she knew if Ivy were somewhere on the plantation and able to make noise, they would have found her already. Still, she hoped.

It wasn't Ivy. A cream colored sedan was parked in the round-about in front of the big house. The owner was knocking on her front door, steadily making a noise, hoping for someone to come. She automatically didn't like the person, even though she couldn't see him. Couldn't, in fact, even tell if it was a "him."

The noise stopped and she could see only the outline of a man in a suit coming around the side of the house. She dropped low, letting the tall grass mask both her and the gun she carried. Two guns actually.

In faint tones, the wind carried the sound of his voice to her. She couldn't make out words but the tone revealed that he was looking for someone, anyone.

Moving softly, trying not to draw attention, Kayla came closer and shortly he made his way around between the buildings and out of her line of sight. Picking up pace, she tried to be sure she stayed where he couldn't see her. But once he moved, he could head in any of a number of directions. He could come around the back of the carriage house or the kitchen and spot her. Or he could make his way to the Overseer's and knock on the door there, though he'd have no better luck with that.

As she peeked around the edge of the carriage house she found he'd left the small quad behind the houses all together. But then sound came from the front, startling her. The man had looped around the big house and was back at the door again, his knocking soft but persistent. His clothes looked expensive, his left hand casually in his pocket when he'd come by. She waited while his right hand paused, then knocked again.

Kayla heard him from where she stood now just inside the carriage house; the sound carried well through these old planta-tion buildings, especially since this one stood nearly empty.

Switching her grasp and wiping her hands on her jeans, Kayla went out into the midday sunshine that flooded the small, grassy area between the buildings. There were noises from the creatures in the grass, but they were obscured by the rasp of the generator as it kicked up and the whir and chug got louder.

She climbed the short, wide staircase and headed across the back porch and through the standard double doors. So many things about Hazelton House seemed ordinary for its time frame.

Kayla was angered by his presumptions; he'd let himself in and turned on lights. Coming around the side and through the archway, she saw that the man in the entryway looking up at the brightly lit chandelier overhead, but he didn't give her time to ponder his presence.

"Excuse my intrusion. No one answered my knock and the door was unlocked." He smiled.

Looking him straight in the eyes, Kayla asked, "Where's Ivy?"

When he only shrugged in answer, she lifted the shotgun and shot him square in the chest.

Blood bloomed on his shirt and face. Lifting his hands as though to look at them, he staggered back a step before falling and beginning to bleed in earnest. Red pooled slowly there in her hallway as he tried to push himself back from her.

She stomped up to him, avoiding the blood that found every seam in the floor, every dip in the old wood. It snaked out, making it difficult to get close, but Kayla tread carefully. "Where's Ivy?!"

"Kayla!"

The sound came from behind her, Reenie's shocked voice and massive gasp coming at the same moment as the man's hand came out to grab an ankle. But Kayla had seen it coming, his muscles tensed in preparation to move, so she deftly sidestepped both his hand and the growing streams of his blood.

The effort proved to be too much and he sagged back. Which pissed her off—if he died, he couldn't tell her where Ivy was.

Carefully tracing her steps backward, she tried not to inhale. Kayla didn't think she'd ever smelled human blood before, she would have remembered the sharp smell. Though she'd been exposed to her own and even others before, the quantity must have made the odor stronger. Once out of his range, she turned and looked square at Reenie and Evan.

Reenie was nearly hyperventilating just from looking. Kayla decided it was a good thing Reenie hadn't shot anyone. She'd pull the trigger, Kayla had no doubt about that, but she was now sure Reenie would hit the mass dead center and then pass right out from having been so good at it.

Reenie's voice squeaked as she ping-ponged her gaze back and forth between Kayla and the figure sprawled on the floor. Though he was clearly dying and though Reenie clearly didn't approve, she made no motion to help him either. "Kayla, what have you done?"

Kayla looked back and saw he was exactly as she'd left him. "I think I killed him."

"Oh, God." At least this time Reenie did something reasonable; she turned away and put her hands to her face. "I need some air."

But Evan stopped her. "You can't go out alone, certainly not now."

She looked up at him, back at Kayla and up at him. "The cops are going to come!"

Evan shook his head. "I don't think so. Gunfire isn't all that uncommon out here."

Kayla had expected the cops to show up, too. She'd been rehearsing what she'd tell them, about how this man was spying on them, how he'd planted the bugs on their property. But she likely wouldn't get to use her speech because Evan was right. They heard gunshots occasionally, and they probably weren't close enough for anyone to either identify the sound correctly nor to pinpoint the direction it came from. She found herself disappointed that she was going to have to call the sheriff and report this herself. Lord knew, Reenie couldn't do it. She'd hyperventilate and the operator would send an ambulance. It was already too late for the man on the floor.

Kayla looked back at him. He'd had the decency to shut his eyes as he died, saving Kayla from his glassy stare. He appeared as though he'd gotten really tired and was taking a half-exhausted, half-drunken nap right there in the entry. But his skin was slowly turning grayer and the pool of blood was a clear denial of her nap theory.

"What happened?"

Like a hand grabbing her and dragging her backward to the present, Evan's voice forced her to turn and look at him.

"He knocked and let himself in while I was still out back. He turned on the lights."

"You killed him because he turned on the lights!?!" Reenie sucked in a huge breath again and bent over to put her hands on her knees.

"No." This could get exhausting, so she decided the best defense was a good offense. "He's inside our home. I killed an *intruder*. Georgia is a 'stand your ground' state. I'm allowed to use lethal force if I feel threatened."

Kayla watched Reenie absorb all of that. As soon as Reenie seemed to accept that they weren't all going to jail for the rest of their lives, Kayla started to breathe a little easier and look around.

"We need his wallet." Kayla considered the man on the floor, wondering if she should pick her way back close to the body and pat him down for it, or if she could convince Evan to do it.

She was quickly stripped of her musings.

Evans voice snapped through her focus again. "What will that tell us?"

"Who he is." She wondered why they didn't see what she did. Then she wondered why she wondered that. No one ever seemed to think like her. Except maybe Charles. And sometimes, Ivy. "How will we ransom him for Ivy if we don't know who he is?"

Reenie moved toward Kayla, eyebrows to her hairline, then

saw where she almost stepped and jumped back. "You're planning on ransoming him?"

"Well," Kayla shrugged. "Sure. I mean we're screwed if they ask for proof of life, since he doesn't have any anymore. But we should be able to maneuver a trade for Ivy. We need to get his phone, too. And we should move his car into the carriage house, or around back." And they should clean up the blood, too, but she didn't say that because she wasn't volunteering.

Reenie had turned a little green and spoke as though reassuring herself really, rather than Kayla. "You're not going to jail. He was in your home, and we can make a case that you felt threatened. You've got Aspergers—"

Kayla immediately cut her off. "I didn't shoot someone because I have Aspergers!"

"Fine. You still won't go to jail." Reenie shrugged Evan's hands away from where he reached for her. "But how do you know that you shot the right guy?"

Angrier by the moment, Kayla gave up thinking that Reenie had come to trust her judgment. "It's not the wrong guy. The fact that there even is a 'right guy' is disturbing. And this is him!"

Evan, at least, stayed calm. "What happened?"

"I asked him where Ivy was and when he shrugged at me, I shot him."

Reenie looked nauseated and closer to tears. "Why?"

"If he's not the one who planted the bugs and checked out the barn, then he's working with whoever did. Look how he's dressed." She pointed to him, unmoved from his dark cherry puddle on the once-pretty floor. That was likely to leave a stain.

"Kayla, you can't shoot a man because he wears a suit!"

She regained her calm, even when Reenie couldn't. When Evan was hanging onto his composure by a thread. Because it was the only thing that would find Ivy. "Look at his shoes."

Reenie gasped again, and Kayla reclaimed some small level of respect for the other woman. As much air as she had sucked down with her repeated deep gasping, Reenie should have passed out well before this. But the other woman's voice turned to a breathy whisper, "Holy shit. They're an exact match, aren't they Kayla?"

Kayla just nodded.

This time it was Reenie who took her arm and provided support and Evan who began to question things. She didn't get the feeling that he was against her, just putting pieces together. "Did he show you his treads *before* you shot him?"

"No." Kayla took what Reenie offered and thought maybe— not definitely, but maybe—things could be okay. "You could see from the sides."

Reenie tipped her head. "How?"

It was Evan on her side this time. "Kayla can."

And she could, though the treads weren't obvious on the nearly shiny dress-looking shoes, there were small rectangular cutouts along the bottom that matched perfectly to the prints found all over the plantation. The size matched, too. Kayla could tell just by looking. She hadn't ever doubted who he was, only if he was going to do something sinister before she managed to shoot him.

KAYLA SLID BONELESSLY into bed in the big house. Evan had argued with her about staying here, but she'd argued back. There was no way she'd ever get any sleep in the Overseer's. Reenie and Evan had already reclaimed her room. And there was nowhere here for them to sleep if they were so inclined.

After the way the day had gone, Evan almost flat out refused to let her stay here. But how would she sleep in another bed? Besides, she harbored a hope that she knew was stupid, but she wanted to be where she was expected in case Ivy should return.

In the end, Evan relented, only because he'd installed the

master deadlocks himself. Because he'd been the one who secured all the windows in expectation of the items that would be on display in the scheduled-to-open-soon museum. Because he had checked every possible entry point and made sure her cell phone was programmed to speed dial him. She'd promised to call the moment she woke up. So she stood in her room by herself, wondering if anyone was outside, watching her lights to see when she went to sleep. Ignoring the feeling of being alone, which she usually liked, but not tonight, she closed her eyes.

The heater reached out with a mild warmth and tried to make up for the missing Ivy, but fell far short. Two nights now, she'd crawled in alone. Two nights she'd taken the gun into the bathroom with her rather than letting Ivy casually stand watch while she brushed her teeth. The constant shuffling of the gun as she got ready almost took her focus from recombing through the day's events for clues.

No one had called the phone they took from the body of Robert Bell. It remained silent even though Kayla managed to unlock the screen with just a few tries. Then later it was silent because she pulled the battery, hoping to stop any GPS tracking, though there was nothing she could do about the fact that any previous tracking would place the final location of the phone here.

Reenie questioned the validity of the name Robert Bell, but it was all they had. The photo on his driver's license matched and Kayla couldn't detect any forgery.

They spent only a little while checking the small amount of documentation on his person. His car was also mostly devoid of anything other than registration. Not even a burger wrapper or a bottle of Tums was anywhere to be found, nothing that identified the vehicle as belonging to anyone in particular. But the registration did match the name and address on the license, so maybe he really was Robert. That didn't help much in the end though, because he really was dead.

Kayla rolled her shoulders to work out the kinks. When she'd shot him she hadn't considered the massive cleanup a human death would require. The three of them had rolled him into an old tarp, and then folded that tarp into another and tied it with rope so that they could move it without further smearing the blood. Planning had been required. Luckily, Bell lay still while they debated.

He was hauled to the carriage house and parked next to his car.

They spent hours scrubbing the floor and dumping buckets of bloody water in various locales away from the buildings. No one showed up to ask them what they were doing. The three of them didn't speak at all around any of the listening devices. They used laundry-safe stain removers to get the red out of the floor as best they could, but they weren't willing to do much more. Kayla was pretty sure that anyone with luminol and a blacklight would be able to see what they had done, but pulling up the flooring or sanding that one spot when they'd already resurfaced and stained the floors recently would be just as damning.

It wasn't that she didn't feel bad about killing a man. It certainly wasn't anything she'd ever done—or even come close to —before. But she contemplated her actions as she brushed her teeth. She thought about the holster and gun that she'd gotten a glimpse of as he fell. She considered the fact that he had a knife strapped to each calf. That Ivy was missing was something she could not avoid.

The man had come here, opened their door, and tested her lights. He did this within days after traipsing around their land and returning even after she'd shot at him. Today, he'd been bolder, pushier.

Though she wasn't proud of what she'd done, though her stomach turned at the thought, Kayla did not regret her actions. She only hoped that Ivy was still alive somewhere and that shooting and killing Bell hadn't endangered her friend in any way.

Kayla fell asleep on the wish that tomorrow would be the day she would find Ivy.

A short while later she was awakened in the dark by an odd smell and a hand pressing down on her.

What someone didn't know was that awakening her in the middle of the night was a mistake.

Coming out of the deep cycle of her sleep to the invasion of another person in her space, she felt the bed shift as she struck out. In her haze, she was stronger than anyone her size had the right to be.

"Bitch!" came in a hissed voice from somewhere in the darkness, and she felt a slap aimed for her face, but her frantic movements batted the attack away with her arm before the blow could really land.

She came fully awake to another voice further away.

"She's autistic. That's why she's reacting that way."

She was opening her mouth to yell, "No I'm not!" when she inhaled the thick and sticky sweet air again.

Suspecting chloroform or something of the like, she held her breath and went limp. Chloroform took a long time to work, which most people didn't know. So Kayla played to the stereotype.

Though waking her in the middle of the night had been a mistake, and she had certainly given as good as she'd gotten, whoever it was hadn't made a second error with the chloroform. They held on tight, keeping the fabric close over her mouth and nose, and so, running out of time and desperately needing to take a breath, Kayla faked a moan.

The bitter flavor flooded her airways making her woozy, but as she moved she managed to sneak a hand under her pillow and hit a button on her cell phone before her skull pushed inward on her brain and everything went black.

21

H azelton House

EVAN'S LUNGS burned from the whip-fast speed of his breathing. But he didn't notice the hard earth, didn't see the overhead light shining down from the edge of the kitchen building, or that he skipped all the steps between his bed and the big house. Not until he made it through the back door and was rapidly climbing the main staircase to the second floor did he realize he'd left without socks or shoes.

He had no memory of coming awake, only of holding his buzzing phone and answering it in a cold sweat. "Kayla?!" He'd been alert as he answered, because why would Kayla even be awake in the middle of the night unless something was very wrong? So Evan was flooded with adrenaline long before she failed to answer his frantic repetitions of her name. He was strung tight before he heard a soft zipping sound and a hushed instruction in a voice that wasn't remotely like Kayla's.

So he'd run, sailed really, as fast as he could, his brain on laser-focus much like the sister he'd come to rescue, so much so that he'd honed in on her bedroom to the negligence of all else. And as he arrived at the open door, empty room and neatly made bed, he heard the noise far behind him and only then registered what he'd heard as he'd hurled himself up the back steps: a car starting out in the front driveway.

Fighting a clammy sweat and knowing better than to waste time by looking through a window he wouldn't be able to jump from, Evan turned and leapt back down the same two turns of steps he'd climbed just seconds before. He never was sure if his feet had hit any of the stairs or if he jumped the whole distance.

Flinging open the front door revealed that the car was already halfway down the drive and gaining speed.

The sedan bounced three times before Evan's feet hit the dirt and gravel embedded from a century of tires and a century of hand-turned wagon wheels before that. The hard dirt beneath him pushed back and held him up, propelled him forward. The car bounced again before he thought to check the license plate. In the dim light he could only see that he couldn't see.

So he ran, thinking about the color of the car. Well out of the range of the lights near the house now, he could tell only that it was a light color, maybe a cream, or a goldish tone. Something with a pale sheen that distorted his view and his ability to make out the lines, lowered his chances of being able to identify the vehicle later.

He ran to the end of the long driveway as the car, already turned onto the main street and having picked up speed with the traction of solid road, disappeared into the deep distance. The glow of the taillights fading at the same time as he finally gulped in air.

Ice crystallized in his system replacing the heavy heat that had kept him going.

He'd made a horrible mistake.

He'd made a series of them. Possibly fatal.

He should never have let Kayla stay by herself. They should never have gone anywhere alone after the first set of footprints had been found. But the prints had seemed rather benign. Their intruder appeared rude, pushy even, but not violent. Taking unwarranted pictures was obnoxious; patent infringement was a gentleman's game. This was suddenly nothing of the sort.

Though Kayla and Ivy apparently liked the heat at night, the weather kept the big house just warm enough for him and Reenie to cuddle together in a nearby room and prevent this. But they hadn't done it. They'd all been swayed by a logical argument.

And when he'd come in the back tonight, he'd gone directly upstairs to Kayla's room. But as he came in the back door, he'd heard the closing of a car door out front. He knew that now.

He'd simply failed to place the sound.

Had he run through the house, or even around, he might have tackled one of them. He might have wrested his sister away. Hurt one of them. Taken one to hold hostage as Kayla had suggested they do with Robert Bell. He could have had ransom. But he had nothing.

He had only his pajama bottoms and his cut-up feet and his empty hands.

"Ev?"

Startled, he turned sharply at the soft sound.

Reenie, exhausted, came jogging up behind him. Though she moved like she was heading out for a workout, he knew by the fact that she was so close behind him that she'd flat out run most of the way. She had shoes on her feet, but the laces were tucked in the sides haphazardly and one had already come loose. She was in danger of tripping flat on her face.

Reaching down, he tucked in the lace. He could do that. He could prevent Reenie from falling and hurting herself, from injuring his family even more than it had been injured tonight. It was all he accomplished.

Reenie had tears running down her face and she didn't bother to ask him what had happened, didn't ask if Kayla had been in the car. She tugged at his hand and pulled him back up toward the house. "We need to look around and see if there's anything we can figure out. If we're lucky someone dropped their driver's license with a valid address."

He wanted to snort, to disabuse her of the notion that they would find anything useful, but he didn't want to steal away the only hope they had. He had virtually nothing on the car. Not the model, make, or year. The hard earth and stone of the drive wouldn't likely yield tire prints. And there was nothing to point him to where his sister had been taken. They were pointed toward Springfield. And the rest of the continental US.

Pulling him by the hand, Reenie led him back to the house, and Evan blindly followed, his mind anywhere but here. He soon found she'd put shoes and a shirt on him and grabbed a sweater for herself, but still never actually tied her shoes. She grabbed their phones and he grabbed the gun he hadn't bothered to pick up when he ran.

When they arrived back at the second-floor bedroom, he got a better look around.

The bed, which had appeared unslept-in at his frantic first glance, was now clearly mussed and hastily turned back up. A shoe—Kayla's—lay on its side in the corner of the room. The other remained tucked under the bed, just to the right of middle, toe pointed perpendicular to the edge, pushed just deep enough to line up with the side slat. That was something Kayla had done. The other had been placed by someone else, likely kicked. Which meant that Kayla had struggled.

Frowning, Evan glanced at Reenie, "What are you doing?"

"I'm trying to find Kayla's phone." She didn't look up, just kept texting. "She downloaded a locator on her phone and mine and Ivy's. Didn't she do yours?"

"I don't know." He answered to the top of her head, then jerked as he started to look over the room again. He reached for the phone in Reenie's hands. "Wait! Don't set off her phone!"

Reenie yanked it back and frowned at him. "It doesn't alert the phone at all. Just pulls up a map and GPS locates it. It's for stolen phones. You don't want the thief to know you're tracking him. Look."

She held the phone up with the map on it. Sadly there were very few roads around the phone's location. But Evan was grateful; this was the best information they had on his sister's whereabouts. "Is it in real time?"

Reenie frowned and pulled the phone closer to her face to peer at the map. "It's supposed to be." Then she huffed out. "The last location this thing has is here on the plantation. Maybe Kayla turned it off to preserve the battery? To keep it from dinging and making noise? That's what I would do."

That would be awesome, Evan thought. That would mean that his sister was alive and of sound mind. Scared maybe, in trouble yes. But not dead.

He pushed that thought away as fast as it came through, in one neuron and right out the other.

Reenie shook her head and pocketed her phone. "I'll try again later."

Evan turned to go. He had other places to search, he wanted to get in the car and see if he could psychically follow the kidnappers. He knew that was as stupid as it sounded, but he had to do something or he would be consumed by the burning in his gut. This had happened on his watch.

But Reenie didn't follow him. And he couldn't—wouldn't—leave even the room without her. It was down to only him and her. They'd been getting picked off. And he'd been too stupid to see that right away. So now he didn't let her out of his sight.

Reenie seemed determined to turn Kayla's room inside out before she left. It was now glaringly obvious that she had been taken from here. Though an attempt had been made to make the room look normal, whoever had her hadn't covered all evidence of struggle. That, too, meant Kayla was likely alive. Evan took solace in the fact that she was useful, smart, and resourceful.

The extra searching didn't help. The room yielded nothing, only that Evan was angry at Reenie for holding him back, for slowing the process. But he couldn't take it out on her when it wasn't really her fault. She simply was acting on her own hunches, and maybe even some logic, rather than reacting to the churning in him that was getting worse by the minute. He could vomit or he could yell, and he could afford to do neither.

Instead, he ripped the covers from the bed, angry with the world, worried sick and taking it all out on the bedding. The pillow collapsed in his rough grip, and he snapped his arm to throw it, angry that it wouldn't shatter, make noise, or yield any satisfaction at all.

But as the pillow hit the ground behind him with a soft thud, his eyes found the shiny object.

Kayla's phone was there. She didn't have it with her.

KAYLA SAT BACK against the cold floor.

Her hands were no longer bound behind her back, but they had been, and for quite some time. Her muscles had acclimated to the position, making every other option hurt. Kayla fought it, working toward a pain-free full range of motion.

Her head throbbed, compounding her problems.

She couldn't see, but that didn't matter much. Without her sight, she didn't panic, she simply shut her eyes so as to avoid even the idea of images and changed her focus.

Something gurgled behind her and then stopped. She'd

heard the noise before when she was first coming around. It sounded like pipes. She breathed in deeply and ran her hands along the surfaces below and behind her. The air felt moist and smelled as though it had been that way for a long time. Though it wasn't foul, it was definitely not her normal above-ground air. The chill in the floor and the wall behind her matched the cement and cinderblock she could plainly feel with her hands, and the occasional hint of heavy movement overhead led her to conclude she was in a basement.

Once she decided that, she converted back to the use of her eyes. Opening them, she sat still waiting for adjustment. There might be a door or a high window, a small amount of light that she wouldn't see unless she waited.

But as she sat still, she heard something else.

Someone else.

Her facial muscles pulled into a frown as her own breathing ceased in an effort to hear more.

And there it was. Though the other person was trying to be silent too, a live human simply couldn't quite pull that off in a quiet environment like this. So Kayla went with what she felt was the only option.

"Hello?"

She heard breath whooshing out of lungs, hands and feet scrambling, indicating that the other person was no more bound than she herself was. Raising her arms to her face, to protect from whoever was clearly coming at her, Kayla was unprepared for the next thing she heard.

"Kay? Is that you?"

"Ivy!"

Diving toward the sound, she reached out, for once in her life desperate to make contact, to touch another human being. But just as she touched skin, shirt, a hand, a knee, Ivy spoke harshly and pushed her away.

"Hush."

Kayla was only confused for a second.

Abruptly, she sat back against the wall, fast enough to be hard, and hard enough to almost knock the wind out of herself. She barely achieved the lazy, motionless look she was going for before the rude squeak of the door added to heavy footsteps.

Light came from above, pouring in from the top of the staircase, showing her that she was exactly where she'd thought—a cinderblock basement, unfinished and rare in this wet clime. That explained the dampness. She'd already deduced she was still in Georgia, and probably not too far from home unless they were in another area far too similar to her own.

There was a shadow at the top, a man, casting out portions of light and obscuring his own face as he did it.

Kayla was relatively certain that it was the same man who'd come into her room and taken her. The build was strikingly similar. She blanked her face, even though she was tucked back in the shadows and didn't think he could see her. Ivy, too, stilled.

He laughed a moment, and Kayla felt her blood chill. It wasn't that his laugh was maniacal. It was just the opposite. He was amused. She imagined it was the same laugh he would use while drinking a beer and watching TV—which showed how little he thought of this situation. Of Ivy. Of her.

"Don't worry." He tilted his head as though trying to get a better look at the two of them and Kayla immediately averted her eyes. She stared boldly at the most innocuous thing she could find—an exposed pipe, right in the middle, not even at a seam—and studied it. It had markings, some kind of writing in white marker and blocky print. She tapped her fingers, counting out how long the pipe was. Six feet, three inches—putting the ceiling height under seven feet down here, an odd six-ten-and-a-half.

He spoke again.

"You two can talk all you want. If she even can talk. There's nothing you can do."

She still couldn't match the tone and timbre to the whisper

from the night before, not yet. So Kayla maintained her focus, wondering about the pipe and now that she was looking at it, could it be of any use?

The man said one last thing, "You know what to do." And then he shut the door, pushing them into a darkness worse than they had been in before. She'd been close to seeing things, able to make out some shapes before he'd light-blinded her.

Now Kayla forced herself to wait. She didn't want to bump into Ivy and crack their heads; she didn't want the man upstairs to think anything he didn't already. And she wanted a moment to review in the darkness the mental pictures she had just formed as Ivy had squinted and held her hand up to block the light.

She wore a large flannel shirt that Kayla had not seen before. Given the size, it was likely that the man or men had given it to her. And given Ivy's propensity for tank tops and shorts, she was probably freezing down here. Kayla wondered how she should go about getting a spare shirt of her own. She wasn't cold, but faking it couldn't hurt.

Ivy had moved her arm oddly, Kayla could still see the snapshot in her mind of Ivy turning her head away from the light and attempting to shield her face. It appeared she didn't want to bend her elbow, and her knees had looked a little bruised. Her fingers looked okay. What Kayla was checking for, and glad she didn't find, were defensive wounds. Bruises along the bone at the outer forearm, anything on Ivy's face. It appeared that she'd fought at one point, maybe struck out at someone, but that it hadn't gone too badly. Not for Ivy, and sadly, it didn't look like she'd done too much damage to the other guy either.

The footsteps upstairs had retreated, and Kayla could hear Ivy coming across the floor to her. She didn't speak, maybe not wanting to alert anyone on the next floor up.

With nothing else around to mask the noise, Kayla could tell exactly where Ivy was; it was almost as clear as sight. So the hands reaching out and touching her weren't a surprise. The arms that came around her were warm, flannel covered and comforting. It was the mouth that found hers in a soft, brief kiss that stole her breath and shocked her to stillness.

But then Ivy held her tight, breathing in and out slowly, her forehead resting against Kayla's. "I'm sorry they got you here."

"We were looking for you."

She could almost see the smile on Ivy's face, and it interfered with the kiss that pressed to her own cheek, the kiss she was becoming more accustomed to. Ivy's voice was almost rough sounding from her attempt to keep it from bouncing off the walls and reverberating everywhere. She spoke into the pocket of space between them. "They thought they covered most of it up. That you wouldn't notice I was gone. But I knew you would figure it out."

Kayla's chest tightened down a notch. "Reenie and Evan didn't believe me for a while. I'm sorry."

A hand went through her hair, smoothing it, reassuring. "It's okay. Don't blame them. These guys tried to make it look like I'd left. I told them my car wasn't running well. So they believed if they tried to start it, you'd all hear. And know something was off."

"It was a good clue." Kayla rested her head on Ivy's shoulder, noticing that her friend smelled like soap. She may be wearing the same clothes, but she'd bathed and she didn't seem hungry. "Did they take your stuff?"

She felt Ivy nod, even as the other woman's arms tightened around her.

Tipping her head slightly, Kayla found her face near Ivy's neck. Curled inside the oversized flannel shirt, she was comfortable and felt safe, despite the fact that she was sitting on the floor in a basement, guarded by a man she didn't recognize. Despite the fact that they had held her friend for over forty-eight hours, she felt fine here. "Did they get your fork?"

Silently, Ivy laughed. "Of course you know about that. No,

they didn't. It's part of the reason I insisted on staying in my own clothes."

She took Kayla's hand and pressed it against her hip, revealing the hard form beneath the denim where she'd stashed it. It felt as though she'd bent it flat; it had been cut from very flimsy metal, part of a set Reenie had picked out for the sole reason of being cheap.

"Good." She could do something with a fork. "Why did they take you?"

"They thought I could build the machine. They weren't sure what to do with me when they realized that I'm pretty useless with the Whitney Device."

"What is it that you 'know what to do'?"

"They think you are mentally . . . off. And I've perpetuated that. They want me to get you to build it."

22

A   *Basement, Somewhere in Georgia*

TWO DAYS LATER, Kayla had managed to accomplish as little as possible. Mostly, she'd succeeded at hiding her reactions to things, but only because Ivy had warned her the men thought she was truly autistic.

The two women laid down each night with their heads close together, stretched out on the sole air mattress. Neither minded.

The first day, Kayla had been given the flannel jacket. Repeatedly insisting that she stay in her own clothing—and smacking out at anyone who suggested otherwise—allowed her to stay as she was.

Ivy had transferred the pilfered fork to Kayla's jeans and accepted the sweats in a show of making nice. She'd used fake, dulcet tones, "Look Kayla, I'm going to wear mine. See? They're soft."

Holding out the inside layer of the fleece, she'd gotten her hand batted away and taken a fingernail to her exposed arm. She'd shrugged at the man and said, "I'll put them on and see if that gets her to cooperate."

Later that same day, when Kayla and Ivy managed to convince the man that Kayla would only wear jeans and t-shirts, she was brought a cheap set of exactly that. The men searched piece by piece, inspecting the women's clothing for . . . whatever they were looking for.

They didn't find it. She'd hidden nothing in them. She'd only wanted to keep them with her, so she pretended an unusual attachment to the clothes. After a short debate, they handed each piece back and watched as she pressed each article flat, folding it carefully into a perfect square and laying it on her pillow. She then rolled the bundle and tucked it under her arm. Her sharp stare warned everyone that she would pitch a fit if they denied her this simple, if odd, comfort.

Though she fought it each day, she let them search the clothes. It was nothing but a ploy.

On that first day, the two women were taken upstairs for a restroom break. The man patted Ivy down after she came out and tried to do the same with Kayla, but she pitched a fit and perpetuated their belief that she was stupid.

She didn't speak except when she was alone with Ivy. And even then she limited herself to a lot of nodding. That first night stood in the middle of the room, in the pitch dark, and waved the fork around. She whispered loudly, "I have a fork. I have a fork!"

Ivy had questioned her over that.

"Did I seem crazy?" Kayla had smiled in the dark, curled face to face with Ivy.

"Well, yes. But you told them about our one . . . weapon."

"And if they come take it, then we'll know that they can see us or hear us."

No one came.

They were kept upstairs the next day with the windows and

blinds all closed. Kayla listened for whatever sounds she could glean. Traffic ran thick and constant in the far distance, indicating a freeway. A smacking call from the yard beyond the window was a fox sparrow—thank you, NPR. She added in the sidewalk not far away—she'd heard the harsh, grinding breaks of a bus stopping outside around seven-thirty that morning, and she figured she was in Statesboro. It was the only place close enough for access to Hazelton House and to have the sounds she heard.

Though she was proud she'd put all that together, it was hard to do anything with it. She and Ivy had no communication with the outside world. Unless Kayla developed a sudden, psychic link with Evan, there wasn't much she could do with the information except tell Ivy.

Kayla had looked off in the distance long enough—listening for sounds but pretending to ignore everyone—that by the time she let Ivy "persuade" her to look at what was on the table she was shocked to see the original Whitney schematic there.

Unable to inspect the old oilcloth, she bided her time. A moment later, she looked up at Ivy, the question in her eyes. She was given a subtle nod in return and she worked to cover the feelings flowing through her. Anger and shock and a sense of violation bubbled within.

These were the people who had taken the diagram from the historical preservation shop. They were the ones who had replaced it with the fake. Though they couldn't get it to work, they knew someone at Hazelton House had.

For a while, she did what Ivy told her to. Looking over the schematic, listening to her friend tell her to build another one. Ivy showed her the gears, the pieces they'd gathered for her. "I tried to do it, Kayla, but I'm not as good as you are."

Unsure what they would do if Ivy was not considered useful, Kayla knew she had to do some of what Ivy asked.

She went back to the table and began drawing a 3D sketch of the original Whitney Machine. She filled in shading and drew arrows, making every third arrow completely random. After about an hour, she smiled and handed over the beautiful and perfectly useless drawing of a machine that would never work.

"It's pretty." He smiled at her. She smiled back. His was blank behind the muscles that moved his mouth. Hers hid a mind constantly assessing and plotting.

Then he turned to Ivy, his voice cutting. "We need her to *make* it. We already have a drawing of it."

"We're getting there."

When Ivy tried to prompt more, Kayla made uninterpretable motions, followed by noises of frustration and anger, until Ivy shouted out, "Scissors! She wants scissors."

"She can't have them."

"Good God. Do you want her to make you a machine or what?" She turned away, "Give them directly to her. I know you don't trust me."

Kayla made her angry noise again, thinking she sounded a little like a baboon. But it was kind of fun and helped solidify Ivy as a necessary object.

She was confident enough that neither man would hurt her or Ivy. Ivy had laid the groundwork and she herself had established that she was unstable and there was nothing they could do that would change that. She'd seen enough far spectrum autistic kids to fake it brilliantly, and anything they looked up on the Internet would match because Ivy had said "autism" not "Aspergers." So Kayla made the noise again and the man sighed and left the room.

He came back with scissors, which he watched like a hawk.

Kayla proceeded to roll and cut paper, demanded glue, and made hollow, scale models of the pieces. She slid her paper axles through holes in the model. The gears spun, fitting together in perfect sync. It would never work—she'd left out a few key pieces. But she smiled and showed off the mechanics. And no

one suspected that she'd managed to snip the hem of her jeans in
several small key places.

EVAN HAD SANDED the corner of the cabinet so harshly that the
top edge was now beveled. He stayed deep in his thoughts about
cabinetry, forcing the exclusion of anything else.

This cabinet wouldn't look like any of the others. They
weren't all identical, because he'd used scrap lumber from
around the plantation. Ivy had parsed it out, Reenie had designed
it, Kayla had funded it, and he'd built it. It had been a group
project and a labor of love, but was now just a distraction.

He and Reenie hadn't discussed it, and he figured the
Hazelton House Museum was on hold until his sister was found.
Mentally he added Ivy—until *Kayla and Ivy* were found.

Reenie no longer complained about their need to stick
together. Glassy eyed, she sat in the corner, also sanding. He'd
given her the work as something to do. Blinking slowly, she
looked at him, then put down the sanding block and walked over
close. "We have to get some sleep, Evan."

He knew that. He felt it. He'd been awake or mostly awake
now for almost forty-eight hours. Even after the initial adrenaline
kick of finding Kayla missing had worn off, he still hadn't slept.

He waited for a ransom demand. He patrolled the plantation
grounds looking for footprints. For visitors, for a car to pull up
and try to take him. He dared them to try.

But no one came. Or called.

No one but the police, who told him exactly what Kayla had
said about Ivy. They said adults could leave. They said he could
file paperwork, but little would be done to find an adult whose
disappearance showed zero evidence of foul play. Evan had
managed to convince them that Kayla's Aspergers was a special
circumstance—that though she was an adult, they needed to start

looking. They'd agreed to a BOLO, but had refused to fingerprint the room.

Though she'd gone missing in the middle of the night, they used her "unusual disorder" as an excuse for any odd behavior. Once that was gone from the equation, all he had was a cell phone and a shoe in the wrong place. They clearly thought he was as crazy as they suspected his sister was.

It was Reenie who'd convinced him to lock the room, so there would still be fingerprints and evidence when the officials realized that Kayla was missing and they needed to investigate. Reenie tried calling every TV station and then the newspapers. But TV was in the city and they weren't interested in what they called a "mentally imperfect adult who wandered off." They wished Reenie good luck but then hung up. The newspapers turned out to just be one, and the local fair took precedence over this apparently uninteresting story. Unless they opened the can of worms that was the Whitney Machine—which they couldn't really do without Kayla—they had nothing to bribe the media with.

Evan was stuck; he feared sleep, feared missing them coming back.

Reenie knew, and her next words allowed him to follow her up the hill and climb into bed, but they did not comfort.

"After they took Ivy, they came back. They checked out the machine again, several times in a few days. They probably thought she knew about it. But now they have Kayla, too. They don't need to come back."

Evan just hoped they continued to need Kayla.

KAYLA HAD BEEN RIGHT, it took two more days. And that was okay.

The cons of taking the extra time had been that she and Ivy were stuck here longer, and that Evan was probably shaving years off his life by worrying about her. At one point she'd considered calculating the physical damage done to his system from her disappearance, but she couldn't seem to mathematically separate this instance from all the times she'd caused him undue stress in the past. She did make a vow to get along better with Reenie in the future, so that Evan wouldn't be stressed by their discord and would finally marry the woman. Reenie was waiting for him to ask, and Kayla knew that if *she* had figured that out, then so had the whole world.

The pros of taking the extra time here were myriad. Right now their captors thought she was an idiot savant. Though there was only one guardian here at a time, there were two of them. She and Ivy weren't mistreated at all, if you didn't count kidnapping and false imprisonment. They were fed well, clothed, allowed to bathe daily and the men seemed to have no real interest in them as anything other than pawns in the race for the Whitney Machine. That might change if the women spent too long here. With time, they also risked their one advantage —the fork.

Kayla had wedged it into a corner in the basement ceiling between the rafters but needed a boost to get it there. They had no bed frame, just the air mattress. No sheets, just one thick comforter to share. And they had Kayla's one change of clothes, and that only because she pretended she would get violent should they take away her precious T-shirt.

In another ploy, she'd felt her way up to the top of the stairs the first night and pounded on the door until it was answered. It was risky to anger the man, but in short, rude sounds she demanded a glass of water. She'd done it the second night, too; until Ivy complained they were all getting awakened every night and could she just have a bottle of water. Each night Kayla drank it and handed over the empty bottle in the morning.

With Ivy prepping their captors and Kayla playing loose with the definition of autism, the men now both believed Kayla to be randomly violent and irrational, an idea they had unwittingly played right into by snatching her in the middle of the night. They pulled her from her bed during deep REM sleep, touching her when she was well aware—even in her deep dream state— that she had gone to bed *alone*. And she had done exactly what this "pseudo-autistic" Kayla would have done. She freaked out and fought like a junkie needing a fix.

These past few days had been the only time she'd been grateful for her abnormal reaction. Without knowing it, she'd pushed the men neatly into the trap Ivy had been building. Of course, she'd been designing it to keep them from grabbing Kayla, too. While it hadn't succeeded at convincing them it wasn't worth it, she was buying both of them a way out.

Kayla hoped.

She'd gone upstairs that morning, her spare clothes in the usual bundle under her arm. She showered alone in the bathroom and brushed her teeth. Emerging with the second set of clothing on and the first bundled under her arm, she even garnered a low growl for the blond.

Each day they offered to take the clothes, and each day she acted like a mother wolf if they were attempting to steal her cub. She veered as far from human as she dared, and with a side helping from Ivy, they bought it all.

She'd built the paper model and spun the gears for them.

They rejected it.

In turn, she rejected the gears they brought her, even though some of them were her own. "Too big." She muttered. The only words she uttered all day except in the dark with Ivy at night.

Yesterday, she demanded Styrofoam, which they found surprisingly fast. One phone call and the second man showed up at the door with big blocks of fine grain blue foam, knives, and a pick.

It was all she could do to keep her eyes from popping out of her head. They'd brought her an arsenal! But they kept too close an eye on the instruments and on her. She was only allowed one knife at a time, though she did eventually manage to get two knives in her hands at once by cutting into the Styrofoam turkey-style. But it didn't gain her anything. She broke the block and the man counted and re-counted all the knives so many times there was no way to slip one away. They were stuck with plan one.

By the end of the day Kayla had produced nothing more than a few cog wheel-like carvings and a pile of dust big enough to make Ivy fret they would all die of "blue lung." She'd also managed to piss the man off. He'd expected results, expected a threat would make her churn him out a Whitney Machine.

He'd expected wrong.

At one point, he pulled Ivy aside, but Kayla was still in earshot. He'd bruised Ivy's arm and shaken her, and it had taken everything Kayla had to appear unaffected. But he was paying no attention to her. Still, she absorbed every word.

"She was much more functional on the plantation. Why is she like this now?"

"Oh? So you admit you were watching us on our own property?" Ivy shot back.

"It isn't *yours*." He growled at her, angry at Kayla's lack of progress and Ivy's attitude. "And your only value here is with her. Why can't she make this damned thing work?"

Bless Ivy, she didn't look scared, just annoyed. "One, it took her weeks to build that thing in the first place, or weren't you watching? After that, she built each one off the last one. Now she has to reinvent it."

It was flat-out bullshit. Kayla kept carving the Styrofoam and suppressed a smile while Ivy ranted on.

"And two, that plantation was her home. She's autistic! She was just like this when she first got to the plantation, too. You took her out of her home and brought her here under duress. You're lucky she's not sitting in a corner somewhere, rocking back and forth. Seriously, it's called 'autism.' Do you not know how to use your Internet? Look it up." Ivy shook off the offending hand, probably worsening her bruise in the process and came back over to Kayla. Without touching, she kneeled beside her friend and smiled. "Do you have everything you need?"

Kayla knew Ivy wasn't referring to the unnecessary blue sculpture. She meant for tonight.

Kayla nodded.

KAYLA HAD LISTENED. As usual, there was only one of them up there tonight. That worked to the women's favor. Kayla and Ivy had the advantage of being underneath, where every footstep could be heard.

She bent the fork, and using the flannel shirt as protection, positioned it just so.

She was nervous as hell and so was Ivy, but they had everything choreographed and rehearsed.

It seemed both refused to think of the consequences if they failed. At the very least, the charade of Kayla as a nonfunctioning autistic would be shattered. She shut down that line of thought as she crawled slowly out of the bed, as though the concrete of the floor would resonate her footsteps throughout the house and wake the man. They had chosen the dark-haired one. He seemed smaller, weaker, less likely to get violent.

Kayla pulled the smallest gear from where she'd rolled it into her clothing. It had seemed a valuable risk. She could still play her role if they found it. But they hadn't. The blond made Ivy pat her down, afraid of what she would do if he did it. He never checked the bundle of clothing she carried like a teddy bear. Never found the gear she'd slipped in while he was manhandling her friend.

Wearing the jeans the dark-haired man had brought her, she held onto her own pair. They were now shredded into long strips from where she and Ivy yanked the cuts Kayla had snipped into the hem earlier. Four of the strips had seams running the length; they would be the sturdiest. Kayla had them in her right hand; the others thrown over her shoulder. In her pocket was a carefully placed, open, and full bottle of water. Over her left arm was the flannel shirt, already folded. Ivy would use the comforter.

She couldn't see, but she knew Ivy was in the bed, on the outside, her arms and legs positioned to hold the covers up as though another person were there with her. The comforter was folded double already. It wouldn't pass scrutiny or bright light, but there should be neither, and they needed only a minute.

Taking a big breath, and knowing they were as ready as they could be, Kayla tucked herself into the corner behind the stairs and started banging on the pipe with the gear.

The racket was awful. If she weren't making it herself, it would have rolled her into a little ball of tears. But she kept banging. She needed the dark-haired man to come down, preferably flustered.

It took longer than she expected, but he did.

The basement, like the house, was roughly square, with the steps leading directly to the middle and creating pockets of shadow on either side. When the door at the top of the steps flew open, the man descended, a nine-millimeter leading the way.

Kayla had not seen that coming, but she wasn't forfeiting their one chance. He expected her to be in the opposite corner, in the bed. So she sent up a prayer for Ivy, and kept banging.

He swept the scene with his gun but not his eyes.

Ivy acted as though *he* had woken her, not the banging. By virtue of being tucked into the shadow on the other side of the stairs, she pulled it off. Her voice was heavy with sleep and she formed her words slowly, as though it took effort to do so. "Why are you here?"

She shielded her eyes from the light.

He must have seen the empty side of the bed, because he

turned and looked directly at Kayla. Saw that she was banging on the pipe. His face hardened.

But it was the opening Ivy wanted. His back was to her, and holding the comforter in front of her, she rushed him. Kayla rushed him too; in the dim light, she aimed and threw the water at his knees.

Too flustered by the odd things happening, and probably charged with *not* shooting the only person who could build the Whitney Machine, he waved the gun, looking startled for just a split second.

It was all Kayla needed. She saw that the gun's safety was on, and it gave her the impetus to move forward without fear. Holding the flannel jacket between her and him, she joined Ivy in pushing him against the wall. She dove low, shoving at his knees.

His wet leg made contact with the fork.

Already bent and pushed partway into the outlet, the pressure pushed it the last bit. And the current surged through it.

Kayla felt a little zing, and shoved at Ivy as they both tried to jump gracefully out of the way but fell backward as though blasted.

It took Kayla another moment to get herself together, grab up the flannel, and tackle the man. The fork sparked as she knocked him off the contact. He wasn't dead, only dazed, but that was all they needed. It seemed forever before the circuit snapped and the fork stopped spitting shards of bright light.

They tied him with the strips of ripped denim. Dragged him, still out of it, over to the pipe, where they gagged him, tucked him in the corner and anchored him there with more of the tough fabric. Kayla used girth hitches and figure-eight knots, knowing they were both secure, and that the man would be unlikely to figure out how to undo them behind his back. She secured even his feet, so he would be unable to make noise unless he banged his head on the pipe. He was in the darkest shadow in the corner, and she hoped the other man looked down here and passed him over.

Kayla checked his pulse and noted that his breathing was regular again as Ivy picked up the gun and commented, "I'm not all that concerned with his survival. He kidnapped both of us and held us here."

They stayed on the move though they talked. Upstairs they found the house empty, as expected, and dark as befitted a standard home on a suburban street at night. They were looking for their shoes as Kayla responded. "I already killed one man. I'd rather not kill a second one."

Ivy stopped dead. "You *what?*"

"I'll explain later. I say we go without shoes."

They found his wallet by his bedside and took his ID along with his eighty dollars of cash. Ivy had the gun and Kayla grabbed the knives. Hiding the weapons as best they could, they took a deep breath and headed out the front door.

Kayla pulled it shut behind her and turned to face the street, only to see Ivy standing on the sidewalk, in her socks, in shock.

An older, white-haired gentleman stared at both of them as though they were monkeys from the zoo.

Why would anyone be out at this time of night? Kayla thought.

Then it got worse.

He looked at each of them for a second before speaking.

"Kayla? Ivy?"

23

Stiltson's Café, Brooklet, South Carolina

EVAN PULLED the car up to the small diner. His mid-grade, mid-aged car matched the others in the lot. Able to see inside the wide windows, he scanned the faces, looking for his sister. When that yielded nothing, he turned to the surrounding businesses. There was a used car lot across the corner. Being used cars, the makes and models were scrambled. Kayla wouldn't like the disorder. Since she didn't like new things, she probably wouldn't eat much of anything at the café either. And that was the least of his worries.

All he had was her cryptic call from an unknown number. She said she'd been "out" for about four hours, whatever that meant. She told him Ivy was fine and that he should bring shoes.

His standard neurotypical brain asked her, "Why would you need to tell me to bring shoes?"

Kayla's Aspy mind continued processing at hyperspeed and

relatively far off the beaten path. "I'll tell you when you get there, get shoes for me and Ivy."

At the first ring, he'd sat upright in bed, thinking he and Reenie had managed a somewhat normal night of sleep. After two full days with no contact, and after he and Reenie had each filed a report, the deputies finally declared Kayla missing. Evan had gone so far as to provide documentation regarding her diagnosis; he gave them copies of everything from Kayla's elementary school though recent therapist visits. He invited the officers to contact her therapist, sworn she hadn't run off with a boyfriend, and nearly threatened the officer.

He'd spent his days stepping in puddles of guilt, waiting for someone to come and take fingerprints from Kayla and Ivy's bedroom. Apparently he'd even failed at that. Though Kayla was finally a real missing person, there would be no waste of black dust or actual time on her case.

They told him she'd turn up.

Evan insisted they were wrong.

She'd done exactly that. So he was waiting at a diner after a brief phone call and a rattled-off address. And a demand for shoes.

He was used to Kaylas demands. But now he had Reenie in his ear, softer, but just as demanding.

"How did she sound? Why are you getting shoes? Don't open the door to their room!"

He couldn't keep up. All along, Evan had hoped that Reenie's pleasantries and ability to handle social situations would rub off on Kayla, and that Kayla's logic and financial sense would somehow influence Reenie. Knowledge seemed to have flowed in the reverse direction. He shook his head and sorted his thoughts.

At five in the morning, he awoke maybe a little too fast. "I *have to* open the door to the room. I have to get shoes for them."

"Why do they need shoes?" Reenie pressed again, from less than an inch behind him, which should have irritated him.

Instead, it made him happy. He wasn't losing anyone else without a good, old-fashioned, hand-to-hand fight.

"I have no idea. Kayla said to."

"Ivy is with her, right?"

"Yes." He grabbed two pairs and handed them to Reenie. The task occupied her for all of half a second, then she trailed him back down the stairs and asked again, "How did she sound?"

While she spoke, Reenie gathered a cloth grocery bag and slid the shoes in as deftly as she then slipped the straps onto her shoulder. She wore a light jacket in the early morning mist and had been ready to go even before he was.

Tilting his head at her, Evan gave her his "really?" look. "How do you think? She sounded like Kayla. Her dial is always set the same."

Reenie climbed in the other side of the car and took care of navigation to the odd little café Kayla had directed them to. Speaking over the growl and hum of the engine starting, she smiled. "Actually, your sister has at least three settings that I have seen. She has normal Kayla, 'lost it' Kayla, and Kayla paying attention to Ivy. Since she's not set on 'lost it' that sounds pretty good to me. I wonder what happened to them. At least they're together now."

Evan followed her directions in the early sunrise. The streets hung with a thin Georgia mist that would disappear before eight a.m. The tension of not knowing how Kayla and Ivy had come to be at Stiltson's Café was much easier to deal with than the tension of not knowing where they were, of praying they were more useful alive, or wondering if he would ever see his sister again. "I assume they'll tell us everything when we get there."

He was glad, too, that it had been Kayla on the phone instead of Ivy. Ivy was an artful liar when she needed to be. It wasn't that he didn't trust her, it was that she might have tried to spare him hurtful details in these early hours of reunion. He was grateful that Kayla couldn't lie. She said she was fine. Had she been hurt, she would have catalogued all of it for him. All she'd told him was to bring shoes.

Evan scanned the area but couldn't find them. Quickly, he realized he was looking for the Ivy he'd seen the day before she went missing. Long, bare legs bracketed by tan work boots and cutoff jeans, brightly colored bra-du-jour showing through a tank, all topped by a long ink-black braid. That woman wasn't here.

The Kayla image in his head was wearing relaxed jeans and a T-shirt that would say something snarky. Or geeky. Or so obscure that even he wouldn't understand it.

But they might not look like that now. Maybe they looked like refugees. Maybe they looked like . . .

The expression on Reenie's face as she opened her door to scan farther told him she was having as difficult a time as he was and his panic ratcheted up by degrees. He couldn't come out here and not find Kayla. He couldn't talk to her on the phone and hear that she was okay only to have her snatched away again.

"Reenie! Get back!"

He yanked her into the car and reached out beyond her, slamming shut the door she had opened. He ducked his head and put the car in gear:

"What—?" She alternated between scanning the area and looking at him like he was crazy.

For the life of him, he couldn't figure why he hadn't thought it before. "What if it's a trap?"

"What are you talking about?" Reenie stared like he'd gone completely nuts.

"There's no better person to use to set a trap than Kayla. If they know anything about us, they know that I'll believe everything she says."

Reenie's expression made it clear that she hadn't downgraded her opinion of his actions from batshit crazy. "She told you she was fine, right? She couldn't perform a charade like that. Go back." She pointed over her shoulder to the diner, which was rapidly disappearing behind them in a cloud of dust as he bolted down a back road that led to God knew where.

"What if they threatened Ivy?" Then he got an idea. "Call her back. She called my cell, but I didn't recognize the number so I answered. Call it back."

Though time seemed to stretch forever, it was only a moment before Reenie's call got through. He could hear the electronic voice responding to her, so he wasn't surprised when she shook her head and said, "Pay phone."

Then she looked at him in that way—the way that said she knew she was right. "It really might be a trap. 'Bring shoes' might have been some code of Kayla's that we overlooked. But this is your sister—this is Kayla—and Ivy. We have to go back." With a sigh, she drove her point home. "If you don't turn around, at least stop so I can walk back."

Evan turned around.

This time, he drove past the cafe, crisscrossing the intersection and looking out for all possible traps. Though he didn't see any, that didn't mean they weren't there.

After parking, he again stopped Reenie from exiting the car. Evan figured they would sit a moment and just watch. If someone was going to approach them, they may have better luck locked in the car, and if someone was waiting for them to go inside, this might just make them a little nervous. "Do you have your gun?"

"Yes, but we can't take it inside a restaurant!"

"I'd rather be alive. I'm perfectly fine with a misdemeanor for bringing a gun into a diner." He looked through the open windows at the hometown crowd getting their daily eggs, bacon and coffee. "Plus, I'd bet my life we aren't the only ones in there with guns."

Just then an incredibly out-of-place Mercedes pulled into the spot next to them.

The back windows were tinted, but the front was clear. An old man sat behind the wheel, wearing a shocking head of white hair and a partially amused expression. He was somewhat hidden from Evan's view by his passenger, a woman who sat facing the driver, her back to the window. Long dark hair fell in unruly waves.

Evan sucked in a breath, it might be Ivy. But . . .

Just then the back window scrolled down, revealing a smiling Kayla. The smile looked a little overbright and possibly forced, but with his sister that might just be the genuine article. Traps forgotten, he was already halfway out of the car and opening the back door to the Mercedes. The give of the handle was a relief— for a moment he'd been certain that it was locked—that his sister was still just as captive as she had been.

But Kayla tumbled out to him, looking much as she did the day before she left. She wore jeans and a T-shirt, her hair pulled back into a smooth pony tail. It figured that even in captivity Kayla would keep her hair neat and in her usual hairstyle.

With pent-up tension gushing from every surface, Evan enveloped her in a massive hug. Nearly crying with relief, he finally stepped back to let her breathe. The hug was for him and he knew it. He saw then that she wore no shoes, just socks—the brand she owned fifty pairs of. Because they fit in a way that she could finally ignore her socks. Evan had no idea it would be such a relief to see those socks.

Whoever had taken her hadn't even taken her socks from her. Kayla was okay.

"Do you have our shoes?"

Of course those were the first words out of her mouth. "Yes." He grinned as he turned to get them and saw Reenie hug her tightly. For a moment he thought about stepping in, about reminding Reenie about Kayla and hugs, but then he decided they would sort it out themselves.

"Here you go." He handed over the shoes and made another covert inspection of his sister. She looked fine. Better than fine, in fact—which was highly unusual for an Aspy away from her home. She hated being away. She needed her things and her routine. "How are you?" He wasn't sure he would be able to handle the answer, but needed to know.

Kayla nodded in return, a common answer for her, just a yes or no even to open-ended questions. But her next statement surprised him, more than it should have. "Ivy was there."

She had latched onto Ivy as the representative of "normal." Ivy made things okay. And Evan had to wonder if Ivy knew that. But now wasn't the time.

He didn't comment as Kayla brushed off her incredibly dirty socks and shoved them into her shoes. He wondered how long she'd been walking around in just her stocking feet as Reenie leaned in the front window and asked Ivy, "Are you going to get out?"

"Not until someone can take this gun from me."

Blinking, and leaping to look, he found Ivy, relatively motionless in the front seat, a nine-millimeter gun trained on the white-haired man.

24

S tiltson's Café, Brooklet, South Carolina

KAYLA SAT next to Ivy in the small booth. The seat was made of molded plyform plastic and wouldn't have been comfortable except that she was feeling good. She was free again. Evan and Reenie were with her. Ivy was beside her. And she was eating a plate of eggs scrambled with real cheddar cheese and hash-browns uniformly cooked to just under completely crisp.

Under the table, Ivy was holding a gun aimed at Reginald Standish the fifteenth. He was the only person she'd ever met who had a stronger family name history than Reenie's.

Around the rectangular table, the five of them were each eating breakfast, Ivy a little slower than the others because she was eating one-handed. Reenie was perched in a pulled-up chair at the end of the booth, ostensibly because she was the smallest, but really because Standish was hemmed into the corner, stuck safely between Evan and the wall.

Kayla couldn't imagine the older man making a break for it. Though he might have, something in his posture said he was willing to sit at the wrong end of the barrel for the chance to say his piece. He also understood where they were and that he would need to put on a good front—as though he were at breakfast with his family rather than out at gunpoint.

Another nod in his favor was his demeanor. He seemed to have Reenie's bred-in feel for propriety. Kayla *knew* tons of etiquette; she could recite reams of "isms" and old family sayings. She just didn't ever seem to know *when* they applied. Standish applied them all. He wouldn't bolt, because that would be unseemly. One simply did not cause a scene in a low-end diner in a backwater town.

Standish was speaking, looking like a combination of a grandfather and an aged knight, not at all like someone who ordered listening devices and kidnappings. He'd started with his history —the Standish family coming to America on the *Mayflower*, traceable lineage, the firstborn son always named Reginald for fifteen generations. He startled Reenie by mentioning that he'd known her grandfather, flirted momentarily with the older waitress who brought them their food, then seamlessly transitioned back to the conversation at hand, never once acknowledging the gun on him.

"You're this generation's Charlene. I remember some family discord about your mother giving you the name. Your grandfather never had an issue with it though. He adored you."

Reenie's eyebrows went up, and Kayla thought to herself "Tell us something we don't already know."

Standish proceeded to do just that. "I helped him with the Whitney Device. He made it work."

Kayla almost spit her eggs. "He did!?"

Evan looked at her and gave a tiny shake of his head. But she didn't stand down. If Standish knew of someone else with a working Whitney Device, she wanted to know, too.

Reginald nodded slowly. "He and I made a business deal for that machine. I funded his research into it."

Shock skittered across Reenie's face. Standish had shocked them all.

But the more she thought about it, the more sense it made. As Kayla considered the pieces she'd found, the ones that had just happened to fit the Whitney Device, she realized it hadn't been coincidence. They were from his machine. He must have scuttled it.

Her eyes darted one way then another while she thought, eventually landing for a moment on the butt of the gun Ivy held. Her new best friend had been quiet the whole meal, carefully keeping Standish locked in place. Later Kayla would ask her if she was okay, but she couldn't now. All she could do was offer a look as a slight smile fell on Ivy's mouth. Her free hand moved over to rest on Kayla's thigh, under the table and just as hidden as the gun. Kayla didn't react on the outside, but knew Ivy was okay.

With her foundation in place, Kayla's attention lasered back to Standish, to ask him about the late grandpa Hazelton, but the older man was still talking, still having a neat conversation in his classy slacks and pressed button-down shirt that even Kayla could see was inappropriate for the diner. He looked like he was visiting poor relations, and the image wasn't too far from the truth. His words reined in her scattered thoughts.

"Edwin got paranoid. Told me he was being followed. That he'd been the victim of vandalism and a few sketchy car accidents." At Reenie's confused expression, Standish elaborated. "He went into a ditch once and into the guardrail another time. He walked away from both, but he thought someone was sending a message. I told him he was a poor driver and needlessly paranoid." Deep regret passed through his features leaving a wake of sadness, "Then he disappeared. They found him later, an apparent heart attack."

For a moment the old man looked back to Reenie, "That's

probably what you remember. That was the official cause of death. And no matter what I said, they wouldn't do an autopsy. I offered to pay for it, but your grandmother refused . . . I think she just had too much to deal with at the time." The way he softened the blow of grandmother Hazelton refusing the investigation made Kayla think there was something more behind it. Like maybe grandma had gotten tired of grandpa's get-rich-quick schemes or just wanted to put it behind her.

Kayla looked up at Standish, more and more convinced that this man was not part of the group that kidnapped her and Reenie. But also aware that her ability to read people leaned very much to the overtrusting side. Until she had proof, she'd leave that decision to the others, and so far Ivy's gun never wavered. Kayla swung her thoughts back to the issue at hand. "Do you think he destroyed the machine?"

Standish nodded at her. As best she could tell, the look was sincere. "After the funeral, I looked around. I found parts—gears, a chain, something I didn't recognize—in the carriage house, but no machine."

"You said he made it work?"

Another nod. "I saw it. But he hadn't figured out how to hook in into the electrical system. The machine kept slowing and eventually stopping when he tried. The sixty-cycle problem plagued him." Looking around the table, Standish acknowledged the rest of them, but kept the conversation on Kayla. "I didn't know what he meant at the time. I didn't pay enough attention; he was the engineer with the big idea and I was the businessman. But after he died and I realized it was a goldmine, I figured I needed to learn."

"I solved the 60 Hertz problem." Kayla volunteered. She'd been thinking that, but had no idea it would pop out of her mouth, true or not. "There was a constant—never mind."

Too late. Standish smiled. "I know. I watched you."

Kayla shuddered. This was going to get ugly; he was going to explain how he'd kidnapped her and why—though she had a pretty good idea of that already. But just then the waitress came back and the way the chatter suddenly stalled was a good indicator that they were talking about something they didn't want overheard, which was stupid in a local, open café like Stiltson's. But once the next round of coffee had been poured and they looked like any family nursing their beverages and clinging to a table for a while to talk, the conversation started up again.

Kayla opened with an accusation. "It's illegal to bug someone's private property."

He frowned, clearly not feeling her wrath. "I didn't . . . listening devices?"

Duh. Unable to think of the proper words, she just raised her eyebrows.

"They were all over the place." Evan leaned closer to the old man, reminding him that Evan was younger and stronger. That he could rip Standish apart for his role in their problems.

"No. I just sent a few guys with cameras to document your progress. It's your machine."

Evan, storms in his eyes, nearly growled the next words. "That's still invasive." There was a subtle beat, a pause in his own internal conversation that showed in his glare. "And how do we know that you didn't ask for anything more than cameras? You had my sister photographed. You sent people onto our property, which is trespassing. And you had my sister kidnapped!"

His voice had risen steadily throughout the clenched-teeth tirade, and Kayla was waving her hand at him across the table. The waitress stopped abruptly a few feet away and would have spilled her round carafe of coffee had she not already dosed half of it out to other customers. The two men at the table behind Evan and Mr. Standish frowned, looking over their shoulders at the odd group.

Kayla smiled at the waitress and motioned for some coffee that she wasn't going to drink. She also pulled Ivy's cup closer and had that refilled as well, since Ivy's hands were busy holding a gun that was likely getting heavy. Ivy had suffered the most in all this, and it wasn't even her plantation, her family memories or her money involved. Kayla leaned against Ivy in a show of solidarity as she smiled and thanked the waitress. She wasn't sure if she got all that right, but the waitress turned and went to the next table. So she pushed another smile to her face and said to the table at large. "I believe it is time to move this conference to another venue."

Reenie, stuck in the fifth seat pulled up at the edge of the booth, tucked her chair in yet again for a customer passing to the back of the small restaurant and sighed. "The plantation?"

Shaking her head, Kayla struck that one down. "Being here, and . . . coercing Mr. Standish is one thing. Moving him to our property would break Georgia and federal laws."

Standish spoke again. "We can go there. I'm certainly not going to press charges."

"You'll understand if your credibility is not at an all-time high." Evan raised an eyebrow as he grabbed Standish by the arm and pulled him out of the booth. "We passed a park on the way in."

This time it was Reenie who objected. "There are kids there. And we have to pay the bill." She patted herself down. "No money."

There was a brief flurry as Standish offered to pay, Kayla refused him, and Evan gave Kayla cash so that he and Ivy could flank the old man out the door. It would have been funny if she hadn't been stuck away from home. She wanted to go curl up in her bed, next to Ivy, not talk to the old man about what he had and hadn't orchestrated. But they couldn't just chain Standish in the basement while they napped. They didn't have a basement.

They pressed into Evan's sedan, which hadn't looked so old until she'd ridden in the Mercedes Standish drove. After a small amount of quiet arguing, which Kayla didn't think fooled anyone from the looks they were getting, Reenie slid into the driver's seat. Ivy released the gun and the jacket to Evan, who only managed to look ever so slightly less like he was concealing a gun. Then she fell, nearly bonelessly into the front passenger spot. The consistent rolling of her shoulder was the only clue that she'd been tense.

Reenie was just backing out of the spot when Kayla yelled, "Wait!" and before the car even came to a full stop, she had thrown open the door and was dashing for the Mercedes. Only as she turned to demand the keys did she realize that she'd left Standish unprotected, unblocked, leaving an open space for him to make a break for it.

But he hadn't even scooted over just a little to keep from being pressed into Evan. Sure, her brother had a gun on the older man, but he seemed almost . . . glad, glad to be squished into the back of a car he probably wouldn't normally be caught dead in. He smiled, held his hands up in the old magician's nothing-up-my-sleeve gesture, and then only after a nod from Evan did he reach into his pocket and produce the keys.

In a moment, Kayla was back in, the fabric-wrapped bundle sprung from the trunk and cradled in her arms. Her baby, back with her at last.

Evan's curious "What's that?" made her smile, and for a moment she was shocked by the matching grin on Standish's face.

"It's the original Whitney diagram. We found it at the house where we were . . . kept."

"What?!" Evan glared at Standish. "You were involved in that?"

"I'll explain."

But Reenie held off all conversation until she located an empty grocery store lot. She pulled into the farthest spot and locked the doors before twisting around and glaring at Standish.

"You kidnapped my almost sister and my friend. So tell me how you are going to *explain* this."

For just a moment, Kayla saw a flash of pit bull on Reenie's face and it made her proud.

The old man took in a deep breath and braced his weathered hands on his knees. "My men did kidnap them but not at my bequest. I only asked for simple, visual reconnaissance."

He pointed to the rolled oilcloth that Kayla was lovingly unwrapping as he spoke. "I've been missing that for several weeks, so I knew something was wrong. But I didn't know how wrong until they stopped reporting in together like they were supposed to. For the past several days one was always absent." Reenie looked like she wanted to interrupt, but Standish didn't let her. He just kept going. "I figured out pretty quickly that Ivy had gone missing at the same time my men started acting odd. Putting two and two together, I got on the case. Hired a P.I. and about 3 a.m. this morning I got the info about the house where they were trading shifts. I hurried right over, gun in hand, hoping the girls were there. They were coming out the walk in their stocking feet as I walked up."

"What?" Evan looked at her pointedly. His vocabulary was severely lacking this morning. Then again, he may not have slept well in about five days, so Kayla excused his inability to put the pieces together.

"Yup. Ivy convinced them that I was autistic, so I got catered to. Well, as much as a kidnap victim can be. I basically dicked around and threw the occasional temper tantrum until we gathered what we needed to escape."

Still slumped into her seat and looking like she was ready to sleep through the whole explanation, Ivy unexpectedly rolled her head back. She really only turned around enough to look at Reenie. "Kayla was amazing. We electrocuted our watcher with a fork and a bottle of water." When she registered the shocked look on the other woman's face, she waved her hand. "He's fine, though probably still vibrating a little bit. He's tied to a pipe in the basement. Shit!" She sat up straight and fully turned, staring at Kayla. "It's after eight. They've had shift change. If number two found him, they could be out looking for us." Ivy's eyes darted between them all. "We have to get back to Hazelton House before they do."

Evan shook his head. "What about Standish? We can't take him to our home."

"Wait." Kayla held up her hand. Looking the old man in the eye, she asked, "If you took this from us, how did you do it?"

"I waited twenty years. I visited Edwin's widow periodically, asking her if she'd come across anything new on the property, remembered anything significant he might have said, maybe found the diagram. She never did. So when the house sold, I watched you all. I kept my eyes on the preservation shop and the Historical Register. The shop employee panned out. The guy I bribed at the Register yielded nothing."

Kayla let him keep going, because so far he matched up. He had details he shouldn't have known unless he was the one to do it.

"When the diagram showed up for preservation, my guy took the original and created the fake as per my instructions."

Kayla nodded, then tapped Reenie on the shoulder. "We can go back to the house."

Even as Evan looked back and forth, Reenie started the car and pulled out of the parking lot. Ironically, it was now Reenie who had more faith in her than her brother.

That came as a huge shock, as did Ivy's tired smile over her shoulder as they exited. It was Ivy who said, "Go back to the café, Reenie? So Mr. Standish can get his car. He'll follow us to Hazelton House."

Although Ivy couldn't see it, Standish nodded. And Evan just looked more perplexed.

Kayla filled them all in on what the old man knew and she'd

figured out. "Standish watched us, wanted to see the progress on the machine. But he didn't bug the place nor have Ivy and me kidnapped. He's been helping us."

Resigned, Evan dropped the gun from its propped position and finally turned off the safety. He, too, seemed tired of holding it, and Kayla realized he'd been carefully aiming it to hit only Mr. Standish should the need to pull the trigger arise. There were too many collateral targets in the car for Evan to have relaxed even an inch.

Reaching out, Kayla took his hand and squeezed it. He'd been having a really bad week. He looked frayed and battered, which was unusual for Evan. With all he'd dealt with in his life, he kept it remarkably together. So she gave him something good. Something in addition to her and Ivy being safe and home and finally wearing shoes.

"He put the extra lines in the fake diagram. He gave us the answer."

25

H azelton House

EVAN HAD his doubts about Standish. There were too many possible ulterior motives in returning the fake diagram with hints about how to make the Whitney Device work.

Though Kayla seemed to think it was proof of his loyalty to the machine and thus to them, Evan thought the old man might not have any thoughts beyond filing a primary patent under his own name. He certainly had the money to be first to the drawing board. And they most certainly did not.

Still Kayla pointed out more that *did* seem to indicate Standish was on their side, but Evan's trust had been completely broken, one piece at a time. The death of his trust should have come earlier, faster, but he'd fought it. Evan had been late to the game, only really starting to question their safety after Georgia Power employee Tom Collins was found in a ditch after being beaten, Evan nearly the last to see him alive.

So his sister's insistence that none of the bad things they'd endured, including her own kidnapping, were the fault of the man who had climbed in his nice Mercedes and followed them to their home, didn't quite convince Evan. Didn't move him to invest in the same man she'd opened all the doors to and welcomed wholeheartedly. She pointed out that Standish wouldn't have mentioned patenting the machine if he was trying to beat them to it. Standish was offering to cover the costs.

Kayla thanked him, then helped Reenie set up a spare bedroom in the main house. Evan then had Reenie help him set up yet another room for the two of them—a room situated between his naïve sister and the old man who, thankfully, couldn't move too fast and easily let Evan search him. Though he'd found nothing, neither had he found anything to trust.

The worst part was that Standish did nothing to violate Kayla's trust. Had he done that, the decision could be made, the man could be forced out, and they could once again close their doors to the outside world that kept trying to burrow past their meager defenses.

Instead Kayla and Ivy had gone to sleep, closing and locking the door to their bedroom. He'd heard not a single peep from them and guessed that they were just happy to be home. They were probably sleeping off a twenty-four-hour tension bender. As they told it, they'd spent yesterday as "normal" kidnappees, then laid awake most of the night waiting for the right moment. After that they'd escaped, captured Reginald Standish as it were, and then spent a long morning at the diner. They'd simply crashed.

Reenie declared the so-called bed—a pile of quilts and bedding the two of them would now be sleeping on—was calling to her and crashed upon it. Standish had taken that hint and declared that he, too, would go to sleep. Evan wanted to doubt him, and probably had looked at him oddly or suspiciously, because by the time he walked back down the hall, the old man's shoes, jacket and cell phone were sitting right outside the door to his room.

There could be no clearer "I want you to trust me" message than that. And while Evan wanted to trust him, he couldn't. Just like he couldn't go to sleep. He sat on the hard wood floor in the hallway, propped in an unused doorway and trying to nod off, easily jerking awake at the tiniest noise. Afraid that someone strange had slunk in, Evan would snap upright and check all the doors. Sometimes he walked slowly up and down the hallway, reluctant to make a creak, but wanting to check just the same.

So mostly he sat and watched the dust play in the afternoon sun filtering through the big windows in the room at the end of the hall. He considered scrapping everything. Was the business really worth this? Was Reenie's family home worth his family? He had no clue when he came here that things would get this ugly, that the family he was trying to build would be put in jeopardy, and that trying to dovetail those two families together would be so difficult.

With a deep sigh, he contemplated actually trying to sleep, but the sigh brought a strong odor with it. Frowning, Evan went downstairs, following the acrid smell. Just as his feet hit the bottom floor he swore once, loudly. Then again. If that didn't wake people, this would: at the top of his lungs, he yelled, "FIRE!!" breathed deep and yelled it again.

Then, pulling the gun from the waistband of his jeans, he raced out the back door. Two figures were disappearing over the hill down to the barn. With the sun in his eyes, he could only make out their silhouettes. But he ran, crested the same hill, and came to a stop.

Planting his feet and sighting the best he could over his heaving lungs, he began pulling the trigger.

∾

KAYLA JOLTED upright at the same time Ivy did. Unable to say what had wakened her, she only knew that it was something powerful. She'd have doubted herself had Ivy not bolted from her own sleep even as Kayla came awake.

Evan's voice tore through her confusion. "FIRE!"

She smelled the truth in Evan's yell, watched as Ivy followed some invisible guide to the door to the room.

Still fully clothed, both of them came completely alert as they skidded into the hallway and nearly ran into Reenie and Reginald Standish, both also sliding out their doorways in their socks. In seconds, they were down the staircase, Kayla grabbing at the older man's arm as he slipped a step and struggled to stay upright. But no words were exchanged, and the four of them were working in tandem even before they all hit the ground level.

"Flour!" Reenie yelled and Ivy ran out the already open back door, shooting to the Overseer's to raid the kitchen. Kayla and Reenie went in different directions, each returning with a fire extinguisher. They'd been required to maintain a certain number in order to open the museum. Though the canister was heavy in her arms, now Kayla was glad they had to have them on hand, and that they'd been obligated to run drills. She'd also learned that the aged hardwood of the house was going to be slow to burn.

As she came sliding into the front room, she saw Standish heading out the front left window where he'd raised the sash and pushed the screen through to the porch. Far too spry for a man of his apparent age, he climbed out just as Kayla heard a series of gunshots.

For a second, she froze, then she registered all the information. Though the shots reverberated through the old house, they came from the northern field. Ivy was heading toward the south, and staying closer. The shots had come a greater distance than Ivy could have traveled. But –

"Evan!" The canister Reenie held slipped several inches before she re-gripped it, her heart catching in her throat the same as Kayla's.

It was Kayla, unable to reach out to her friend, pulling the pin on the canister she held, who comforted Reenie they only way she could. She spoke from belief. "It's Evan shooting. Not the other way around. He'll be back in a moment." Then she aimed the nozzle with her left hand, holding the clamped trigger and supporting the hefty mass of the extinguisher with her right, and started killing the thick orange flames that snuck through the leaks in the doorway.

Reenie, pulling her own pin, started through the window, heading to the front where the flames were heavier. But Standish stopped her. Reaching through for the extinguisher, he told her "go" and Reenie instantly capitulated, bolting out the back and pulling her own twenty-two from the waist of her jeans as she disappeared over the porch, her sock-clad feet eating the distance.

The deep and continuous swoooosssshhhhh of the second spray canister assaulted Kayla's ears through the thick old wood of the front door. Kayla hit the small flames that tried to escape into the house, to get away from the heavy assault coming at them from the front, and took in all the details. For all the smoke that was made, the wood had burned very little. Evan would want to repair it rather than replace it. There were places where the formerly straight lines had been hollowed away but not many.

For the first time Kayla feared leaving. This was her home, and suddenly she had changed; she was no longer just helping until Reenie and Evan were ready to run the place on their own or just getting lost in building the Whitney Device. This was *hers* and she was going to defend it, with her fire extinguisher, with her brains, and with her gun again if necessary.

"You can open the door!" Reginald Standish called from the

other side. So she wrapped her hand inside her shirt and quickly grabbed at the knob, twisting and yanking it before it could burn her through the fabric.

There stood the old man, sooty from head to toe, his only set of clothing—his nice suit—ruined. But he smiled. "It isn't too bad. Come out here and we'll soak it down to make sure there are no stray embers."

Behind him, Ivy sprinkled flour and stomped on it as though she were performing some odd wiccan ritual. Kayla wouldn't have put that past her friend, but she didn't need to look twice to see that Ivy was covering and stomping out stray sparks. Though the door and porch hadn't suffered much, leaving a stray ember could light them up again later in the night. Ivy was already pulling her phone out and asking Kayla if she should call the fire department. "We want this checked by professionals."

But Kayla couldn't say yes, not until . . . there they were: Reenie and Evan, arms around each other's waists, guns hanging limply at their sides. A sharp head-to-toe check left Kayla relatively sure they were both undamaged. So she moved to the next order of business. "Can we call the fire department to come check the damage?"

Clearly weary to his bones, Evan checked the door frame, the flooring on the porch and the surrounding areas, his heart clearly hurting. There were times when Kayla thought he knew the vagaries of the world, that he had a grasp on the machinations of man that generated war, but he couldn't understand that people might harm homes and furniture. With his own hands, he generated pieces that would survive long beyond his own mortality. For the first time Kayla saw the house as he did: an enduring testament to time gone by, to a once-glorious history, to craftsmanship almost unparalleled in the age of technology. And her heart hurt for him.

She shifted focus, inviting them all out onto the porch so she and Standish could spray the last of the foam inward and around the frame. "The question is, if we call the authorities will we need to be concerned about anything other than a fire?"

"Nope." He shook his head.

Nodding, Ivy stepped away and dialed as Kayla shot the extinguisher and yelled over the resultant noise, "So you missed?"

EVAN GRINNED. "NOPE."

He hadn't laid anyone out cold, but he'd seen one of them stumble and fall, then watched as the other man stooped to pick him up. The first man, leaning heavily on the second, still moved well enough. Evan didn't foresee a murder charge, but then again, there was a body buried under the floorboards of the third to last slave cabin. He explained, "I clipped one. If someone goes combing through the grass, they'll find blood, but otherwise, no worries."

They called, waited, and took care of a few details. Kayla laid her socks over the railing to dry. The empty canisters were set aside, left out to show the firefighters. Evan went out back to comb the grass and found all but one of the shells his gun had ejected. And after washing his hands thoroughly and changing his clothes in an attempt to get rid of any lingering cordite smell, he made his way from the Overseer's back to the front of the house.

Unworried about the timing—the local fire department was not only volunteer, it was distant—Evan made sure everyone had the same story. Everyone agreed, realizing his version allowed for arson, but didn't point out the gunshots and subsequent wounding of one of the offenders.

Standish was the only uncertain link. Kayla eyed him sideways as Ivy leaned over from her seat on the bottom step and fidgeted by pulling and peeling some grass.

"I'm in. No worries," the older man said calmly. He clearly picked up on the unease. "Call me Reggie, my friends do."

Just as Evan was wondering who this man's friends might be, Reginald—Reggie now—continued. "We need to explain my presence. The real story won't do anyone any favors."

Evan nodded. "Stick close to the truth, that helps. So you're an old friend of Reenie's grandfather, you showed up last night, and stayed over when it got late." Evan looked from face to face, hoping the story was close enough to real that Kayla could speak it without stumbling. They each nodded back at him, some more blankly than others. Between them, Evan was willing to bet they had maybe the equivalent of one person's good night's sleep. "We're all tired because we stayed up talking with our new friend Reggie here."

Again, the nodding appeared contagious, moving from one head to another though no one spoke.

"I'm going to head out and buy more fire extinguishers. The fire's out, it wasn't big and we don't necessarily think it was arson. I'll get back while the firefighters are still here, I think. I'll let you all decide if you think they should wait and speak to me or not."

"Y'all," Reenie corrected him absently, but she nodded again, looking like she was going to fall asleep while waiting for the firemen.

Evan headed for the car and took off down the driveway. He was as tired as the rest of them, but unlike the others he had to do something. Beneath his palms the steering wheel felt more solid than the rest of his reality. And the decisions he'd been making were coming home to roost.

He'd just left all three women with only an old man. Though they had guns, they weren't nearby since the fire department was on its way. And though he didn't think Reggie Standish himself posted a threat, Evan was unsure just what resources the man had at his disposal and was just as uncertain about his motive. Kayla took Standish at her own combination of face value and cold logic. Her gut instinct was always to trust, so she relied on facts more than anything. Because of that, she was often right in her decisions, usually the first to see when something was wrong with someone, not because she felt it, but because the person was statistically acting out of character. Right now the numbers made Kayla trust Standish. Evan wasn't quite there yet.

Evan didn't like leaving them alone, but they needed new extinguishers. If they didn't have them by nightfall, there was a good chance one of the arsonists could turn up after dark and—with no way for the occupants to fight the new fire—laugh while it burned.

The other side, whoever they were, had escalated. So Evan was out buying a shitload of extinguishers, leaving the house relatively uncovered. The fire department was none too fast. A quick check of his watch showed him it had been twenty minutes since Ivy's call and he hadn't yet passed the trucks on the road.

Since the whole story wouldn't come out, the firefighters wouldn't stay on standby, and that meant the occupants of Hazelton House would have to fight whatever came their way by themselves.

The old asphalt passed in rhythm beneath the equally old tires on his car. There was no good decision here. Stay and protect now or run to the store and protect against the future. Both threats were subtle and uncertain. Evan had chosen action.

Just then, he heard the sirens in the distance and a moment later two big trucks came into view. The sirens were overkill, the fire already out. At this point the plantation just needed a good inspection. But the drivers weren't rushing too fast, not pushing the other cars out of the way.

Evan watched them pass, clinging to his belief that he was doing the right thing.

Behind the fire trucks several cars had packed in, following the cleared path, staying out of the way.

He wouldn't have noticed, except the third car back was a shiny silver sedan. Nicer than the old beater cars and trucks folks around here kept. It stuck out, but the issue was the two men inside, both polished, both wearing gray suits. Both turned to look at him as they passed, as though they recognized him.

26

H azelton House

KAYLA MIGHT NOT HAVE BEEN there had Evan not called her cell moments before the trucks rounded the corner and told her to look out. She immediately noticed the silver sedan and saw that it was out of place around here.

The two men in suits in a single car were definitely out of the norm. Though some around here did have "suit jobs" as Kayla had always called them, this was not an area where people carpooled. Certainly not in the early afternoon on a Tuesday.

Thanks to Evan's warning, she had run down to the edge of the property, waving the fire trucks up the driveway as though she were a distraught homeowner.

Directing the trucks into the long drive, she subtly turned and took note of the passing traffic.

The two suits got a good look at her, her soot- and foam-soaked clothes, her bare feet, her likely filthy face. But they probably already knew what she looked like. Only now she knew what each of them looked like, too. And in her mind she had a catalog of their features to share with the others. She would sketch them, something she could do reasonably well.

Kayla trudged back up the long drive, far behind the two blaring red trucks, a smile on her face.

Once they assessed that the fire was completely out and there were no stray, burning embers about, the firefighters took notes, called the sheriff's department, and soaked down the surrounding wood—just in case. The fire chief had come to investigate. Apparently, just the location of the fire was indicative of arson, and he had a deputy take notes as Kayla told what she knew. One bulky-clad firefighter flirted with Ivy, telling her what a good job she'd done stamping out the stray sparks with flour. He basically suggested she'd saved the whole plantation, and he'd done it with a goofy grin on his face. Kayla's focus was pulled from her interview by the unfamiliar knotting sensation in her stomach. At least Ivy had a smile on her face, showing she understood what fell from the handsome man's lips was utter bullshit.

The officer droned on, asking questions that didn't need answers. So Kayla responded with short phrases and shrugs that offered nothing of value. Sure, it could be arson. No, she didn't know anyone who would want to burn her house. Yes, she'd been asleep when the fire started. Of course, he could wait for her brother who would be back any moment.

The sheriff's deputy didn't think it at all odd that Evan had left to buy more fire extinguishers. Kayla told the man how Evan had run out the back door, thinking he'd seen someone, but that he hadn't. The officer didn't seem to think there was much he could do in the situation, so he confirmed that belief by doing relatively little.

With her help, he traced Evan's steps out the back door. She walked him up to where they could see over the small rise, deliberately planting her foot over a 9mm casing she spotted in the grass. It hadn't been visible until she'd been nearly on top of it, but she mentally marked the position so she could come back for it later. "My brother said he thought whoever it was went over the hill, but when he could see—my guess is from right about here—there was no one."

"Hmmmp." Another sound of disinterest, but the man made a few notes on a cheap touch pad, searching for the location of several letters while Kayla tried desperately not to point out that a qwerty keyboard was universal and he should know where all the letters were by now. But he managed to get his few thoughts down and make a useless commentary. "If there was someone who went that way, I don't know how we'd track them."

Kayla was tempted to point out several ways that one could, in fact, track people, or at least make an effort. But that wasn't in her own best interests, so she made a noncommittal noise of her own.

"Do you know where those woods go?"

She honestly didn't and made a mental note to learn it. "No. Other properties probably. Our border is just into the trees. But I don't know if what's back there is privately owned or industrial or even government park properties."

He raised his eyebrows once then started back to the house, leaving her to follow, to take her foot off the shell and trail behind him. At least he wouldn't see it, not that this man would get suspicious if he did. If she told him they'd been taking target practice at the broad side of the barn, he'd probably nod and say, "Hmm" and ask if they could hit it from here.

As they came around the front of the house, Evan arrived with six large red fire extinguishers in the backseat. Kayla wondered what the bugs were picking up. She wondered if that guy was still bound in the basement at that stupid house. She wondered if Reggie was going to go back and check on the kidnappers, or if he'd called someone or if he even still trusted the someone he might call. After all Number One and Number Two had failed him.

Pushing her mind back to the present, she saw that the fire inspector was asking Evan questions, but he repeated much the same story she'd already told. No one seemed to smell the cordite or the lies.

In the end, the fire inspector stood at the front steps and scratched his balding head. "Looks like someone threw an ID—incendiary device—onto your front porch." He pointed around the burn marks. "This is gasoline or the like. But it looks like a prank rather than a real attempt to destroy the house." He scratched his head again.

As Kayla watched, Evan's anger bloomed. "He sealed our front door shut with fire. That's not just a prank!" The muscles in his jaw clicked. That was a bad sign.

"Yeah, well. He didn't douse the house, didn't seal the windows or even the back door—"

Evan cut him off, righteous anger probably ruining his ability to censor himself. "Oh, so that makes it okay?"

Kayla stepped in front of him, nearly running into Reenie in the process. Apparently, she wasn't the only one who thought Evan needed to shut his trap before he spilled all the beans and went to jail for shooting someone. Her brain scrambled ahead along the trail it was on.

"Ev." She kept her voice soft, the sound echoed in Reenie's own warning. But the fire inspector was talking again.

"Look, Sir, I'm sorry. I know you want something stronger than that. And I know there's nothing right in this. But it's arson, not attempted murder."

With Kayla's and Reenie's hands flat against his shoulders as though they could actually hold him back, Evan nodded.

And like that, the encounter was over. They were told that there were businesses that did fire cleanup but the firefighters legally weren't allowed to make any recommendations. Even then they admitted that they didn't know anyone who specialized in fire damage to historic homes.

In a surprisingly short period of time, the hoses were rolled up and the trucks had trundled down the driveway.

Dark was falling on them, and Kayla wondered what was out there, watching them, listening in.

They checked the front door. Though the bolt turned and caught, there were several gaps where the fire had eaten down the wood. Drafts wouldn't be a problem for a while given the season, but they safety dictated some action.

Evan and Reenie trudged down to the barn for a piece of plywood. Their intent to board up from the inside in order to do as little damage as possible and yet leave the outside of the house looking as intact as possible. Almost an F-you to the guys who had burned it. Though there were no faces or names for their attackers, Kayla knew who they were.

Dinner was late, a solemn affair of macaroni and cheese with veggies on the side. They had made it for her, Kayla knew. Everyone was trying to keep her as close to routine as possible, trying to keep her from freaking out and melting down.

She wanted to tell them she wasn't that fragile, that she felt great and the changes to her routine were offset by a wild excitement that came from not knowing how each day was going to turn out, from knowing that she was doing well. She had escaped being kidnapped, found a new ally, gotten arsoned and put out the fire before any real damage had happened. She actually felt secure in their insecurity and desperately wanted to convince them all of that.

But they wouldn't believe her. She'd flipped her lid a little less than a month ago and Evan had needed to talk her back to the world of the sane. She couldn't blame them for not believing her, so she ate her macaroni then trailed everyone back to the big house to get ready for bed for the second time that day. At least it was dark.

Reggie answered his phone with, "Come around the back." And he started walking that way.

Just as he opened the door to a man in a suit and tie coming up the back steps, Kayla saw the man utter "Shit." And step down. He looked up at all of them standing in the doorway. "Crap."

As greetings went, it wasn't the best. But Kayla liked it. "That step is weak."

He smiled at her, even as Ivy's arm tightened around her waist. His grin was lopsided. "I think it's actually broken now."

Looking, Kayla couldn't see the damage, but she believed him.

"Who is this?" Evan's harsh voice came over her shoulder just a moment before his arm did. He pushed her out of the way, gently, but a push nonetheless.

Reggie softly moved, forcing Evan to step back and exhibit at least the movements of a politeness he didn't feel. The older man gestured the other closer but didn't let the man any farther than the back door. "This is Marcus, my IP lawyer. . . . Is it all right if we all have a discussion? Maybe find a table and chairs?"

Evan was still leaning forward, blocking the way, his face near Reggie's. "You don't let people into my house. You don't have that right."

Reggie nodded only once, not as tall as Evan, but not cowed by his height, his strength, or his anger. "I didn't want the bugs to pick up anything. Not even that we have a lawyer at the house. It's your decision."

Kayla's mind swirled with possibilities that were better off answered. "What's the lawyer here for?"

Evan looked stern. Ivy and Reenie looked curious. Kayla figured she knew where this was headed but she wanted to hear it from Reggie himself.

Another short nod was all that preceded his voice. "I didn't move fast enough to protect Edwin. And while I'm not stupid enough to think that some papers on file will stop any of these people, I do believe that if we can take away their gains, then we can help slow it down. And maybe they'll stop on their own."

"How do we do that?" Kayla asked before Evan could. Evan would be snide, operating from his current anger. And he had every right to it. Kayla knew how that felt, and she knew that righteousness made it that much harder to let go. So did helplessness. Evan had suffered from both this past week and opening his home to a lawyer brought in by the man he still wasn't convinced had nothing to do with his sister's kidnapping was stretching him pretty thin.

Reggie did the smart thing and acknowledged them both. "We incorporate and we file for a patent."

"You don't get her patent." Evan was already a dog in the fight.

Reggie, genteel as ever, clasped his hands behind his back, rocked slightly on his heels, and nodded. "I don't want the patent. I don't even need to be part of the company. But I'm going to fund it if you'll let me, and I'm going to make you big enough that you're harder to hurt. That was always my intent from the beginning."

"Bullshit."

"Evan!" Kayla blurted it and was surprised to again find herself in accord with Reenie, who was wrapping her arms around brother-dear and pulling him back.

Evan shook his girlfriend off. "Look, if that's what he wanted in the beginning, why didn't he just show up on our doorstep and ask? Why the photos and the sneaking around? He's in with the people who bugged the place and took Kayla and Ivy—" here he stopped and looked pointedly at the two women, as though they needed a reminder—"and *now* he wants to write up a contract?"

Another nod from the distinguished older gentleman.

Kayla had to admire him. He only ever admitted that Evan was right, that his points were valid, then calmly made his own. The fact that he'd done the same this morning with a gun trained on him for more than an hour only solidified her belief that at least *he* believed what he was saying. *He* believed that Marcus Winters, appointed lawyer, was here to help.

"I had to check you all out. I didn't know if you were going to even get the thing to work, or what your intentions were for it. For all I knew, you were going to sell to Big Oil the moment you had a chance."

Reenie looked back and forth, the idea of restraining Evan all but gone from her thoughts. "Is that even an option?"

Reggie nodded. "Absolutely. All you have to do is let them know you're interested. They'll tie you up 'til kingdom come. Kayla will never patent anything again, and they'll own this patent and all the rights associated with it. But they'd rather pay you than kill you."

Reenie seemed to consider that, so Kayla stepped in. "But in the meantime we watch them jack up prices while we know there's a better way. We watch them get rich off our enterprise and we do what?"

Reggie shrugged. "I guess run the plantation. But they may take that from you, too. At the least they'll want the Whitney history out of here so no one ever makes the connection."

Reenie frowned. "Why would they care about the plantation?"

"They won't want anything about the existence of the device getting out. You'll likely have gag orders that you'll agree to as part of the settlement. Your relatives knew Whitney. The plantation leads to Whitney, Whitney leads to the device. And the device is already embedded in urban legend—"

"What?" This from Evan, but he was the only one who was surprised.

"Haven't you heard that Whitney made a 'free energy machine,' and that he hid the designs?"

It was Winters who nodded. Kayla hadn't, but she didn't get

time to ponder that as Winters nearly spat out, "Is that what we have here?"

No one answered him.

He looked from face to face, each as impassive as the next, and when everyone remained studiously blank, he grinned monkey-wide. "Holy crap."

That went well, Kayla thought. By not answering, they'd all answered him. But her thoughts were interrupted by Marcus Winters, setting down the briefcase he'd been quietly holding and popping it open. He pulled out a tablet and with a swipe of his finger he opened some program. But then he stopped, wiped his face, and put the device back. He grabbed a notepad and pen. He held them up. "This is unhackable and never connects to the Internet. How many patents can we file for this thing? We need to patent the shit out of it and build a company to protect it right away."

When no one spoke, Winters did again. "You have to sell to Big Oil or patent, or you're all going to be dead soon."

27

T
he Main House

"I'M SORRY." Evan watched as Reenie, ever polite, questioned Marcus Winter. "Did you just threaten us?"

"No, ma'am." He still stood there in the rear parlor, pen and paper in hand, ready for any notes they might give him. "I'm only stating the facts as I know them."

Reenie squinted at him, and Evan considered pulling her back, but then again she was asking all the same things he would. Reenie's eyes hardened. "And how do you come by these facts?"

"If you have a computer handy you can look up Carlos Tuanama." He spelled it for them as Reenie pulled her phone from her back pocket, indicating that yes, she did have a computer handy.

Watching Winter's face for any signs that she'd thwarted him, Evan was hard-pressed to see anything but grim reality.

"Tuanama owned a large section of oil-rich land in the Andes. Tell me about his daughter."

Reenie waited a minute then spoke softly. "She went missing six years ago, was ransomed, then a month later her body was found."

"That's his oldest daughter. Tell us about his wife." Marcus Winter's voice was soft, and Evan read that as meaning he didn't like talking about this. Or maybe Winter was a solid actor and he just wanted them to think that.

Reenie sighed and spoke again, even though Kayla and Ivy were now hanging over her shoulder reading off the small screen with her. "Same."

"You can look it all up. But the same thing happened to each of his family members, one by one. Then Carlos himself disappeared." He pointed at the phone as though they should double-check that, too. Evan preferred analyzing the lawyer for tics, signs, tells. But he couldn't find anything he could use.

"The thing is,"

Evan's head jerked at the sound of Standish's voice joining in. "Carlos wasn't ransomed; he wised up and went underground. He somehow got his hands on evidence linking the hitmen to one of the big players in International Oil, and he brought that man to court here in America. Where—after multiple threats and attempts on his life—Carlos disappeared again. This time, each of his surrounding neighbors was sent one of his body parts." Standish ducked his head and tucked his hands behind his back. His usual "delivering important information" stance, Evan noted. "At least, that's what we believe. Only a few of them reported it. But there are still many missing parts to be accounted for, and the neighbors all started selling quickly."

Standish looked pointedly at the lawyer. "Tell them."

Something passed his features. Clearly, he wouldn't voluntarily reveal what Standish was pushing for. "I know about this because I helped on Tuanama's case. I was junior lawyer." Winter's jaw clenched. "When Tuanama went missing, I took copies of the documents and posted them on the web—"

"I remember that!" Ivy was shocked and she looked to Evan, who offered a slight nod. He, too, remembered the leak of the documents, but had no evidence that the man standing in front of them was responsible.

Marcus's voice was full of regret this time, but aside from the pause, he didn't acknowledge their interruption of his story. "I was threatened. Slapped with so many lawsuits I could never unbury myself, though only some had actual merit. I received threats, and then . . . my mother died a concerning death, though I can't prove anything. I was living with her as her caretaker at the time, she was elderly, and I was the likely suspect. I was jailed and bail was set ridiculously high."

"What?" Ivy again. But Evan knew what was coming.

"I was cleanly framed. I have no idea if the lawyers took advantage of my mother suffering a natural death or if they actually killed her. The DA decided to make an example of me, and they tied me up for months. When I got out, I ran. I tried my luck with Standish here, thinking he'd either send me back or help me out. He'd helped Carlos. . . . and here I am. You can look up the lawyers in the Tuanama case."

There was a silence for a moment, during which Reenie worked on her phone. She then held up the screen showing them all in tiny detail a clear picture of the legal team. Winter was there, listed under a different name, lighter hair, different cut. But it was him. Over the top of the phone, Reenie's eyes locked with Evan's. And he asked the question he thought had to be asked.

"So you're yet another person with a target on you and you're aiming that target at my house, as though we don't already have enough red laser dots on us?"

It was Kayla who answered for Winter. "They can't find him."

Evan asked, "And you know this how?"

"Because he's alive. If they could find him, he'd be gone. But he's here."

Reenie watched it all and didn't like it one bit. "Can we just scuttle the machine?"

This time she looked to Kayla; the machine was Kayla's project, patent, baby. But it wasn't worth their lives. Was it?

Kayla was shrugging. It was clear to everyone that she didn't want to abandon it. Her sense of worth was tied to the future she could see. And she could see well beyond this machine. She could probably calculate the percentage loss of their carbon footprint just in the time they'd run the three Whitney Devices here on the plantation. And she could surely see the impact of having the machines out there, running constantly.

That was the thing about Kayla and Charles and her other friends like her. To an Aspy, the end goal was everything. If it was growing a business then everything worked toward that singular focus. For Kayla, the goal was that tomorrow be better than today. It had been cars and safety mechanisms for a while. Then it had been conversions for motorcycles for clearer emissions. She'd always had to see a positive end in order to work.

The irony was that she didn't see the people right near her sometimes because she was too busy striving for her bigger goal. That they all might wind up in real trouble to bring the machine to light could just be chalked up as the cost of business.

It didn't matter. Marcus was shaking his head. "Scuttling the machine doesn't mean anything."

The four of them looked to him, but only Standish stood unconcerned. He already knew what was coming and Evan hated being in the group that was last to the fountain.

Marcus continued, although he did seem a bit contrite. "Whoever they are exactly, they know the machine is here. And they're well aware that at least one of you contains the knowledge to build it. I'd argue that their knowledge was imperfect, in that they took Ivy first and tried to get her to build it. But now they know for certain."

"How does Winter here—" Ivy started but let the protest fade off.

Standish put his hand up, as though holding the younger, probably stronger woman at bay. "I brought him entirely up to speed. He needs to know what he's dealing with in order to help."

Marcus barely acknowledged the blip in the conversation. "Once they realized Ivy couldn't build it, they went next to Kayla."

Kayla nodded.

Evan's heart pinched. But it pissed him off sometimes that she saw some things so much faster than others did yet couldn't seem to grasp when Reenie was being sincere. He tried not to show his irritation but failed. "What, Kay?"

Ivy frowned at him.

That was good. She understood that he was being pissy to his sister. And she didn't like it. She'd been on Kayla's side now for several months. Kayla needed that. And he hoped the other woman wouldn't burn out on it the way he sometimes did. He hoped she wouldn't wind up carrying the baggage of butting heads with those she loved, just because she defended someone they didn't understand.

Luckily, Kayla didn't pick up his ire at all and simply turned to explain. "They screwed up in taking Ivy . . . but they didn't screw up again. They beelined for me the second time. So whatever they didn't know before, they know now."

In his head, behind his heavy sigh and closed eyes, Evan swore a blue streak. They all might be in danger here, but Kayla was clearly going to be the main target. And if these guys had figured anything out about her, then they would have realized that the standard threats wouldn't move her. So there would be bad guys coming after them in new and odd ways and Kayla was likely already in someone's crosshairs.

He could have a nightmare and chances were good it would be a better option than this. After all these years of just him and Kayla standing up to the world, he couldn't lose her. And beyond that, she loved this machine. He couldn't ask her or even tell her to let it go. And he didn't want to. He might not have Kayla's end-goal drive, but he did know that if nothing changed, nothing would ever change.

His words came out as a beaten consent, rather than the battle cry they should have been. "Screw the high price of gas. How do we patent?"

Winters, finally, motioned toward the table.

Apparently, Evan had asked the triggering question, leading the other man to understand that he finally gained some ground or had been accepted and it was time to sit like civilized people.

Winters spoke while he arranged his papers. "Kayla is in the greatest danger. As the owner of the knowledge, that's who these people will come after first. If she owns the patent and the company, then after they dispatch her, they can then follow the beneficiaries right down the line until they find someone who can be manipulated." He looked at Kayla, and the grim nature of his stare turned Evan's stomach. "You're the inventor, so—"

"No, Whitney invented it. And Reenie's grandfather put further work into it, too. So, I worked on it, but I'm not the sole inventor."

Marcus wasn't swayed. "You're the only one alive who contributed to the design. You are the current owner of the intellectual property."

Lovely. That was a brilliant *thought.* Evan held back an actual groan.

They all looked to Kayla.

Kayla nodded. "So Whitney and Edwin Carroll and me?"

Marcus shook his head. "They're dead. Only you."

Evan felt his muscles freeze at the thought.

Ivy's voice cut through the haze he was seeing. "Well, that's sucky."

Leave it to an ex-stripper with a Ph.D. to use "sucky" to describe this situation.

But Kayla missed all the emotion running rampant around her, leaving Evan to field the innate fear that went with wondering if someone was right outside the door. With being concerned that there was now a bug inside the house, maybe in this room. He kicked himself for being so slow, but for the first time he thought maybe it wasn't a thing, but a person.

"I need your phone. And any recording devices you have." Evan blurted to Marcus.

The lawyer didn't even blink, just handed over one of each and said, "I'm kind of surprised it took you this long to ask. You can pat me down, I'm not wearing any weapons or doing any kind of recording." After a small pause, he sat back and kept going. "Kayla will hold the patent, but we need to create a corporate board to own it. Remember, everyone who owns the machine is at risk. So who's on the board?"

He looked at Kayla first, then one by one at the rest of them.

Evan raised his hand, volunteering himself. Kayla nodded. "Reenie, too. If you want. Your grandfather is part of the design team, you should at least get some credit or royalties or something."

"No." Evan put his foot down. He couldn't keep Kayla off the list but he didn't have to have Reenie on it, too.

"I'm in." Reenie's voice was soft, but sure. She didn't stiffen, she didn't get angry; she simply gave him a sad smile. And that killed him more than anything.

Evan's eyes sank closed.

He'd never been able to save anyone he loved.

His parents had died. They were two folks who loved a good party and lived in a world of social networking back when that meant appetizers and martinis with friends. His father's blood alcohol had been just over the legal limit the night they put the car into that tree.

He hadn't been able to stop the school kids from bullying his very intelligent sister. Though he'd put a damper on it for a while, he'd graduated and hadn't been able to do much other than tell a few younger friends to watch out for her. But while they'd done a passable job, Kayla had been exposed to small ridicules every day at school.

He hadn't been able to get his socialite mother to see the wonder in her daughter. She only saw a girl who hated dresses and parties and didn't have many friends. He had never been able to get his father to enjoy anything about her other than the fact that his only daughter could calculate baseball statistics fast enough to impress his friends.

He couldn't keep Reenie out of debt and clearly he couldn't keep her name off the corporate documents. And while his heart hurt, he realized he loved Reenie so much that some of it was eased. He nodded at her and let her squeeze his hand. Reenie loved him enough to take some of the weight. Even when the creator of all that stress could never change it, and in fact had created all these problems just by doing something amazing. He allowed the small amount of weight Reenie's gesture lifted from his conscience to disappear into the ether to never be borne again. He had enough to carry.

∼

KAYLA SMILED AT REENIE. Good for her. The machine was trouble right now, but the device was Reenie's family legacy and she deserved something for the contribution Edwin Carroll had made. It was the least the universe could do to make up for the fact that her grandfather had been taken away from her, likely murdered over this same device.

Kayla looked to Ivy and Reggie. "You, too, if you want."

Ivy looked a bit shocked. "I'm not family. I didn't invent it, I didn't build it."

Kayla pulled her friend's hand from where she was waving it, palm out, as though to ward off the patent-monster. "You don't have to be on if you don't want to. But you *did* help build it. You brought me food and made me get some sleep and drove me to Cleveland more than once. You made it possible for me to make the machine possible."

Ivy blinked rapidly, and it took Kayla a moment to realize the dark eyelashes were batting back forming tears. Kayla offered a sadder note, too. "You were kidnapped over it. You're part of it. Also that puts three different family names on the corporation. The further our reach, the stronger the patent."

Ivy smiled at her, the tears gone. But she looked to Evan and Reenie. "Y'all are family. You can vote and I won't be offended if you say no. But if you want me, and if my name adds strength to this sucker, put me on."

Kayla looked to Reenie and Evan. Their fingers were interlaced, Evan's tight on Reenie's more accepting ones. "Reggie, too."

Reenie nodded. But Evan reacted swiftly and fiercely. "No! He doesn't get to come in here with photographers or worse and walk out with a piece of this thing!"

Kayla shrugged. "He's already a part of it. He gave us Edwin Carroll's design, he made it possible. And most importantly, as soon as he goes home, they can't kill us all in one house."

That made Evan start to shake his head as though that would remove the nasty thoughts. He was mad at the situation, but there was nothing for him to hit. She wished she had a two-by-four and a sanding belt or a hand saw for him. Maybe he'd feel better after obliterating a board or something. But she didn't have that. "Marcus, too."

"What!?" Evan almost jumped out of his seat at her. He would have if Reenie hadn't held him back. As it was, he looked at Kayla like he was for the first time truly contemplating having her committed.

Reenie's face changed though. She was thinking, and she tugged at Evan's hand. "Kayla's right, honey. Even if we add both of them we would still have a controlling percentage." She looked to Marcus, "Right, we can do that?"

"I can add a document that deals with the sale or any alterations to the patent, so that it must be handled by the entire group and that power of attorney may not be signed away by any of the owners." He scratched something in a Sanskrit-looking scrawl on his legal pad. "I don't need or want to be on it."

"And that's exactly why I want you on it." Kayla looked him right in the eyes. "You'll be tied to both us and the device. You can't sell it, so you'll have to protect it."

28

T he Back Parlor, Hazelton House

"SHOULDN'T WE GO SOMEWHERE ELSE?" Ivy put her palms flat on the table and leaned forward. "If we're all targets, shouldn't we split up?"

Kayla rested her hand on her friend's arm, still surprised by the warmth she felt from that simple touch. "We can't do this over the phone or Internet; we know we've been hacked. We all have to be in one place, at least for a while. And this is the best place. There are so many doors and windows and egresses that we have the best chance of escape. And we have to protect the plantation, the devices."

"Can we at least get some big dogs?" Ivy set her forehead on the table as though the smell of burnt wood and the fumes that lingered from the extinguishers had done her in, worn her out.

Kayla perked up. Why hadn't they thought of that before? "That's a great idea!"

When Evan agreed, she knew the world had gone to hell.

He'd never permitted a pet; he had her. She was the thing he had to feed and check up on and take care of because it couldn't take care of itself. Not that that was completely true, but adding a dog—something else he'd be responsible for—had always been something he insisted would never happen. His easy acquiescence now showed how far down their world had spiraled.

Kayla saw Reenie slide her hand to his and squeeze. "Tomorrow morning? The shelter?" But she was looking at Kayla.

Kayla heart clutched tight in a moment of sharp happiness. Things were in the crapper, but she was finally getting a dog!

Evan sighed. "Get four."

Her mouth dropped open, as did Ivy's. Reenie smiled. Kayla's chest tightened again.

Marcus cleared his throat. "That's a good idea. Dogs are harder to circumvent than security systems."

Kayla noticed he didn't say "'impossible," but he was talking again, cleanly steering them back to the topic at hand.

"We'll need someone to draft the designs for the patent."

"I can do it." Kayla perked up again.

He smiled at her, softly with some sorrow in it. "It's for patent and corporate designs. We'll have to find another—trustworthy—professional to bring in."

She wondered why he hadn't added "sorry, honey" or patted her on the head. She was opening her mouth when Evan beat her to it.

"She *is* a professional. And we already have enough people in this little cabal. No one tells anyone else." He glared at each person in turn, which Kayla thought was wasted because no one had any desire to spread this any further.

Marcus eventually gave in, and a while later they all signed what Kayla pegged as rudimentary incorporation documents. The sole purpose of this little company was to control and protect the device. Then he turned to Kayla.

"What do you want to do with this machine?"

She looked from side to side not knowing what to say and her answer came out with that same tone. "I want to power my house? . . . and be left alone."

Marcus looked at her weird. Well, he should have known better than to ask an Aspy such an unpointed question. "Do you want to sell the design to a factory to produce them? Or create your own manufacturing plan? Do you want to run seminars to teach people how to build their own? How do you want to get it out there?"

She hadn't thought that far ahead. "I thought we could post it on the Internet?"

He shook his head. "There's no money in that."

She had money. She didn't need money. People needed power. And the earth needed less carbon dioxide.

As Reggie smiled, Winter got the hint. But he turned first to the older man. "Is this okay with you?"

Exasperated, Kayla frowned at him. "Then why did you ask me?! Reggie's fine with it."

"Mr. Standish may want a return on his investment. Why don't we let him answer?" Marcus turned and looked at the older man who was now grinning broadly.

"You heard her. Let's put it on the internet!"

Marcus burst out. "But, sir. You'll lose thousands, maybe millions of dollars on this! I can't advise it."

Shut up, Marcus, Kayla thought, but bit her tongue, closing the portal of escape for the words inside her head.

Reggie smiled sweetly at his young lawyer. "So? I have money. And they already took this away from me once. More importantly, they took my friend, and look what they did to you. I think a little healthy revenge is in order."

"You may not have any money left when this is over." Marcus muttered under his breath.

"I heard you, young man. And I don't care."

"All right." Marcus Winter, Esquire, gave up the fight. "Next order of business, then. Kayla, you need to teach a master class in how to build this thing. ASAP." Then he turned back to the group. "Who's going to learn?"

"Everyone but you." Kayla smiled.

Reenie's eyebrows went up. She probably thought that was pretty ballsy. Ivy was trying not to laugh and Evan was simply in agreement with her.

Marcus just nodded. "Then we all go home and get some sleep. The rest of you reconvene tomorrow, bright and early. I need all five of you able to build a working model by end of day."

He packed up the few things he'd taken out of his briefcase, snapping it closed and turning for the door with a few "thank yous" and "goodnights" as though they had simply had him over for drinks and appetizers.

Reggie stood, too. "I'm going to follow him. Two cars are harder to get. I'll be back tomorrow morning at seven?" He looked to Kayla and she nodded, though Reenie grumbled, "I hate you both."

Then it was just the four of them again. All dead on their feet. All ready to crumble.

Suggesting she was the least in need of sleep, Ivy volunteered for the first shift of watch. She would sit in the hallway and read, walking a circuit of the house every twenty minutes to half hour. In three hours, she would wake Evan, who was already as far down on the watch list as he could stand to be.

All four of them got ready for bed in shifts, and Kayla was tucked under her covers alone, unable to sleep, when she heard the voices in the hall.

"Get some sleep, Evan. I'm here. I'll defend her with my life."

Kayla blinked at the vehemence in her friend's voice.

"Why?" Evan asked back.

It's what she wanted to know, too.

Another sigh from Ivy. "Because, she makes the world better, and we can't let anything happen to her. Because this has to be done. Everyone's tired of high gas prices and even more, we don't deserve to be jerked around by big companies because we don't have other options. Some people can't feed their kids while these companies are posting record profits. I've always hated it, but I didn't have a viable alternative. So I didn't do anything. We're the David here, but I'm in this."

"We're going to take down a Goliath, aren't we?"

Kayla could almost see Evan, slumped against the wall next to Ivy, not sleeping like he should be. "Or we'll die trying? . . . You would really save Kayla over yourself?"

Maybe Ivy had nodded. Kayla didn't hear anything. Not until, "In case you you've been too slow to figure it out, I'm in love with your sister."

"W𝐀𝐈𝐓, why does this piece go here?" Evan was two seconds from swearing a blue streak.

Though Kayla was a brilliant mechanic and electrician, she was a terrible teacher. Her answers were often "because that's how mechanics work" or something equally pointless. Her teaching method appeared to be: build a demo model, then ask the "students" to build one from scratch and point out what they'd misplaced or why their model would blow up the earth or such.

Evan felt bad for Reenie and worse for Ivy. Reenie—the architect—had a good sense of three-dimensions and mechanics. But Ivy was the artist. She was the one who'd commented early that she liked the standard 'repetition and variation' of the gear design.

In spite of this, Ivy had held it together best. She also sported the most band-aids. Reggie had smiled his way through failed model after failed model. He smiled despite Kayla's obvious frustration with all of them. And he soothed her by saying that if she wanted to give her machine away, she had to be able to teach other people how to assemble it or else she'd end up as a line worker, building each one by hand.

Evan had latched onto that, more than once mumbling, "Be nice, Kay, or you'll die in a factory."

He felt he'd finally achieved a decent grasp on the mechanics when Reenie tapped out. She stood up from where they were all hunched up, building like the factory workers he threatened Kayla with becoming. His sister wasn't quiet about her discontent, not with them or even the lighting. He knew Kay saw deep irony in building Whitney Devices under lights powered by the grid.

Reenie called a halt to the whole thing. She stretched, putting her hands low on her back and arching with a sigh. "We need lunch. And dogs."

Reggie nodded. "I'm buying."

Kayla, instantly forgetting to be irritated at her failing students, perked up. "Lunch or dogs?"

The older man shrugged in a gesture that looked young on him. "Both. Dogs keep you safe. I need you all safe."

No one mentioned that the whole point of this exercise was to make sure that if anything happened to any one of them, or particularly to Kayla, that the knowledge of the machine didn't die with them.

Kayla nodded. Then smiled. "I'm getting dogs!"

Evan's eyebrows went up and he felt like she was ten again. "*We're* getting dogs, Kayla. All of us."

"Why can't they be mine? I always wanted a dog."

He'd always talked her out of it and he continued to do so now. "Do you really want four dogs?"

She made a classic "I dunno" gesture, "What's the difference between one dog and four dogs?"

"Three dogs." He kept his expression flat, not wanting to say that people who didn't see the difference between one dog and four dogs shouldn't be allowed to have dogs in the plural and maybe not at all.

"It's still care and housing and food and vet bills. Plus, extra dogs keep each other company and the added cost of each subsequent dog is cheaper." She prattled.

Evan would bet that she already knew the percentages of cost of care for each additional dog in both money and time. He caved. "So, what kind of dogs are you getting, Kay?"

Her grin made it all worth it. Made him glad they were getting dogs to protect her. Dogs of the canine, corporate, and legal varieties. Kayla would have more dogs than she even knew.

"Pit bulls." Of course she already had that level of certainty. "They're incredibly loyal, very protective, great family pets, and everyone's afraid of them. Also they have a bite pressure on average of 1600pounds . . . per square inch." She grinned a little bigger at that last comment, almost as though she were envisioning one of her kidnappers with one of her pit bulls squarely clamped to his ass.

Reenie smiled, too, truly warming Evan's heart. "There are also a lot of pits at the shelter. So we should be able to find you four of them."

Kayla nodded. "Ivy and I talked about it last night."

Here they went, Evan thought. But at least they were scattering tools and gears. Kayla was taking a handful of important pieces and loading them into her backpack. He and Reggie would stay behind, wait a half hour, and order pizza. The ladies were going after the dogs. Everyone would take Whitney Device parts with them—make it harder to track down the right pieces if anyone came after them.

Ivy suggested getting dogs of different ages. Two older and two younger, so that they wouldn't all get old at the same time. Wisely, Ivy didn't use the word *'die'* and Kayla stayed happy. The women all went out the door with Evan's thoughts following them.

Ivy was good for Kayla. And that was good for him, too.

Even more, Reenie was good for him. He rolled that around in his head quietly for a few minutes. Then Reggie suggested that Evan make up for some lost sleep last night. The older man didn't know Evan had the middle watch last night, meaning he got no single decent chunk of rest. But Evan refused. He still didn't quite trust Reggie alone in the house. So he took Reggie to the Overseer's House and sprawled on his sofa, offering the older man the use of the recliner.

They sat there in silence, and Evan almost relaxed.

THE HUMANE SOCIETY wasn't a humane society. It wasn't even an animal shelter. No, they were in back woods, Georgia, and here the sign read "Dog Pound." Kayla cringed. Ultimately though, it wasn't much different than the few animal shelters she'd been in over the years. The kennels were nothing to marvel over, but they were big and clean enough.

Reenie squinted her eyes at the din—it seemed every dog in the place started barking the second they opened the door to the kennels, but she looked down the line and muttered, "Won't be hard to find four pits."

The place was full of them, and still Kayla had a hard time choosing. Some had their ears and tails clipped; others didn't. And once she made initial choices, she had to put the dogs together and see how they would get along. That was more daunting than the rest.

When she was a kid and had campaigned for a dog—a quest she always failed at—she had studied up to show her parents she could be a responsible pet owner. She hadn't forgotten a thing.

She checked the dogs to see who licked her hand, who barked

well, and how well trained they had been prior to arriving at the shelter. Did the dog take well to Kayla issuing commands then pushing the dog into a sitting position? That turned out to be harder than she'd anticipated. While she had read all about it, she'd never had the opportunity to work with a large pit bull before. You didn't just push their backside to the floor when you said "sit"—it turned out they were harder to move than that.

The dogs ended up choosing each other. The two older dogs were apparently brothers, and the two younger dogs had come from the same place. The bigger dogs were in charge, clearly, with the younger female dogs being only slightly cowed by them. But no one peed on the floor, which Kayla knew was a good sign. They all licked. They all liked her as well as Reenie and Ivy.

And they were all taken away for a flea dip, a rabies shot, and a spay or neuter. They would be ready the next day.

Kayla wanted them sooner, but kennel regulations said that no animal could leave the shelter until fixed.

Reenie pointed out that pizza delivery time had already passed and they should head home. Plus, the extra day gave them time to get collars and bowls and beds and food. Kayla didn't mention that she had a list, but her stomach grumbled—loudly —just then, and the three women reached a mutual agreement to head home.

They headed back to the house, Kayla in the middle of the backseat, leaning forward to share in the conversation. She couldn't think of the last time she'd done this, and her only real memories of being involved in car conversations were when it was just her and Evan or her and her Aspy friends. In this group, though, she felt perfectly at home. They let her have her turn and only occasionally showed off some weird dynamic that everyone else had picked up on except her.

They spoke only of dogs on the drive back. No mention of the Whitney Device, nor the need to learn to construct them. They discussed dog names, Kayla settling on Curie and Goodall for the girls and Newton and Faraday for the boys. Reenie and Ivy both shook their heads.

They were headed toward the rear parlor of the big house when Evan stuck his head out the back door at the Overseer's House and waved to them. Kayla found Reggie at the table, a napkin in hand and a partially decimated pizza in front of him.

Her stomach growled again as the smell hit her; even from here she could tell the food hadn't quite cooled off yet. She was reaching for a piece, a plate of no concern to her, when Evan put a hand on her arm, "Kayla."

His voice was grim and Kayla snapped around to look at him, pizza and grumbling stomach forgotten.

"Look." He held out his cell phone.

It held a picture of her, Ivy, and Reenie, climbing into the car. Kayla looked at Ivy and Reenie, both of whom were washing hands and grabbing paper plates. Reenie was wearing a pink, fitted T-shirt and jeans, Ivy—in her usual tank top—had on a blue bra. Just like in the picture.

She looked up at Evan.

"It came in just as you pulled up."

29

H azelton House

THEY WERE SUPPOSED to be sleeping. Evan had taken first watch, worried about that picture on his phone.

Back and forth he'd gone. Whoever 'they' were, they had been watching the plantation all along. They had planted listening devices. Reginald Standish had confessed—not that it had come as any real sort of apology—to paying people to photograph the machine. Evan knew and had known they were all being surveilled. So he couldn't figure out why *this* picture bothered him so much.

Then it hit him as he sat there alone, back to the wall.

'They' now knew the occupants of Hazelton House were aware they were being watched. The picture changed the game from covert to flat out open. The message was "I'm watching you." And maybe a little "I can get to you."

His stomach turned. When he'd thought things couldn't get

any more wrong than they already were, he felt the ratcheting down in his gut that said, yes, they can. The threat was made worse because it was a *great* picture. Kayla was clearly talking to Reenie and Ivy, and the women were smiling. Which added another layer to the message: "You forgot that I was watching."

Evan sat with his head in his hands. He made his rounds and found nothing going on at the house. But he wished for the dogs to be there already. He wished for a loyal friend with excellent hearing and sense of smell. But for tonight, he was the dog.

He'd only gone in and woken Kayla for her shift because he was so very tired. But once in his own bed, he found himself unable to sleep. He radiated enough anxiety to wake Reenie, her soft voice mumbling through sleep, "What's wrong?"

He should have told her to go back to sleep. He should have lied. But he couldn't. He didn't want Reenie to be just a person in his life; he couldn't handle her being an extra dependent almost the way Kayla was. If this was going to work, he needed a partner. He needed to be able to unload without judgment, fear or guilt. Yes, he felt a desperate need to protect her, but if they couldn't share the burdens and help each other through, then he'd screwed up the past five years, of his life and he was living on a plantation that he partly owned with a woman who would never be more than a temporary bedmate and passing friend. He needed more.

So he threw caution to the winds, "What's not?"

Reenie scored her first point. "It's something specific. Is it the picture from tonight? That really freaked you out."

Not his choice of words. Certainly he was more manly than someone who got "freaked out" but . . . "Yeah. It did. I finally realized why."

"Because they called us on it?" She was awake now, on her side, head propped in one hand, her free hand searching for his and lacing their fingers together. "They aren't trying to hide that they're watching anymore. I'm concerned they'll come right up to the front door and . . . I don't know."

Two points for Reenie.

"Me too. I'm worried about Kayla."

She nodded, a small movement he could make out from the dim light seeping in around the windows. "We're protecting her as best we can. We're getting dogs; we're all taking turns at watch. Now that you can build a machine, we've made some progress. Ivy and Reggie and I will go back tomorrow and continue learning. That will help, too."

He squeezed her fingers, soaking in the heat of her palm against his, and understanding that though her hand was smaller and though he would step in front of a bullet for her, she had her own strengths. Strengths he didn't have himself, strengths he needed. "You and Ivy held up well today. Kayla is a crappy teacher."

"Yeah, she is."

"You did a good job of teaching her to be better."

"She got better as the day wore on." Reenie scooted closer to him. More points for Reenie. "It all rolled off Ivy's back. But then again, Ivy's in love with her, I'm not."

Evan laughed. "You heard that the other night, huh?"

"Heard what?"

He sat upright, accidentally losing the link between their hands. "When Ivy told me she was in love with Kayla. You didn't hear that?"

This time she laughed. "No. I didn't need to. The problem is, Kayla does. It's hard enough to pick up that kind of stuff when it's aimed at you. Kayla often misses the obvious right in front of her. If Ivy doesn't tell her, then she'll never know. I'm considering dropping some very pointed hints or questions next time I have Kayla alone."

More points for Reenie. But he wasn't done. "You two seem to be doing a lot better."

"Yeah. I'm starting to understand her better. And truth be told, she's adjusted to me, too." She tugged him back down. "Until we all moved here, I didn't understand. You said she 'had Aspergers' and was 'fiercely independent' and then you watched over her like she was your kid. It didn't add up. You left a lot out."

In the dark, lying in bed, he blinked the encroaching realizations back. He probably had left a lot out. Chances were he'd never examined the entire construction of their lives. He'd lived it. Some of it was innate: when to step in, when to back off, how tied he was to Kayla. "I'm sorry."

"No need to be. It made sense to you, and it's finally starting to make sense to me." She tucked herself into his shoulder. "If the rest of this shit would go away, she'd do really well here, I think."

"You want her to stay with us? On the plantation?"

"Of course. Her and—if she wants it—Ivy."

Game to Reenie.

He *was* sorry. He'd misjudged her so many times. He'd doubted her when in many instances he hadn't given her what she'd needed to perform the way he'd expected.

For a few minutes, they lay there like that. Her tucked into his side, his arm around her, his other hand absently playing with her fingers while out in the hall Kayla stood watch, keeping them all as safe as they could be. The resentment and the worry melted away and Reenie felt closer than just beside him.

Ironically, it was a perfect moment inside the worst time of his life. He was literally afraid for the lives of the people around him. He had only a passable plan to get out of it. And inside, he was as calm as he had ever been.

"Reenie, are you still awake?"

"Of course." She moved into him, aligning their bodies, kissing him deep and long.

They had made love only once recently, while Kayla and Ivy were missing and the sex had reflected the tension they had both felt. Though it had released some pressure and allowed them some sleep, it hadn't been the real deal. He kissed her back but then stopped.

"No?" She asked, her voice soft, worried but not frightened that he didn't want her anymore.

"Yes. But first . . ." He took a deep breath and found no doubt, no fear lurking in his shadows. He smiled. "Will you marry me?"

"YOU DID IT, REENIE!" Happiness seeped through her and Kayla beamed at her future sister-in-law.

Reenie sported her own Cheshire grin. Kayla thought a good part of it was not due to completing her first working Whitney Device, but was permanently etched and shining as brightly as the diamond that Evan had given Reenie this morning. He'd brought it out during breakfast. Reenie looked surprised, commented that she'd already said yes, but seemed thrilled nonetheless. Apparently, her brother had stashed the ring a while ago and just today brought it out.

"Yes!" Now Reenie jumped up and did a dance, while Reggie grinned and Ivy stuck her tongue out. They each had yet to complete a working device. Reggie had all the parts in place but hadn't adjusted for the shadow constant yet. If Reggie hooked up to the house, he'd burn out all the major appliances by tomorrow at the latest.

At least he understood the sixty-hertz problem. He had a rudimentary idea of what it was and that it had to be adjusted for. Ivy could only recite back the words others had said. Luckily, Ivy was determined. It was possibly the only thing going for her.

Stretching out, Reenie finally stopped her victory lap through the cramped carriage house. She avoided several machines, including the one Evan had rebuilt this morning as practice. It was chugging away in the corner, attached to nothing, to Kayla's great dismay. If they were building them, they should *use* them.

Instead they were apparently taking Reenie's completion as a signal for a break.

Kayla remained disappointed until the dogs were mentioned. And this time it was elected that Reenie and Evan stay home and keep an eye out while she, Ivy, and Reggie fetched the four dogs.

She almost opened her mouth to comment that Reenie and Evan should be sure to keep their eyes on their surroundings rather than each other. But her brother had told her a long time ago that if her comment involved sex, and if there was more than one person around, she should just hold her tongue. So she did. Besides, she was going to pick up her puppies.

Leaving Reenie and Evan to do whatever they were going to do, and also to hopefully make some lunch, they headed out. Sitting in the middle of the back seat again, Kayla made it about fifty feet out of the driveway before she began to panic.

Ivy twisted around in her seat, looking back with a frown etched on her pretty features. "What's wrong?"

Kayla considered lying, but since she sucked at it, she decided against. "They sent pictures of us. They followed us. I'm worried they'll do something to my dogs."

She shouldn't have called them "my dogs," they really should belong to everyone, but she named them and she thought of them as her babies already.

"There's nothing we can do until we get there." Kayla didn't like the look on Ivy's face.

The shelter was another thirty minutes away; places were few and far between out here in the back wilderness and the shelter served the whole county. Kayla was starting to really panic. If she were 'them,' she'd get the dogs.

No, she would *kill* the dogs, to send a message. Kayla played out scary visions of her dogs—already precious in spite of being new—dead at the shelter. She imagined returning empty-handed.

Her breathing kicked up. A hand touched her forearm and

she fought the instinct to yank back. It was Ivy; the touch was warm and Kayla breathed in, focusing on the soft fingers against her skin.

"Kayla, there is something we can do." Holding up her cell phone, she started to make it better. "Hi, I'm Ivy Lopez. I'm calling to check up on my friend's dogs. We stopped in and adopted four pit bulls yesterday.... really? That wasn't us. We'll be in shortly... . Yes, Kayla Reeves is with me ... She'll be glad to show ID."

Kayla's breath went out as relief claimed her. She felt in her pocket for her small zippered wallet that contained ID, cash and a credit card.

Ivy sighed, too. "You have good instincts, Kay. Someone came by to pick up the dogs, but couldn't prove he was Kayla Reeves." She squeezed Kayla's hand. "Apparently, it's odd for a person to just come in and get four pits, so they had the cops run a back-ground check on you."

"What?" Kayla's head jerked just a little. The shelter people thought she needed to be investigated?

"They do it with all people getting more than two pit bulls." Reggie volunteered. "I wondered about that last night and looked it up. They want to be sure you aren't starting an illegal dog fighting ring."

"Oh." She relaxed again, feeling like a spring bouncing back and forth. "I wouldn't do that."

"And now they know that." Ivy smiled at her. "And our dogs are safe."

Kayla leaned back and let her head rest against the seat. It would be okay. They would pick up the dogs, then take them to the nearby pet superstore, and get real collars and food and beds. Her credit card would get a bit of a workout today. Since moving into Hazelton House, she'd lost the nickels and dimes of her old life. Her puppies were going to run her a pretty penny, but she didn't care.

When they arrived, the four dogs were prancing around the

office, waiting for her. Kayla hit her knees and started laughing as she was licked left and right. In the background she heard Ivy at the counter checking out the dogs.

The woman in the beige shirt nodded at Ivy. "I recognize you both from yesterday. But which one of you is Kayla Reeves? Legally I have to see ID."

Kayla held up her hand from where she still crouched on the floor, covered in dogs. "That's me." She stood to ferret out her ID. The dogs all followed her over to the desk, each of them trailing a cheap nylon leash. Kayla couldn't have been happier. She flipped out her driver's license, signed the paperwork and petted dog heads with her free hand.

It was Ivy who thought to question the clerk and managed to look completely confused, as though she had no idea who would do such a thing. "So who came and tried to pick up our dogs?"

The clerk shrugged. "Two men in jeans and T-shirts. I think they were in here yesterday, after you were. They may have overheard us running the check on you. That way they would know that y'all were getting four dogs and maybe thought they could get around regulations."

It all sounded very reasonable to Kayla, and very much like it could be '*them*.' "What did they look like?"

The woman who ran the place looked at the deputy who sat in the corner chair, apparently just being there. "They were average height, one had dark hair, one blond." She shrugged, "You can look at the footage if you want. We got a camera." She pointed up into the corner at an unobtrusive video recorder, which Kayla and Ivy both absently looked directly into.

Sitting behind her desk, the clerk tapped at her mouse. Her system and monitor were less than state of the art, but seemed to get the job done. Before they knew it, they were watching grainy, jerky footage of the two men trying to pick up her dogs at ten a.m. this morning, the time the clerks had said yesterday the dogs would be ready.

Ivy pinched her on the arm while Reggie looked over the clerk's shoulder, but Kayla stayed silent. Though neither man obliged by turning around and looking into the camera, it was clear to all three of them that these were the two men who had kept them at the house. Reggie's eyes met hers; he knew, too. He recognized them. At one point, he'd hired them and trusted them.

Ivy played dumb quite convincingly. "That's just nuts. We heard they make good family guard dogs." She clasped her hands in front of her, and somehow it looked normal. "Thank you so much for not letting our dogs go to a fighting ring!"

"No problem, ma'am." The woman replied about the same time as the deputy spoke up from behind.

"That's our job. To keep the dogs out of illegal fighting scams." He gave a short nod of acknowledgement. What exactly he was acknowledging, Kayla was unsure. But she nodded back and smiled.

After loading the dogs into the backseat, they took off for the pet store. This was the kind of shopping Kayla liked. They got no-tip bowls and four beds—Kayla picked out the type and Ivy chose the colors.

The stuff didn't all fit in the trunk of Reggie's sedan, so the dogs crushed into the back with two fifty-pound bags of dog food shoved into the footwells and grinned the whole way back to the plantation.

Evan and Reenie helped them unload animals and supplies and Reenie only flinched a little at the idea of the dogs in the main house on the pretty floors. But they'd had their nails trimmed and they didn't gouge the wood.

Each of them took a dog by the leash while Reggie hung back, walking just behind the crowd as they fanned out over the plantation. Kayla and Evan made a sweep around the barn. When they got back to the main house, they could see Ivy, Reenie, and Reggie down by the front stone wall, and Kayla turned to her brother. "Evan, you're holding something back. What is it?"

He nodded. Not a surprise.

Evan didn't answer. Instead he held up his phone. He'd gotten another message—another picture from the same number as yesterday.

But this picture wasn't of them.

This picture was of a live Robert Bell. Robert Bell, who was now decaying under the floor of one of the slave cabins.

30

H azelton House

THE DOGS HAD BARKED NONSTOP the first few hours, driving Evan crazy. Then it had subsided to random single responses to squirrels and maybe deer. There were a ton of animals on the plantation even though they owned none other than the dogs.

Ivy and Reggie finally got their machines working. They all set a routine, where each of them built a Whitney Device each morning. Then they would scuttle the machine, taking pertinent parts with them, and go about the remainder of their work.

Reenie and Evan decided to get back on track with starting the museum. Though they wouldn't be able to open without getting the issues with the Whitney Device and their safety resolved, there was only so much they could do about it. Kayla and Reggie were on top of getting the machine out to the general public. Ivy floated in between working with the device and the plantation.

Evan upgraded their phones to a single business plan with one-touch calling. It was more secure than a walkie-talkie line, but faster than dialing. This meant they could—within the borders of the Hazelton Plantation—roam free with a dog and a walkie.

Like prisoners, they checked each other out before leaving the house. Dog at side, phone on, a test run, a plan.

He was working in the barn, Faraday at his side, when Reenie's voice came from the main house telling him that Marcus was on his way. They were now officially incorporated, so naturally there was more paperwork to sign.

Not moments later, Ivy's voice followed. "Leaving Kayla in C." Carriage House—they had made a code for each, not difficult to break, but something that didn't have them announcing exactly where everyone was all the time. "Joining Evan at J."

His eyebrows went up. She was headed his way.

After a moment, he stopped sanding and headed to the doorway where he could see her coming over the rise and down the hill to the barn, Newton at her side. Newton was either well trained or completely in love with Ivy; either seemed equally possible. He paced her, always in a perfect heel. Evan waved even as he wondered, *Who would work so hard with a dog and then give him up?*

Even before Ivy made it to the barn, the phone beeped again, Kayla's voice ringing bell-clear across the waves. "Leaving C, heading to A." She'd be in the big house with Reenie. Reenie would be designing marketing materials and Kayla would be gathering the drafts to show to Marcus Winter when he arrived.

The lawyer had been working for two days to the exclusion of everything else to get the patent papers ready.

Ivy came through the doorway; immediately Evan lifted his phone to report her arrival. That was another essential piece of checking in. If there was anyone else there to check you in, they had to do it. Kayla had added that rule to help prove you were where you were supposed to be. In addition to the GPS on the phone, they should know where each other was at all times. Of course, phones could be shut off and everything would be out the window. But as long as the phones were on, it worked.

It also meant anyone who could hack a phone system would know where they were at every moment as well. But Evan had pointed out that these people already were keeping better tabs on them than they were themselves; the least they could do was keep up.

Ivy smiled at him as the dogs sniffed each other. According to Kayla, they had been housed together at the shelter; the caretaker reporting that they had become friends at first sight. So why they had to sniff each other's butts now was a mystery to him. He was glad Kayla had claimed the dogs. He just had to make sure they got fed on a regular schedule.

"I came down to talk to you about not beveling the edges of these."

Evan's head popped up. Excellent, Ivy was talking about something that didn't involve the machine or death threats or . . . hell, he didn't even know if Kayla had told her about the man she shot while Ivy was missing. He stuck to the topic at hand. "Why wouldn't we bevel them? This was a house with money. The rest are all beveled."

"Sure, but this is a display in the kitchen area, and those items weren't high-quality show pieces. This is the place to show off other furniture from the time, more the norm for the general population, and certainly not out of keeping with the set up that we have."

He nodded, knowing he was going to have to do some re-planning.

Evan and Ivy worked through matching what she thought would be historically accurate for a kitchen house with what he had already constructed, and he found the work loosened the knots he'd developed—just a bit, but he breathed a little easier, and his shoulders relaxed just a bit.

He hadn't received a picture since the one he showed Kayla. That helped, too.

Kayla was drawing schematics. She was going to post them on the web. Sell them to manufacturers. That helped, too. The further she could fling this thing, the safer they would all be.

Then his shoulders tensed again: the safer they felt, the more dangerous it was. They had to stay vigilant. *He* had to stay vigilant.

Ivy was heading back up to the main house and suggested he come with her. He had to head back anyway to sign the new round of paperwork Marcus Winter was bringing. He changed the topic on purpose.

"Have you said anything to Kayla?" He didn't add "about your feelings" or "that you're in love with her." He didn't have to. Ivy picked up on it.

"Not yet. I'm hoping for a good time."

He'd done that, too, and had suffered through thinking there wouldn't ever be a good time. But then he'd found it, right when he least suspected it. In the end, Evan had no advice, only his own opinion. "For what it's worth, I think you stand a good shot."

That earned him half a smile. "So she hasn't said anything about me, that way?"

"No." He wasn't going to lie. "But I haven't outright asked and she doesn't volunteer things like that. Never has. Her last boyfriend she dated for six months and broke up with him before I even learned he existed. So it doesn't mean anything. Kay doesn't gush. You know that."

She laughed. "But right now, it would sure be easier if she did."

"She wouldn't be Kayla if she did."

Ivy elbowed him. "Don't go throwing around logic when I'm

waiting for the right moment to declare myself to someone who will be honest with me whether or not it hurts my feelings."

She was right about that. Once Ivy opened the conversation, she'd be in it. Just as he was about to comment, the phone beeped again, Reenie's voice coming through. "Marcus and Reggie are here."

Ivy hit her button. "We are already on our way."

Evan felt a tickle at the back of his neck and turned to look over his shoulder.

IT WAS TOO QUIET. Kayla didn't like the silence.

She'd handed Marcus Winter her copies of the drafts of the machine this evening, and he'd driven off with them.

It was exactly what he was supposed to do, but she hadn't liked it. It was eight p.m. when he left. Ivy had cooked dinner for all of them, Reggie staying until the last minute. The conversation at the meal felt stilted to Kayla so she figured the others had to be positively nuts from it. She'd asked Ivy later and confirmed it.

But then Winter handed Reggie the incorporation documents to file with the county. And the lawyer got into his car and headed up to Washington, D.C. He didn't trust the mail service and didn't want to wait to get the patent filed. He wanted a receipt in his own hands.

All of that made sense. Kayla didn't trust the post office, but the problem was that she didn't quite trust Marcus Winter either. And if he wanted to file the patent in his own name, he had all the documentation to forge it.

She rolled around in the bed, crossing over onto Ivy's side as she did. Half the time, one or the other of them was on watch. Since she didn't sleep well without Ivy beside her; she didn't sleep half the time. So she rolled back to her own side, wondering what Ivy would think if she came in and found Kayla in her space.

Since real rest wasn't on the menu, Kayla ran down the next day's plan. She would draw up how to hook up the battery and gas generator to the machine. She'd test it on Reggie and Ivy. As the last two to finish construction of their own Whitney Devices, they were the best guinea pigs for her plan. If they could follow the instructions, anyone could.

She and Evan had talked about how to get the device out to the public. She'd been serious about posting it on the web, but knew only a few would be willing to construct something that seemed to run on so little. The solution had been to give the machine an apparent energy source.

It had taken a while, but she and Evan worked out a hybrid system that used a minor amount of gasoline on a small side generator. This was hooked up to the machine, which was also hooked to a rechargeable battery of a significant size. People were familiar enough with hybrid cars to believe in the gas-to-battery-and-back scenario she proposed. She declared her machine ninety-seven percent efficient, and adjusted the shadow constant to fit.

They hoped it would be enough to be enticing, making people want to download the schematics and build one. It also had to be within the realm of the believable, or else only a few people would even be willing to consider it. Her strength would come in numbers. So she had to ride that fine line between the real truth and getting the machine out there.

Kayla had no idea how long it would take to reach some kind of critical mass; they were in danger every moment until they reached that point. But that was a thought for another day. She rolled over again and tried to sleep.

Sleep still evaded her, and she planned the next morning and how she was going to build—or have the others build—several machines around the place and hook them up as the power source. She hadn't figured out a good way to get one working out at the barn. It was too far away, there was no way to police it, someone might take it at night, which defeated everything they were working for. Having Evan reassemble it every morning and disassemble it every time he left was a self-defeating move.

She got up, first sketching out and then trashing an idea for a mobile unit. Kayla was sliding back under the covers, and thinking that Ivy had about five more minutes on shift when she heard Goodall growling from downstairs.

Loud barks erupted as all four dogs raced to the back entry of the house, letting the intruder know they weren't welcome. Next came the distinct sound of Ivy pounding down the hallway toward the noise.

Kayla's own feet were on the ground, her hand automatically sliding under her pillow for the twenty-two there. Not as proficient a weapon as Ivy's nine-millimeter, but useful nonetheless.

She followed Ivy's path and arrived moments after Ivy had flung open the back door. Holding Curie by the collar, she let Goodall and Newton head out. Faraday had turned to look at Kayla and she grabbed him, too, imploring him to stay, praying he didn't realize that he was stronger than she was.

Evan and Reenie nearly barreled into her as they arrived, Evan barefooted and Reenie sliding on her socks. She'd need to rethink her footwear.

They all looked at each other, wondering who knew what.

Ivy spoke first. "Someone was there."

KAYLA YAWNED her way through the day.

They'd all stayed up the night before, checking windows in every room on every floor. Never moving anywhere without being part of a pair or without each pair having a dog at their side.

They didn't find anything that had been touched—not that they could tell.

In Kayla's mind, that made it worse. If they knew, they could make a decision, maybe get back to sleep.

But thirty minutes after dashing out the door, Goodall had returned, panting but seemingly happy. Newton followed less than three minutes later. They inspected both the dogs, but found nothing of interest: no marks, no muddy paws suggesting where they had been.

All of them weary to the bone and too wary to do much, they headed back upstairs.

Evan's watch had begun, and Kayla was finally able to curl up and get some sleep.

She slept more soundly than she'd expected and was surprised to find herself waking up in a tangle of arms and legs with Ivy. But the interruption and the hard time getting to sleep had taken their toll.

Ivy spent the morning painting one of the second floor bedrooms for display. She'd gone to see Evan in the barn and consult on the remaining pieces he was building. They ate lunch all together, with Kayla reporting on her progress building the machine outside again.

"I'm through assembling the machine, and the hookup of the gas generator and battery combo. But I have to house it to keep anyone from getting in without at least alerting a dog, and that's going to be a bitch."

Ivy chewed her sandwich thoughtfully, so Kayla wasn't surprised when she asked, "Can we set it up so people can put power back onto the grid?"

It was Evan who answered. "Nope, not in this incarnation. The sixty-cycle problem isn't too big a deal here, once we get it. But on the grid, we'd have to phaselock and that's way too much to deal with now."

Kayla nodded, she'd thought about exactly that. "Plus you

have to sign on with the power company. Most systems only pay you a fraction of what you pay for power." She paused, "which makes sense, since you then become the wholesaler. But in the meantime, they charge you full price every month for the power you draw, then at the end of the year credit you—at the lower rate —for the power you put onto the grid. So you can easily run a surplus onto the grid and still wind up owing them money."

"Really?" Ivy put her sandwich down for that one.

Kayla didn't. "Yeah, I looked it up. Seemed like it was worth figuring out the phaselock until then. We'll just take people off the grid entirely. I wonder if the Amish will be able to use it?"

The Amish used gas generators sometimes but would never hook into a system like the phone lines or the power grid.

"No Amish yet, Kayla." Ivy touched her arm and kept her from trailing off. "They aren't a big enough market to accomplish what you want."

Kayla saw exactly what Ivy had done. She knew she'd been neatly steered back on track. And she didn't really care. Ivy was good at that.

After they cleaned up from lunch, she headed outside, Ivy trailing her, helping with the last of the work. Faraday stayed with them, his leash staked to the ground with a bent piece of metal that both kept him in place and also allowed her to release him quickly should the need arise. But it didn't matter, the newly adopted dog seemed to have nowhere better to be than at her side.

Ivy held parts and tools for her, the heat finally soothing rather than baking as it had just a few weeks ago.

Midafternoon, Reggie called to let them know that Marcus had arrived in D.C. and filed the patent in person. Ivy was musing out loud that he could have changed his name to all the papers and filed it as his own.

Kayla was shaking her head, having finally figured out why Marcus wouldn't do just that. "You have to be the true inventor to file it. And he could lie, but it would put him back in Big Oil's crosshairs."

Just then the photo of the receipt popped up on her phone, marked as filed by Marcus Winter for a patent for Kayla Reeves. Underneath the picture it read, "On my way back." She showed Ivy, who smiled and happily admitted to being wrong.

Then she frowned. "We keep saying 'Big Oil', but who is that really? I mean there are a small handful of companies, it could be any of them."

Kayla nodded. She had this very conversation once with Reggie when everyone else had been asleep. She passed on what she knew. "Reggie said that the term 'Big Oil' refers to the group of companies and that the group has consultants, who in turn employ contractors, who in turn hire the people who 'get things done'."

Ivy handed over a connector as Kayla hooked the small gas generator she was tying to the Whitney Device. "So no one's really responsible for things like this and it's really difficult to tie it to any of them."

"Yeah," She checked her cables one last time and connected to the car battery she was using for the first run. "It means we'll never really be able to take them to court, unless Marcus can find another link. But he found one before and he only got so far up the chain before shit rained down on him."

Ivy nodded and Kayla asked if she wanted to do the honors.

With a flick of her wrist, Ivy looked like a pro starting up the Whitney Device the old way—manually. The generator would do that in the future. Kayla flipped switches and started up the entire connection. They watched it run for a few minutes, then quickly set about constructing a small house for it.

"Why do you keep looking over your shoulder, Kay?"

At the worry on her friend's face, Kayla laughed. "I don't hear anything or suspect anything if that's what you think." She watched her words all day, but they were being freer in range of the listening devices now. "It's Evan. If he sees me, he'll give me another lecture on the proper way to use hand tools. You, too."

Ivy laughed at that, the smile genuine and deep. It lit up her eyes and her entire face in a way that made Kayla pause and catch her breath. She stared at her friend for a minute.

Kayla had experienced that skip of the heart before. Of the handful of times it happened, it had never lasted. Twice she'd had a boyfriend for more than a year, but the little things, the pieces he missed and didn't understand about her just wore down the relationship. And always, that catch of breath had happened right when she met someone. It never came from someone already embedded in her life, in her heart.

Ivy had kissed her before, but since Kayla hadn't known what to do with it, she waited it out. When it hadn't happened again, she'd written it off. But here it was, Ivy's smile, her dark gaze locked with Kayla's, and that feeling of a hiccup in her heart.

It took a conscious thought about how to react. Smile back.

It wasn't as if it was difficult to smile at Ivy, it was that her natural reaction was to sit there, stunned, and not really respond. But once she thought about smiling at Ivy, she couldn't stop it.

She grinned while they finished building the housing together, working in a seamless fashion, Ivy knowing what she wanted even before she did. Kayla smiled through dinner and thought she caught Reenie and Evan looking at her funny, but she wasn't sure and they didn't say anything.

With Reenie on the first watch, Kayla and Ivy were both supposed to sleep. And they did. It worked until Ivy flung off the covers and headed out to the bathroom at the end of the hall. Kayla listened to the running water, the closing door, and the footsteps that told her where exactly Ivy was. So she was on her feet when her friend opened the bedroom door and found her standing there.

Ivy sighed but didn't say anything. And Kayla felt it coming.

In two steps, Ivy was right in front of her, then Kayla felt soft hands frame her face and pull her close. She gasped at the feel of Ivy's lips on hers, stiffened at the shock of lightning in her system, and melted underneath the storm that followed.

She was kissing Ivy back when the deep barks sounded from the first floor. Almost simultaneously, Reenie yelled for all of them, and Kayla heard footsteps pounding down the hallway. Before she could even assess what just happened, her own feet were racing down the stairs, right behind Ivy.

31

H *azelton House*

THE BACK STEP WAS BROKEN. Evan knew it had been a problem and now the old board had given up and split in two, jagged edges pointing toward the middle. Probably someone running had leapt onto it at high speed; from the looks of it, that someone went right through.

Shit.

The Whitney Device stayed tucked into its safe house, neatly hidden in the angle of the porch and the back side of the house. It was the obvious choice.

Evan headed down the steps, now avoiding the second one because he had to.

Looking at the lock—a relatively cheap key-and-number combo—didn't yield any clues. The housing looked untampered with.

He glanced up. The moon was just a sliver, not giving up

enough light to check for tracks. And even if it had, there was a good chance he'd cleanly erased them as he came over here and crouched down, looked for clues that he wouldn't find at night anyway. Maybe he'd have better luck in the morning.

Evan was standing up, stretching his legs, and musing how he had simply raced down here without forethought, when fear brought him fully upright. "Reenie! Ivy! Go check the front. What if this was just a distraction?"

Both women took off running, three dogs following. The canines at least seemed to enjoy the games of "bark at the intruder" and "run around the big house," Evan not so much.

As he scanned the dim horizon, he heard them reach the double front doors, and though he couldn't hear what they said, the tones carried well on the night. Neither of them seemed upset, which allowed his shoulders to relax just a fraction.

It was Kayla who was still uptight.

From the looks of her, she didn't even notice that Reenie and Ivy had dashed off. She stood on the back porch, turning slowly in a circle, her eyes scanning everything. At last they settled on him, delivering her worry directly into his system.

"Evan, they didn't come for the machine." Pointing to the housing she'd built earlier that day, Kayla asked him, "There are no marks on the wood or around the lock, are there?"

He shook his head, knowing that in a moment she'd explain how she arrived at that conclusion without even looking at the very thing he'd just inspected. Her gaze trailed away from him and her focus hit the middle distance, as though she were seeing the action unfolding here. "The dogs barked once and we all ran. Whoever it was barely got away and surely didn't have time enough to do two things."

Evan nodded. So far, so good.

Reenie and Ivy appeared behind Kayla, and some part of her brain must have catalogued that, but she gave no outward appearance of sensing their presence.

"Whoever it was broke the step as he ran off the porch. So he couldn't have gone to the device. He wanted something here on the porch." She turned, scanning the porch, and closed the door in Ivy and Reenie's faces. "Look, Evan."

He climbed the steps, peering where she pointed. Even in the dark, he could see the faint gouges in the wood. As though it were silk or velvet, Kayla ran her fingers along the door frame. "He was trying to get inside."

For a petty moment, Evan put aside what that meant and considered the repairs. It was easier to be mad about putty and paint than to be scared or concerned about someone jimmying the old lock.

The dogs had saved them and suddenly Evan no longer begrudged the extra scraps Kayla had been sneaking to them at meals. He opened the heavy door to find Ivy and Reenie standing right where they'd been.

He was starting to explain what Kayla had figured out when the other two suddenly looked over his shoulder. Turning, Evan saw Kayla walk off the porch. She missed the broken step cleanly, without a falter in her stride; anyone watching from a few feet further away would have no idea the step was even out of commission.

In her socks, she made a beeline for the back corner of the house, and standing there, facing the wood slat siding, she began to speak. The three of them stayed still, straining to hear the words.

"You can come for us, but it won't matter. If you stop the patent, which you already know we filed for, it won't matter. You can even kill us, it won't matter. The machine is already out there. Too many people know. And there are many who can build one from scratch. There's nothing you can do. But if you come for us, know this: we'll be ready."

Kayla had been speaking directly into the bug.

KAYLA FELT LIKE CRAP. Evan had chastised her for making her bold statement without first consulting everyone. She hadn't thought of that, but she still didn't think it was in any way the wrong thing to do.

Then he made them run drills. They'd been too haphazard, everyone sliding in socks and pattering on bare feet, all running to the same place. It was unorganized, and worse, maybe unsafe.

Though he was right about all of that, it still felt like punishment.

Go to your room. Lay down. Sleep in your clothes. Now think about where your shoes are.

Once they'd practiced that, he reorganized them. Ivy and Reenie would take the front door, regardless of where the commotion was; Evan and Kayla the back. Once the front and back doors were secured, each team would sweep counterclockwise through the ground floor rooms to be sure nothing was amiss.

He made them run the drill five times before finally going back to bed.

In the morning, Kayla helped Evan with some sanding, then they quickly assembled a Whitney Device in a cabinet that Evan built for just that purpose. He braced and locked it before they trudged in for lunch.

Reenie looked perfectly chipper, the lack of sleep not bothering her at all. In the face of all that bushy-tailed wakefulness, Ivy looked even more tired and Kayla figured she looked about the same herself. After eating, she declared it nap time for the two of them and took Ivy's hand, pulling her out of the Overseer's kitchen and into the big house.

She heard Reenie behind them telling her brother that she'd be making vendor calls from the main house anyway and to let the girls sleep. Evan pulled the dogs inside, cooping all eight souls inside one building, which either meant they were safer or they could all be blown up with a single good plan.

Even so, what she told the listening device was true. Reggie knew. Marcus couldn't build it himself, but he had all the info, and if he put it into the right hands, someone else could. And there were two patents—one for the device itself and a second, "new use" patent for the hybrid technology she'd added to make it look like it was using fuel.

She turned the corner toward the room she shared with Ivy, her feet dragging, sleep stealing over her before she was even tucked under her covers. But a hand grabbed her and pulled her back. Off her feet a little, she rocked into Ivy, who pressed a fast kiss to her mouth and then declared that she was exhausted. Before Kayla could move from the spot she was suddenly rooted to, Ivy slid into the bed and disappeared into slumber.

Kayla was jealous and a little frustrated. She'd been exactly that tired herself, but the kiss had startled her. Still, she climbed in and felt the sheer bliss of crisp, cool sheets and the comfort that if anything happened, the machine was already out there.

KAYLA WOKE up to the sound of Reenie and Evan speaking somewhere downstairs.

The slant of the light told her she'd been asleep for at least a few hours. She stretched and started to roll over before she took into account the body next to her. Ivy was still deep under, so Kayla stayed quiet.

The voices downstairs filtered up without the benefit of clarity. Though she couldn't understand exactly what was going on, when the door opened then closed, it became clear that Evan had stepped out. She could almost see him, traipsing down to the barn—his favorite place to be on the plantation. He had no desire to help with the hordes of people coming through the future museum. He didn't even want to run classes, though he probably would until they could hire someone else to handle it.

So Kayla lay there drowsily, and sure enough she heard a faint beep and Reenie's voice. Evan had arrived at his destination and was checking in.

She drifted in and out of consciousness, not knowing when she fell asleep again, but only coming aware when Ivy nudged her shoulder. "Someone's at the door."

The words were hushed—rushed—and Ivy wasn't looking at her. She looked at the bedroom door as though it were a portal to the front porch.

A knock came again; Kayla heard it clearly. It was followed by the beep of the phone and Reenie's voice, which became clearer as she came out of the back parlor and entered the grand space of the central staircase. ". . .the door. . . . police officer. I'm answering it."

Kayla and Ivy's attention snapped to each other as they heard Reenie pull back the large front door and in her best Southern Miss voice ask what she could do to help the officer today.

There was no way Evan would arrive in time.

Kayla, already out of bed and peering through the back window at the police cruiser parked there, motioned quietly to Ivy. Without talking, they each grabbed a gun and slipped over to the servants' staircase. Bracing themselves on the walls, they came as fast as they silently could, unable to hear Reenie as they snaked through the back walls of the old house.

By the time Ivy and Kayla made it into earshot again, the officer was standing in the front hall, fingers hooked at the waistband of his deep-blue uniform, exasperation painting his features. "Ma'am, I need to ask if you've seen this man."

Just then, Kayla got her head around a corner and saw the officer holding up a paper photo. Reenie shook her head and the officer explained. "This is Robert Bell, he was last seen in Effingham County and never arrived at his destination in Savannah. We're checking areas in between."

Reenie shook her head again. "I haven't seen him." Then she gestured to the road out the open door behind him. "We don't get many visitors. I'm sorry."

Kayla tiptoed around the edges of the room, Ivy right behind her. They reached the open arch that led into the foyer, the voices loud on the other side of the wall. They were too close to talk, so Kayla mouthed a few words to Ivy, who nodded. Then, gun ready, she rushed the officer.

"Don't move!" Ivy nearly yelled it, but she appeared right behind Kayla. Quickly, Kayla put the officer between herself and the barrel of Ivy's gun.

He was responding to the threat, trying to knock Kayla out of the way, but aware that he had a nine-millimeter aimed at his head. He acted as though he was confident Ivy could hit him, too. Her right hand darted out and slipped off the snap on his gun holster. Quickly, too quickly for him to react with Ivy drawing down on him, Kayla slipped her fingers into the space and pulled the gun free. Stepping back, she handed it sharply to Reenie, who looked bewildered but followed along.

Kayla then pulled the cuffs from his utility belt and ordered Reenie to cuff him.

He fought only slightly, his eyes darting from Kayla, now standing square in front of him but out of reach, to Ivy, still steady, still with her Glock trained on him. Reenie slid the bracelet around his wrist and ratcheted it down. As she reached up to pull his other arm into place, he tugged again, protesting just a little, his eyes darting to Ivy.

Kayla spoke. "You know Ivy has a bullet chambered. You don't know if she'll shoot you or not, but you're fully aware she's a crack shot, aren't you?"

He pressed his lips together for just the briefest moment, a tell if Kayla ever saw one. "No ma'am, I don't know what's going on here." Then he stood straighter. "If you'll release me and explain, I won't press charges. No one has gotten hurt . . . yet. But you're at least up for assaulting an officer."

Kayla smiled. Reenie finished restraining him and stepped back out of hand and foot range. She startled when she backed into the edge of the open door and scrambled to close it.

Ignoring his comment, Kayla ran a test. "You should look down. There's a discoloration in the grooves between the floorboards. Do you know what that is?" She didn't give him time to answer. "It's blood. Specifically, Robert Bell's blood. You can cooperate, or you can join him."

Ivy and Reenie exchanged a glance, and Kayla knew enough that they were questioning whether or not she was crazy. She wasn't. She was just smarter than him. And she wanted him to know it.

32

H azelton House

"WHAT'S YOUR NAME?" Kayla asked the man as calmly as she could.

"Don't have one." His lips had stopped pressing together and he was as relaxed as he could be with his hands secured behind his back. Kayla enjoyed the irony of him wearing his own cuffs.

His eyes had narrowed when she commented about the blood in the floorboards. But this was as close to him flat-out stating who he worked for as was likely to come.

As the two other women darted their eyes back and forth at the swift change in the dynamic, Kayla watched his leg muscles. He wanted to take advantage of the momentary distraction and lunge at one of them. Even with his hands immobilized, he seemed to think he could accomplish something. She shook her head at him; *don't even try it.*

She heard the back door open, and Evan must have seen her back before much of anything else.

"Kayla?" but before she could answer him—she wasn't going to turn around for a conversation—she heard him startle and ask, "Ivy?"

He'd seen the gun that her girlfriend still had trained on this sucker. She liked the sound of that—girlfriend. Her lips curled in a little smile and the "officer's" eyes narrowed again.

Ha. She'd freaked him out a little with her smile. Let him wonder. His eyes focused in the distance, not on any one of them. But she wasn't fooled. He was ready to act, and he was trained.

Evan came into view, clear even though he was in her periphery. He whispered to Reenie, but Kayla didn't catch it. She only caught Reenie's answering shrug and remark, "I don't know, but he seems less and less like an officer."

"He's not." Kayla assured them.

"How do you know?" Evan asked her.

But it was Ivy who chimed in first. "He basically just admitted it, though not in so many words."

Evan looked at the three women, then back at the man, who for now remained unmoved.

Ignoring her brother for another minute, Kayla focused on the man in front of her, making sure her voice carried. "I won't be charged with assaulting an officer, because you aren't one. What you may not also know is that I shot Robert Bell. I asked him where Ivy was and I only asked him once. Before you make any moves, ask yourself if you're willing to die and disappear."

Then she shifted her voice, but not her focus, to the others. "He's a little too stupid. This area isn't zoned for police, we only have the sheriff. Then he parked his car around back. The real police park out front, they want people to see the car, but lucky for us, his is already hidden." She smiled at him, a cold but satisfied curve of her mouth. "And no one but no one has reported Robert Bell missing."

∿

EVAN KNEW SHOOTING him certainly would have been easier. It even seemed at times as though Kayla shot Robert Bell just because she was frustrated and recognized him as "foe." But he knew that wasn't true.

Ivy had been missing, they had all been stalked, spied upon, and wire tapped, and Kayla hadn't even known if her friend was alive. There had even been good evidence that these men were no strangers to killing those in their way. It had been a sound decision—if you could look at it through a purely logical lens. Which apparently, Kayla had.

Evan wanted that lens now. He wanted to look at this man who wasn't giving them anything, not verbally or via evidence either. His badge was stolen from a Savannah police officer whose name was Gruber, but this man wearing Gruber's badge gave them nothing else.

Being the only male, Evan was given the job of checking him for a wire. That was thankless. Evan found nothing, but hadn't done the most thorough of checks. When Kayla pushed him, he responded with, "Look, if he's willing to wear a wire up his ass, then they can just hear what I have to say."

The problem with letting this man live was that he needed to be watched like a hawk. He was a professional. There was every possibility that he could get himself out of the handcuffs in a few seconds if left alone. It had been eight hours since they'd captured him. And there had been too many questions. Could they let him pee in his pants? There would be the smell and the cleanup and the damage to their nice wood floors. Could they just not feed him? And if they fed him, how should they do it? Unlocking his hands was not okay by anyone's estimate. Who knew that holding a captive would be so problematic?

Then again it clearly wasn't easy; even Kayla and Ivy had escaped captors who were prepared for them—people with guns, plans, and a network. So Evan wasn't sure how he now stood a chance at detaining this man for long. The real question was, how much damage would he do when he went?

Kayla and Ivy had left their captor tied up in a basement . . . and electrocuted. Evan didn't like his probable outcome by that math.

He sat in the hallway and watched the man sleeping. It was entirely possible he was faking, waiting for the exact moment to spring. Evan wasn't sure he'd be ready for it. It was far too easy to rest, to watch, to wait without tension.

For a moment, he considered what it would take to sneak the man out of the room, save them all the trouble.

There had to be a better way.

Kayla's feet appeared at his side. "Your three hours is up. My turn."

"Damn straight." He looked up at her and grabbed his water bottle, his book and started to stand.

His knees hurt and his body didn't want to unfold. Joint by joint, he came upright while Kayla plopped, in lithe Indian style into a pretzel. He reminded himself that he loved her. That this was for her as well as for a greater good. It didn't make his knees feel any better.

When he was standing, looking down at the top of her head, he felt a surge of envy. And he debated a moment before speaking it. Not sure what kind of resolution it would bring, if any.

"Kay, you're the only one cut out for this."

She nodded, automatically knowing what he meant. She could read. She could draw, diagram or build, and still keep a sharp watch as her primary focus. She was also more consciously aware of what the man was doing and what that might mean. If he started to shift, to prep for a strike, Kayla would see.

She never fit in, and so she studied other people, knew the

statistics about how people acted, and recognized what was out of the norm. Her general disadvantage was a huge advantage here.

"Kay, you can't watch him twenty-four seven. But we need that." He looked at her for a minute. "We need a better solution. I'll be back at the end of your shift."

"You need sleep." She wasn't mean about it, just factual. "Take four hours. I'll still be good."

Of course she would. She was also giving him two full REM cycles. She'd read up on it once in hopes that if her family had to wake her, they could do it at the best possible time and avoid a smack to the eye or a kick.

Evan leaned down, ignoring protesting joints. He hugged her tight and thought for a moment that someone needed to tell Ivy about the sleep cycle thing. It would save her some grief.

KAYLA MADE it partway through her book. Pen in hand, she jotted notes inside the back cover, enjoying the irony of reading a how-to guide about creating a how-to guide. She had to deliver information about the machine and she clearly needed help. She needed to make instructions and videos. She considered getting the parts manufactured and selling a kit. Her research said there weren't that many people with spare gears around.

Kayla looked at her book; it was thick and tall, obviously a text of some kind. Not one of those cute little paperbacks Ivy liked to thumb through. Though Ivy understood why Kayla didn't read fiction—there were too many idioms and metaphors that she tended to take literally and miss the entire point of the story —Ivy loved her stories. Kayla had once found Ivy tsk-ing over a paperback whose cover sported a carriage and winding floral vines. When asked, Ivy had complained the stated color scheme hadn't become popular until a good twenty-five years after the story was set. Kayla had responded, "Of course" and assumed it was the same thing as if someone got a numerator and denominator transposed in an equation in one of her texts.

Still, she longed for something fashionable, like an e-reader. People always looked at her oddly when she just opened a manual on the bus and started to read, or when she would pull one out of her bag while waiting in line. Some days she wanted to wear a shirt that said "I have Aspergers. Go away."

She reached down and picked up her second pen—one blue, one green—nestled beside the present Reenie had bought while Evan was on first watch.

The man rolled over in his sleep, the blanket pallet looking none too comfortable. Though he appeared very much dead to the world to the casual observer, Kayla knew he was anything but. He'd been awake for about twenty minutes now. While he had actually slept for a while, he'd woken and even in his half-woken state had known to fake his change in consciousness. Kayla was waiting for him to try something.

His shoulders gave him away when he woke. Then his breathing had gone from truly deep and even to the faked kind that pretty much everyone did when they were pretending to sleep. Granted, he was better at it than most, but he still didn't have the innate kind of rhythm that was the hallmark of true sleep.

Now the rollover had moved his hands out of the limited frame of sight Kayla had from her position just outside the doorway. He knew that, too—what she could see and what she couldn't.

Subtly, while she turned the page, Kayla checked her watch. Evan would be here any minute. He was always prompt, something inherited from neither parent. Kayla assumed her own innate need to be on time was a symptom of the Aspergers, but Evan's clearly wasn't. Maybe he'd just become that way to help her with her schedule. Her mother had never quite understood.

Evan was a good brother. The best.

And—though she wasn't quite ready to mark it down as real yet—she seemed to now have Ivy, and also Reenie, who would soon become extended family.

The man shifted again, still appearing dead asleep to anyone who wasn't paying close attention. From the new set of his shoulders it looked as though he'd managed to either jimmy the cuffs open or dislocate a wrist and slide out of one. Either way he was free and biding his time.

"Hey sis." Evan called to her in low tones from down the hall. He was emerging from the door to the room he was sharing with Reenie and he looked sufficiently rumpled to indicate that he'd managed to sleep rather deeply for at least some of the time. He probably hadn't faked it either.

"Hey, Ev." She motioned him toward her and his bare feet made little noise on the hardwood hallway.

As he stopped in front of her, he smiled, clearly better off than he'd been four hours ago. "So, what are we going to do with our mystery guest?"

Though she didn't speak loudly, she didn't make much effort to keep her voice low. "We need to tie him up better. And we need to get in touch with his people and let them know we have him. See if they'll trade for him."

Evan nodded. "Should we truss him to something? We don't have any exposed pipes in the rooms." He smiled. "I know you're fond of those."

She responded with a quick grin of her own. "They do work quite well for keeping people stationary. But a good iron bed should do the trick. Maybe with cinderblocks on it to help weight it down."

Clearly Evan's brain wasn't at full speed because he looked concerned.

"What?" she asked.

"I was just thinking about whether these old floors can hold up that kind of weight. But that was stupid."

"Yeah. This place has great bones." She knocked on the hard-wood floor. "The weight won't be a problem."

But as she spoke, she saw a shadow behind Evan.

Quick as lightning, the man rushed out of the room, headed right toward Evan's unsuspecting back.

Kayla reached down.

33

U*pper Hallway, Hazelton House*

As QUICKLY AS SHE COULD—AND she was fast, she was ready—
Kayla threw herself to the left. This changed the man's line of
attack. Evan was no longer between them and could no longer be
thrown into her.

Just to make things a little better, she'd nudged Evan with her
foot as she toppled over. Okay, maybe it had been more like a
kick. Evan must have heard the barely two footsteps of warning,
and between Kayla lunging one direction and her foot giving him
more than a hint, he went the other way.

Now their captive—whose hands were indeed free, which
pissed Kayla off—was aligned only to the wall that had been
directly at her back. He started to change directions, but as he did
he spotted her hands coming up. And he saw what was in them.

She knew the moment he figured out this wasn't going
to work.

The man's feet left the ground in the attack he'd already committed to, but his eyes started to close as Kayla smiled and pulled the trigger.

Two prongs shot out, striking through his shirt, and the charge that followed made him jerk like a dry fish. His leap lost its grace. His muscles lost the tension of training and traded it for a contraction associated with pain and voltage. He hit the wall without striking either of his two intended targets and jerked twice before his eyes opened only to roll back.

Kayla looked at him. He was definitely asleep this time.

Evan rolled to his feet from where he'd hit the floor. He lacked all the grace of the intruder, but he also hadn't had to be Tasered, so Evan came out ahead. "Damn Kayla, you must enjoy electrocuting these guys."

She frowned. "I am developing a pattern. But it beats the alternative."

He held his hand out for the stun gun, "Can I see that?"

"No." She shook her head. "Reenie bought it for *me*. You have one, too. And besides, that's kinda fun."

"Dial down the glee, Kay." He sighed at her. "Grab his hands?"

"I'll take his feet." While she knew she wasn't the stronger one, she was the one best prepared for him waking up and lashing out. She'd be more attuned to the changes and hopefully less likely to take a foot to the kneecap.

They had already removed the man's shoes, his uniform shirt, and all the fun things on his belt. The sharp objects revealed only the normal police items plus one burner cell phone that didn't even have a single number programmed into it.

In her frustration Kayla made no concession to her captive's head bumping nor to any scratches that his back might get. Sadly, Evan had redone these floors and they were smooth as a baby's butt.

Reenie and Ivy rounded the top of the stairs as Kayla and Evan disappeared into the room. Kayla imagined they saw only the one limp foot she had dropped, dragging backward, horror-movie style. When they came pounding into the room, crowding the doorway as they both tried to push in, she concluded that her guess was right.

"What happened?" "Huh?" the two women talked over each other, looking confused.

Evan dropped the man's hands, his head hitting the floor with a distinct thunk that Kayla found satisfying. "Kayla Tasered him. Thank you for that, Reenie."

Unsure if her brother was being sarcastic, she smiled at her future sister-in-law and said sincerely, "Yes, thank you, Reenie." Then she dropped the man's foot with another satisfying thunk.

She looked from one of them to another. "Well, we don't have time to put an iron bed in here to keep him in place. I'm thinking tie-down straps should loop through cinder blocks nicely and be very hard to get through without a knife or sharp object."

The four of them looked at each other. Reenie's face reflected concern; apparently she was just as upset about kidnapping as people being kidnapped. Kayla had no such problem. "We need to do it before he wakes up, or else someone gets to taze him again."

Ivy tilted her head. "Someone will get to Taze him again. He won't be out much longer unless he's sustained a brain injury. Or the Taser stopped his heart. What? I read up."

Reenie smiled ferally. "We have four. One for each."

"Damn," Was all Ivy said in response to that. "Are you going gunslinger, or do I get one?"

There was a laugh in answer, followed by, "You get one." Then, "I suggest you and I get the straps and let Evan carry the cinderblocks."

A short while later, Reenie and Ivy came through the door, a faint sheen of sweat on their foreheads. They had looped the straps through one cinder block each and used that to lift. It didn't make the blocks lighter, but it did make them easier to carry. "That's a good idea."

Evan appeared in the doorway behind them, showing off his manly prowess by carrying two cinderblocks. He had broken a sweat though.

Kayla stood over the man, her stun gun reloaded and at the ready. Though the others had been quick, he started to show signs of coming around. Still aiming at him, Kayla directed the blocks to towels she had doubled up to protect the hardwood. She pushed the blankets away from the double door to the terrace and into the area visible through the doorway. Then she explained how to tie him up so he had a little room to move, but so his hands couldn't reach any of his limbs. It wouldn't do to have him untying his knots.

Getting him situated included waiting for him to come around. It took a little while, but when he did, he formed a clear sentence, "What time is it?"

Kayla didn't answer, just concluded him to be alert and so she Tasered him again. She did ask if anyone else wanted the privilege first. They didn't.

This man had come into her home, posing as a cop and clearly with some other purpose. She had no remorse as his muscles clenched and he flopped a little. His unconsciousness rendered him very compliant, if heavy, while they trussed him up. This time it took long enough for him to come around for Kayla to get impatient.

She kicked his foot a few times until he first grumbled, then growled. At last he opened his eyes and asked again what time it was.

Evan pointedly looked out the window and said "Midafternoon. Why do you ask?"

The man looked away.

He definitely looked worse for the wear. His pants no longer bore the nice pleat he'd entered the house with. His T-shirt was a little stained, and it looked like he'd drooled a bit from being Tasered. Sucked to be him. Maybe he should rethink his career path.

But then he looked them in the eye again and asked more pointedly, "What time is it?"

"You want a clock?" Kayla asked, looking at him sideways.

"Never mind." His jaw clenched.

She turned to Ivy. "Wanna get the clock from next door?"

"What?!" Both Ivy and Reenie looked at her oddly.

Kayla looked back at him. "The man wants to know the time. Let's not have it be said that we are bad captors." Her grin was half-hearted at best.

Reenie frowned. "I think the sheer fact that we are captors means we don't owe him much."

"True." Kayla smiled again. "But we can be a little nice. Ivy, you want to get the clock from next door."

"But—"

Kayla cut her off, then imitated Evan's sigh nearly perfectly. "Just get the poor man a clock. Please."

As soon as Ivy left, Kayla looked at him again, maybe with a little glint of crazy in her eye. "If you try to escape again, I'll reach for whatever's handy. It may be a frying pan, or that Tazer or it may contain bullets. I won't feel any remorse regardless of the method necessary to stop you. If you try to escape and you drag those blocks and scratch the floor, this guy—" she pointed behind her to Evan, "will kill you—slowly and painfully. He may use you to rebuff the flooring, among other things."

She was answered with a single terse nod and a glance over her shoulder as Ivy arrived with the seventies-era wall clock that had come as part of the décor. Without saying anything, Ivy knelt by the one outlet that had been added to the room some time ago. Since this wasn't a room they planned on showing right away, the wallpaper remained. Small birds flitted amid the paper flowers. Kayla wanted to barf. The clock fit right in. The constant ticking, which would be interminable in the otherwise silent room was an added bonus.

Ivy didn't say anything, just stood and resumed a spot near Reenie, so Kayla continued. "We'll be speaking to your people soon. Do you have a message for them?"

Behind her, she heard shuffling and a short near-snort from Evan. They hadn't discussed this. But the man didn't need to know that.

His expression morphed, one eyebrow up. Not serious. "Tell them I'm at the fucking Shangri-la and not to come. I'm having a fantastic time."

She smiled. "Will do."

Kayla left, the others trailing behind her, leaving the man strapped to cinderblocks and unable to touch any two of his extremities together. If he wanted to scratch his face, he could use a shoulder.

Kayla was satisfied.

~

"WHAT WAS THAT?!" Evan's hiss was the only answer he could find to his dilemma. He wanted to yell, but he didn't want the man to hear him. They couldn't leave the house; they'd already left the man partially untended. Evan wouldn't be that surprised if he ran up the stairs right now and found empty straps and the terrace doors open.

Kayla gestured for them all to come closer. "Let him think we're disorganized, that he can play us against each other."

"What about contacting his friends?" Evan was mad; she had no right to make a blanket statement like that. "We should have voted on that!"

Kayla nodded, much calmer than she should have been given the way he was yelling. "We didn't have time to vote first, I just thought of it. And the fact is, we can still vote. I only told him we were contacting them, no one has actually done it yet. I wanted to see what he'd say."

"And?" Reenie's hand gently laid across his forearm. How she stayed calm—or at least calm-ish—through all this was beyond him.

Kayla looked at his fiancée now, "I think there's a message in there. Maybe the word 'Shangri-la' or that he's telling them not to come for him. If we talk to them and we decide to deliver the message, I think we should do it word for word. What do you think?"

Now he was pissed, but he knew he didn't really have anything to be angry about. Kayla had played some good cards. But he lashed out for what he could. "What about the clock? There's a cord, he can break the face to make sharp pieces . . ."

Ivy seemed to sense that he was just venting rather than asking legitimate questions. Kayla started to launch into, "Well, if he—" but Ivy cut her off. "If he can get to the clock, he can get to other far more dangerous things than some cheap plastic and a cord."

"Fine." The word pushed its way out between his clenched teeth. "Should we vote? Do we contact them?"

Kayla raised her hand, needing no time to think it over. "I say yes. We need to find out what his code means."

Evan looked at the other two. Reenie shrugged. "I don't want to bring down bad shit here, but it seems to be finding us anyway. I don't think contacting them will make it any worse. If we're lucky we can trade him for something useful."

Ivy shook her head. "I have no vote. I keep waffling. I'll do whatever anyone else decides."

Evan looked at all three of them and made his decision. Keeping the man was a pain in the ass. And furthermore, the man would eventually make a break for it, possibly—or even probably—hurting one of them in the process. "Contact."

He stepped in before anyone else could. "I'll do it."

Kayla just nodded again. "I'm going to upload schematics. I told them we already had information out there, so now I need to go put it out there before anyone figures out that I lied. Then Ivy and I are going to film a how-to video for the net and post that."

Evan took Reenie's hand. "That leaves you on watch first. Are you good?"

"Sure, just let me get my stuff together so I can work."

Kayla and Ivy had already disappeared, so he consciously let out a breath and stole a far too brief and far too hungry kiss. If they could get through this, then marriage should be a piece of cake. Whatever went wrong, they would always be able to say to each other, 'Remember when those hitmen were after us? We did okay then, and we'll do okay now, too.' They just had to get to later.

After Reenie was settled in the hallway without incident, Evan made a quick check of all the straps. They seemed just as tight as they had been before. The man didn't scowl or speak, just stared into the middle distance.

Things were as good as they could be.

Evan left Reenie there, wishing he didn't have to, headed down the steps and—skipping over the broken one—out to the back corner. Standing there, facing the house, he took a deep breath then spoke calmly.

"We have your man. He says 'Tell them it's fucking Shangri-la and not to come.' You know how to reach us."

There would be no answer, so he turned and walked away to wait.

34

T *he Carriage House*

IT SEEMED FITTING to film in here.

Ivy pointed out that she should be in the video, too. Someone should translate the tech-speak, she said. Kayla figured having Ivy in would also dial down any weirdness from her own personality as well.

So, piece by piece, they demonstrated gears and cogs, then proceeded to film how to put the machine together. Kayla had the small gas generator and battery standing by. They couldn't show the Whitney Device exactly as it was. It needed to look hybrid—normal—so people would build it. But the efficiency alone had to be high enough to attract builders and buyers.

There were already a handful of downloads and comments on her dinky websites. Ivy had already managed to duplicate the site in a number of unlinked places. It wasn't beautifully designed, since none of them knew how to do that. But Kayla already had a few comments. One person wanted to know where to get parts. One said he already had one running. He'd sent a picture—an elderly gentleman, an engineer from the old days, a tinkerer at the ready when she'd needed him. He reported a great efficiency rating and was telling all his cronies.

The adjustment, the one she'd called the shadow constant for so long, was now just a number. Just a report about what speed to run, how to align, no longer a concern or a sticking point.

They worked without breaks. Ivy turned on the wattage when she was on camera, smiling and generally glowing on screen. And when she leaned over to point out a gear, Kayla wondered if some people weren't going to tune in just to get a look at that bright green bra under the white tank top that was both too pale and too cute for this kind of work.

Kayla worked hard because she had plans for more. This evening she was going to start drawing up plans for a heat-pump model. She would advertise it at just over double efficiency. They also needed a video about running an entire house on a Whitney Device. People needed to know they had to make a binary decision—pay for power or run completely off the grid. She had lots to do.

They worked until Reenie announced dinner.

Dinner conversation was not sparkling. It was a rote hunt for a solution regarding their captive. Though tempting in its simplicity, not feeding him wasn't an option. But feeding him was decidedly problematic. Plates, silverware, anything solid really, could become a weapon or at the very least a mess. In the end, they'd decided on a protein shake—only a straw and a big plastic cup.

Later, Kayla and Ivy took their food into the upper hall to relieve Evan of watch. The man sat there, tied at all four corners, and sipped his possibly nasty-tasting protein shake. He watched the women and the clock the way a cat lies in wait.

And Kayla watched him.

KAYLA KEPT VIGIL THAT NIGHT, letting Ivy, Reenie and Evan get some decent sleep.

She didn't have room to draft anything from her cramped spot in the hallway, but she could edit video. She watched footage, making preliminary cuts and splices so that at least her time wasn't wasted. Besides, she had her suspicions and she wanted to wait them out.

Around eleven, when everyone else had been asleep for more than an hour, her prisoner became slightly more alert. It was subtle—he was good at concealing it. What he didn't know was that he was sitting in front of someone who couldn't interpret if he meant good or ill, who couldn't distinguish most sarcasm from regular speech, but who would notice even the smallest changes.

He no longer slumped, but inch by inch worked his way up to nearly sitting. His shoulders moved a bit, as though he were ready to go full "Hulk" and snap his bonds. Kayla didn't see that happening. Maybe he could move the cinderblocks, but she rested easier because he wasn't beefy enough to operate with four blocks weighing him down.

She made edits, wanting to go into the room, but not having an excuse. He was interesting to watch, slowly shifting and flexing. She tried to imagine alternatives—maybe he was just fighting sore muscles. So why not stretch outright? But he was subtle, thinking she didn't notice what he was doing.

He wasn't one of the captors from when she and Ivy had been taken. She'd sent his photo to Reggie to see if he was another rogue employee, but that had come back negative. That didn't please her. It meant that this was more than just one or two guys operating on their own.

Kayla was about to rip a hole into Big Oil, and she was going to do it even knowing they had unlimited resources. Their people could come like the tide. But she was going to fight the tide—

right now, by watching, by playing underhanded, and by hoping she'd done the right thing.

At 11:30 she picked up her phone and tapped out a message to Reggie. At midnight, she subtly hit one button and sent it. All the while she wondered if this man was as good at watching her as she was at him.

Just after midnight, he became openly tense.

Though he tried not to give it away, he heard the sounds of Reggie's car at the road, stopping, door slamming in the far distance. Kayla wondered about that. Hazelton House was the only exit from the road along this stretch. Unless someone was coming here, there was no reason to stop along the street.

The man's head twitched, came up just a sliver of an inch higher as though he was listening. His eyes darted to the clock and she wondered whether she should feel vindicated. But she wasn't there yet. And she didn't even know what "there" would be.

She was convinced his message was a signal of sorts. Someone may have watched him come in, known that he hadn't come back out. But maybe not. Maybe his message simply explained why he hadn't shown up for his next appointment.

So she listened to Reggie come up the drive, and watched her captive. Reggie came on foot, slowly and around the side, just as Kayla instructed. And when the dogs barked, she jumped. She shouted for Evan, just as planned, and he went racing by, leaping over her legs and paperwork, aiming himself down the back steps to check out what had triggered the dogs.

Kayla looked at the man, and back down the hallway, then back at the man.

His tension had multiplied. His eyes darted from her to the clock.

She stood, ready to run. She knew what Evan would find, and she had to tell him ...

With a sharp look revealing the man's arms flexed at the end of their tethers, she stepped out of view of the doorway. It was a risk, losing sight of him, but she thought he was waiting rather than preparing to bolt. So she took that chance.

She bolted down the stairs, running into Evan at the bottom. He was starting to yell up to her, "Don't worry Kay, it's—"

Only at the last minute did he comprehend her frantic hand waving and her finger pressed to her lips. *'Nothing'* she mouthed to him *'It's nothing!'*

"It's nothing." His tone was solid but his face scrunched up.

She nodded and pointed at herself. "*I know*" she mouthed, then said out loud, "Are you sure?"

"Yeah, must have been an animal." He continued at her prompting, still a bit confused. She hoped it didn't show in his voice. "I went out and checked. I think it was just a . . . animal or something."

"Okay." She handed him a page she'd written out, explaining the clock and Reggie waiting downstairs. Then she turned around and headed back to the spot she had abandoned. A quick glance into the room was all she needed before settling herself as though the dogs had been startled by nothing of consequence.

Their captive was sitting straighter, his expression less tense. He was definitely awaiting something, but Kayla wasn't quite sure what or when. She prayed she'd played her cards right and hoped he believed the commotion was his friends coming for him. She was hopelessly bound not knowing if she'd gotten the timing right at all.

She worked for another hour, Evan staying downstairs with Reggie, keeping the sound at a minimum, not letting on that another person had arrived. Periodically, Evan would come halfway up the steps and look over the landing. "Do you need anything, Kayla?"

"No, I'm fine." She tried to stay neutral; she may have added Reenie's accent or Ivy's shoulder shrug. Those were things people did when sounding normal. Unsure if she'd nailed it, she hoped that anything she screwed up or misplaced got written off as her own personal weirdness.

The time came and went and she began to wonder if she wasn't as smart as she thought she was. She'd been so sure that the message was a code. But there was no way of knowing if someone would come tonight, or if they wouldn't even try to get him back for another couple of days. Even if it wasn't a code, they could still come. At any time.

And that wasn't good. She needed something from him first, and all her hopes were bundled with the commotion Reggie caused and the clock in the room. Earlier, she had adjusted the Whitney Device attached to the house. She'd reset the constant, letting it run just a little faster than usual. Not enough to harm any of the large appliances, but enough.

It was another thirty minutes before he started getting visibly angry.

At nearly 2 a.m. he began yelling.

"HEY!!!" He hollered it out to no one in particular. "Now!"

Reenie and Ivy burst out of their rooms, but Kayla waved them past, told them that Evan was downstairs. Kayla returned to studiously ignoring the man. She wanted to see his clock, but she couldn't look without making a real move.

He was fully agitated now, his breathing heavy as he muttered, "It's well past four now."

She spliced another section of footage and waited. *And no one came even though you told them 'now.'*

Finally, he spoke directly to her. "You. Come here."

"No." She refused on principle. She couldn't make it too easy for him; he'd get suspicious.

"Yes." He countered.

Kayla stood her ground.

"I'm negotiating my own release." His eyes locked on her, blue —and human for the first time. "Please."

"I don't trust you." She didn't, but she walked into the room to stand in front of him. "I need to know why I'll let you go in the end." Then after a moment's debate, she added, "I'm pretty sure your message was a code."

"You didn't deliver it?" His eyes widened for a moment then flitted around the room, landing on one spot then another. Maybe he was rethinking his position.

"Of course we did. We wanted to see what would happen. But nothing has happened, has it?" She shook her head, the movement exaggerated so she could read the clock out of the corner of her eye, 4:37. "It's late. Are your friends overdue? Or did they come, then decide to leave you? Because even the dogs quieted down." He wouldn't be able to argue that. "Did they plant a bomb or something? Because that would kill you, too."

The words tumbled free, the speaking of them being the first time she'd considered a bomb, really considered that this could easily get bigger than her cat and mouse with the fake cop tied in front of her. They had been sending spies in ones and twos. Even the kidnapping was an attempt to get information. But killing them? Killing them all?

There was no good reason not to blow them all up.

So she shifted tactics. "If you want to negotiate release, we'll need something in exchange and something that shows you won't come back." And she'd need to give them all a reason not to just take out the whole lot of them.

35

Dining Room, Hazelton House

EVAN LOOKED up from the table.

Kayla was coming down the steps, her eyes roving the scene, checking the table person by person. Reenie and Ivy had wandered down a while ago. Reggie was staying out of sight of the man upstairs.

Evan had initially been distrustful of Standish. But then he was distrustful of most of the people in Kayla's life at first. It had been hard on him to watch out for his sister from a distance these past several years. But he'd gotten his own life, met Reenie, and fallen in love. Now he was back to find that it was just as hard to protect Kayla from up close.

What was easier was sharing it and realizing that Kayla had grown up. She was no longer his younger sister who got ostracized in school for a combination of factors ranging from poor social skills, to straight up strangeness to keen intelligence. What he saw now, through this better lens, was that she was really like any other younger sister. He'd watched out for her, and still did—still fielded and vetted the people in her life—but as adults it had become a give and take. What Kayla added—strong business sense, organization, moral support—was just as much as he did.

So maybe they didn't have the same breakdown as normal brother/sister pairs did, so what? And while Kayla had given not only her savings and some brilliant business plans to Hazelton House, she'd also designed the device that was threatening to bring death like a tsunami.

Just another day in the Reeves family, he thought.

Kayla's words surprised him. "He's asking to negotiate his release."

"What?" Reenie jerked up from the paperwork she was typing out for Reggie, clearly shocked.

Nodding dejectedly, Kayla sat down hard. "I then asked if his people were going to just blow us all to hell, and he implied that wasn't an impossibility."

Reggie smiled at her.

To anyone else, that would be taken the wrong way. Maybe the old man had a touch of the Aspergers himself. But Reggie's voice was soft and soothing. "We've been working on that."

Evan chimed in. "I had the same thought earlier and didn't want to worry everyone. But when Reggie showed up and we had to stay down here, we started planning. Reenie's typing up agreements and plans and emailing Marcus as we go."

"Will email be enough?" His sister wasn't as concerned with stopping a bomb as she was with making sure the bomb didn't shut down the machine.

So once he'd taken Curie and made a few passes around the outside of the building, he'd felt a little better. He'd failed to locate anything he recognized as a bomb. While he knew it wouldn't look like Wile E Coyote's bundle of red dynamite, he wasn't exactly sure what it *would* look like. Still, he didn't find anything bomb-like. Then he went around again, looking for places the ground had been disturbed, checking extra close around the machine. Once he'd examined everything he could, he gave up, came back in and ran his doomsday scenario by Reggie.

Evan passed their progress on to Kayla. "Reggie has a password with Marcus that will make the email a legal document in his absence."

Kayla perked up, looking from Evan to Reggie. "You can do that? That's really cool. So what are you setting up?"

Evan took her hand before he spoke. Even though he knew he didn't need to soften things for her, he did anyway. "Wide, public release of the machine in the event of our deaths. Something big, something they won't be able to completely clean up or shut down."

Nodding, Kayla looked to Reenie, then finally to Ivy. Ivy seemed to have been waiting for acknowledgment, but without any rancor. "We're all good with that."

Reenie nodded back at her. "I'm writing it up. It's not the way we wanted to release the machine, but it makes things happen if no one here is left to do it. And by ensuring that, their position becomes better if we stay alive."

Squeezing her hand again, Evan got her attention. Then he pointed at Reggie. "Standish here is putting a large chunk of his money in trust. In the event of our deaths, that trust will reward people handsomely for putting as many Whitney Devices out there as possible."

He watched as his sister jumped up and ran around the table, a kid at the best birthday ever. All because of a death clause. Just another day in the Reeves family.

She hugged Reggie and the old man smiled as he hugged her back. "I figure we ought to fund the trust even if we live. Let's go big."

She squeezed him again and stood up straight. "So do we go

tell them about the contingency plan or negotiate prisoner release first?"

Reenie's eyes darted back and forth and she looked at Kayla like drugs were a major part of the equation. "Um. I vote we save our own asses first."

They came to an agreement about wording. Reenie printed it out, and the four of them left Reggie in the kitchen with the dogs. Reenie opted to read, speaking awkwardly to the corner of the house. "I'm here to inform you that as of fifteen minutes ago, legal and binding documents have been filed. Each of us, upon our death or disappearance, will have all our worldly goods converted to cash and . . ."

Evan smiled, Reenie had gotten rolling. His future wife telling someone high up in a nasty organization just how and just how badly they were going to get screwed if anything happened to any of them. He loved her more than yesterday. Less than tomorrow.

While her voice kept going in severe monotones, she turned and offered him a small smile. He wondered if they could hear a bit of that grin on the other end of the line.

In just a few minutes, she finished, and they all stood silently, looking at the small bump on the siding as though it would suddenly speak back, offer instructions or countermands. But communication was one way and one way only. With a shrug, Reenie headed back inside, the rest of them trailing.

Reggie greeted them with a questioning look.

Evan shrugged, then turned to Kayla, "Shall we go negotiate prisoner release?"

Kayla lowered her voice. "He's been sitting up there for a while, stewing. Which I think is good. I told him he had to trade us something for his release and he has to prove to us in some way that he won't be back. . . . And he thinks it's almost 5 a.m."

Reenie frowned and pulled out her cell phone. "But it's only just after two."

Kayla smiled. "I know."

THEY CLUSTERED THERE, at the edge of the doorway, Kayla looking over their prisoner.

He either was actually still tied or else he was good enough to make replacement knots look exactly like the ones she had bound him with. If it was the second case, she figured he deserved to escape.

Deciding he wasn't much of a problem, she stepped further into the room, Reenie and Ivy spilling in behind her. The four of them naturally lined up like a roadblock. If this guy was going out the door he was going through at least one of them.

"You have something for us?" Kayla asked.

His eyes went to the clock, again telling Kayla she'd played that well. The only thing he'd asked about was the time. So she'd reasoned time was important to him and if she messed his up, she might get something from him. She hoped the next few minutes would yield something valuable.

"Yes. I'm ready to negotiate."

36

*S*econd Floor Hall, Hazelton House

KAYLA LAUGHED. "One name for one knot undone is not a negotiation."

His face remained impassive. "You get four names or four pieces of information."

"No, I don't. I get one." She frowned at him. "You only need one knot undone to get out. You give me four. Then I'll release you."

They went back and forth, finally agreeing to Kayla's demand. He wanted out; they didn't want to keep him. He saw the wisdom in trading information on people who had screwed him over in exchange for an early escape.

He gave them three names, one associated with botched inspections and cleanup in the Gulf spill. He also gave an account number that had incoming payments traceable to accounts linked to Big Oil. Then he looked them in the eye. "Chavez

Mahoney hired me to hit you. That's free. Because he's ditched me here."

"Alias?" Reenie asked even as her fingers flew over her keyboard, checking his intel for any accuracy.

Ivy snorted. "Chavez Mahoney?"

"Now release me." He demanded, tugging hard at the straps, moving the cinderblocks a bit, showing that he could.

"What's your name?" Kayla countered.

"I was ordered to gather intel, and to take out any dog or person in my way. I'll still carry it out, if you fail to either release me or kill me within the next sixty seconds."

Kayla was glad for Reggie's last will. Marcus had already e-filed it. It wouldn't post with the county yet, but it would register with a recorded drop in the middle of the night.

Kayla nodded. "It was a code right? Shangri-la?"

"Doesn't matter. If I missed my check-in, they were supposed to come for me. Fifty seconds." He held his bound hands up as far as he could.

"What was the time frame?" She tilted her head, hoping she didn't sound like she really cared.

"Before 4 a.m."

Her heart started to race. "And what was going to happen?"

"Break me out. Take out the dogs. Find me, preferably not my body. Twenty five seconds."

Evan looked at her, "2 a.m.?"

"Yeah." Her eyes stung, and before she knew what she was doing she was pulling her gun out. She swung suddenly toward him. "Would they just leave you? Or blow the place with you in it?"

A shrug was his only answer, and Kayla pushed the rest of them out of the room. She drew her gun, and aiming it at him, used her other hand to release one of his wrists. Then she backed out of the room, gun still on him.

"Where are you going?" The man hollered after them from his spot on the floor.

"To clean up. It's nearly 2:30." But as she started down the staircase, Kayla heard noises from the room behind them. It took less than a second to figure out the man was already partway out of his bonds.

EVAN SAW Reggie pop up out of his seat from over Kayla's shoulder. The old man didn't ask any questions, just reached down to remove a hefty looking gun from an ankle holster and joined the party.

When Evan made it to the bottom of the staircase, he told Reggie, "There's a 4 a.m. deadline."

One brief look at his watch had Reggie sucking in his breath. "Not long."

Kayla looked at all four of them, "If I were them, I'd take the machine and the computers."

"Shit." It was a sweet voice. Reenie hugged her computer tighter to her, then considered a spot to hide it.

With a flick of his head, Evan signaled Ivy, who understood and immediately followed Reenie. Ivy's gun stayed poised in her hands and Evan hoped it was enough.

Immediately, his attention was pulled back to Kayla, who was already out the back door, Reggie following her because somebody ought to.

Evan began stalking the perimeter from the inside of the house. He heard Reenie and Ivy arrive at the base of the stairs then begin riffling through things on the table, but he didn't go check. He had to trust them to take care of themselves.

Cautiously, he checked out each window, carefully scanning the horizon, breathing low as though that would make any sounds come clearer. He was rounding the front corner when he heard Kayla and Reggie come inside, snippets of their conversation floating to his straining ears. For a moment he wished they lived in a normal house, not a 200 year-old mansion that came stocked with bloody clothes, handwritten confessions, and dangerous schematics hidden in the walls and under the stones.

As he moved to the next window, he realized that this was not the first time the machine had brought madmen to the doorstep of this house. It wasn't even the second time. But it had to be the last time.

He heard loud thumps from the back and slips of words in Kayla's voice saying something about removing gears. Footsteps told him that the others had split up and were checking the rest of the house, hopefully scanning the dark horizon in all directions as they went. Each reported that all was quiet.

At least the ground floor was. Upstairs, thumping told him the fake cop had ceased to care about the threat to his person if he ruined the hard wood floor.

As they stood there, all of them looking at each other, each with guns drawn, the thumping stopped. A moment later they heard the French doors open and the sounds of the man leaving from the second-story balcony were both impressive and unmistakable.

Kayla's mouth quirked. "I really thought I tied him better than that. At least he's got to be starving, that protein shake wasn't worth much."

They stayed there, guns drawn, all five of them in a cluster in the middle of the old house, until Evan realized the folly in that. "This is a good way to put Reggie's last will into action, guys. Let's split up."

～

ALL QUIET ON *the western front*, Evan thought.

He and Reenie had slunk softly across the back to the Overseer's House. Well, as quietly as they could with two large and sometimes snuffling dogs in tow.

They periodically checked the front lawn through the windows in the smaller home, then the side windows that faced away from Hazelton House. Reenie paced nervously.

He wanted to put his arms around her, but he wouldn't do anything that didn't leave his hands completely free—not as 3 a.m. rapidly approached.

She sighed, not in exasperation or confusion, but in bone-weary resignation. "When will this end?"

He could only shake his head. "I truly don't know."

All his life, he'd felt his purpose was to deal with the things that came at him. Life happened *to* him. Aside from his work—which he honestly partially picked because of the ability to follow Kayla around if need be—the only thing in his life he felt he'd actually chosen had been Reenie. And even that hadn't been easy. He'd held onto that ring for a long time, knowing what he wanted but not knowing if it was the right thing to do. He didn't want to give Reenie a future that slowly wore them down until there was nothing left. And that's all he'd been able to see when he first put the two women together and watched their oil-and-water dance.

But they had surprised him. In spite of all the craziness, Kayla only had one episode when she'd come close to shutting down. She'd been kidnapped for Christ's sake and she'd come through just fine. She was more open about saying what she was feeling, and she'd learned to better interpret people while they'd been apart. When he thought about it, he realized she'd been calling him less frequently these past few years, leaning on him less often than usual. And he had taken more control of his own life, gone out more, been interrupted less. He'd found Reenie.

She held the gun clasped in her hands, her engagement ring winking at him. He was pretty sure she polished it every day. She dug in the dirt, she clasped a gun, she took notes for a last will and testament and she loved him enough to find ways to not only get along but actually become friends with his strange sister.

So what if she shouldn't be allowed near a credit card or an account ledger?

Reenie kept pacing, seemingly unaware of the turn of his thoughts. She was wearing him out just from watching, so he went over to the old wingback chair and sat down.

He didn't know how long he should expect to wait. Their prisoner—held in place more by their watchful eyes than by their jury-rigged containment system—had fled. Because of that, the information well had run dry.

He looked at his phone; they were due for another checkin in five more minutes. The time dragged, his system tired but on an odd buzzing alert. Reenie and the dogs all wandered nervously, but Evan couldn't tell if the dogs had anything to be edgy about besides Reenie.

His brain was fading, his breaths deepening, and his eyes starting to drift close when it sounded like his world exploded.

37

T he Overseer's House

IT TOOK his brain a moment to register the pandemonium that he heard. It wasn't so much an explosion as a series of them. Gunshots.

From the back of the buildings. At the main house?

He heard glass breaking in the distance. The dogs had gone nuts the moment the first shot was fired, making it harder to distinguish what was happening outside from what was going on inside.

Reenie hit the deck at the first shot and he, too, had rolled his ass right out of the recliner. For some reason he looked at his phone and saw that the time was just after 3 a.m. They had hit their mark and still managed to come right as the group was starting to relax.

Several more shots were fired in rapid succession, and he and

Reenie realized something very important: No one was firing at them.

Everything was aimed at the big house. Since neither he nor Reenie had fired a single return shot, it was relatively unlikely that anyone coming up even knew they were here. If they played their cards right, that could be used to their advantage.

Using hand gestures—probably very improperly—he signaled to Reenie that he wanted her to stay here and cover him.

She frowned, waved her hand back to him, and he tried again.

Still, Reenie shook her head at him before scooting toward him. She stayed low, an odd look on her face that—only when she got close did he figure it out—was exasperation.

She blinked twice and held her gun aimed away from him. "We can talk, you know."

Yeah, he should have known.

Two more shots rang in the distance, and he heard glass breaking again. Instead of fearing for lives, which he wasn't able to do for fear he'd break down, he got mad about the glass. The windows on the house had survived almost 200 years unbroken. They had warped and started to droop the way old glass does, an authentic look that couldn't be duplicated by contemporary measures. And some idiot was shooting them out.

After suffering an involuntary flinch, Reenie looked at him again. "What were you saying?"

"I don't think they know we're over here. I should be able to sneak out the back and around the cook house and see if I can get a better shot off before they find me."

She looked at him blankly. "You were trying to say all that with gestures when you don't know sign language and have never been in the army?"

He wanted to smile and call her a smart ass, but another shot rang off, this one clearly coming from the big house. Evan prayed like hell that it was Ivy, Reggie, and Kay shooting back.

His thoughts were interrupted again by Reenie saying, "I'm coming, too, Ev."

"No." It was dangerous and he didn't want to worry—

"Oh, okay." The sarcasm embedded deep in her tone told him what was coming. "I'll stay here and not cover you because I can't see you once you round the corner. And I'll stay by myself and do nothing just because you don't want to worry. Oh, and if anyone comes storming in here, I'm either toast or a hostage. Yeah, that sounds like a great plan."

He sighed as another bullet went soaring in the distance. "Are you done?"

"Are you?" She stared at him.

He sighed. "Yes, Let's go."

Together they shifted out the back door, listening to the seemingly random volleys of shots. Luckily, no one screamed. From where it sounded like the shots were originating, whoever it was wouldn't be able to see the back door to the Overseer's open. That should be obscured by the kitchen house, and if he and Reenie could sneak in without being seen . . .

Then again, if they were seen, he might just die tonight. But since he might just die tonight anyway, he squeezed Reenie's hand and looked her in the eyes one last time. They were exposed there in the small back courtyard between the buildings, but it needed to be done.

"I love you. I want to marry you."

She squeezed his hand back. "Then let's go shoot these a-holes."

God bless Southern women.

He crouched low into the tall grass and tried not to let the movement give him away. A slight wind had kicked up, which he was hoping would work in his favor for getting into position. Then again, it would work against them for shooting people.

Holy shit. He was going to go shoot *people*.

The only thing worse he could think of was getting shot by these people, or watching one of the others get shot by them.

He looked up at the main house for a moment and saw a rifle barrel poking out a broken window from the second floor. He imagined Ivy at the other end of it, sighting something. Someone.

Evan's imagination must have been pretty good, because he saw fire shoot out of the tip just as he heard the blast. And in the distance he heard something yelp. Another smatter of fire was returned and he watched as a spot of wood along the siding splintered and rained down.

Reenie had gotten ahead of him and was almost inside the kitchen building.

He heard her voice in his head. *Let's go shoot these a-holes.* He slithered in behind her and she headed for the window, Evan still right on her tail.

Just as they arrived, the glass shattered over them.

His eyes closed instinctively and his hands came up for cover. He tried to dive in front of Reenie, but only did half the job, the glass came so quickly.

By the time he opened his eyes, both of them were dressed in tiny shards. It littered hair and shoulders; some clung to shirts or jeans like snowflakes. His arms bore a thousand tiny cuts and so did hers. Blood ran from above Reenie's right eyebrow, and she wiped at it absently as she commented, "Well, that was lucky."

"Lucky!?" He hissed.

She nodded, "Now we don't have to shoot out our own window and give ourselves away." She was already moving. She didn't stop to wipe at the blood again or check for injuries. Someone was shooting at her family and her house and . . . Evan scrambled to keep up.

He never had qualms punching someone who needed it. He figured he could even handle a knife in a fight, and he brandished the gun with ease. But when it came down to it now he was following her. Reenie was keeping mostly out of sight, but the barrel of her gun slowly slid between two shards remaining in the frame and her eye lined up right behind it.

Evan did the same at the other corner, and he waited.

It didn't do them any good to fire at things randomly; they'd only give themselves away.

Nothing moved.

No shots rang and the night stilled while everyone waited.

Evan wondered if Eli Whitney knew that he'd died for that machine. That in destroying Hazelton's livelihood he'd dealt a near death blow to a man who was already wounded by Whitney cuckolding him. He wondered if Edwin Carroll knew who had come after him and why. The man seemed to; he told Reggie he thought someone was looking into it. At least Reggie would now do everything in his power to keep the same thing from happening again.

In the distance, Evan saw something flutter near the edge of the barn, but he held his fire.

Then, the figured stepped a little further out and materialized into the shape of a man.

Evan reminded himself that all of his own people were accounted for, aimed and pulled the trigger.

His bullet left the barrel just a moment after Reenie's.

KAYLA WATCHED the man in the distance come around the edge of the barn. She was sighting him when she watched him jerk, not once, but twice, and drop like a stone.

It only took her a second to figure out the shots had come from her side.

Evan and Reenie were outside. She just hoped they were under cover. That was hard to tell though. They could be on the roof of the Overseer's. They could have snuck around the kitchen house, or into the kitchen house, or they could be on the roof of the kitchen house. So many options . . . most of them exposed.

She ducked instinctively as fire was returned. Okay, so there was more than one guy down there. She'd already figured that out. In fact, she calculated they were looking at a minimum of five guys, one of whom was probably their fake cop.

Though it appeared her side had the distinction of drawing first blood, the shooting could go on all night unless someone put a stop to it. If Evan and Reenie had nailed that guy, then they had drawn attention to themselves.

And why had no one in the house been hit?

She crouched behind the wall while Ivy lined up another shot. Reggie was still down at his post in the far room on the first floor. Kayla knew because she could hear his shots.

If she were planning this tactical assault it would have been just that: tactical.

If you wanted to kill people, you came in with enough guys, armed them all with rifles, and went for head shots. Whoever was funding this endeavor had enough cash to make that happen. There should have been five to eight men out there, strategically located, communication system in place. Each of them would sight a person in the main house and once everyone had a bead, drop them all at once.

No one would have had a chance to get away. It would have been nearly silent and it could have been several days before anyone found the bodies . . . except Marcus knew where they were. And there was a plan to go into effect upon their deaths. So as soon as Reggie failed to check in at the appointed time, Marcus would go broad with it. These guys knew that. Add in that there were already several zealous converts from her websites and there was no longer any reason to take them all out.

So shooting all of them wasn't the plan.

On her hands and knees, Kayla made her way out of the landing area. She headed to the bedroom on her left and entered.

Car ties and cinderblocks littered the floor and the balcony door still stood ajar, just as she had hoped. Slithering out onto the porch, she clung to the puddles of shadow near the wall and moved into place before she could change her mind.

Once she stood, she'd be an easy mark. But she was betting her life that they weren't actually shooting *at* the occupants of Hazelton House. Still, it was in her best interest to move the target somewhere else.

Then, with a deep breath, she popped up and started yelling for all she was worth.

"That fake cop you sent us gave us names. He gave us account numbers. We can find you all!"

As soon as the words left her mouth she realized that she'd just given them cause to take her out. So she started reciting the words the man had spoken, verbatim. She yelled out the account number he'd given them. She yelled out names of employers. She had to work quickly, talk fast, make sure they had more reason to shoot that fake cop than her. She wanted to get them to turn on him, make him have to shoot his own way out of here.

He'd already turned against the others, and his orders had been to take out anyone in his way. Her guilt was at an all time low. When she wasn't immediately killed, she peered down the back hill, trying to make out shapes in the dark. As she watched, the shadow of the man that had fallen the first time started to get up.

Another came around near him, staying low. He started to help the wounded man, but someone from her side laid down fire and it didn't happen. From where she stood, it looked like he was being dragged away, certainly still alive.

Kayla started yelling again.

She recited the intel about the oil spills and about the purposefully bad inspections. About the jobs the fake cop had claimed to perform. She rattled off dates Reenie had found and deposit dates into the account.

And then Kayla ran out of verbal ammunition.

She stood there, looking out over the shadows of her plantation home and she was struck by the stark beauty of it. By the idea that for several hundred years, people had stood on this balcony and looked out over this land. And they did it when there was no running water. They did it when there were no power tools or TVs, without decent lighting or even proper food preservation. They did it when babies were born and often died on the same day. And they were just as devious as any man alive today.

The first Charlene Hazelton had killed her own baby in this house, so that her husband wouldn't see the child belonged to another man. She did it to hurt the baby's father, and she did it because she seemed to have a cold, hard streak in the middle of her heart.

And here Kayla stood, two hundred years later, a gun in her hand, alongside Charlene's many-times-great granddaughter, fighting over the same machine that started it all . . .

She had no more words to protect herself. And she was low on bullets, already well into her second clip. She stood on the porch and waited for some sort of resolution.

None came.

No one moved.

So she didn't have a warning and didn't have time to react.

It seemed the moment she heard the sound of a bullet tearing out of a gun from not too far away was the same moment she felt it rip through her chest.

Kayla heard the scream and could only assume it was her own.

Reacting purely on instinct, her hands clutched at her shirt and felt hot, thick liquid pumping down the front of her. It took a moment to process that it was her own blood. Her fingers started to grab at it, as though she could hold it and push it back into her system.

She felt gray and odd. Thoughts passed through her head,

but ran too fast to be grasped. Stars started sparkling at the edges of her visual field, and she suddenly felt that gravity had cranked itself way up.

Needing to sit, she did her best to make a smooth transition to the floor boards, but she wasn't sure she handled it so well.

It all must have happened very quickly, even though to her mind the sounds were slow and long, like a record played too slowly. Because she heard Ivy scream in response. Ivy wasn't hit, the sound was angry, not pained, and it certainly wasn't afraid.

In that moment, Kayla knew that losing her was the one thing Ivy was afraid of. Now that the possibility of that was off the table, now that it had become definite, Ivy had no fear at all.

Kayla heard her yelling that she was going to get every one of them. Ivy went through the broken window on the landing, judging from the sound. Though Kayla's eyes slipped closed by some unseen force, she heard Ivy's feet on the roof over the back ground-floor porch, then a thud onto the ground. Ivy must have jumped it, much the way the fake cop had.

Then, feet pounding, the yelling of promises, and before she had even cleared the edge of the kitchen building, gunshots, as Ivy went screaming across the plantation, hell-bent on revenge.

Kayla opened her eyes just enough to see she was right—the shadow of Ivy firing into the night as she moved closer and closer to the threat was the last thing she saw before unconsciousness claimed her.

38

S*avannah Memorial Medical Center*

EVAN SAT CRUMPLED in the unforgiving chair, Reenie on one side of him, Ivy on the other. All three nursed cheap Styrofoam cups of coffee that was stale even though it had been made on the spot by the vending machine.

Ivy's coffee was full, steam still rising off the top, and she blew on it, probably in an effort to maintain some normality. From the look on her face, she was just as concerned as he was. Evan assumed she was in even deeper with his sister than he'd originally thought. In just a few short months, her worry had grown to equal what he'd built up over Kayla's lifetime.

Ivy wore a scrub top and three bandages. Her pajama bottoms had been cut away to make space for the dressing that wrapped her lower right leg. She had gauze around her right bicep and another on her left hand. All three were due to bullet wounds; all three had grazed her. Lucky son of a bitch.

Reenie sported butterfly bandages as well as the occasional small row of stitches marching along her otherwise unblemished skin.

Evan had his own band-aids, butterflies, and glue. The staff practically had to hold him down to keep him in the ER.

He, Reenie, and Ivy had raced here behind the ambulance that had taken so long to arrive. The EMTs found that Reenie, ever practical, had towels pressed to Kayla's wound. She'd turned Kayla over and found the exit hole and stopped that up, too. Ivy had come running back, dripping her own blood in the process, and proceeded to pray to every God Evan ever heard of and several that he hadn't. She'd done mouth-to-mouth when Kayla stopped breathing.

It went on for an eternity. Once the EMTs had gotten hold of her though, the pace became manic. The paddles came out, and the backboard was strapped on before Evan had even seen it arrive. They shuffled Kayla down the steps like they were robbing the place, each with one hand on the board, the other doing something vital.

And then the ambulance doors closed and she was gone.

Evan stood there, stunned before he even realized they told him they were going to Savannah Memorial. Effingham didn't have a level one trauma unit, and Kayla was definitely level one. They didn't mention that she'd already died once. Twice, if Reenie and Ivy were right about her breathing stopping before the EMTs came.

He didn't remember following the ambulance here. But he did remember the turn onto "Feel Better Drive" and being affronted by the stupid name. He remembered the three of them falling through the ER doors and thinking they were going straight to where Kayla was, only to all be stopped like thieves and thrown into ER jail for their own injuries.

Evan had been the first out. And he'd found the previous argument of "stay in the ER, she won't be out of surgery for a while. There's nothing you can do" to be far too painfully true. So Reenie and Ivy's arrival was recent, and they had warm coffee to show for it. It took longer to put them back together than it had for him. Or else the ER staff simply saw that he would not be contained for long, and he was released to come contain himself in this horrid plastic chair and wait for word of his sister.

No one spoke and his thoughts wandered.

For a while he veered into anger. Why had she stood out there and yelled everything? Clearly she'd thought she was informing them of what her cadre already knew, but why? Did she think they would just leave and know there was nothing they could do about it? Maybe she had. Kayla had always been on the "knowledge is power" side of any argument.

Ivy turned and started to speak, her words sounding almost too loud for the otherwise empty room. Maybe because the three of them were huddled close in three adjacent chairs even though they had the entire waiting room to themselves in the early morning. It appeared only Kayla was in need of surgery at this hour.

Evan had to focus on Ivy, force his concentration in order for her words to make sense.

"There was blood by the barn. But by the time I got there everyone was gone."

Reenie looked across him, completely missing him as a person, as she too turned her attention to Ivy.

"It looked like they dragged several people away, alive or not. . .." She shrugged.

This time Reenie's eyes flicked to him. "Once again, we have to get our stories straight." She picked up the phone and Evan could see the name "Reginald Standish" across the screen.

Her voice was tight. "Reggie."

The older man had waited behind at the house. Thus he'd probably already been interviewed by the sheriff's deputies. They would have had to respond to an emergency call that was clearly the result of a gunshot. Reenie nodded while she listened, her tension loosening visibly as she spoke. Eventually, when she tucked the phone back into her purse, she looked as though her shoulders carried less of a load. For that, Evan was grateful.

"He cleared out the cinderblocks and the straps before the deputies came."

Evan breathed his own sigh of relief. He hadn't even considered the mess left behind. Had anyone official stumbled into that room, it would have been clear that it was designed for holding a prisoner. In short order, they would find enough evidence to see that, in fact, someone had been held there recently. And that could have opened a can of worms that could have led someone to check the floorboards of the slave cabins. But without the appearance of the cinderblocks and straps, there would be no reason to suspect anything.

Even in his relief, Evan felt sick to his stomach.

He'd helped hold a prisoner. Though the reasoning had been sound—and he'd do it again in the same circumstances—he couldn't help noting that he'd held a man against his will. He shot at humans and was pretty sure he'd hit two. He would likely never know if he'd killed them. He preferred not knowing.

"Reggie told them everything starting with the dogs barking and gunshots flying. And except for what Kayla said."

Evan nodded. That was an easy enough lead to follow. They had agreed before, that if anyone asked why they were all holding, it was because of the robbery, then the fire. The deputies had already been out once. No one should be surprised or suspicious that they were all sleeping with their guns. The assault had been forewarned.

But Evan didn't know if they would survive the next one. What lie could they possibly tell the deputies next time?

There wasn't time to think about it.

A doctor was coming out of the double doors at the end of the hallway and Evan was on his feet before he understood what he was doing.

The doctor's face was a plane of acceptance and exhaustion. Evan braced for the worst.

～

KAYLA PLAYED with the bed covers.

"You told them I yelled?" She looked at her brother.

She hated this. She'd been moved from the ICU finally. She was in a normal hospital gurney now, with fewer things tying her to the bed, but she was captive nonetheless. An IV ran into her arm, a slim tube with prongs blew air up her nose as though her lungs didn't work. Her ears had begun to ache from having that slight but constant pressure from the nasal tube. Her right hand was tied to a board, and several bags hung from the tall metal pig tail at the head of her bed. Her finger wore a white laundry clip with a red light that monitored her oxygen levels. Her chest was covered in foam stickers with metal snaps that led to even more wires, this time running to the left side of the bed, and making an incessant beeping each time her heart beat. Thank God her heart had a good sense of rhythm.

They told her that now that she was out of the ICU she'd be able to get up and around a little bit. That was clearly a joke they all thought was hysterical. She couldn't even just go to the bathroom, because budging even one wire would set off alarms and people would rush into the room to save her from getting out of bed.

She knew; she'd tried it once. And nearly had a heart attack as she was swarmed.

Twenty minutes later, she'd been wired neatly back into the bed and still had to pee.

Now Evan sat at her side, providing further unnecessary

policing, and all she really wanted was to go home. She could watch her own machine better than anyone here.

"I told them I couldn't hear what you yelled."

She nodded. "I told them word for word what I yelled."

Lowering his voice and leaning in, Evan stared at her. "Shit, Kayla. You told them that? Why?"

"Because they can look into it. Once the trail leads far enough —and we already know that it does—they'll turn the investigation over to the FBI." She made a series of perfect pleats in the sheet, the argument with her brother the best relief she'd had all day. She'd been bored out of her skull since she woke up.

"That's going to bring a load of publicity down on this."

"Which is exactly what we need. Publicity is going to get people interested in the Whitney Device and get more working machines out there." She looked away. "I was content to go plugging along with my websites and just working around getting sabotaged at every turn, but they brought this to our doorstep with deadly force. I'm done pussyfooting around."

"Pussyfooting? Is that your word of choice?" He smiled at her.

She grinned right back. "Yes, yes it is. We have been pussyfooting."

His expression turned somber once more, the startling transformation revealing that a serious thought had just passed through his head and wiped out everything in its path. "How did you tell them that you came by this info?"

"I told them that a cop came to the house—"

"Jesus, Kayla!"

"Wanna let me finish?" She sighed and tried to adjust her pillow. She couldn't reach since her hands were bound by wires and tubes. She had a fleeting moment of sympathy for her one-time prisoner. "I told them a cop came to the house, and I answered the door. I recognized that he was fake—I told them he wasn't a very good fake cop." Which was only untrue because he was grossly out of district.

"And that I unexpectedly drew his gun on him. And I made him tell me why he was there and why we had been arsoned the week before. I made no mention of any of the rest of you in that."

Evan's phone rang. Without moving away, he answered it, then began to look alarmed. But the volume was up, probably because his hearing was shot from all the loud power tools he worked with and Kayla heard everything. So she interrupted. "I told them where to find the gun. It will have my prints and the fake cop's prints on it, unless you guys touched it?"

There was a distant rumble of Reenie's voice relaying that question, followed by a faint chorus of 'no's.

Kayla smiled. "It turns out, this is all about the machine. Who knew?"

39

H azelton House, Opening Day

IT SEEMED as many people came to see the machine as came to see the plantation itself. Kayla stood to the side and watched the public come to visit. She wore jeans and a T-shirt, but she was the only one.

Reenie was dressed as the mistress of the plantation. Had they opened on their original planned date, she would have sweated her way through the layers of crinolines and fine fabric that bounced in simple harmonic motion as she walked. Well, she *sashayed* or whatever. It's apparently what you did when you put on one of those dresses. It was inevitable, Ivy said, and that was just part of the reason Kayla refused.

Also, she couldn't put on a corset as per doctor's orders. Thank you, God.

A bullet through your left lung nicking the heart muscle was a good reason not to bind your ribs and reduce your lung capacity. Pain was another good reason, though Kayla was relatively sure she'd feel it from a corset regardless of the bullet hole.

Ivy came by, in house-servant gear—a beautiful but simple gray dress topped by what resembled a fluffy white shower cap. They told her the name of it, but Kayla had forgotten. She didn't have a head for those kinds of things.

There had been a media onslaught after the shooting. Evan, Ivy, and Reenie had refused all interviews, leaving that to Kayla and Reggie. Once Kayla was home, Reggie put his people to work lining up TV time slots and interviews. She'd now been quoted in most major news outlets and had been seen on two of the big morning shows. They all came here and sat down for an interview in a room Reenie and Ivy had refurbished plantation-style. They said it lent charm. Kayla said it lent a place for two people to talk in front of a camera setup.

There were some requests for the talk-show circuit, but Reggie handled that. He was in Chicago right now, sleeping off what he referred to as a three show bender. Kayla had watched several of the interviews and he seemed good at it. She didn't understand half the questions the couch jockeys asked. These people wanted to know about Reggie's personal life, about his late wife, about Edwin, and how Reggie felt. She preferred the news outlets, where she stated facts and talked about the Whitney Device and how it had been found—none of this 'What's your favorite color and will you be manufacturing Whitney Devices in that shade of green?' Kayla shook her head because it hurt just thinking about it.

"So, can you sell me one of these?"

Though it had been preceded by heavy footsteps, the voice seemingly came out of nowhere and Kayla jumped, feeling the pull deep inside her chest. She looked up to find a beefy man in jeans and an untucked button-down shirt.

"Sorry." He shoved his hands down into his pockets. "Didn't mean to startle you."

"That's okay." Kayla felt each sound form in her mouth; the feeling of talking to strangers had always been a little unnatural to her. But she knew everyone started out as a stranger, and she pushed her way through. "We do have a website. You can order one there."

Thinking that would be the end of the conversation, she started to turn away, but was startled by more words.

"I just thought it would be nice to own one built by the inventor." He looked at her more closely. "That's you, right?"

She nodded, only to recant a moment later. "Well, I just tweaked Eli Whitney's original design. But since you can't get Whitney to build you one . . ."

Reggie was already manufacturing them. He'd seen the opportunity when the media blitz hit. They still gave away the schematics for free. They sold build-it-yourself kits, too. But there was a market for plug-in versions and Reggie had invested heavily to get that up and running.

There had been no profit from any of it yet. But, as of 9 a.m. today, they had income from Hazelton House.

The parking lot was full and they had stuffed each of the three first tours to capacity—Ivy, Reenie and Evan each heading in a different direction and rotating through the different buildings. Even Evan was in plantation gear, suspenders and old-timey shoes included.

The man spoke again. "I know your time is valuable, but if you'd be willing to build me one, I'd be honored. And I'd pay whatever you're asking for the work." He offered up a shy smile. "I think these things are going to change the game and I get to tell everyone I met the inventor."

Kayla was taken aback. Suddenly it hit her that she'd become a minor celebrity. What a mess. But since there was nothing she could do about it. She nodded and offered to look into it. Then she added, "Are you waiting on a tour?"

"My wife and kids came for the tour. They want to see about soaps and buggies and that kind of thing. Sheila's real excited about getting a mint julep at the end."

Reenie's idea, Kayla remembered.

"But me, I came for the Whitney Device. They say you found the plans in the hearth? How does that work?"

She wound up showing him the stone. It was carefully set at an angle, revealing the pocket underneath. A reprint of the original Whitney schematic hung on the wall along with Reggie's slightly altered version that led to Kayla's breakthrough. In halting sentences, she told the man about the steps they'd taken. "Do you want to see the original Whitney Machine? It's in the Carriage House."

It, too, was part of the tour. A nearly complete—nonfunctioning—device, made from the parts and gears she had found in this very spot.

The man asked intelligent questions, obviously a bit of an engineer himself. Kayla happily answered him, the words no longer forming like bricks in her mouth, but tripping happily out without worries about counting sentences.

They talked about the machine and she told him about her struggles with the shadow constant. About cannibalizing the old tractor in the barn to link the device to the generator so that she could actually run things.

When the tour finished up, the man pulled his wife and three kids out of the way and introduced them to Kayla. Though the middle child, a boy, responded politely, he didn't shake her hand or meet her eyes. And she recognized it.

She didn't ask the parents. Kayla knew better than that. She'd been talked around most of her life. "Do you have Aspergers?"

"Highly functional autism with asocial disorder." He didn't say yes or no. Of course not.

She didn't hold out her hand for a handshake. "My name's Kayla. I have Aspergers."

He nodded, though he still didn't look at her face, he moved his gaze to her feet and then her knees, his eyes darting all around. He moved even as he stood still, almost undulating in the breeze. "We've been watching you on TV. You built the machine."

"Yes, I did. Do you build machines?" It would get him started, she knew. Though it was a yes/no question, it wouldn't be answered as such.

"I draw. I paint. Sometimes on the walls. Mom has to tell me which walls I can paint on. She marks them for me with a pencil. She used to mark them with a Sharpie but I can't erase it for pencils or watercolors, and it bleeds through both acrylic and oil paints." He kept talking, pausing only when his big sister commented on how talented he was and when his parents asked if she would like to join them for drinks.

So she sat at the table with them, inside the boundaries of the old forcing house, where Reenie and Ivy had set up a café with two mobile carts to serve drinks and cookies.

She listened and she watched as the two kids running the small food service delivered soft drinks and mint juleps. While she sat there, the first tour ended, and the people waiting near the front entrance and on the front lawn were herded in and divided up for the second tour. Ivy smiled and waved as she walked by, clearly busy with the inundation of guests. She didn't seem to resent Kayla for sitting and chatting while she worked her butt off.

Kayla left a while later with the man's card in her pocket so she could get back to him about building him a Whitney Device with her own hands.

She had her own work to do.

≈

ONE MONTH later

KAYLA SAT AT HER COMPUTER, the desk along the wall sitting just out of the spill of light from the large windows looking out over the front of the plantation.

"It's Monday. Time to stop working." Ivy's voice came from behind her.

Four full weeks of tours and they were finally finding their groove.

She and Ivy had moved to the third floor, their previous digs proving problematic. It seemed impossible to keep people out of their side of the floor when other rooms there were open. They now had a suite of rooms here, and as Ivy liked to point out, great legs from going up and down the stairs all the time. Kayla still preferred the servants' staircase that led directly to the kitchen.

They'd all learned quickly to rope things off. Lock doors. And even gate the driveway. They took Mondays and Tuesdays off, but spent their first break turning away visitors who drove all the way to the front and even knocked on the closed door, not paying attention to the online info about days and hours.

"You've been in bed all morning. What do you care if I work?" Kayla was making updates to the websites. She was crafting a letter to her mailing list.

"Whatcha got there?" Ivy came into view at Kayla's side, her arms crossed under her breasts, her legs bare in the pajamas of boxers and T-shirt that she always wore.

Kayla smiled up at her. "We just crossed 700,000."

"Wow."

They both knew that was just the email list. There had been a burst of interest from all the TV activity and newspaper articles. Though that initial acceleration had tapered off, more kept coming.

When she first came home from the hospital, Kayla

searched the plantation and pulled four listening devices in addition to the two Evan had already ripped out. Ivy went with her and spoke into each device just before Kayla yanked it, telling the listeners in no uncertain terms exactly where they could stick it.

There was still a possibility that there were more devices. But the sweep they'd done had been thorough, and certainly nothing remained in the areas where they lived and worked. Kayla still checked for new ones each week, just to be sure that nothing new popped up.

There was one set of footprints out by the slave cabins, and Robert Bell's body had disappeared. But nothing since then. Kayla was pretty certain efforts had been directed elsewhere.

The internet at the plantation tended to crash for no reason, and Kayla wound up hacking her way around it. When she was on television for an interview, there would be an unusually high number of glitches with the broadcast functions for that station. But the signal always got through somehow.

Ivy broke through her thoughts. "We have to try on dresses today."

Kayla groaned. The last thing she wanted was to attend a dress fitting.

"We promised." Ivy reminded her gently.

She knew.

As Reenie's bridesmaids, they were obligated. Since Kayla couldn't care less about the dress, Reenie had picked them out herself with help from two sorority sisters, but Kayla and Ivy had to get tailored; there was no way around that.

Ivy changed the topic to a better one. "Are you sending out adjustments again?"

Kayla nodded. She had a plan and was already on recalibration number two. Out of seven.

The design they were selling had a dial that changed the amount of gasoline feeding into the system. And bit by bit they were showing Whitney Device owners that they could get the same power output from less and less gas.

Adjustment seven would involve unplugging the system entirely, and they would give the owners the manual-start process.

Ivy had written a series of emails, detailing how excited they were to discover that the device didn't need as much power input as they thought, and how owners could follow the steps included to help save on fuel costs. It was Kayla's job to write out the instructions, and she just finished. She also had the responsibility of sending out the mass emails.

"Step two is done." She smiled up at Ivy.

Without smiling back, Ivy pulled the chair over from her own desk. Ivy's spot was directly under the window. She enjoyed having a distraction while she worked. "You realize that you got your shadow constant all wrong, don't you?"

Kayla frowned. She realized no such thing. "I got it right. It gets adjusted as we go, but I got it right."

Ivy softly shook her head and took Kayla's hands in her own. "You missed it entirely."

"What?"

"It isn't even the number. You needed that to make the machine run, and you had to find out how to make it work for you. But that's not the real shadow constant."

"What do you mean?"

Reenie's voice hollered up the stairs at them. "Don't forget, we're leaving in thirty minutes!"

Ivy hollered back, but then continued with Kayla. "It's them." She pointed to the computer screen showing the message that her email had been sent. "It's the people. We had to figure out how to get them involved. How to not get squashed like Whitney and Edwin Carroll did. And how to get the people to come along. How to get them behind this."

"Oh." Ivy was right. "They're the ones who are going to carry this. They're going to use this technology to run cars and even the power grid one day."

"Yeah. We're the initial push. We figured out how to get it out there. But it's out there now and it's up to them. They're the Shadow Constant."

You need another book!
Good and Evil isn't always black and white.
"Provocative . . . Spellbinding . . . Gripping . . ."

OR get the full set! 4 novels and two short stories with the exclusive "TWISTED" at a fraction of the individual cost.

ABOUT THE AUTHOR

At heart a biologist and avid student, AJ writes about the possibilities that keep us up late at night. Previous novels have won numerous awards including a Booky Top Ten Fiction Novel of 2011, several USA Book Awards for Best Fiction of the Year and Best Suspense of the Year, multiple Best Audio Fiction of the Year awards, as well as others. Audio formats have even garnered 2 Audie Nominations. AJ also writes the "Archives" Hybrid Novel Series for Game Nation.

For more information
www.ReadAJS.com
AJ@ReadAJS.com

www.ingramcontent.com/pod-product-compliance
Lightning Source LLC
Chambersburg PA
CBHW030928020726
47498CB00001B/164